THE AGE OF MAGIC

TALES OF ALBION: BOOK 2

R.K SUMMERS

Published by Inspired Quill: March 2024

First Edition

Content Warning: This work contains non-graphic mentions of kidnapping, pregnancy, death, and assault.

Chief Editor: Sara-Jayne Slack
Cover Design: Chris Era

Typeset in Dante

Paperback ISBN: 978-1-913117-09-2
eBook ISBN: 978-1-913117-10-8

Printed in the United Kingdom
1 2 3 4 5 6 7 8 9 10

Inspired Quill Publishing, UK
Business Reg. No. 7592847
https://www.inspired-quill.com

Praise for R.K Summers

The Old Ways

While one can certainly read The Old Ways *simply for the pleasure of encountering the incredible world that Summers shapes, the storyline itself is captivating. I mentioned before the dark topics that Summers explores through the choices and circumstances of his characters, and I stress that the events that unfold never seem too predictable or too rushed.* The Old Ways *is a fantastic fantasy read dedicated to exploring both the nuances of faeries and the worlds they inhabit and the consequences of choice.*

If you enjoy tales of surprising depth, I highly recommend The Old Ways.

– Hannah Anderson,
Epicstream

The author has woven her own particular magic into this adventurous retelling of Thomas Rhymer. Like any fantasy worth its salt, The Old Ways *submerges us into a whole other world, which means a whole world full of characters to get to know.*

I was always going to love this one. It has faeries and talking horses and magical realms and everything. The Old Ways *would make a lovely gift for fantasy fans and/or a selfish treat!*

– A Bruce Eye View

My usual is a medieval era against Tolkienesk creations. This one is in the right era and made a refreshing change from the norm. I have never enjoyed a faekind read like this!

– P. Holloway,
Reviewer

They told me I can't dedicate a book to a cat.
So I didn't.
I dedicated it to *two* cats.

Thissy "Thistickles" & Luna "Loony Battlecat"
See you both on the Rainbow Bridge

"I miss being human"

"IT'S CLOSING!"

The shriek rang clear through the circular stone room.

"Not yet!"

The sorcerer almost lost his grip on his staff, palm so slick with sweat. The huge, glowing portal above them rippled with power, yet grew smaller and dimmer every second.

"Do something!" commanded the woman, beautiful face twisted with anger. The portal reflected blue in her cold grey eyes. "It's closing, Maleagant, *do something!*"

"I—can't—it's not enough—!"

The portal fluttered like a failing heartbeat, and with a final, feeble pulse, it shrank into nothing.

The air grew still as the unnatural wind died away, and the woman furiously swept her hair from her face.

Maleagant tried to tear his eyes away from where the portal had throbbed with potential only moments before. Now, only the royal-blue ceiling painted with silver moons and golden stars stared back at him. Numerous jars, cages, and vials hung from steel chains around him, swaying gently to stillness. A muscle twitched in his clenched jaw.

"Damn it!"

The sorcerer threw a copper basin to the floor with a snarl, while the woman threw herself down on a throne. Green-grey eyes glared at him. Though smoke-coloured hair fell in waves around her face, her young, smooth flesh remained unmarked by age or sorrow.

"Nothing came out this time," she said, and her voice carried intonations of both consolation and blame.

Maleagant ignored her.

"If only I had more power," he snapped. He swept his arm across his work table, hurling every glass jar to the floor. Contents hissed against stone when they smashed. Two-tailed rats scurried for their nests.

With a sigh, the grey-haired woman slithered up behind the sorcerer. Looping her arms around his waist, she purred in his ear.

"Calm your temper, now," she cooed. The tension in Maleagant's shoulders slackened. He smiled over his shoulder, and then turned to face her. He laid his hands on her hips. "We'll get what we need soon enough."

"My sweet Carman," he said. "I need more power to open the gate, and he's the only one who can give me the potency required."

"I didn't mean him," Carman said, a smirk curving her lip.

"Oh."

"*Oh*, indeed."

"But we need to be careful. The beasts that have already come out of the portal will be nothing compared to him if we don't have suitable bindings."

He stroked her cheek with the back of his fingers.

She airily waved a hand.

"Out of sight, out of mind," she said. "As long as they're gone from here, I don't care what peasants they feast on."

"And if a certain *someone* follows the trail back to here? Back to us?"

"Then all the better," Carman said, her smirk turning truly wicked now. Maleagant's brow knitted in confusion. Carman turned away, gesturing around her.

"I've been thinking, all these experiments have been

missing one key... a catalyst," she said slowly, circling the room. Maleagant waited and watched.

"We thought enough blood would suffice," she toyed with a jar on a workbench, inspecting the cluster of fat, slimy leeches within. "And it appears so. The portal opens for a short time."

"Long enough for something to escape, but not long enough for us to find who we want," Maleagant interjected.

Carman rewarded him with a smile, though her cold beauty made it seem more like a sneer.

"Then we need to stabilise the gateway, leave it open long enough for you to cast the blood-to-blood spell and summon him out. I think we will need magic," Carman said.

"I *have* magic," Maleagant pointed out.

Carman rolled her eyes. "Not enough. We need *true* magic. True power. Straight from the source."

"Are you suggesting..." Maleagant's eyes narrowed, then immediately widened in horror when the truth of her words sunk in. "Impossible."

"*Why?*"

"Do you even realise what you're suggesting? To steal magic right from the source would be—"

"Not *steal*," Carman interrupted. "Just... *tap into*."

"Still impossible," Maleagant said. "Just gaining access would be hard enough. Subduing would be even harder. But then to 'tap into' the source of all magic in Albion? We might as well offer our necks for the noose now."

"But if the source were to come to *us?*" Carman approached with an alluring sway to her hips, the way she always did when she wanted something from him. "Everyone wants something, even *her.*"

Carman's face twisted on the last word. Maleagant said nothing. Carman inhaled slowly and plastered the smile across her face again. Forcibly.

"If we have something she wants, she'll come looking for it. And you know *who* would follow her anywhere. You can finally have your revenge, and I can have some magic. At last."

Maleagant sighed. The muscle in his cheek twitched again as he ground his teeth.

Carman pouted, and purred. "You've been working so hard. You need some time to relax." She draped her arms around his neck. Maleagant took in a deep breath, tilting his head back, eyes closed. Carman smiled again.

"Come upstairs. My sister will clean up in here," she said, lips brushing his ear. Maleagant nodded. *"Isolde!"* Carman's voice rang hard and loud. Maleagant flinched at her sudden shrill tone, still so close to his ear. "Come here, *now!*"

THE COMMAND RATTLED through the halls until it reached the ears of a mousy-haired girl, scrabbling at the loose but heavy stones blocking up a doorway. Her knuckles were bloody and raw from where they'd scuffed the stone. The old spoon she used to scrape her way to freedom was only small, and she'd lost more than one fingernail for her efforts.

Just a little longer. A little more.

At the call of her name, she jumped.

Oh no.

She pushed the cabinet to cover her work, quickly wrapped a cloth around her knuckle, grabbed her broom, and scuttled down the hallway.

She poked her head into the study, "Yes, sister?"

Carman took Maleagant's hand and led him towards the door.

"Clear away this mess," she said, idly gesturing with her free hand. Isolde sighed. Carman turned her steely gaze on her at once.

"What was that?" she snapped. "You'll do as you're told, understand? Unless you want to end up like our dear dead sister."

Isolde shivered as the memory of a white, screaming face rose before her eyes. Cold, green lake water. Tiny bubbles emerging from her mouth and nose like glittering fish. Mother and Father nowhere around.

Poor Vivienne.

"I'm sorry, Carman," Isolde mumbled.

"Don't forget, you're here because *I* saved us. If it hadn't been for me, we'd still be begging on the streets, or worse." Carman sneered, and Isolde silently nodded and approached Maleagant's workbench.

"Once I have magic, little sister, we can have a better life," Carman said in a voice brimming with false fondness as she passed. "One where you won't have to work so hard."

Isolde didn't miss the sneer that told her otherwise. Things would never change.

The door swung closed behind them, and Isolde turned away and sat by the grate. The last few embers smouldered there. She sighed again, rubbing her hands together over the dimly glowing coals.

"It's good to see you again, little mouse," uttered a soft voice. Smiling, Isolde turned.

"Sorry, Broc. I didn't mean to wake you," she said.

A skinny badger in a silver cage stretched and yawned. His square cage, suspended from the ceiling by four thick, study chains, lazily swung when he moved.

"You didn't. It's impossible to get any sleep in here," he said. He scratched his head with his claw and sighed. "That's a new one."

"Hm? Oh." She covered the raw burn on her arm.

Broc folded his front legs but said nothing more.

Isolde approached his cage, smiling. "Stop fussing, Broc, you'll get ticks. Here." She reached into her apron and pulled out a small handful of wriggling earthworms. When she pushed them through the bars, Broc stared disdainfully at them.

"Eugh," he said, pulling a face, but then proceeded to pick up a worm in his claws and nibble on it.

"I'll see if I can get some honey cake from the kitchens," she said, turning back to warm herself by the dying embers.

"I miss being human," Broc moaned. "I want proper food. And wine. *Good* wine."

Isolde made a soft noise of agreement. "At least you're stuck in one shape, rather than a dozen. He turned me into a snake just last week. My jaw still doesn't close properly." She rubbed her chin absent-mindedly. "What happened tonight?" she asked quietly.

He broke his gaze from the last worm to look at her.

"It stayed open for a short while, but no monsters this time," Broc said, lowering his voice.

Isolde breathed a sigh of relief. The last beast to escape had been... she shivered, hoping she'd never encounter it again. Though she'd never forget the sight, the stink, the sinister sound—

"Your sister has given him an idea on how to fix their problem, though," Broc's voice broke into her thoughts. "It might not be long before they succeed, but they need help from someone. I didn't hear exactly, but it might be best to keep an ear to the ground."

"I've been working on the—" she glanced over her shoulder. "The tunnel. I think a few more nights should do it, I can smell fresh air through the stones."

"Are you sure you want to leave?" Broc asked uncertainly. "She is your sister, after all."

"I know," Isolde said. "But ever since Vivienne died, she's treated me like... I mean, she's acted like..."

Isolde sighed. She was nearly sixteen, she wasn't a child anymore. If Carman truly wanted to keep her safe, then why did she bring her to this awful place? Why fall in with that *awful* man? No. Her sister only wanted to keep her confined. Subdued. *Enslaved.*

"If I can find the key, I'll get you out of there," she said aloud.

Broc nodded.

"If you need to, go without me," he said, standing up on his hind legs and gazing at her through the bars. "They don't know we're friends, they wouldn't suspect I had anything to do with it."

"They'd torture it out of you if they even *half* thought

you'd seen me, no doubt," Isolde sighed. "I wouldn't leave without you, Broc. Not ever."

Broc lowered his eyes, humbled. Isolde weakly smiled.

"I should clean up this mess before Carman calls for me again," she said quietly, getting to her feet. Broc stretched with a long yawn.

"I'd help, but there's not much I can do. Unless you want to tie me to a stick and use me as a broom?"

Isolde laughed despite herself. Her quiet, forbidden mirth seemed to clear away some of the cobwebs in the dark tower.

CHAPTER I

"We are no longer safe here"

Samhain night found the Glenthorne woodlands burning bright with life. Herds of fauns galloped between the trees, laughing and shouting, chasing a troupe of giggling wood sprites. Alongside them, mysterious merrows swam through the brisk rivers, shimmering blue beneath silver moonlight.

Wine flowed and musicians played with hearty vigour. As the forest came alive with the earthy scent of waning autumn, a gathering of seelie faeries danced in the heart of a glade. Even the creeping, chilly fingers of approaching winter couldn't dampen their giddiness.

Upon an enormous tree stump – cleverly carved into an elaborate throne – the Queen of the Old Ways oversaw in silence the end of the pagan year.

Mab glittered in her finery; a black and amethyst gown glimmering with jewels and magic. Her dark hair bounded free in loose curls, decorated with sparkling crystals. Rose lips curved into a smile, even as her dusky eyes swept the glade.

"They're pleased you've joined them this evening, Your Grace," Lightfoot said, from her left. He'd sat by her side all evening, watching the festival. "I know you've been ill at ease these last few moons."

"As I should be, Lightfoot," Mab said. "The sacking of Fernbank shook everyone, yet it was much too direct to have been a simple act of banditry. And then there is the matter of this mysterious sickness. Elphame has escaped this plague so far, but for how long will it remain outside the city?"

Lightfoot seemed unable to retain his heavy sigh. Mab turned her sharp gaze on him.

"There are black deeds happening in Albion, Lightfoot. Someone is attacking villages under seelie and unseelie domain alike," she said. "I sent a company of extra guards to each of the outlying villages, and a small troop of scouts south to Fernbank three days ago."

"What does Queen Morrigan think?"

"We spoke at length. She will stand with us, should war come once again to Albion," Mab sighed. "But our peoples have seen too much of that already."

Lightfoot reached over and put his hand on hers.

"We must discover the source of these attacks, and stop them before they can escalate to open war," she said, a trace of urgency in her tone.

"And we will," Lightfoot reassured her. "Fear not, Your Grace. But not tonight. Tonight, we honour the gods. Please, be merry."

He smiled at her. Her gaze softened, and she returned his smile.

"Forgive my melancholy," she said warmly. "You are right. Tonight is a time for celebration."

A hesitant movement towards her caught her attention. Two young seelie approached her throne, both bowing as they stepped closer.

"Your Grace," the young man spoke first, his voice trembling. He cleared his throat and straightened. The young woman beside him gripped his hand, gazing at him with devout adoration. "We are honoured by your presence."

Mab gave him a gracious smile and nodded, beckoning him closer with her taloned fingers.

"We have a request to beg of Her Grace," he continued, glancing down at the young woman on his arm. Mab cocked her head, and gestured for him to continue. "Rosy—I should say, Rosetta and I wish to marry, and we seek your permission."

Mab paused. Blinking, her right hand unconsciously crept to the third finger of her left, and rubbed the grey indent there.

"What is your name, child?" she asked quietly.

"Oren, Your Grace," he said.

She looked between the pair. They were young, bright, full of mirth, and giddy from the night's festivities.

"Rosetta," she said. The young woman glanced at Oren, then approached her queen with a practised curtsey.

"Your Grace?"

Mab stood. "Walk with me, child."

Rosetta looked surprised, but nodded and followed Mab as she stepped through the crowd at a casual pace.

"Oren appears quite taken with you," Mab said. Rosetta beamed. She was well named; her hair was as red as any autumn rose. The pointed tips of her ears poked neatly through her flaming locks.

"You think so, Your Grace?" the girl glanced back at her beloved. Mab smiled.

"Indeed. Do you love him, truly?"

"I do, Your Grace," Rosetta said warmly.

"What do your mother and father make of the match?"

"Oh, they're very excited, Your Grace," she said, then went on. "My brother too, he and Oren were childhood friends. I always thought he was too protective of me, especially after—"

Rosetta broke off. Mab frowned.

"After?"

"I... should not say, Your Grace," Rosetta mumbled, looking abashed. "Forgive me, I misspoke."

"Then misspeak again."

Rosetta twisted her hands. Mab noticed she was avoiding her eyes. Her cheeks and neck flushed red to match her hair.

"I was only a child at the time, I can barely remember. It was... during the reign of the Dragon King."

Mab faltered in her step. She managed to pass it off as

stepping over a patch of mushrooms.

Rosetta went on, "The Dark Prince had sent soldiers to arrest our family. My brother escaped."

Breath caught in Mab's throat. *Could fate truly have such a cruel sense of irony?*

The memory blossomed in her mind; the boy had indeed escaped, and managed to make his way to the castle where a seelie colony had hidden away, bringing the news to Mab herself. News that had caused Mab to return to Elphame to stop the needless execution of the family. Though successful in her endeavour, the following days – and nights – had wrought themselves on Mab's heart forever.

"Has he ever hurt you? Or have you ever hurt him?" Mab asked suddenly. Rosetta looked momentarily surprised.

"Your Grace!" Rosetta looked affronted. "Never! We love each other so much, that I would rather die than hurt him. And I believe—no, I *know*, he feels the same."

Mab sighed. *Love is a vicious mercy.*

She paused mid-stride and took Rosetta's hands in hers.

"Then go in peace and be wed, with my permission. And my blessing," she added. Rosetta beamed and immediately ran back to Oren, leaping his awaiting arms. Their joyful shouts echoed through the crowd as they raced off.

Mab felt warmth in her chest spill into a smile, and returned to her throne. On her left, Lightfoot chuckled. She glanced at him, pleasantly curious.

"What is it?" she asked.

"They truly love each other, Your Grace."

"I can see that, Lightfoot. But they are young and therefore inexperienced. I must be sure of these matters before I permit anything."

"Understandable, Your Grace. But..." Lightfoot hesitated. Mab's brow furrowed.

"Yes?"

"I worry about you, Mab," he said. She baulked at the use of her name. He only used it when he was feeling particularly fatherly. "I watch your face when you sit alone, when you think no one can see you. The Dark Prince is imprisoned. He can't harm you anymore."

Mab's gaze softened.

"Harm is my last worry, Lightfoot," she said softly, and rubbed the indent on her third finger again; the mark had never truly faded. Lightfoot scowled.

"Your Grace!" The soldier who had shouted ran toward her, face flushed, his hand tensing as if longing to grasp his sword. Gasping and muttering, seelie parted to allow him room. "Your Grace, the wards around the festival have been disrupted."

Mab's disposition hardened. She stood.

"Show me," she said, and the soldier immediately turned, leading Mab through the crowd of frightened seelie to the outskirts of their clearing.

"HERE," HE SAID, pointing to the suspended empty talisman cages hanging from the branches. Their crystals smashed and strewn among the grass, their glow flickering to nothing. Mab's eyes danced between each one. She had meticulously set these charms to ward off any approaching threat.

Lightfoot appeared behind her, just as she knelt to collect the scattered shards of crystal. Rising again, she turned back, carefully inspecting a fragment, now nothing more than colourful, broken glass.

"We are no longer safe here," she said. "Call back every soldier from within the wood and form an entourage to return the people to Elphame."

"Your Grace, that seems a little rash," Lightfoot said, his voice steady. "Surely there are no threats to us at present?"

"After what we have just been discussing?" Mab countered. "Someone has destroyed my wards using powerful magic. Return the citizens, I will—"

Several screams drowned the rest of her words.

Without hesitation, her fingers aflame with magic, Mab darted through the trees back to the clearing.

Rosetta lay prostrate over Oren's twitching body while blood spurted from a clean slice across his throat. Mab stared down at the dead boy, her eyes narrow with fury. She clenched her fist, extinguishing the fire. *Who is here?*

Muttering rumbled through the crowd like distant thunder. Tension gripped the seelie, like a colony of rabbits scenting a fox. Lightfoot and half a dozen of her soldiers appeared behind her.

"Your Grace?"

Mab ignored her advisor, and instead raised her eyes to the crowd, seeking that which was unfamiliar.

The glint of a dagger blinked in the crowd. A shrill squeal – fright or pain? Mab acted without thought.

She thrust her right arm towards the assassin, brandishing her fingers as she would wield a whip. Her seelie screamed and darted aside, as several writhing tree branches snaked into the crowd. Mab curled her fingers into a beckoning fist, and the branches wrapped around the stranger and dragged him forward on his knees, his head bowed low.

The white bonfire from the festival cast a ghastly pallor over Mab's face. For a moment, she looked monstrous; ancient and furious.

"You *dare* come here with your wicked intent?" she growled, her voice a slithering whisper.

The stranger looked up. Mab baulked. A seelie—no, an *unseelie?* His face rippled, almost unperceivable, but it was there. A tiny flicker of magic, making him both seelie and unseelie at the same time, and yet...

Mab gestured, and the magic dispelled. A glamour, a false face, given to hide his identity. She would have sensed him otherwise.

Mortal.

She could see him at last.

"Who are you?" she demanded.

He said nothing, yet with a crooking of his lip into a cruel smile, Mab immediately knew he had not come alone.

A blade sang. A strangled cry rang from the crowd. Mab looked up sharply. More seelie fell to hidden blades. Three dead on her left. Two more on her right. Another two ahead of her.

Mab released a scream of fury, and chaos erupted in the glade. Her delicate fingers squeezed into clenched fists, and sharp pillars of ice burst from the ground, forming a freezing ring around the glade.

Guards flocked forward, finding opportunity in the chaos to fell the mortal assassins before they could take any more seelie lives. Anyone with a knife in their hand met with a bloodied end. Steel rang like tolling bells, and the mirth of the festival dissolved into crippling terror. The night had begun with such delight, and ended with blood and fear.

Seven assassins lay dead, and the remaining six soon kneeled before Mab, bound and struggling, blades pressed to their throats.

The Queen of the Old Ways glared at her first captive. He gazed back at her with a cocky, ugly smile.

Mab gave a simple nod. Blades thrust through their thin armour, and each assassin fell; their deaths only a small payment for the amount of seelie blood they had shed.

"Your reign is ending, Wolf-Queen," the last assassin before her sneered. Soldiers closed in around him but, with blazing eyes, Mab held up a hand to stop them running him through.

"No," she said. Her quiet voice still somehow rang through the glade, silencing even the sobbing seelie who mourned their fallen kin. "Not this one. Take it back to Elphame for questioning."

Her glare could have incinerated him as the guards dragged him away.

This should not have happened.

This would not happen again.

Movement caught her eye. One of the assassins twitched in his death throes, moaning as his lifeblood pooled beneath him. Mab held up her hand and gestured, and his head twisted back, his neck snapping with a hideous sound. He slumped, finally dead, in the spongy moss.

I will make sure of it.

CHAPTER 2

"Oft she runs the wilds"

T HE *DANCING KELPIE* rang with loud laughter and music. Thomas Rhymer sat in a quiet corner, doing his best to avoid the stormy glares of the missionaries of the New Religion.

Having recently come to Ercildoune and taken rooms at the inn, the missionaries had tried with dogged determination to catch Thomas alone. He'd so far managed to escape their questions, but he knew it wouldn't be long before they caught up to him. He had nothing for them; he and his family would soon be leaving this realm for Albion.

Romans had brought the New Religion to Britain. Every day, they pressed further and further into the countryside, smashing the ancient standing stones and slaughtering the berobed priestesses where they stood.

The Old Ways had no safe place in Caledonia anymore.

Breaking into Thomas's morbid thoughts, Robb Goodfellow wobbled over to their table, carefully balancing three mugs of golden ale. As he plopped into his seat, cheeks distinctly redder than they had been earlier, he slid one of the mugs towards Thomas.

"That ought to put the smile back on your moping face," he grinned.

"I'm not moping," Thomas said defensively. "I'm just

going to miss this old place." He cast his eyes around the small, lively room. Úna, now the landlady of the *Dancing Kelpie*, with three grown-up children of her own, and a husband deep in his cups at the bar, caught his eye and gave him a flirty yet harmless wink. Thomas cracked a smile and returned it.

"When do you leave?" Logan asked, interrupting Thomas's thoughts again. With his nose buried in his mug, his voice echoed louder than Thomas would have liked. He cast an anxious look at the missionaries.

"The day after tomorrow," Thomas took a swig of his ale. "In fact, I should probably get home soon."

His voice trailed off into silence as he noticed the missionaries whispering to the young serving lass, their eyes determinedly fixed on him.

Robb and Logan noticed his distraction and turned to glance.

"Have they come to you yet?" Robb asked, suddenly sober.

Thomas shook his head and lowered his eyes to his mug. The ale was sweet and crisp, but it couldn't wash away the sour taste in his mouth.

"Not yet," he said.

"I heard," Logan leaned in conspiratorially and lowered his voice. "They were waiting for Matthew Hopkins to get here. They do their preaching first, then when Hopkins arrives, they start knocking on doors and asking questions."

"Knocking *down* doors, more like," Robb put in.

Thomas inhaled slowly.

"I thought Hopkins was down south?"

"*Och* aye, he were. But since his sister died of consumption, he's been moving further and further up our way. Some of his so-called *witch hunters* were seen pestering old Maggie Aitken last week."

"Why?" Logan asked.

"Something about her herbcraft," Robb shrugged. "Don't know why they bother, the old girl wouldn't squash a gnat if it landed in her soup."

"Thissy goes with her to assist with births sometimes," Thomas said. "It's why we've waited so long to leave. She wanted to be here for when Morag McKie had her baby."

He took a swig of ale and sloshed it around his mouth before swallowing.

"By the time Hopkins arrives, we'll be long gone," Thomas went on, although he couldn't disguise the uncertainty in his voice.

"How is Thissy, by the by?" Robb asked. Thomas appreciated the tactful change of subject.

"Aye, she's fine in herself," Thomas lowered his voice. "But her magic only comes in fits and starts now. She can still use it, but it's like it's… waning."

It had only been that morning when she struggled to conjure enough simple sparks to light the fire. Yet a few hours later, just as he was leaving, she lit half a dozen candles with barely a blink.

"Once we return to Albion, her magic will come back properly."

Logan and Robb nodded sympathetically. Although both were human with no connection to magic or Albion, Thomas trusted them to the ends of the earth with his family's secret.

Ten years prior, when Robb's infant son had come down with a terrible fever, he'd offered every scrap of coin he owned to Thissy if she could save him. She took no coin, only asked that Robb and his family could keep their secret.

Before their mortal eyes, Thissy had used her magic to cool the fever and soothe the infection that had caused it. After some clever herbcraft, the boy was hale within a few days.

Logan had simply stumbled upon Thomas throwing playful sparks at Thissy's backside one afternoon, barely five autumns past.

After some wild gibbering about going to the priest, Thomas had invited Logan in for some tea, and told him everything. Thissy had scolded Thomas for being so careless, and Logan had sworn himself to secrecy.

Both men had since been close family friends, and fine

secret-keepers.

"She insisted I come here tonight to say farewell before we go," Thomas took another gulp of his drink. "But I think it's time I take my leave."

Robb and Logan glanced at each other, dejected.

"Stay for one more drink, Thomas," Robb pressed. "At least hear a story from Baird; he's just setting up, look!"

Thomas looked to where Robb was pointing, to see the gaily dressed minstrel downing the last dregs of his tankard and picking up his lute. Having just recently arrived in Ercildoune – shortly after the missionaries, in fact – the minstrel had spent the past few nights drinking in the *Dancing Kelpie* and telling his tales to all who would listen:

A fierce pirate king who married seven women and murdered all but the last, who shrewdly discovered his grisly secret; the clever daughter of a vizier from far away, who tricked the cruel sultan into listening to her tales for one thousand and one nights to escape execution at his hands; a prince who threw a mealy worm back into a river, only to return several years later from war to find it grown to enormity, and wrapped seven times around a hill near his home.

"I don't need to hear stories, I've already lived enough adventures," Thomas said, yet turned to face the minstrel.

Baird strode out to the front of the bar, and the tavern quietened. A patron sniggered, and Úna gave his ear a sharp nip to silence him. Thomas grinned at her.

"Thank you, dear lady," Baird bowed low to her. "And thank you for your hospitality, fine food, and strong drink. It's not often a lowly minstrel is treated with such grace and dignity."

He strummed his lute, then fiddled with some of the knobs, and strummed it again, looking happier.

"*To the east lies Aryndel, the cathedral on the moor,*" he sang, voice high and somewhat feminine, yet soothing. "*To the west is Brackenpeth, the home of barbarian shore.*"

Thomas's ears pricked up. Brackenpeth? He'd seen that

name on a map of Albion, many years ago. How would Baird know of that place?

"To the north hides Trimsaran, where mystic men grow white."

Thomas sat straighter, staring at the minstrel with rapt attention. Perhaps Baird also had faery blood in him? Had he too crossed the bridge?

"To the south lurks Wicklewood, there, dead boys go to fight."

As Baird finished with a flourish, and the tavern gave him a round of applause, Thomas failed to suppress a shiver; Wicklewood had been where Mab had left Erlik's cage. Few people knew that. Could Baird just be posturing? Repeating tales and legends that had slipped from Albion into the mortal realm?

But Baird had no intention of finishing there.

"Ah, yes, Wicklewood," he said to a now silent audience. Thomas had to admit, he knew how to get the crowd's attention. "A dark forest, lurking not far from here, past a bridge that leads… to another place."

"He knows how to tell a story, doesn't he?" Logan whispered to Thomas. Robb turned and nodded in agreement, before returning his attention to the minstrel.

"A place ruled by a powerful, mysterious, and beautiful queen," Baird lowered his lute and made his way around the room. He cuffed the chin of a particularly winsome girl, who giggled.

"I speak, of course, of Mab, Queen of the Old Ways."

Thomas, who'd been nose-deep in his mug, choked. He lowered the tankard and emerged, dripping and coughing. Robb thumped him on the back. Baird seemed not to notice.

"The Heart of Magic Itself, bound to human form by the Old Gods," Baird continued, clearly loving the attention of his rapt audience. "Yet not content to remain as a woman; oft she runs the wilds, in the guise of a huge white wolf with blazing red eyes and fur as soft as down."

Thomas couldn't help himself. He snorted a laugh, trying desperately to withhold his shaking shoulders. Logan kicked him under the table.

"Sorry," he whispered back, voice thankfully not loud enough to carry over Baird's. The minstrel kept going, and Thomas swallowed gulp after gulp of ale until the mug and the story were both finished.

"Well, I'm glad I stayed for that," Thomas grinned, standing. "I'll be sure to tell Mab what mortals are saying about her these days."

"You're leaving?" Robb stood as well. Thomas nodded.

"I still have things to pack up," he said. "Thissy will go mad if I leave all the heavy lifting to her and Tristan."

Logan also got to his feet after draining his mug. Albeit a little unsteadily.

"Thomas Rhymer," he said, voice just a shade too loud. "I wish your family nothing but happiness and good health for the rest of your days."

Thomas smiled and grasped Logan's outstretched hand.

"It's been an honour, my friend," he said warmly. He turned to Robb. "And you as well. Never did I expect to make such good friends. I wish you both good days and good lives."

Thomas hadn't even heard Úna approach, yet she appeared by their table with a warming smile.

"I overheard," she said. "Logan isn't exactly quiet when he's had a few in him."

Thomas grinned, and his friend scowled.

"I'm going to miss your face in here," she said, pulling him into her embrace and planting a kiss on his cheek. "Best of luck on your travels, and I hope to see you back one day."

Thomas pulled a face of mock seriousness. "Oh, of course," he said. "I couldn't go too long without seeing you, old girl."

Úna gave him a playful punch in the arm and then returned to her patrons. Baird had started a bawdy song about the unspeakable and worldly skills of a fisherman's daughter.

After bidding further goodbyes, Thomas silently congratulated himself as he left the *Dancing Kelpie* for keeping his eyes dry.

A better life awaited them, he reminded himself, a safer

life. Where Thissy had her magic back and could use it without fear of persecution, and where their son could come into his own magic without having to hide it.

CHAPTER 3

"Leave us be"

DARKNESS AWARDED HIM no favours as he headed home, but his eyes, sharper than they were when he'd been human, found no danger in the shadows. The lights of his home beckoned, and he knew Thissy would be waiting for him. He sped up, eager to feel her warm lips on his.

"Thomas Rhymer?"

Thomas froze. His hand crept to his dirk as he turned.

"Yes?"

His heart dropped. The missionaries had followed him from the tavern. His hand tightened on the hilt of his knife.

"We have some questions for you, if you don't mind?" one of them approached carefully, a false smile decorating his face.

"I do mind, in fact," Thomas said, and feigned an enormous yawn. "It's late. I'd rather be home to my wife and son."

He turned away.

"Well, *in fact,*" the other pursued, speaking a little too loudly for Thomas's liking. "We have questions for them, too. Your wife, in particular."

Thomas sighed. A light appeared in the window of a nearby house; someone had woken at the raised voices outside. He turned back to the missionaries. Letting go of his dagger, and raising his hands, he offered them an amicable smile.

"Listen, gentlemen," he said. "It's very late, I'd rather we not speak of this out here."

"Then perhaps we can come to your home and discuss it there?"

"I'm afraid that's not a good idea, my wife is… not well. It's better that she rest. Perhaps you could come next week?"

"But aren't you leaving town in a few days?"

Damn.

Thomas sighed, "I don't know what you want from us, but leave us be. We'll be gone soon enough. This is a peaceful village, people worship who they want, they don't harm anyone. I suggest you move on."

"I'm afraid that's not possible," the first said. "Witch Finder Hopkins will be here soon, and he already has plans for this village. And it's… *oddities.*"

His eyes drifted past Thomas and into the darkness behind him. Thomas frowned and followed his gaze.

There, looming out of the dark night, rose Mab's Hill. Atop the steep embankment lay a circle of standing stones, and a great unlit bonfire garlanded with wildflowers. One of those old stones had cracked and fallen at the moment Thomas had first met Thissy.

"No," he heard himself whisper. He turned back to the missionaries. "You can't touch it, it's sacred."

"It's *sacrilege*, Mr Rhymer," the second one spat. Thomas took a step back. He had never seen them get angry before. He'd never considered they would, but now realised just how dangerous they were. One word from them, and Hopkins would have their entire village put to the torch.

"We have no quarrel with the New Religion," Thomas said quietly. "There are plenty of worshippers here, and they live peacefully alongside pagans. Leave them be."

"Thou shalt not suffer a witch to live," the first missionary said.

Thomas shook his head, "My wife is no witch."

"Strange that we didn't mention her, yet you jumped to her defence straight away," the second man gave Thomas a smug smile.

"Leave us be," Thomas said one final time, and turned away.

"Witch Finder Hopkins will be arriving soon, Mr Rhymer," one of them called after him. "We'll wait for him, and then you can expect a knock on your door."

By which time, we will be gone.

They didn't pursue him this time. Without realising, his pace quickened, and he walked until the darkness, rather than his misery, swallowed him.

CHAPTER 4

"There can be no delay in this"

MAB STOOD WITH her arms folded, drumming her fingers and unable to hide her expression of disgust as gaol guards dumped bucket after bucket of water over the assassin. *This process is repugnant,* she thought to herself. *Yet wholly necessary.*

Half-conscious, the man slumped in his chair. His head lolled to one side, and one eye cracked open to look up at Mab.

"Wh... what's going on...?" he croaked.

One more bucket of water sloshed over his head, and the assassin cried out in shock and discomfort, panting for breath. He wriggled his arms, but they'd been tightly bound behind his back.

"Mercy!" he begged. Mab held up her hand to indicate the guard stop the torture for a moment. She circled the assassin, glaring down at him with enough ferocity to reduce him to ashes.

"Mercy?" she hissed. "You have spilled seelie blood, and you *dare* beg for mercy?"

"Qu—Queen Mab?!" the assassin's eyes widened and he shrank back. "Oh gods! I—gods preserve me, I swear—P-please, Your Grace—I wasn't... I couldn't—"

Mab narrowed her eyes and snapped, "Enough! Who sent you?"

"Please, Your Grace, I was bewitched."

"I know," she gestured behind his head. "And now you are free of the enchantment. You will tell me everything."

"Please, you must… I beg of you, Your Grace, have mercy. I—"

He choked and coughed, like his tongue had swollen in size. Gagging, the assassin leaned forward as if trying to be sick.

"W-what have you done to me?" he gasped.

"Now you cannot lie. Tell me *everything*. What is your name?"

"Joren, Your Grace."

"From where do you hail?"

"Stonehaven, Your Grace."

"Who sent you?"

"A sorcerer. P-please, Your Grace, I'm only a baker—"

Mab scoffed. "And a sorcerer would send a *baker* in place of a true assassin? A *baker* would seek to enter a seelie circle for such black deeds?"

"He bewitched us. He bewitched us all," Joren said. Mab leaned forward, her face unnervingly close to his.

"Tell me of this sorcerer."

"Y-yes, Your Grace," Joren coughed to clear his throat. "He… he sent missives out to all the abled men and women of my village. He said if we went to his stronghold, he would give us jobs that would pay more than we'd otherwise make in a lifetime."

"Where is this stronghold?"

"Near Loch Aber, Your Grace. He calls it The Iron Keep."

Mab straightened at once. Silence overcame the room just as an unfamiliar feeling overcame *her*; a deathly cold shiver of icy fear. She took in a sharp breath, her eyes boring hard into Joren.

"The Iron Keep?" she repeated.

"Yes, milady," Joren nodded.

"Who is this man? What is his name?"

"M-Maleagant."

Mab inhaled deeply. She chewed the inside of her lips.

"Your Grace?" a gaoler's face appeared through the bars of the prison door. "Steward Lightfoot requests your urgent attention."

With the rattle of keys, the door opened.

Mab threw a filthy look at Joren.

"Very well. I have heard enough, besides."

"What of the prisoner, my lady?"

"Allow the physician to tend to him. Keep him imprisoned, but send a courier to his family to let them know he is alive."

"Th… thank you, milady."

Mab barely turned back to him.

"Do not *thank* me."

She gestured, a clawed snatch of her taloned hands, and the prisoner howled in pain. He writhed, desperate to free his arms to clutch his now tongueless mouth. Mab didn't turn back to look at him.

She swept out of his prison cell and through the rest of the dungeon, lightning crackling in her eyes.

✧   ✧   ✧

MAB STOOD STRAIGHT-BACKED, rigid as a statue. The guard beside her looked sickened.

Lightfoot bustled around the ugly, bloated body lying prone before them. Carefully poking the swollen and purple flesh with a wooden rod, checking the blank, white eyes, and examining the thick, sticky tongue. Although the corpse belonged to a fairly young man, his hair was steel grey. Thin, spidery fingers of frost dressed his eyelashes; he must have died sometime in the middle of the night.

"The sickness?" Mab asked.

"Perhaps, Your Grace," Lightfoot said reluctantly, pulling off his gloves. "It definitely appears so. But the question is *how*."

With no one awake at this hour, only Mab, her guard, and

Lightfoot stood in the empty street, speaking in hushed voices. A night-watchman had almost broken his neck tripping over the corpse, and then once again in his haste to inform the palace guards.

"This is the only fatality within Elphame's wall from this illness," Lightfoot said. "Either this man has come from one of the outer villages, or—"

"Or the disease has come to the city," Mab finished grimly. She inhaled. "May I examine the body?"

Lightfoot nodded. Taking the torch from her guard, Mab lifted her skirts slightly and kneeled beside the corpse.

As she stretched out a hand, Lightfoot stopped her.

"Careful, Your Grace," he said. "We don't yet know how this sickness is shared."

Mab nodded, and hovered her hand over the body. A frown creased her brow.

"What is it?"

"I am unsure," she said slowly. "I sense something… unnatural. I believe this…" she paused, then stood again. "This sickness has not originated in our world."

Mab tipped her head back, her gaze still fixed on the distorted corpse.

"This plague is the Mortasheen."

Lightfoot froze. The muscles in his throat rolled as he swallowed hard. There was only one way to contract the Mortasheen.

"The Nuckelavee… but *how?*"

Mab repressed a shudder. "I did not think it would ever roam Albion."

"Where does it come from?"

"The only place truly fitting for a monster who breathes death," Mab said slowly. "Annwyn."

Lightfoot, less able to hide his fear, noticeably shivered.

"There is something foul stemming from the Iron Keep," she said. She flicked her fingers, and the carcass erupted in flame, collapsing into ash and dust like a broken sandcastle.

Then, to Lightfoot, "Come with me."

MAB CAREFULLY WATCHED the man standing before her. Shrouded in dark clothing, unshaven and untidy. Not overly handsome, yet not so misshapen as to draw attention. Neither young nor old, simply a man who would be forgotten the moment he passed from sight.

An unequivocally useful quality for a spy.

"You know the way?" Mab asked.

He nodded without a word.

"There can be no delay in this," she pressed. "You must return as soon as you discover Maleagant's purpose in the Iron Keep, along with any information you can find regarding the Nuckelavee."

"I will not fail, Your Grace."

"May the winds speed your steps."

The spy nodded once more and turned. Mab sighed as she watched him leave.

"Are you well, Mab?" Lightfoot asked, lowering his quill as he sat by her side, composing polite letters and writs.

"Such subterfuge is unbecoming," she said carefully. "I trust your judgement, although I will not ask how you came to be so closely acquainted with a Fianna spy."

"Subterfuge is necessary this time, my lady," Lightfoot said. "If we send an army, it would be an invitation for open war. Besides, Derne is an impeccable agent; one of their finest, I believe."

Mab made a noncommittal noise. Lightfoot smiled.

"You're still worried," he said kindly.

Mab frowned, "I am not," she said, yet lowered her thumb from chewing the nail. "Merely cautious where caution is due. If Derne should fail—"

"He won't," he said. He leaned over, took her hands, and rubbed them. She smiled, weary and accepting. "Please stop fretting. Derne will come back with news to soothe your mind."

He kissed her brow, and then returned to his work. Mab sighed again.

"I sincerely hope so," she said.

CHAPTER 5

"Not fair, using magic"

T HOMAS RHYMER LOWERED his quill. The ink on his letter to Alissa still gleamed. Sprinkling a fine dusting of sand over the letter, he suddenly realised this could likely be the last contact he ever had with his little sister.

He'd take the letter into town in the morning before leaving for Albion, and find a courier heading for Port Neasaig.

He swept his eyes over the words again, congratulating her on the birth of her third child, a girl this time, and wishing her a long and blissful life with her candle-maker husband.

Despite knowing he would never see his sister again, he felt strangely at peace. She was safe and happy, and no worse off for having been kidnapped and enslaved all those years ago. She'd always retained her cheerful attitude.

Yet she had never come into her magic, and was ageing at a faster rate than Thomas. The thought was not a pleasant one. *But she's made a happy life for herself,* Thomas thought mildly. *She won't need me anymore.*

"Have you packed your grey tunic?" called a voice from the other room.

Thomas hesitated.

"Yes?" he called back hopefully.

Thissy appeared in the doorway, holding up said garment.

"Really? Because I've just found it rolled up under the cat."

Thomas gave her what he hoped was a charming smile.

"Oh, *that* grey tunic," he said, blowing sand from the letter before folding it and stuffing it into an envelope. He stood to take the tunic from his wife, and she put her hands on her hips, a playful smile still tugging at her lips.

"I'll do it now," he added meekly. Thissy made a noise of assent and pecked his cheek as he passed her.

Walking by the largest window in the house, he caught a glimpse of their son at the very end of the garden, nearest the forest edge. Quiver flung over his back, each arrow he fired perfectly hitting their mark.

Thomas still remembered when he'd catch the boy, barely ten years old then, intently concentrating on a pantry door while he fiddled with a bent pin in its lock.

Five years on, the lad would still be scolded for sneaking into places he shouldn't, or peeking into chests and trunks he had no business with. Though there was no badness in his intent. Only playful mischief. Thomas could never find it in his heart to scold him too harshly, and his son's nimble fingers had continued to make short work of any lock he could get his hands on.

"Tristan!" Thomas called, half-hanging out of the window. "Come inside, you still have packing to do."

Tristan turned, the fading red sunlight catching in the fair hair he'd inherited from both parents, and the grass-green eyes of his mother.

"Just a little longer!" he called back.

Thissy appeared beside Thomas and stuck her head out the window.

"Only if you can hit that branch up there," she called, pointing to the highest branch of a nearby oak tree.

With a carefree cry of "Ha, easy!" Tristan drew an arrow, nocked it, and fired.

Thissy casually gestured, the move easily disguised as scratching her nose. Tristan's arrow diverted its course, whistling through the leaves and into the air, missing the branch by a good few feet.

Tristan slowly lowered his bow and turned to stare at his mother with a stony look, while Thomas chewed his knuckle to keep his laugh contained. Simple magic like that came easier to her. Easier to misdirect something that already existed, than conjure fire from nowhere.

"Oh, that's a shame. I suppose the wind must've caught it," she said lightly, smiling.

Grumbling, Tristan unstrung the bow, coiled the cord to place it in its oiled pouch, and trekked back to the house. Thomas greeted him at the door.

"You should know not to play games with your mother," he said. "If she can beat me, she can definitely beat you."

"Not fair, using magic," Tristan muttered.

"Privileges of being your mother, I'm afraid, *a páiste*," Thissy said absent-mindedly. Thomas chuckled.

"Go on, go pack. You can go back out later, if there's still enough light," he said.

Tristan obeyed, and disappeared upstairs into his bedspace. Thomas momentarily cast his eyes around the house. He and Thissy had worked hard to provide a spacious home for their son to grow up in; with Thissy working as a skilled healer and midwife, and Thomas providing game to sell, in addition to some coin and precious items left over from his adventures in Albion.

It'd be a shame to say farewell to their beloved home, but something better awaited them across the bridge.

"I'll load the wagon in the morning," Thomas said, and Thissy nodded. He wrapped his arms around her waist and held her close, breathing in the sweet scent of her hair.

"Do you think we'll reach Elphame in time?" her words came muffled against his chest.

"For Tristan's sixteenth? Of course," Thomas said, smiling. She broke away and looked up at him.

"But if we're not there by the time his magic manifests, it never will," she said. "You weren't, and you had to almost die under the light of the Godsbane Moon for yours to appear."

Thomas closed his eyes as a wry smile crept onto his lips.

"Thank you for bringing back such wonderful memories," he said dryly. "But we *will* be there for Tristan. Stop fretting, my love. It'll be fine. We still have a week."

"Now that Morag's had her baby—"

"Oh, Morag's had her baby?" Thomas interrupted. "You *never* mentioned."

Thissy playfully swatted his arm.

"Hush, I was excited for her. I wish I could stay for the celebration, though."

"I know, *a ghrá*," he kissed her forehead.

Thissy smiled, stood on her tiptoes and kissed him again. She had just turned away from him when a loud thump at the door startled them both.

"You see who that is," Thissy said, "I'll make some tea."

Thomas cleared his throat pointedly, and she looked at him. He grabbed a white linen hat from a nearby table and tossed it to her.

Just in case, he smiled. She nodded and tugged the hat over her pointed ears and tucked in the golden strands of her hair. Tying the strings loosely under her chin, she left the room.

Thomas approached the door as the thumping sounded again, more urgent this time. He'd barely opened it when the person standing there almost fell into the house.

"A little late for houseguests, Robb," Thomas closed the door behind him, a little unnerved by the anxious look in his neighbour's eyes.

"Thank the gods I got here first," he said, gulping down air. Robb owned the farm about half a mile away; he must have ridden hard all the way, judging by his red face.

"Robb, what a pleasant surprise," Thissy smiled as she returned to the room. "Would you like some tea?"

Robb immediately tugged off his hat in her presence.

"Ma'am," he acknowledged her, "Thank you, but I'm afraid there's no time." He turned back to Thomas now. "I know you're leaving tomorrow, Thomas, but you should go tonight."

Thomas laughed, "We're hardly packed, Robb. We still

have a lot to do."

"You said you were finished." Thissy frowned.

Robb waved his hands before Thomas could bluster an answer.

"No! You need to leave as soon as you can!" he said. "Hopkins has arrived early; he's in the village right now. He's taken rooms at the *Kelpie*, and he's already taken Baird in to question."

"The minstrel?" Thomas almost laughed with incredulity. "What's he got to do with anything?"

"That stupid tale he span last night, of course," Robb said.

Thomas shared a quick glance with his wife, heart hammering in his throat.

"Those missionaries said they'd wait for him to arrive," he said. "I thought we'd have more time."

Robb went on, "He's started asking questions about this house as well. I think he's coming here next."

A muscle twitched in Thomas's cheek.

"Tell Tristan to grab what he can," he said to Thissy, while she anxiously pulled the hat tighter. "We leave tonight."

TRISTAN GLANCED BETWEEN the shirt in each hand, finally deciding to pack both. His short daggers had been lovingly tucked into his satchel, and he'd decided to carry his bow and quiver for ease.

His father had tried teaching him swordplay in his youth, but Tristan's fingers were much more nimble and dextrous than his. Tristan found, as he listened to his father's stories and re-enacted them against the old straw dummy, that his skills lay in small knives and bows. Something where he could use his sharp eyes to detect movements. Finding his opponents weaknesses. Striking from shadows. There was much less danger in that, he'd always reasoned.

Why strike head-on and risk a sword in the gut? Strike from the side, from the shadows, take them by surprise. Under the arms, and the neck, wherever there's a break in the armour.

Growing up, his parents would tell him stories from his mother's homeland before he went to bed. His mother usually omitted the more gruesome details, so he often asked for his father to tuck him in at night.

Tristan would pull a face and point out how, if his father had parried this way or feinted that way, he wouldn't have been stabbed so often.

His father would laugh, ruffle his hair, and sheepishly ask him to not tell his mother the stories he'd been sharing.

Mouser stretched on the bed, splaying its claws and yawning.

"I don't know if you're coming with us, wee one," Tristan said, giving the cat a quick scratch behind the ears. It responded with a purr and a quiet meow.

Tristan's heart sank a little; he loved this cat.

"I'll ask Mother if you can come along," Tristan said, and Mouser rubbed his face against Tristan's hand before giving him a loving nip.

He'd just finished rolling up his best tunic when his mother burst into the room.

"Tristan—good, you're almost done," she said, looking unnerved.

Why is she wearing a hat? Tristan wondered absently.

"Come, we're leaving tonight."

"Tonight?" he repeated. "Why?"

"Things have changed, we're not safe here anymore," she said. She beckoned him.

Realising there'd be no time to ask about the cat, Tristan threw his satchel over his shoulders, scooped Mouser up into his arms, and followed his mother downstairs.

"Ahh, the lady of the house, I presume?"

The voice slid to his ears, oily and affable, and sent shivers down Tristan's spine. With an aggressive hiss, Mouser leapt from his arms and ran out of the open door. Tristan wished him a silent, miserable farewell.

Tristan appeared behind his mother to find a strange man

in a wide-brimmed hat standing at the open door. His father and Robb Goodfellow both twisted their hands beside him. Tristan gulped. This was obviously why they had to leave so suddenly.

"Supreme Witch Hunter Matthew Hopkins, at your service, Madam," the stranger announced, inclining his head towards Thissy, and removing his hat.

"Mister Hopkins," Thissy began, a tremor in her voice belying her courage.

"*Witch Hunter* Hopkins, if you please, Madam."

Thomas narrowed his eyes as Hopkins entered without invitation and took a seat. Thissy affected a smile.

"Forgive me. May I offer you some tea?" she asked politely.

"No, thank you," Hopkins said, opening his satchel and pulling out several sheaves of parchment, an inkwell, and a long, pointed quill. "My apologies for intruding, I heard you were unwell. I trust you are feeling better?"

Tristan frowned at her. She wasn't sick. Then he saw his father widen his eyes significantly at her behind Hopkins's back.

"Oh, I—" she coughed once into her hand. "Yes, thank you. Much better."

"Good, good," Hopkins trailed off. His eyes found Tristan. "Is that your son?"

Thissy put her arm around Tristan and nodded without a word.

"Handsome young lad, strong-looking."

Tristan stood up a little straighter. *This was the terrifying witch hunter everyone feared?* He thought to himself. He looked like someone's grandfather, with his white hair, kind eyes, and warm smile.

Yet silence reigned thick and heavy over the room. Robb swallowed hard, twisting his hands still.

"I have a few questions I'd like to ask, if you don't mind," Hopkins announced, gesturing for Thissy to sit.

"Actually," Thomas said. "We're quite busy at the

moment, we're leaving Ercildoune."

"Oh?" Hopkins raised an eyebrow politely. "Where are you off to?"

"*An Gearasdan*," he said, a little too quickly. Thissy squeezed Tristan's hand, though he couldn't tell if it were to reassure him or to warn him.

"You'll have to forgive me, I'm afraid your accent is a little thick," Hopkins said with a smile.

"Fort William," Thissy said politely. "My husband sometimes slips into his native tongue."

She gave him a loving gaze. Hopkins *hmm*'d and scribbled something on his parchment.

"That's quite a journey," Hopkins noted.

"Three days," Robb said quietly, as if wanting to be helpful.

Hopkins ignored him. "But you have such a lovely home here, why leave it?"

"Tristan turns sixteen next week," Thomas said. "We heard there were jobs there for a strong lad like him. At the garrison, you know. Soldiering," he finished lamely.

"Hmm. And he didn't decide to follow his mother's profession?"

Again, silence fell across the room.

"As a healer, surely? Well, a doctor," Hopkins went on, when no one spoke, making a note and leaning back as if to watch Thissy's reaction. "I've heard plenty of tales from people in the village about how you cure their sick and wounded family members. Miraculous recoveries, I've heard. Almost... *magical.*"

CHAPTER 6

"You tortured her to death?"

N O ONE SPOKE. No one dared. Hopkins' grandfatherly and kindly demeanour had begun to crack.

Thissy internally cursed. She knew the villagers wouldn't have meant to say such things. To them, she was just a particularly effective wise woman, and Thomas a fine hunter. Only the Goodfellows and Logan Macleod knew their family's secret.

"My wife is skilled with herbcraft, Hopkins," Thomas said in a low voice.

Don't antagonise him! Thissy thought desperately. Thomas looked up at her.

"Herbcraft? Interesting," Hopkins said. "Modern physicians are men. Science and medicine are gifts from Our Lord. And Our Most Holy Father only graces that knowledge to menfolk. We usually find that *women* physicians have gained those forbidden skills from... other sources."

"I—"

"People tell me odd stories about this household," Hopkins stood and looked around. "Strange lights in the night. Odd noises, funny coloured smoke from the chimney. No known attendance at the church, even for your so-called wedding. I heard you undertook *Pagan* rites instead."

Thomas balled his hands into fists.

"And then there's your unexplained disappearance all those years ago," Hopkins had lowered his voice so much, Thissy could barely hear him. "You vanish for seven years, and return with a..." he cleared his throat and glanced at her, "*foreign* bride. I understand your mother died shortly after that, did she not?"

Thissy swallowed hard. Margaret Rhymer had indeed passed away, barely three months after Thomas' return. Seven long years of wishing and wondering what had happened to her children had taken their toll on her health, and she held on long enough to see her son come home. But in the end, not even Thissy could heal a grief-heavy heart.

"Strange," Hopkins went on. "Your mother's passing was almost twenty-five years ago, yet you don't look a day over thirty. Now, how do you explain that?"

"I told your missionaries to leave us be," Thomas said quietly. "We mean no harm, this village means no harm."

"Harm doesn't come into it, I'm afraid, Mister Rhymer," Hopkins said. "Thou shalt not suffer a witch to live. Margaret Aitken knew that, and she went into Our Good Lord's light in—"

"Maggie's *dead?*" Thissy interjected. "How? When?"

"I'm afraid she wasn't strong enough to survive my—our rigorous questioning," Hopkins said. "She passed away this morning."

"You tortured her to death?" Thomas growled.

"She was a witch."

"She was a *midwife!*" Thissy hissed, barely able to speak through her rage. "A frightened, harmless old woman who you humiliated and tortured! I can barely stand to look at you. You will leave my house, Mister Hopkins."

"*Witch Hunter* Hopkins, Madam!" Hopkins raised his voice, drowning out her enraged whisper.

"Don't you dare speak to her like that," Thomas snarled. Hopkins ignored him.

"I knew there was something strange about you, about this house," he said in a low voice. "And I will have the truth of it. By God, I swear it."

Thissy felt rage like she'd never known storming in her chest. Maggie Aitken dead, and the man responsible standing there, in her home, cold as a winter morning. "Mother, no—" Tristan began, and tugged her hand. Thissy pulled away. She began untying the laces of her hat.

"I am no witch, *Mister* Hopkins," she said. She ripped off her hat, revealing her pointed ears and strands of fine-spun gold in her hair. "I am a faery of the Seelie Court, Thistledown of Elphame, wife to the Champion of Elphame, protected by the might of Her Grace, Queen Mab, the Heart of Magic Itself. And you are *not* welcome in my home."

Without another word, Thissy thrust both arms towards Hopkins. Green fire flared at her fingertips, and a pulse of powerful, forceful magic lifted the witch hunter off his feet and threw him against the wall.

With a groan, Hopkins staggered to his feet, clutching the wall for balance. He pointed a shaking finger at Thissy.

"I knew it! *Witch!* Rhymer's wife is a witch!"

He pushed Thomas aside and threw himself out of the door.

Thomas slammed it closed behind him and locked it.

"'*Rhymer's wife*'," Thomas snorted. "You're not even a person to him. Scum-sucking, low-born… Tristan, do you have everything ready?" he said.

Tristan nodded, his eyes and mouth wide.

"Good, go wait by the horses. The wagon will be too slow. We travel light, and we leave now."

With a brief look of awe at his mother, Tristan did as he was told.

"You've been holding out on me, my love," Thomas said, throwing some bread and fruit into his saddlebag. "I thought your magic was fading?"

Thissy felt her strength leave her with every word he spoke. The room span around her and she slumped forward, her fingers gripping the back of the chair for support. Thomas thrust the sack into Robb's hands and bounded across the room to catch her before she could fall.

"You would say something stupid like that, wouldn't you?" she mumbled with a weak smile.

"You rest up, I'll prepare the horses."

He gently lifted her to her feet and half-carried her to a seat by the window.

"Hopkins might come back," Thomas replied, scribbling Alissa's name on the envelope containing the letter and sealing it. "But he'll never find us where we're going."

"What about Robb?" Thissy laced her hat back on, and wrapped her cloak around her shoulders. "What about his family? Hopkins has seen him here; he'll go after them next."

Thomas paused. He turned to his friend, who had paled so sharply he now resembled a beech tree.

"Robb," Thomas said, taking the sack of food back from him. Robb turned his wide eyes from Thissy to Thomas. "You've been such a good friend, and I'm sorry to leave it like this. Here," he handed the letter over, as well as a bulging purse of coins. "Alissa lives in Port Neasaig, take your family there. Find Alissa, tell her what happened. She'll put you up for a while, until it's safe to return. Actually..." he dug out another purse from his satchel. "Take Logan and his daughter with you too."

"Will you be alright?" Robb asked, casting another glance at Thissy.

Thomas nodded, "Aye, we'll be fine. You go take care of your family."

"And you take care of yours," Robb nodded and left.

Thissy stood, heaved her satchel onto her shoulder and approached the door.

"This isn't how I imagined it would be," she said, throat choked with tears. Thomas took her arm to steady her.

"I know, my love," he said, also taking her satchel. "But once we reach Albion, everything will be alright."

CHAPTER 7

"They're still inside!"

TRISTAN BUSTLED QUICKLY around the stable, tying his saddlebag to his patient chestnut gelding. Mouser had appeared once to butt his head against Tristan's leg, and then vanished into the darkness. Tristan miserably hoped he'd find a new family to look after him.

He kept thinking back to the moment his mother unleashed her magic. He's seen her cross, certainly. But for small things. If he spilled the milk, or ripped his shirt, or forgot to bring in the eggs. He'd never seen such *fury* in her before. And the *magic!* That raw power that had emanated from her hands with such a simple gesture.

Epona snorted and stamped her feet, eagerly demanding attention.

"You know," Tristan said grumpily, not looking at her. "If we were to have this conversation next week when I'd be sixteen, I could actually understand you."

Epona snorted more frantically and reared back with a screeching whinny.

"What's the matter with you, girl?" Tristan grabbed her reins. "Father will be out be soon—"

Epona whinnied loudly, her eyes fixed on something past his shoulder. Tristan turned, and his heart dropped like a stone.

A honey-coloured glow crested the hill. The sound of

shouting reached his ears.

"Oh, no. Mother, Father!" Tristan called, cursing the youthful lilt in his voice.

Both ran from the house, burdened with as few possessions as they dared.

"What is it?" Thomas asked as Thissy approached her own grey horse to load her bags. Tristan pointed at the horizon, where now a small group of people had appeared, marching towards their house. Thomas cursed.

"Hopkins is back, with his friends," he muttered, and shoved Tristan back into the stable.

"There, girl," Thomas soothed as he quickly patted Epona's nose. She snorted again. "I know, it'll be fine," he said.

"I hope Robb doesn't get hurt," Thissy said, stroking her horse to calm its fretting.

"He'll be fine, he's smart," Thomas assured her. Then, after a quick disbelieving glance from her: "Well, smart enough, anyway."

"Burn it down!" a clamouring voice rang through the darkness. "Burn it to the ground!"

"Stop! You can't!"

"They're still inside!"

"No, don't! They've never harmed anyone!"

The clamour of voices pitched through the oncoming night. Smoke stung their nostrils and eyes. Tristan approached the front of the stable to see half the village out there, Thissy and Thomas behind him.

Thissy's face became pale and stricken as the witch hunters flung torches at their beloved home. The thatch caught the fire quickly, devouring the wood and straw like a glutton at a feast.

Hopkins stood at the fore of the crowd, eyes glowing red from the flames. For someone so godly, Tristan marvelled at how much of a devil he looked, eyes blazing, lips asnarl in fury.

The rest of his missionary lackeys stood behind him, bearing more torches and various tools of witch-hunting. Bodkins glinted like sinister daggers in the night. Some bore huge bibles and read aloud from the pages.

The rest of the village stood behind them, cursing Hopkins' name and crying out for the Rhymer family.

"Come, Tristan," Thomas whispered in his ear and pulled him away. They mounted their horses and left the stable as quietly as possible.

Tristan suddenly realised, as they quietly trotted towards the forest, that their mortal lives in Ercildoune truly were over. He paused and took one last look at the house, their home, *his* home, now a burning bonfire, flames clawing higher into the rapidly darkening sky.

Everyone thinks we're dead.

It was a very disorientating thought.

Thissy hissed his name from the shadows, and he followed the noise reluctantly. His mother might be going home, but Tristan was leaving his forever.

✧ ✧ ✧

"IT HAS BEEN two moons since we sent Derne, *why* have I waited so long?" Mab cursed herself, pacing back and forth.

"None have returned, Your Grace," Lightfoot said heavily. "Derne and the others. Every spy we've sent to the Iron Keep has vanished."

Mab sighed, and rubbed her brow.

"You are being diplomatic, Lightfoot," she said. "They are dead, defected, or worse."

"You mustn't blame yourself," he approached her throne. "Spies were the best way of discovering Maleagant's plan."

"What of the scouting party to Fernbank?"

Lightfoot hesitated, then lowered his eyes. Mab sighed again and turned away.

"Not a word, Your Grace," he said quietly. He paused, as though loath to give her yet more bad news, then went on. "We have had other reports, Your Grace. About the Mortasheen."

Mab's eyes snapped to him.

"Three outer villages have reported the sickness," Lightfoot read from his sheaf of parchment. Mab watched his eyes scanning the words, growing wider as they moved further down.

"Has Aoife found anything yet? Any remedy or countermeasure?"

"Nothing yet, Your Grace," Lightfoot replied. "She and the other herbalists – as well as the healers – have been scouring every book in your library. Any mention of the Nuckelavee is catalogued and checked thrice, but there seems to be no record of a cure."

"They must keep searching. There must be something," Mab said.

"There's more, Your Grace," Lightfoot said hesitantly. Mab pinched the bridge of her nose.

"Sightings of the Nuckelavee?" she asked. Lightfoot swallowed and nodded.

"And others," he said. "A headless horsewoman. Fearsome white hounds with blood-red eyes. Bean Sídhes freely roaming the countryside. Púca attacking farms and smaller settlements. A herd of cattle was found drained of blood. And a group of fishermen have seen a—well, *something* in the rivers."

"In the rivers?" Mab repeated. "I have no dominion over the waterways. Has Melusine not sent word?"

Lightfoot shook his head. "Nothing from her as yet. But merrows are being found washed up on the shore and on riverbanks, mangled beyond recognition. No one has seen what's been causing it, but the wounds suggest the Each-Uisge."

Mab shivered. Unlike kelpies, which would show occasional compassion or could even be tamed, the Each-Uisge was a vile, dark creature, with thoughts only on how to fill its belly. A great horse, skin green and slimy, with reeds for its mane and tail, and sharp gnashing teeth to devour any fool who came too close.

"Albion is being overrun with monsters," Mab stood and began pacing again. "This all stems from the Iron Keep, I know it." She paused. Lightfoot looked up from his missives. Mab chewed her lip. "I need someone who is utterly loyal to me, so there is no chance of deceit or betrayal. Someone who is clever and quick, but strong enough to escape should the situation turn sour. I need…"

She paused again. Lightfoot frowned.

"I have no other choice."

"Your Grace?"

Mab stood, her shadowy gown sweeping around her like an embrace of midnight.

"I will ride out with my wolves," she announced. "To clear my head."

"As you wish, Your Grace," Lightfoot bowed and turned from her, ushering the last few courtiers from the hall. Once alone, Mab closed her eyes and hung her head.

This is a foolish venture, she thought to herself. *He will not do this. Not without recompense.*

"Faolan," she called.

The soft ticking of claws against stone heralded the arrival of an enormous white wolf with blazing red eyes. She smiled as it padded towards her, stretching out her hand to stroke its head.

"Mistress," the beast nuzzled her fingers with its cold nose. "What need have you?"

"Come with me, Faolan," she said. "I require company."

Faolan's head bobbed as he followed her. She swept out of the hall, trusting Lightfoot to take care of duties in her absence.

"You are distressed, Mistress," the wolf noted, his voice a guttural rasp. Mab ran her fingers across his head.

"As should you be, Faolan," she said. "We ride to Wicklewood."

The wolf released an involuntary growl.

"Mistress," his voice took on a warning inflection. "Is that wise?"

Mab led him to the stables, where she mounted an enormous gleaming white stag, his velvety antlers twisted and sharp. A soft crown of snow now lay upon Elphame as winter had settled itself around them.

"Perhaps not, *a sheanchara*. But necessary, for Albion's sake. You will need the rest of your pack," she added.

Faolan growled again, then threw back his head and howled. The chill sound rent the chillier air, echoing across the stone courtyard.

Mab spurred her stag into movement, galloping out of Elphame's gates. Faolan and a half-dozen other wolves loped behind, following their mistress to the place that wise creatures avoided.

CHAPTER 8

"Play by the rules"

T RISTAN COULDN'T SLEEP.

The ride to Albion had been arduous, and he ached all over. His fingers numbed by cold and sleet, his back stiff and sore.

He remembered how excited he'd been when he first learned he would, one day, travel to the land of his mother's stories. He'd been a small child then. Curious and playful, he would imagine himself on his sixteenth birthday, a man in his own right, striding across the fabled bridge; bright, wrapped in ivy and bursting with colourful flowers, stepping into a world of wonder and magic.

He never thought for a moment he'd be drudging across a sodden, half-collapsed overpass in the middle of the night, running away with his tail between his legs from a man who'd burnt their home to the ground.

Not exactly the grand arrival I imagined, he thought bitterly.

The sleet had finally died away, and at last they slowed their horses to a stop. Thomas had gathered enough dry twigs and kindling, and Thissy ignited them with a spark of fire to warm and dry them. After a quick supper of bread and cheese, they'd unpacked their bedrolls, set up their tents, and laid down to sleep.

That had been a good few hours ago. Tristan sat outside

his tent, poking the dying embers of the small fire. The sky had cleared now; no clouds obscured his view of the crystalline stars. He released a sigh, and his breath escaped him in a cloud of mist. He listened to the sounds of the night forest around them, interrupted by an occasional rumbling snore from his father in the other tent.

Tristan stretched. Epona dozed calmly nearby. Despite the quiet stillness around him, Tristan felt his body ring with lightning. Fine wonder he couldn't sleep; everything had happened so fast. It seemed impossible that only hours ago, he'd been firing arrows at a tree, free of the cares that plagued him now. The stench of burning thatch clung doggedly to his nostrils.

A glimmer of white between the trees caught his eyes and broke his reverie. *Is that snow? A reflection?*

Frowning, he stood and stepped through the tents, remembering to grab his bow and quiver from beside his bedroll.

BLUE MIST ROLLED across the forest floor, and the bracken underfoot shielded any noise he made. Further in he wandered, breathing deep the scent of petrichor and ferns, the glinting white *something* always just out of sight.

He picked up his pace. Bracken and thorny bushes snagged on his tunic as he walked; he ducked beneath a low branch and vaulted over a fallen log.

Tristan stopped.

A white stag and doe lifted their heads, calmly chewing the forest debris. They gleamed brilliant, cleanly white in the darkness, so bright they glowed. They didn't shy away as he grew closer. He held out his hand, and the doe snuffled at his fingers with her cold, wet nose.

He smiled, and ran his hand over her muzzle. Despite the cool air creeping around his neck, Tristan felt warmth spread from his chest to the very tips of his fingers and toes. The stag grunted, and nudged the doe's hindquarters. She bleated and ignored him. Tristan gazed into her round, black, beautifully sad eyes.

She nuzzled into his hand. Touched by something strange and old, he kneeled before her. He bowed his head briefly, and she bumped her nose against his forehead.

The stag turned away, and the doe whined. She gazed at Tristan, and then turned to follow her mate, pausing to make sure he was still there.

Regaining his feet, Tristan chewed his bottom lip. Those doleful eyes near broke his heart. He felt as though he'd been tested, and been found wanting. Should he follow?

As soon as the thought entered his mind, the doe snuffled and lifted her foreleg.

I'm not going far, he reasoned.

Nodding to himself, he followed the stag and doe deeper into the woods.

✧   ✧   ✧

EVERY STEP TOOK Tristan further into darkness. He pushed a branch aside, only to knock another into his face. He wiped his damp brow with his sleeve.

He stopped.

The stag and doe were nowhere in sight. His heart in his mouth, he looked around for any flashes of white, but he saw nothing; only the green and brown of the forest.

"Shit," he said under his breath. He licked his lips, eyes darting.

Heart thumping in his throat, Tristan pushed his way through the thicket, when the ground beneath his feet gave way, and he fell.

He tumbled down a steep bank, grazing every inch of his body, crashing into a tree trunk and through undergrowth, finally landing in a crumpled heap at the bottom of a mossy bank, unconscious.

✧　✧　✧

IT TOOK A long time for Tristan to wake up. When he did, he thought himself delirious to find a pair of slender golden eyes staring at him. Something tickled his nose and he scrubbed it furiously, holding back the urge to sneeze in the creature's face.

Head pounding and body aching, Tristan groaned and sat up.

"Ceridwen's Cauldron, you look *dreadful*," said an amused-sounding voice. Tristan blinked.

A long-haired cat sat before him, gracefully licking its front paw. A pair of curving goat-like horns sprouted from the shaggy bark-coloured fur of its head. It wore a thin rope around its neck like a collar, from which hung several charms and trinkets.

"Is someone there?" he called. The sound of his own voice rattled in his head, and he groaned again, pressing the heel of his palms into his eyes, finding ice crystals on his face.

"Just me," the cat blinked at him and lowered its paw. Tristan frowned.

"Mouser?"

"No, but I know a few."

"Cat's can't talk," he said dumbly. The cat flicked one of its ears back, and its eyes narrowed into deadpan.

"Well, you're obviously an expert," it said snidely, and stood up to circle him. "You've the scent on you, but it's faint. Got any eggs?"

Tristan twisted around to watch the cat, "Eggs? No. Scent of what?"

"Magic, *amadán*," it sighed. "The scent lingers on your skin but you've barely dipped your toe in the pool. You should *plunge*."

"I thought cats hated water," Tristan said smugly. The cat returned to its place in front of him, fluffy tail swishing through the leaves.

"Don't get smart, it doesn't suit you," the cat said with a slight narrowing of its golden eyes. Its voice was surprisingly deep for such a small animal. "Why are you in this forest, anyway?"

"We're heading for Elphame," Tristan found no reason to lie to the cat.

"Elphame?" its tail quivered with excitement. "Why, I haven't been there in years. There used to be a woman there who kept the fattest chickens..."

The cat seemed to lose itself in a delicious memory, so Tristan took the moment to stand up and assess his surroundings.

The twinkling mist had burnt away, and more than a hint of dawn brushed the sky. Still, the forest remained an evergreen maze to him.

His heart thumped hard in his throat. *Mother and Father will be looking for me. I should find a way back up the bank.*

Yet Tristan was utterly lost, and just thinking about trying to find his way back to their camp made his battered body hurt even more. He looked up at the tree in front of him. He could have sworn it had writing on its branches. It took him a few moments to understand it was a signpost.

"Have you seen my bow?" Tristan suddenly realised. The cat gave itself a little shake. The charms around its neck jingled pleasantly.

"In the bushes," it said.

"Where?"

"Well, I can't exactly *point*," the cat snarked. "Behind you."

Tristan turned, but his head swam. Waiting until the world stopped spinning, Tristan leaned down and pushed aside the foliage until he caught sight of treated wood. He grabbed it, but his heart immediately sank; the string had snapped.

"Travelling light, I take it?" the cat leapt up into the tree, claws scrabbling at the bark as it went, and perched on the branch pointing to Woodcroft. It scratched its horns against the tree trunk, much like Tristan had seen bucks do to shed the velvet in the spring.

"Hmm?" Tristan asked miserably, too focused on his snapped bowstring.

"No belongings. No satchel. No horse," the cat purred. "Good thing, too. *Cat Sidhe* and horses don't get on very well."

"Mhm," barely listening, Tristan blinked a few times and shook his head. It was stupid to cry over a bow. He could get it fixed. Or get a new one.

Still, unwilling to part with it, he wrapped the broken string around the limbs of the bow. A few steps forward and he found his quiver, half his arrows scattered around it, pitiful and broken. The others no doubt somewhere up the bank. He slid the bow into it as far as it would go, then bound it with its own string. It was the best he could do for now.

Giving himself a shake, he turned and decided to walk in the direction he thought he'd come from. The cat jumped down and walked silently beside him.

"Fall like that could've killed you," the cat said.

"I'm tough-skinned."

The cat laughed, "We'll see."

Rustling leaves broke his thoughts. He spun around, making himself dizzy. The cat hissed and immediately bristled.

"I didn't realise how close we were," the cat growled. "I should have smelled him a hundred miles away. That's your fault, for distracting me. If you want to go further in, you're on your own."

"Why? What's—"

Fur on end, the cat darted away into the forest before he could finish.

Tristan watched the cat bolt, finding himself slightly crestfallen at its absence, and took a few slow steps forwards. Rubbing his still sore neck, he caught sight of something silver glinting through the trees. His heart leapt. *Epona's mane! They found me!*

He rushed through the trees towards the sight. Skidding to a hard stop in a clearing, his heart thumped even harder against his ribcage. There were no animals around, as if they, like the cat, sensed danger in this small glade. Only a small, cramped cage – rusted with age and use – lay here.

A ragged man sat cross-legged in its centre. It seemed too small for him to comfortably stand up straight, yet not so small that he was restricted in other movement. His head had snapped up the moment Tristan had burst through the foliage, and now his dark eyes narrowed in suspicion.

From what Tristan could see, his clothes, obviously once fine and expensive, were now old and worn. Tristan took a few wary steps forward, wondering who this man could be. Before he could make up his mind, the man spoke first.

"Who are you?" the man asked. He looked tired, his timeless eyes lined with care and fatigue. His thick, dark hair fell far past his shoulders in dirty waves. Upon seeing Tristan hesitate, he frowned.

"Oh," he said. "Never mind, I can tell." His voice was cracked and dry, though Tristan now noticed the accent was well-educated and refined.

Tristan looked around, wondering what would happen if he just ignored him and left. The prisoner seemed to guess his thoughts, and broke into a dark, sneering laugh.

"Why did you come alone?" he asked, and leaned forward slightly "I would have thought your father would want to—"

"You know my father?" Tristan blurted. *Perhaps this man is one of my mother's people?*

The prisoner raised an eyebrow.

"Don't you know who I am?" he asked, looking slightly offended. Tristan swallowed hard and shook his head. He took a step forward, despite his better judgement.

The prisoner snorted and leaned back in his cage again. He paused.

"So..." he cast his eyes behind Tristan. "You're here alone?"

Tristan nodded again.

"What's your name?"

"Tell me who you are, first," Tristan countered. It was always good to be wary of strange men locked in cages; most of the time they were there for good reason. The prisoner glared at Tristan, as if deciding if he was being stupid on purpose.

"Very well," the prisoner huffed. "I'm the former Lord of the Unseelie Court, Prince Regent of Elphame, and Dragon King of Tír-Na-Nóg."

Tristan was barely listening. Only one word caught his attention.

"Former?" he repeated. The prisoner sighed hard.

"Yes, *former*. Do you think the people of my kingdom take orders from a wretch in a cage? I've been *deposed*, idiot child..." he made a derisive noise in his throat. "You're definitely a Rhymer."

"How do you know my father?"

"No fair, *amadán*. Play by the rules," the prisoner said. "You tell me your name, now."

Tristan chewed the inside of his mouth.

"Tristan," he said. "How do you know my father? And why are you in a cage?"

The prisoner yawned pointedly.

"You ask a lot of questions."

"I'm a curious person. Why are you in that cage?"

The prisoner huffed and rolled his eyes. He paused, then lowered his gaze to his lap.

"The woman I love put me here," he said quietly.

"Why?" Tristan pressed. The prisoner sighed again, looking irritated now.

"If you let me out, I'll tell you."

"How can I trust you?" Despite his words, Tristan's hand drifted to his pocket, where he kept his bent pin. The prisoner looked mildly affronted.

"You have my word, *amad*—Tristan."

Tristan narrowed his eyes in suspicion.

The prisoner leaned forwards again, clutching the bars of his prison. Eyes gleaming, he sat up a little straighter. With what seemed like an unconscious thought, his hand went to his chest, and grasped something hidden under his weathered shirt.

"You can trust the word of a prince," he said slowly.

"Did she trust you?" Tristan asked. The prisoner – or prince – blinked.

"What?"

"Did she trust you?" he repeated. "The woman you love."

"She…" the prince paused. "I don't know. Maybe she did once."

A wild howling echoed loudly behind him, and as the foliage rustled, several wolves burst from the bracken and snarled at Tristan. They were fearsome, enormous beasts, larger than any wolf Tristan had ever seen, their fur milk-white; their growling like the low rumbling of thunder; red eyes glinting hungrily. Tristan staggered back.

"No!" the prisoner leapt forwards and reached through the bars of his cage to grab Tristan, but he'd stepped too far out of reach. He turned and fled into the darkness of the wood, never looking back to see if the wolves were pursuing him.

CHAPTER 9

"Think on it now, then"

"**M**ONGRELS," ERLIK SNEERED. The wolves growled at him, circling his cage. One approached and snapped at him through the bars, its lower jaw matted with blood; Erlik pulled his arm out of biting reach.

"Our mistress bade us guard you, Poison-Hoarder," the wolf rasped. Erlik laughed, and retreated again when the wolf snarled at him.

"And you perform your task so diligently," he said. "Mab would be proud."

"The Old Gods gave us a hunger, we must hunt to satisfy it," another wolf growled. Erlik tutted mockingly and shook his head.

"And what would your mistress say? Betrayed by her most trusted, most *faithful* lieutenants."

"But you did not escape, and our mistress remains safe. The boy has fled, he will not return. You will not escape your prison, Poison-Hoarder," the wolf paced in front of Erlik.

"Stop calling—only Mab calls me that," he said quietly. The wolf gave a deep, throaty laugh.

"Feeling maudlin, Poison-Hoarder?" he asked. Erlik threw the wolf a venomous glare, then huffed and lowered his eyes to his lap again.

"Look to better yourself. Our mistress approaches," the

wolf barked suddenly. Erlik's head snapped up at once. He inhaled deeply, and her overpowering scent burned his nostrils with the bitter tang of wood smoke and nightshade. His eyes began to water. He blinked them dry in case she mistook it for tears.

A magnificent white stag strode out from between the trees, though Erlik was certain he hadn't heard its hoof beats approach. The stag grunted in distress upon entering the glade, and its rider tugged the reins to quieten it. More wolves accompanied, the largest of the pack loyally at her heel as ever.

She dismounted, her black boots silent as snowfall on the mossy earth. Her fur-lined cloak swept around her like smoke, but it couldn't hide the rich purple gown she wore, nor the black corset cinched about her waist to accent her enticing curves. She glittered with crystals and silver jewellery, as though she'd been borne from black stars. A band of silver vines wound around her hand and fingers, and a delicate headdress of silver chains and onyx stones flowed through her dark hair. Her eyes burned with passionate fire, sparkling like moonlight on a snowy bank.

Erlik took in another deep breath and let it out again with a somewhat hungry smile as she approached. He held out his hand to her without thinking, and retracted it again immediately when a wolf snapped at him. Erlik glowered at the beast, and looked up at Mab again. Wolves surrounded her; her guard against a dragon in his cage. His scowl melted into a smile as she kneeled down to his level.

"Not a word for decades," he said, not unkindly. "And now you come."

"Not a spoken word, perhaps," she said. "I have heard your voice every day in my mind. You say my name so often, it is difficult to ignore."

Erlik noticed there was no harshness or bitterness in her voice, and he smiled inwardly.

"Then why haven't you come to me until now?" he frowned, then tilted his head back and closed his eyes. "Ohh… of course. Now you *want* something."

The wolves around her snarled at him.

"Have a care how you speak, *Nathair*," one of them growled. "She is the Mistress of Magic, show her every respect!"

Mab stood and approached the wolf, running her gloved hand over its head. The beast was so large, and Mab so small, that she had no need to lean forward or kneel down to stroke it. The wolves surrounded her in a protective circle.

"Faolan, take your pack and scout the area," she said to the largest wolf. "I will call for you when I am finished."

The beast hesitated for a moment. Then bowed its head in respectful acknowledgement, and turned away, followed by the others.

Mab waited until the wolves had completely vanished from sight before looking back at Erlik. He smirked.

"Alone at last," he said. Mab kneeled down and reached through the bars. He watched her hand and narrowed his eyes slightly, but she only wiped a smear of dirt off his cheek. He looked at her suspiciously, and her lip crooked into a smile.

"Indeed," she said softly, and stood up again. Erlik watched her, admiring the way the weak sunlight glistened in her dark hair and exploded in the jewels entwined in the locks.

"You *do* want something," he asked to her back, and she stopped and looked over her shoulder at him. His voice became a familiar low growl. "Well, so do I. I want my freedom."

Mab sighed. For a brief moment, Erlik thought he saw a flicker of fear cross her face. But it passed almost as quickly, and he realised it must have been a shadow or a trick of the light.

"Say something, Mab."

"The Iron Keep has become occupied once more."

Erlik faltered. He hadn't heard the name of *that* place in a long time. Icy fear slipped down his gullet.

Clearing his throat, he affected a tone of nonchalance, "That mouldering old ruin? Only an eyesore. It was abandoned centuries ago, you know that," he said casually. Mab turned around fully to face him.

"'Tis no longer a ruin. It has been rebuilt," she said.

That icy fear spread its touch across his whole body. He repressed a shiver that had nothing to do with the weather.

"By whom?" Erlik asked with a frown. *Surely not…?*

For a moment, he wondered if Mab was indeed there to release him. *She needs me. She must. Or she wouldn't be here.*

"A sorcerer. I am told his name is Maleagant. Do you know of him?" she asked. Erlik exhaled in relief, his original fears unfounded.

"Never heard of him," he said. He sniffed and pretended to look thoughtful. "I suppose I may be able to help."

Mab's mouth twitched into a knowing smile, and she leaned to gently stroke the bars of the cage. Erlik carefully watched her expression.

"And what would you want in return?" she asked. Erlik laughed, and leaned his back against the bars as casually as possible within his confines.

"Gold, land, power," he reeled off, smiling. Mab shook her head.

"You have no love for wealth, you never have," she said. "Tell me truly, what do you want?"

Erlik's smile slipped slightly. *Are you serious, Mab?*

"To be with you," he said, as though it were the simplest thing in the world. "Don't you already know that?"

Mab's warm smile vanished. She sighed and turned away, and he caught the look of disappointment on her face as she did so.

"Erlik," she said softly. It was the first time she'd said his name since arriving, and hearing it in her voice was intoxicating. "You are too predictable. You are like the shadow on a sundial, forever turning in the same cycle."

Erlik tore his eyes away from her. His sorrow gave way to anger.

"What do you want from me, Mab? Why have you come?" he snapped. "To torment me?"

"No," she said quickly, turning back and kneeling down to

his height. "I truly do need you—your help."

A glimmer of mischievous excitement rippled through him at her words, quashing the irritation that had risen up at her rebuff. He didn't let it show. *Let her think I'm angry with her.*

"What do you *need* me to do, then?" he asked in a low voice. She twisted her hands for a brief moment, her eyes darting.

"If I release you…" she paused. Swallowed her words, then began again: "I fear there is something sinister occurring in the Iron Keep. I need you to go there, discover its secrets, and return to me with your findings."

"Why me? Why not just storm the Keep? Or send spies?"

"I considered the first option," she admitted. "But to send an army would be an invitation for open war. I cannot risk that. Enough blood has been shed already. There are strange monsters running free throughout Albion, and the Mortasheen is striking down my people. And Maleagant has sent bewitched assassins to kill me—"

"*What?* When? What happened, were you hurt?"

Mab shook her head, and again he caught a slight hint of a smile. "After such an attack, I opted for a more covert approach. I sent spies to the Keep to discover his intent. I assumed, to fight one so sly as to send ensorcelled assassins, I must respond in kind. Yet none of my spies have returned. I fear they have either betrayed me, or are dead."

"So you're sending me because I'm *expendable?*"

"Of course not," she rounded on him. "I want you to go because I know you would not betray me. Because I know you are the strongest and cleverest man for this task. I was foolish to send spies, when I should have sent a trickster."

Erlik allowed himself to smile openly.

"And what happens after?" he said quietly, gazing at her.

Mab froze.

"What?"

"If I do this thing you ask," he began again. "What happens to me afterwards?"

Mab's brow twitched into a frown.

"Am I forgiven? Am I to be returned here? Tell me."

"I…" she paused. "I do not know. I had not thought on it."

"Think on it now, then," he braced himself, almost daring himself to ask. "Would you… or, would we…" he trailed off, losing his nerve.

Her violet-taloned fingers gently grasped the bars.

"Give me time, *a múirnín*," she said as she cast her eye over his tattered clothes and overlong hair. Her head tilted.

"Oh," she whispered, almost to herself. "Look at you."

Suddenly self-conscious under her gaze, Erlik ran a hand through his hair and plucked away a few stray threads from his scruffy clothes. Mab smiled.

"You will think on it?" he asked quietly, his dark eyes boring into hers.

"I will."

Mab stood up and looked down at him. Erlik grabbed the bars of his cage.

"No! Don't leave," he said. He wanted – he *needed* – more time with her. Mab said nothing, but turned to mount her stag.

"Please!"

Mab stopped. His heart jumped.

"Please," he said again, softer. "Stay. Just… just a little longer."

She faced him again, her expression unreadable. Was that… pity? Love, even?

When last they spoke, she admitted it herself. He'd heard those words from her own lips.

I love you.

"Have you changed?" she asked quietly. Erlik lowered his eyes. How could he even answer that? He didn't know who he'd been before, and he didn't know what he was now.

"I don't know," he admitted. "All I know is what's in my heart."

"Which is?"

"That I'd never hurt you again," Erlik looked up at her. Her eyes sparkled, but there were no tears falling. How could there be? She never wept. Her lips parted slowly.

How he longed to feel them on his again. Just one more time...

"Faolan," she called. The alpha stepped out of the bracken almost immediately. Erlik glared at it. Had the beast been listening?

"You are relieved of your duties. You need no longer guard the Dragon King. You and your pack may return to your hunting grounds. And," she added. "You must tell no one of this. Do you understand?"

Faolan hesitated and glanced at Erlik, who frowned in confusion.

"Mistress, I assure you there are no better guards to the Poison-Hoarder than my pack. We—"

"I know, Faolan," Mab smiled, and ran her hand over the wolf's head. With a snarl at Erlik, the wolf howled at the sky, and led its pack away. Mab took the reins of her stag and turned back to Erlik, approaching his cage again.

She hesitated.

"This is no doubt a terrible idea. I fear I may come to regret this," she said slowly. More to herself than to him. "But sometimes recklessness is required."

She pulled the cage door, "Come." It opened easily at her touch. Erlik stared at her, but didn't move.

"I thought you said—"

"I am not taking you back to Elphame. There would be chaos. But I do require your help, whether I like it or not. Unless you would rather stay in there?" Mab added coolly.

Erlik slowly crawled forwards, unable to fully stand until he was free of his prison. He pushed himself to his feet with his hands, bones creaking and cracking as he straightened. With a low groan of soreness, he stretched his cramped, aching body. Everything burned as blood flowed back into his limbs, his stiff back and legs worst of all.

Mab watched him, face contorted into a wince, but there was a definite spark of pity in her eyes. It both thrilled and infuriated him. Erlik gave a breathless laugh of relief, relishing in his freedom. Then his knees buckled and he stumbled forwards, but Mab grabbed him and kept him upright.

"Oh—steady!" she said quickly, as she wrapped his arm around her shoulder to keep him on his feet. "You must take things slower. You *have* been in there for seventy years."

"Seventy-six," he corrected, his words coming muffled as he pressed his mouth against the top of her head. "Thank you. You've no idea how I've longed for this moment."

Mab paused and pulled away.

"Come," she said, leading him away from the cage. "There is a pool nearby. What you should have longed for is a *bath*."

CHAPTER 10

"Just a trinket."

THOMAS ROLLED OVER onto his back and yawned. Stretching, careful not to wake Thissy, he got to his feet and stepped out of the tent to welcome the morning air.

A pink sky greeted him when he stepped outside. The sight of it, framed by the swaying treetops, along with the heady scent of the earth and the quick chattering of birdsong, drove from his memory the sight of watching his home burning, and Hopkins's twisted, sneering face.

At least we're all alive, he thought. He turned back inside to gaze at Thissy's slumbering form. She was a marvel. He smiled, remembering when he'd first returned home from Albion with her.

His mother had frozen solid as he'd strode through the door. He'd worried for a brief moment that her heart had given out, until she dropped the bowl in her hands and staggered towards him.

"Thomas…" he remembered the break in her voice as she threw her arms around him and hugged him so hard he thought his ribs might crack.

Thissy had shyly crept in behind him, and Margaret, eyes so blurred with joyful tears, barely saw her.

"Mistress Rhymer," Thissy cleared her throat quietly, and Margaret's gaze turned to her. Though her smile slipped a little, more out of surprise than disappointment, one glance at Thomas's shining, proud face, and she pulled Thissy into a bone-bruising embrace.

Thomas's laughter had drawn Alissa's attention, and she burst into the room. Barely registering the shards of broken clay on the floor, she too dashed to him and fiercely hugged him. Wildly sobbing and of course calling him every version of stupid she could think of.

Thomas sighed and smiled at the memory.

As though she could sense his gaze on her, Thissy opened her eyes and smiled lazily at him.

"Good morning," she said through a yawn.

"Indeed it is, when I wake up next to such a beautiful lady," he said, kneeling down to kiss her good morning.

She swatted him playfully, still half asleep, and sat up.

"We should reach Elphame shortly, if the weather stays fine," Thissy said, lacing up the front of her dress. Thomas nodded, thinking more on his rumbling stomach, and watched her approach Tristan's tent to wake up.

"It's winter here, we should've brought warmer clothing," Thomas yawned, noting the chill in the air and rubbing his arms.

"Tristan," Thissy peeled back the tent flap. "Time to wake up."

A pause.

"Tristan? *Tristan!*"

An arrow of panic lanced through Thomas. Memories of his mother trying to wake Alissa so many years ago flooded his mind's eye.

Thissy lurched out of the tent, eyes scanning the forest.

"Tristan!" Thissy called, fully awake now, her voice mirroring the panic Thomas felt. "Tristan, where are you?"

The words echoed back to her, mocking. No reply save the twittering of disturbed birds.

"*Tristan!*" Thomas's voice, deeper than Thissy's, echoed only louder with no reply from their son.

"Where is he?" Thissy spun in circles, eyes scanning the

trees, frantically twisting her hands. "Who took him?"

"No one, look," Thomas pointed at the single pair of footprints in the dirt. "He's just wandered off. He can't be far, come on," Thomas said.

Though he tried to keep his voice calm and soothing, inside he blistered with fear. It had been years since he'd faced the horrors of what Albion had to offer, but that didn't stop his heart from thumping against his windpipe.

Nothing in Albion could be as deadly or dangerous as Erlik, he reasoned. *Besides, he's imprisoned; he couldn't possibly escape the cage Mab put him in.*

Yet the wicked laughter of a mad god-prince kept invading his mind. He shook himself mentally.

"Come," he said again, striding to Epona to wake her properly, leaving their tents and bedrolls as they were; everything of importance was still packed up.

Thissy chewed her lip as she mounted the horse behind Thomas. She took the reins of Tristan's horse – the grey gelding he'd nicknamed Grisel as a boy – and carefully led it to walk beside her. He kicked Epona into movement, and she trotted off, each pair of eyes scanning the surroundings for any signs of movement.

"Where could he have gone?" Thissy said, and Thomas caught the bleak fear in her tone.

"He's a curious lad, my love," he replied, gently patting her hand on his waist. "Don't fret, we'll find him."

✧   ✧   ✧

"Ow!" ERLIK CRINGED away as Mab dabbed at the abrasions on his chest and shoulders with a tincture-soaked cloth.

"Stop being such a child. Hold *still*," she insisted, and gently pulled him back. She upturned the green bottle onto the cloth and patted a nasty graze on his shoulder. Erlik hissed with pain and shirked away again. Sighing, Mab gave him a patronising look.

"You are being very difficult."

"It *hurts*," he whined, and reluctantly returned to her. "Why don't you just use your magic?"

"You know fine well why," she said, soaking the cloth again. Mab raised an eyebrow and adopted an innocent look when he moved out of her reach again. "Unless you *want* to be poisoned?"

Erlik huffed and said nothing.

Mab sighed and continued cleaning the wounds on his shoulders, as Erlik watched the waterfall that fed the pool by which they sat. The cascading water was oddly mesmerising, the way the fading golden light skittered across the gentle waves.

"Almost finished," Mab said softly at last. "Then you can clean yourself up. Leave your clothes in a pile over there."

"You first—*OW!*"

Mab had dabbed hard at a deep cut on his chest, which stung viciously.

"Whoops."

Erlik scowled, though there was no menace in his gaze.

"How did you even get these wounds?" she asked with genuine curiosity.

Erlik shrugged, "Disagreements with your wolves. Throwing myself against the bars for freedom. Moments of despair when I thought there was no point in living anymore."

Mab stared at him in horror, her face growing more ashen with every word. Her breast heaved and she swallowed hard. Erlik held her gaze, almost daring her to speak.

"What happened?" she breathed.

Erlik swept his eyes over her face. *Look at those eyes. A man could drown in them.*

"I fell," he said slowly. "In and out of madness. I'd lost everything. Most of my children were dead. The only one still alive hated me. I had nothing left. No home. No family. No love. *Nothing.*"

Mab swallowed but said nothing.

Erlik went on, "Some days were better than others. I

would go months, *years*, where I didn't even know my own name."

Her trembling lips formed his name, as though to remind him. Her brows were drawn in despair.

"Sometimes I thought I heard your voice," he said. "Talking, singing, anything. It brought me back. Grounded me. Made me remember. Remember what I'd done, to your people, your city. To you."

He closed his eyes now. Blood flushed into his cheeks. He turned his face away.

"I realised I could hear you, your thoughts, from so far away. It kept me sane. *You* kept me sane."

She stared at him for a long time. His heart thumped when he realised he'd frightened her into silence.

"Was I right? Did you think of me every day?"

She cleared her throat and stood up.

"Call for me when you are done," she said, turning her back on him. The formality in her voice hurt more than he cared to admit.

Erlik pulled off his breeches and sunk into the pool. The water was ice-cold, but the sweet crispness eased into warmth as blood flowed back into his still-aching limbs.

MAB STOOD BY her stag, idly patting its neck. She had surprised herself by freeing Erlik, despite having come to this forbidden place with every intention of speaking with him and leaving. Even in this dirty, dishevelled state, she couldn't deny the way her heart leapt whenever he said her name.

And his story chilled her to the core. Had she pushed him to this? Left him there too long? His fragile grip on sanity was so tenuous. It frightened her. How had it become so? It had not always been. When they first met, when they first kissed, first confessed their love. Her heart danced in her chest.

Seeing his face again after so many years forced old, painful, bittersweet memories to resurface. Yet he seemed so repentant. So... *sincere*. Was it a trick? A ruse to lower her guard? Or was there truth in his sorrowful words? He had always been silver-tongued, even in their youth. But perhaps, now, after so long, she could allow herself to trust him. Trust his feelings. Trust her own.

And – infuriatingly – he was right. She *had* thought of him every day.

Get a hold on yourself, Mab, she thought sternly to herself, rolling her eyes. *You are a queen, not a bashful youngling.*

She shook her head, closing her eyes. She had come to ask his help against Maleagant, nothing more. Once the threat had been dealt with, she would… he would…

"Mab?"

She looked back. She stroked the stag once more, and returned to the clearing.

"That was fast—oh! I thought you were finished."

Erlik was still in the water. Mab quickly averted her eyes, but had already caught a glimpse of the droplets of crystal water clinging to his chest. She turned her back to offer him privacy.

"You didn't leave me anything to change into," he said. The smugness in his voice needled her.

Mab waved a hand without turning, and a small pile of clothes appeared beside the pool. There was a sloshing of water and a gentle rustling of fabric. "Are you done?" she asked.

"Yes," came his voice behind her. She turned, a little faster than she intended, and nodded as she took in his appearance: the shirt hung on him like a sack. Her gaze softened and her shoulders dropped.

"Very well," she said, and beckoned him to follow. "Come, there is a pot on the fire."

MAB LADLED THE watery vegetable broth into a bowl. Plucking at the overly-large shirt to make it hang better on his slender frame, Erlik sat opposite, eyes flickering between the food and her. As soon as she handed him the steaming bowl, he snatched it from her hands and gulped down the broth, ignoring the blistering heat on his lips.

Mab cleared her throat, and Erlik lowered the bowl and swallowed his mouthful. He wiped his mouth with the back of his hand, looking nonplussed.

"What?" he asked. With a knowing smile, she offered him a wooden spoon. He took it begrudgingly and started to eat in a more civilised manner. Mab watched him until he had almost finished, when he lowered the bowl and shifted uncomfortably, scratching the back of his neck where his long hair tickled.

"Will you cut my hair?" then quickly added, "Please?"

Mab smiled and ran her hand through his recently washed hair. It fell far past his shoulders when clean and dried off a little. Erlik held back a shiver; her fingers brushed the back of his neck.

"If you like," she said, then gestured to her own lengthy tresses. "Though I suppose if we leave it much more, it will be longer than mine." Her voice carried a teasing inflection, but with fondness intertwined. Erlik buried his sudden burst of affection beneath a scowl.

Mab shifted to sit behind him, and after a few moments, he heard the unmistakable sound of a blade. Her nimble hands moved deftly, and Erlik had to repress another shiver.

Finally, she lowered the scissors and brushed the cuttings off his shoulders.

"There," she said. He ran his hand through his hair; it was still a little longer than he was used to, but he said nothing. If it pleased Mab, then he wouldn't complain.

"Thank you."

"You are welcome," she smiled at him and stood. "Finish up, and I will find somewhere for you to sleep."

"You're not staying?"

"I will be back soon."

"Wait," Erlik's eyes scanned the glade. "Where are my old clothes?"

Mab nodded towards a pile of rags, and his heart leapt into his throat. He ran over and rummaged through them for a while until finally, he found his treasure: a silver ring on a chain, which he slipped around his neck and tucked into his shirt, hiding it from sight.

He turned to find Mab watching him with a raised eyebrow. He said nothing, and silently hoped she wouldn't question him.

"What did you take?"

Damn.

"Nothing," he lied quickly. "Just a trinket."

To his enormous relief, she didn't press him. She simply made a *hmm* noise and nodded.

"Very well," she said. "Stay here, I will be back shortly."

She left the glade in silence, and Erlik returned to the fire.

"I HAVE FOUND somewhere for you to sleep tonight," Mab announced as she returned. Erlik hastily shoved the chain and its treasure back under his shirt. She beckoned him, and he stood, though his balance was still unsteady.

"Are you still sore?" she asked. Erlik stretched, and his bones creaked and popped; he winced.

"A little."

"Do you need help?"

Erlik grimaced and shook his head.

"You just need a good night's rest," she said. "Follow me."

Mab led him back to the pool, where she gestured at the waterfall. The water parted like curtains, revealing a large cave behind. Erlik watched as Mab made her way towards it, delicately stepping over the streams and rocks to enter. Mentally shaking himself, Erlik followed quickly before the water could close behind her.

"'Tis simple, but it has everything you will need for now," she said, moving to light numerous candles. As flickering light filled the cave like fireflies, Erlik took in the small bed, wash basin, and fire pit.

"Will you stay with me?" he asked, and she shook her head.

"No. I must return to Elphame." Erlik sat down on the bed and ran his hand over the downy pillow. He suddenly realised how comfortable he would be, lying on something soft and warm for the first time in almost a century.

"I will come back tomorrow," she continued, and Erlik looked up, surprised. "There are many things we need to discuss."

She paused, chewing her lower lip.

"There is one more thing," she said slowly. "At some point during the night, your strength and magic will return," she said. Erlik's brow knitted. Mab continued, "I only ask that, when they do, you do not use them against me, my people, or my allies. This sorcerer, this new threat, is greater than any quarrel between us. I need you on my side, and I cannot lose you as an ally. Do I have your word?"

Mab leaned forwards, her face so close to his that he could see himself reflected in her eyes. Erlik gazed at her and cupped her face, gently rubbing her cheek with his thumb.

"You have my word," he said softly. Mab narrowed her eyes.

"I will not ask for a Binding; that is a magic I will forever abhor," she said. Erlik's hand dropped from her cheek. Her words felt like a red-hot brand against his heart.

"So I need you to swear to me, I need to hear it from your lips, you will help me, and you will not use your magic against me for your own gain."

"I swear it," he said sincerely. "Do you want me on my knees? How can I make you trust me?"

"Deeds, not words." She said no more. Erlik followed her to the edge of the cave.

"I will see you again tomorrow," she said. In a moment of weakness, Erlik took her hand and kissed her palm gently, closing her fist around the kiss as though to keep it hidden. Mab looked up at him, surprised.

"I—" she cleared her throat. "Goodnight, Erlik."

He smiled, "Goodnight, my love."

CHAPTER II

"Come away, human child"

 RISTAN RUBBED HIS arms against the wind. Certain now the wolves had stopped pursuing him, he'd found himself on a rocky beach. He cursed his curiosity. *Why did I walk so far? Why did I speak to the prince in the cage?*

Grumbling to himself, he'd sat for a while and contented himself with watching the waves incessantly chew the shoreline. The shadows grew longer as the day stretched on.

"You realise Elphame is in the other direction, don't you?"

Tristan's heart jumped a thousand yards in shock. The *Cat Sidhe* sat beside him, delicately nibbling the claws of its front paw.

"I thought you'd ran away," Tristan said dryly.

"Not far," the cat replied, slowly blinking at him. "But far enough. *Cat Sidhe* will always run from a dragon. Like most sensible creatures, I imagine."

"I didn't hear a dragon," Tristan said. Surely he would have heard the beating of enormous wings or the roar of a creature ten times his size?

"That's because you're *not* a sensible creature," the cat said. "I quite like the coast. Wolves don't come here as much. Got any eggs?"

"Not since the last time we spoke. I like the coast too," Tristan said. "My mother used to take me, when I was very young. I made mountains in the sand."

"I steal fish from the fishermen's nets," the cat said, as though this was a way of relating to him. Tristan threw the cat a wry smile.

They sat in silence for a while. The cat's eyes grew blacker as the sun crept towards the horizon and slowly sank beneath it.

Tristan finally stood, brushing sand from his breeches, and said, "I really should be going." He glanced about him, wondering which way he should attempt. In brushing himself down, he'd suddenly realised how bruised and battered he still was from his fall in the forest. Perhaps he wasn't as tough-skinned as he'd told the cat.

"If you're still looking for Elphame, I'd head in *that* direction," the *Cat Sidhe* nodded east. "Though it's a long walk without a wagon or a horse."

"I suppose I'd better make a start, then," Tristan said. "Care to come with me?"

The *Cat Sidhe* bristled and said, "As delightful as that sounds, it's time to hunt."

Tristan released a small laugh. He was growing more and more fond of this strange creature.

"As you wish," he said. "Perhaps I'll see you at Elphame one day."

The *Cat Sidhe* gave him something of a smile, showing off his pointed teeth.

"Perhaps you will," it shuddered, fur bristling, "if Mab ever deigns to get rid of those awful wolves of hers."

Without another word, the *Cat Sidhe* turned and leapt away into the darkness. Tristan silently wished it luck in its hunting.

Tristan shrugged and turned east. The sun sank lower as he walked, and the sand beneath his feet gave way to pebbles and then rocks that made him slip and stumble. He walked on, trying to ignore the gathering darkness. His legs ached with exertion and bruises.

The night sky above glittered with a thousand diamonds.

The crashing waves sent the briny smell washing over him with every break. The scent was somehow comforting, as if someone had just wrapped a warm blanket around him, despite the frosty air.

Suddenly, out of the darkness, just up ahead, his eyes caught a dim glimmer of faint blue light. Tristan stopped. The light was accompanied by the pleasant sound of laughing. He gulped and looked around, then approached the light and laughter.

As he grew close, he noticed the light hid behind a cluster of rocks. Laying down his broken bow and empty quiver, he leaned against the largest boulder and pulled himself upwards to steal a glance. As he did so, his foot slipped, and the small tumbling of pebbles sounded like the crashing of boulders.

He heard women gasp and stop laughing. With the sound of splashing, the blue light vanished. Tristan scrambled forwards, but there was no one there. The women were gone, and Tristan sighed softly as he sat himself down and stared out at the black, silent ocean.

"Hullo," a soft, silvery voice whispered. Tristan nearly slipped off the rock. He regained his balance and looked around. A dim blue light shone from where the water gently slapped the stone, and Tristan crept towards it, slipping on the stranded seaweed as he approached.

As he crested the rock, he lowered himself to his belly to look down into the water. A white-haired head shyly lifted up, and a beautiful girl gazed at him with violet eyes. Tristan stared, and the girl giggled and pulled herself higher, closer to him.

Her arms were long, sinewy, and strong, and thin membranes of white, scaly fins clung to her forearms like waterweeds. She wore nothing to hide her bare chest, and Tristan felt heat rush to his cheeks. He averted his eyes, but found himself staring, not at a pair of feet, but a long, powerful fish tail beating against the tide.

Tristan felt his heart give a thump. His mother had told him stories of these creatures. Beings with the upper bodies of beautiful women, but the lower bodies of fish.

The merrow laughed shyly, and put her cold, webbed fingers against his cheek to direct his gaze back to her face. Her hand was slimy, but Tristan found, once he looked again into her violet eyes, he didn't care. More merrows appeared around her, glowing blue under the moonlight. They laughed and crooned as they pulled themselves up onto the rocks and surrounded Tristan, caressing him and pulling him down to them.

He felt himself slip into the water. He bobbed there like a cork, held adrift by the merrow's strong arms. With a quiet splash, the other three slid back into the water with the grace of seals.

"Come away, human child," the first merrow sang in her silvery voice.

Cold water seeped into his clothes and soaked his hair as the merrows pushed him beneath the surface of the waves. They followed him underwater, smiling sweetly and caressing him with tender fingers.

Water flooded his mouth and up his nose, and yet he found he couldn't move. His arms were paralysed, and his legs wouldn't respond to the commands of his waterlogged brain. Seawater filled his lungs. Sharp pain stabbed his chest. The merrows didn't relinquish their powerful grip on him, dragging him deeper down, despite his struggles. Their laughter seemed less sweet now, their eyes blacker, their needle teeth in rows like sharks'.

Tristan opened his mouth to scream but only bubbles escaped and more water rushed in. *Air!* he begged in his mind. The merrows closed in, circling and crooning in their husky voices. He felt himself sinking, deeper and deeper, pulled down by his own water-sodden body and the strong arms of the first shy little merrow, who now leered hungrily at him.

Suddenly, a vivid orange light appeared through the black water like a burst of sunlight. The merrows squealed and scattered like flies, as a great splashing announced the arrival of Tristan's saviour.

Through the darkness of his half-closed eyes, he saw a figure swimming downwards, gracefully piercing the water like an arrow through the air. Arms wrapped around him, gripped him tight, pulled him higher, towards the blissfully open air.

Tristan and his saviour broke the surface of the water with a great slosh of waves, coughing and spluttering and splashing. The stranger dragged him out of the water and onto the pebbles of the beach.

"Here, get your slimy backsides back to Melusine, you scaly water rats!" shouted a thickly accented voice. There was a loud plunging splash; it sounded like the stranger had thrown a heavy rock into the sea.

Tristan gulped down the air desperately. He rolled onto his front and vomited seawater onto the shore. Pushing sodden hair out of his face, he blinked furiously to stop the salt from burning his eyes. His breathing ragged, his vision slowly returned.

"You mad?" asked the stranger, who Tristan could properly see now by the flickering light of his torch. "You tryin' to get yourself killed or somethin'?"

Tristan tried to say 'thank you', but when he opened his mouth to speak, he found he could only cough up more seawater.

"Here now," the stranger said, sounding concerned. "You don't sound so good, let me fix up somethin' for you."

The stranger sat beside him and pulled his satchel open. Tristan vaguely heard the clink of bottles and various mumblings, followed by a victorious *"ha!"*

"Wait here, try not to move if you can, and wrap yourself in that blanket in me satchel."

Tristan obliged, and, still coughing, pulled a blanket – that seemed too large to fit into the satchel – out of the stranger's pack and flung it around his shoulders. Warmth immediately seeped into his bones.

After a short while, the stranger returned carrying an armful of sticks.

"Th-thank you," Tristan managed to cough out. "You

saved my life."

"Aye, well," the stranger looked uncomfortably humble. "Don't take much to scare them scraggy pests away. Just need a bit of old Brigid's Kiss. *Fire*," he added, when Tristan stared blankly at him.

"M-my name's Tristan," he said, sitting up straight and squeezing water out of his shirt and hair.

"M'name's Lir. Lir of Ériu's Isle. Come by these parts to fish of a night time, there's a good spot just along by the— here," he snapped his fingers in front of Tristan's eyes. "You listenin'?"

Tristan blinked. He'd been gazing thoughtlessly at the ocean, feeling an odd sort of longing.

"What?" Tristan dragged his attention back to Lir, who frowned.

"Hmm, them water rats must've drowned you fairly bad," he said. "Looks like you've picked up a touch of Sailor's Fever. Just the after-effects of Melusine's beauties. It'll pass, don't worry."

Lir took a healthy swig from a leather hipflask and offered some to Tristan.

"Best get you away from the water's edge," he said as Tristan took a gulp of whatever was in the flask. It burned his throat. "Once a merrow takes a shine to you, she'll be after your bones for a while. Come on."

Lir shoved the sticks he'd collected into his satchel, along with the jar of *something* he'd pulled out earlier. Tristan grabbed his bow and quiver from the water's edge and followed him along the beach. Lir's torch spread a circle of light around them. The warmth from the fire and the blanket enveloped Tristan like a loving embrace.

"I've never met a merrow before," Tristan said, casting a glance back to the rocks. Lir laughed.

"Bet you never want to again, though, eh?" he said. Tristan snorted in agreement. "How did you come by Tumblin' Bay in the first place? Wouldn't be most folks' idea of a night time stroll. Here seems fine enough."

Lir stopped abruptly and dumped his satchel. He sat down and dug out the sticks he'd collected, gathered them into a pile, and thrust the flames of his torch into the wood. The fire crackled and took root. Tristan watched enviously. *I could do that with just a gesture when my magic manifests. Eventually.*

"I got lost," he said aloud. His voice was croakier than usual and he coughed once more to clear it. It didn't help. "I was chased by a pack of wolves in the forest, and I ended up here."

"Wolves?" Lir repeated with a snort. "You must've rightly pissed off some royal folk to get wolves chasin' you."

Lir shuddered, and Tristan nodded even though he didn't quite understand. Lir stoked the fire with a lump of driftwood and pulled out the little bottle and a small cast-iron pot from his bag.

"That satchel," Tristan said carefully. "Is it… enchanted or something?"

Lir gave him a sly smile, "What makes you say that?"

"It seems to carry a lot more than it should," Tristan stared at the bag. Wholly unremarkable, it seemed like the same kind of satchel that his mother used when she gathered her herbs. Lir laughed hard and crushed up some herbs from the bottle.

"You're a sharp lad, even after your little swim with Melusine's beauties!" he said. "Aye, it's enchanted. Long story though."

"I've got time," Tristan smiled. Lir laughed again.

"Aye, I suppose you do. Alright then, long time ago, got myself into a bit o' trouble during a storm. Little boat I were in, the *Kingfisher*, went under. Found meself washed up on this tiny little island, so small you could see one end from the other!"

Tristan nodded as he listened. Lir set up three sturdy posts around the fire, bound together with strong twine, and hung the small pot between them. He invited Tristan to inhale the fumes that rose from the pot. He did so, and an earthy scent arose from the crushed herbs.

"Well it just so happened that a lovely lady lived on that

island, all alone there. And she'd grown ever so lonesome, so I kept her company for a while, if you know what I mean."

Lir winked and grinned. Tristan smiled. The fumes began soothing his still aching lungs. He found it much easier to breathe now.

"I managed to build myself a new boat so I could go back to fishin', and she gave me this satchel and enchanted it, made it bigger on the inside or somethin'."

"And she didn't mind you leaving?"

"Nahh," Lir snorted. "She knew I were a fisherman at heart, couldn't keep me in one place for too long. Start gettin' cabin fever, you know? I need to be out on the sea."

"Was she a seelie then? Or an unseelie?"

Lir shook his head, "Not that I ever noticed. Pointed ears, right? Or them glowy eyes the unseelie sometimes get when they're happy? And she were happy a *lot*, I tell you now!"

"So she was just… human? I didn't know humans could do magic."

"Aye, some can. They call it Mab's Blessing. Don't see any blessing in it, meself. Anything the Wolf Queen offers is more like a curse, if you ask me."

Lir shuddered and fell quiet.

Tristan spoke up, "My family were heading for Elphame when I got lost. Do you know the way?"

"Aye, I know the way," he said. "Tír-Na-Nóg is closer, though. We could head there in the mornin' and take a carriage. Might be easier on the legs. Not a young buck anymore, you know?"

Tír-Na-Nóg? Tristan thought. *That prisoner in the cage mentioned he used to be the prince there.*

He was about to ask about him, but a shadow at the other end of the beach roused his attention instead.

"What's that up there?" Tristan asked, pointing towards the other end of the beach. Tristan quickly realised it was a huge cliff. Lir looked over his shoulder, and Tristan swore he saw him shudder.

"That's Mab's Hill," Lir said quietly, and a shadow passed

over his face. Tristan suddenly realised for the first time since meeting him, Lir looked afraid. He didn't seem to like Mab very much. "There's hundreds of them, all over Albion. As far as I'm concerned, any man fool enough to climb up there and light that fire deserves everything she does to him."

"Why? What happens if you light the fire?" Tristan asked. Curiosity had taken hold of him, yet he touched his bow out of instinct. Lir leaned in closer, the firelight dancing on his face. He lowered his voice dramatically.

"If you light the fire on Mab's Hill, then she'll come for you."

"So?"

"*So?*" Lir repeated, looking aghast. "Silver Wheel, lad, like you want to go summoning the Beldam?"

"What are you talking about?"

"The Beldam! The Virago? The Kingmaker and Kingslayer? The Wolf Queen? She Who Rides The Battlefields?" Lir ticked off the names on his fingers as he went. Tristan raised an eyebrow.

"You're just saying *words* now," he said, unimpressed.

Lir dropped his hands and frowned, looking disappointed that his act hadn't frightened Tristan.

"She still scares *me*."

"So what's so bad about Mab coming for you?"

"Wouldn't wish it on any man, if I'm honest," Lir shuddered again. "Last poor sod that lit the fire had his eyes torn out."

"*What?*"

"Well she don't take too kindly to bein' summoned like that," he said, pleased he had Tristan's attention again. "So she took out his eyes and replaced 'em with wooden ones. Took his tongue and his teeth as well, 'swhat I heard. And his heart. Suppose the poor bastard thought himself lucky to be thrown on the fire after that."

Tristan folded his arms.

"You made that up," he said. Lir shook his head gravely and took a deep swig from his hipflask.

"Wish I had, lad," he said. "You should get some sleep. We'll head off for Tír-Na-Nóg in the mornin'."

Tristan nodded and thanked him. He lay down on the pebbles, his eyes fixed assuredly on the cliff, trying not to wonder if there was any truth to Lir's stories.

CHAPTER 12

"Every man has his price"

ERLIK LAY ON his bed and sighed. The scent of Mab still lingered in the air. He inhaled deeply, trying to recapture her presence. The cave's stone ceiling offered no comfort.

Softness soothed his aching body, and he closed his eyes. Darkness encroached on the mouth of the cave, and he briefly wondered if he should light the fire pit for warmth, but it was just so comfortable lying there—

"Not exactly a royal bedchamber, is it?" asked an obnoxious voice.

Erlik's eyes snapped open and he sat up at once. His gaze met a sneering man standing at the mouth of his cave.

"Who are you?" he growled, standing. "What are you doing here?"

The stranger casually looked around. Erlik watched him, realising with a sickening jolt that he had no weapons. *Need to rely on my wits alone for this.*

"It's a shame she didn't invite you back with her," the stranger said. "Or even stayed the night with you here."

The stranger took a few steps around the cave, using his long staff as a walking stick. His red and gold robes slithered over the slick rocks. Despite the obvious expense of his clothing, and the way he looked with disdain at the simple furnishings, Erlik couldn't help but notice the slimy, overly-smug look that hung about this man, like a servant who had risen above his master.

The stranger forced a condescending laugh.

"Oh, forgive me, I haven't introduced myself," he said. "My name is Maleagant."

He bowed low, but kept his eyes fixed on Erlik's.

"The sorcerer?" he asked, swallowing his anger. "I hear you're burrowed away in the Iron Keep."

Maleagant nodded, forcibly smiling, and banged his staff twice on the ground. A small, cushioned chair sprouted up from the rock, and Maleagant seated himself upon it.

"Your mongrel wife tell you that?" he asked.

Erlik snarled and leapt forward, a red haze descending over his vision, but Maleagant raised his hands in apology.

"Forgive me," he said, without sincerity. "Sometimes I speak before I think."

He smiled at Erlik again, and gestured for him to sit down too. Despite a growing, burning hatred for this foul little man, he obliged.

"What do you want?" Erlik asked again. Maleagant brushed down his robes unnecessarily.

"I understand your, ah, *lovely* Mab brought you here," he said. Erlik narrowed his eyes. He didn't like the way he said her name. "She's a terribly beautiful thing, isn't she?"

"She is not a *thing*," Erlik snarled at once, glaring at Maleagant.

The sorcerer gave his awful, contrived chuckle again.

"No need to be so defensive. You can keep your little she-wolf. She's too hot-blooded for my liking. I have other plans," he said.

"What plans?" Erlik asked. "If you intend to harm her, I'll—"

"You can't do anything. You have no weapons, and no magic. Not at the moment, at least. Which is why I've come to you tonight, so we can talk like civilised men. Your temper is just as bad as hers, I hear."

Erlik growled quietly, and Maleagant smirked.

"What do you want with her, wretch?" Erlik asked.

"She's coming back to see you tomorrow, yes? No doubt to ask you to infiltrate my keep and spy on me for her," he said, leaning back in his chair.

"And you want me to convince her otherwise, I suppose?"

"On the contrary," Maleagant said, plastering a large, false smile on his face. "I think it's a wonderful idea, I'd welcome you to my keep. But I want you to bring her with you."

Erlik leaned forwards, a threatening look shadowing his face.

"Why do you want her?" he growled. "If you—"

Maleagant cut him off with a heavy sigh.

"You *do* insist on threatening me, even though you're powerless."

"Why," Erlik spat out each word like they were poison on his tongue. "Do. You. *Want.* Her?"

Maleagant picked at his robes fussily, a muscle spasming in his cheek, "That's *my* business."

"Then play your little sorcery tricks with someone else."

"Oh, my dear man," Maleagant laughed, his oily voice thick with delighted menace. "Haven't you yet wondered how I know her plans? How I knew where to find you? I have my own spies that have crept into her crystal city. Every man has his price."

Erlik stared at him. Blood pounded in his ears, but Maleagant continued, obviously noting the look of fear that briefly passed over Erlik's face.

"And if my spies have access to her council chambers, where else can they penetrate, I wonder? Her inner sanctum, perhaps? Her own personal bower?"

Erlik leapt to his feet and lunged forwards, but Maleagant held up his hand. Erlik felt his arms yanked back and he stumbled. He looked down; thick manacles had appeared around his wrists, linked to chains that bound him to the wall. He pulled at the chains, but they were thick and forged strong. The flesh on his wrists began to viciously sting. *Cold iron.* Erlik looked up at Maleagant with a poisonous glare.

"She'll never come," Erlik growled, shaking his head.

"You underestimate her feelings for you, my dear man. She will come, because *you* will ask her," the sorcerer stood up and banged his staff again. The chair disappeared, as did the shackles around Erlik's wrists.

Maleagant gave a mocking bow and, with a flick of his wrist, vanished. Erlik glared at the empty place, rubbing his wrists where the cold iron had burnt him. His initial hatred had been well-justified. Erlik spat at the ground out of spite, then gently touched the ring resting against his chest.

I'll warn her, he thought. *If she must come with me, at least then she'll be prepared. I won't let her get hurt, not because of me.*

With a heaving sigh, he lay back on his bed, flexing his fists. A flickering flame flared at his fingertips, then vanished.

Erlik sat up again, staring at his hand, willing it to reappear.

"Come on," he muttered. His hand trembled with the force of his effort. "*Come on!*"

Nothing happened. Erlik cursed and threw himself to his feet. He paced like a big cat in a cage.

He lifted his hand to run it through his hair. But stopped. Smiled.

Magic burned through his veins again, and he relished in the feeling. Gesturing at the fire, he commanded sparks to leap into the braziers on the walls.

Unable to sleep, thoughts whirring and buzzing like a thousand wasps, he sat on the edge of the bed and watched the fire devour the logs in the pit, listening to a solitary howl on the wind.

With his magic returned, he truly could protect Mab now. He smiled to himself; he could practically hear her say *I can protect myself.*

He needed fresh air. A walk. Anything. He stormed to the mouth of the cave. Noting the cool night air fresh against his skin, he summoned a cloak and swept it around himself, heading out into the night to clear his head.

CHAPTER 13

"There's too many of them!"

"TRISTAN IS A smart lad," Thomas said as he walked on ahead to push foliage aside to make room for Epona. The forest seemed to have become, if possible, even more dense the further they walked. The sun had set, and cool air kissed their skin. "He'll know if he gets lost to head straight for Elphame."

"He doesn't know the way," Thissy said quietly, and Thomas heard the catch in her throat, as much as she tried to hide it.

"He'll ask for help," Thomas said. "Everyone in Albion knows the way. Someone is bound to help him find it."

"What if he runs into a *bean sídhe*? Or a *púca*?" Thissy argued. "Or something worse?"

Thomas stopped and turned to look at her.

"Thissy," he said firmly. "You're just scaring yourself. Tristan isn't stupid and he has his bow. He's more than capable of looking after himself."

She sighed and rubbed her forehead, closing her eyes in defeated despair.

"I know, I just..." she trailed off and said nothing more. Thomas gently took her hand.

"I know you're worried, but—"

Thomas broke off at the sound of wild howling.

"Wolves," Thissy said, turning in the saddle. "We must be near their hunting ground."

"We'd better keep moving, then," Thomas said, and walked on. "We don't want to disturb them."

They continued on in silence for a few minutes, until the howling echoed again. It seemed closer this time. Thomas' hand unconsciously crept to his sword. Despite the knowledge that Mab's wolves would never harm them, he couldn't ignore the unpleasant feeling around the nape of his neck.

Something rustled in the bracken.

"Stop, shh," he said suddenly. Epona snorted at the abruptness. He lowered his voice to a whisper. "There's something there."

His grip tightened around his sword. His heartbeat thumped against his ears. Thissy's hands clenched tighter around the reins of her horse, ready to conjure any magic she'd need.

An enormous white hound burst out of the bushes to their right. Red-eyed and copper-eared, the beast dripped froth from its huge jaws as it snapped at Thomas. Epona reared up, whinnying in shock. Thissy clung tightly to the reins, but not tight enough. She slipped and fell from the horse with a grunt.

"Thissy!"

Thomas rushed to her aid while Epona reared up again, beating at the hound with her front hooves. The creature, over half her height and just as wide, brushed off the blows, and snapped at her flanks. Epona screamed in pain as a dewclaw – more draconine than canine – caught her heel.

Thomas drew his sword, as Thissy waved her hand with a cry of *"dóiteán!"* to conjure a ring of white fire to surround them. Epona limped away from the edge of the circle, and Thomas moved to soothe her as best he could.

The hound howled again, and its call for help was met by the baying of more of the monsters. Thomas and Thissy found themselves at once surrounded by the beasts.

All but the largest seemed wary of the fire. It snapped at the flame, and its deathly cold bite extinguished it momentarily, and although flame bit into its fur, the dog shook off the fire and stepped through the circle.

The others followed, their bodies so cold the flame couldn't take root. It sputtered down to nothing, leaving a circle of blackened grass.

Thomas scanned the circle of hounds, seeking an opening. But even if he could see one, how could they flee? The beasts were huge, and would surely catch up to them in moments.

A hound lunged at Thissy's throat. She ducked back and the beast soared over her instead. Skidding, its vicious claws gouging huge fissures in the earth, it snarled, turned, and lunged again. It almost undershot its mark as Thissy moved backwards, but this time it managed to wrap its enormous jaws around her boot and drag her down. Shaking its shaggy head, the vile dog yanked her away from the others.

"Thissy!"

She scrabbled at the earth, too twisted to gain an opening to cast magic without searing off her own foot. She kicked the monster in the face with her other boot, but it shook off the blows.

Thomas swung his sword and buried the blade deep into its skull. The beast shuddered, and slumped. Thissy scrambled away, her foot bleeding and half-crushed from the dog's powerful jaws, but it gave a clear indication to the others.

Attack.

The circling hounds dove forward as one. Through a flurry of teeth and claws, Thomas barely felt any pain. All he could hear was Thissy screaming in frustration as bolts of fire flew through the air, rapid unaimed attacks against the raging animals.

Then, through the baying of hounds, the crackle of fire, and Epona snorting and whinnying as she too fought against the beasts, Thomas heard the rolling echo of thunder. Teeth and claws left him, and lightning slashed at the sky.

The hounds whimpered and backed away, short tails lowered and hind legs shaking. Thunder rolled over the sky again and, with a sudden downpour of rain, a bolt of lightning struck the earth close to the hounds.

The earth exploded at the point of impact. A fountain of dirt erupted and showered Thomas and Thissy with dust and burnt plants. They staggered back, Thissy stumbling and limping over her injured foot, and threw up their hands involuntarily against the blast.

Yelping and falling over each other, the hounds scattered, leaving their prey bruised, torn and battered. Thomas turned to see Thissy still on the ground, shredded and panting. Gasping for breath, he scanned the trees for more signs of the animals.

No more, he thought. *Safe.*

Until he caught a glimpse of a hooded figure through the trees. His heart dropped hard into his stomach. *The hounds' master?*

The hooded figure raised a hand to the sky, and the rain died away with one final rattle of thunder.

Relief flooded Thomas. It must be her! Who else could command the skies?

"Mab!" he called, and pushed himself to his feet. "Mab!" he shouted again. "It's—"

He staggered towards her, but she took a step back, turned away, and fled into the trees. His brow furrowed. *Why would she run from us?*

He didn't dare follow. Perhaps she wasn't meant to be so far from Elphame? The minstrel Baird was right about one thing; she loved to roam the woodlands, even when it wasn't advisable. But he didn't have the time or strength to wonder about Mab's evening excursions. They'd meet again soon enough, when they finally reached Elphame.

He turned to Thissy, who pressed herself into his arms, and he ignored the burning pain of his open wounds. They carried each other to a sheltered grove where they could dry off and tend their wounds.

✧   ✧   ✧

ERLIK THREW HIMSELF back into his cave. Near certain Rhymer hadn't seen his face, he'd ran all the way back, hoping the idiot wouldn't follow him. Thankfully, he seemed to have grown some brains and had decided to stay with the leaf-eared woman. How typical, he thought, that he should go out to clear his head and encounter *him*. The Old Gods truly did have a wry sense of irony. Erlik scowled at the ceiling, as though they could see him.

He leaned against the wall and grimaced.

Why *had* he saved Rhymer? He felt unclean.

He knew Mab had some affection for the boy. Perhaps even love? That maternal tenderness that she offered so freely to her people. Erlik had sworn he wouldn't hurt her again. He couldn't bear to see the despair in her eyes if she learned her Champion had been torn apart by Cú-Sith hounds.

Erlik shuddered.

The Hounds of Annwyn were running free. The Iron Keep was occupied again by a sorcerer with an unnatural interest in Mab. Erlik repressed another shiver, one that had nothing to do with the raindrops sliding down his face from his wet hair. He knew why a sorcerer like Maleagant would want her.

The Heart of Magic Itself, Erlik thought. He sat back on his bed, running a hand through his hair. A rush of anger swamped him, and his heart gave a hard thump. *Why does everyone forget she's a woman, not just a tool? He won't use her. I'll tell her everything; we'll be prepared when we face him.*

Erlik lay back and closed his eyes.

And I just won't mention that I saved her Champion. Ever.

CHAPTER 14

"You will come at once"

ONCE MORNING HAD broken, after a quick breakfast of kippers, Lir led Tristan up a steep sandbank and onto a cliff overlooking the beach. From this great height, Tristan could see the expanse of the forest, and marvelled at how far he had walked without realising.

I bet Mother and Father are worried about me, he thought miserably. *There's no point trying to find them. If anything, heading to Elphame is my best route.*

"You alright, lad?" Lir broke into his thoughts. Tristan started, and nodded.

"Just thinking about my parents."

"Good folk?"

"Aye," Tristan sighed. "The best. I just wish I hadn't wandered off. They'll be looking for me."

"Anyone with a decent lick of sense will be heading for either Elphame or Tír-Na-Nóg these days," Lir said. "Those will be your best bets, I reckon."

"What do you mean?"

"Been a lot of attacks recently," Lir said darkly. "Smaller villages, you know? Some on the roads and such. Mostly at night, though," he added with a slight grin, when Tristan reached for his bow.

"Bandits?" Tristan prompted, but Lir shook his head

gravely.

"If only," he said. "Bandits are easy. Stick a sword in a man, and he dies. But the things attackin' folks now..." Lir shivered. "Albion used to be a place of magic. Now it's a land of monsters."

Tristan swallowed hard.

"Hasn't Mab done anything? Or whoever rules Tír-Na-Nóg?"

"Queen Morrigan?" Lir shrugged. "If either of them are doing anything, it's not working." The fisherman gave Tristan a sly smile. "But the tricks you learn on the road aren't easy to forget, lad. Especially the ones that'll save your hide. You saw how those merrows reacted to fire. Every creature has its weakness. Spend enough time fightin' them off, and you'll find out what it is."

Lir led Tristan over the cliffs with much more pleasant conversation after that, and as the day wore on, Tristan grew to like the fisherman more and more. His accent sometimes made him difficult to understand, but he laughed often and told Tristan stories that kept him entertained.

Tristan shared his tale of leaving home, sharing his fears of Hopkins, and the sadness at leaving his beloved cat. He silently wished he'd encounter the *Cat Sídhe* again. Yet Tristan's mind couldn't stop returning to the prisoner in the cage. He wished he'd discovered his name.

JUST AFTER MIDDAY, the walls of a city came into view. It lay in the shadow of a deep valley which was strewn with huge, sharp boulders, and seemed to stretch on forever. Lir took in a deep breath and sighed.

"Look at it, lad," he said, beaming. "The fine city of Tír-Na-Nóg."

A pair of enormous gates was flanked by a row of stern guards, each bearing a lance from which fluttered a white banner.

Lir and Tristan joined the ever-moving jostle of people

entering the city, like water flowing through a crack in a wall.

Inside, the city was a bustling hive. Tristan couldn't keep his eyes still as Lir led him through the streets. He'd never seen such a busy place. Bumping into too many people to apologise to, he finally walked accidentally headlong into an enormous man. He looked up to see the giant glaring down at him, baring all three of his broken, yellow teeth. His brow overhung his small eyes and his huge nose looked broken.

Tristan stammered his apologies as the giant flexed the muscles on his huge, meaty arms. Thankfully, Lir grabbed Tristan by the arm and pulled him into the sanctuary of the crowd.

"Careful of the ogres, lad. Not the brightest flames, but they'll pummel you to the ground if you look at 'em the wrong way," he said in a low voice. Tristan gave a nervous laugh and quickened his pace.

Despite his encounter with the ogre, Tristan couldn't help being awed at the city. Banners and flags waved from every window, and colourful motley performers danced and leapt on every corner, surrounded by laughing and applauding citizens.

"This way, lad," Lir called, when Tristan stopped to watch an extremely bendy man twist himself into a bizarre shape. Tristan caught up with him just as Lir was stepping inside a little house on a street corner.

"I'll put—"

"Lir of Ériu's Isle?" asked a commanding voice. Tristan spun to see several guards in white cloaks.

"Uhh… aye?" Lir gulped. Tristan stared at the guards. Their armour gleamed white-gold.

"The queen has requested your presence immediately," said the first guard, and Lir giggled, high-pitched and shaky.

"There must be some mistake, for sure. What would the queen want with a lowly fisherman?"

"There is no mistake. You will come at once. And you will bring your companion."

The guard snapped his heels together and gestured for Lir and Tristan to walk ahead of them. Tristan gulped and looked at Lir, who gave him a nervous glance, then both fell into step with the guards, suddenly feeling as though the sun had lost its warmth.

✦　✦　✦

TRISTAN STAYED CLOSE to the fisherman as they were escorted through the narrow streets.

"You alright, lad?" Lir asked quietly. Not trusting himself to speak, Tristan nodded. *I'm about to meet the queen of Tír-Na-Nóg, and I look like I've just fallen out of a boat.* He nervously flattened his hair and tried to pluck stray threads from his tunic.

TRISTAN'S EYES WERE immediately drawn to the white banners that hung from the castle. The symbol of a golden bird in flight emblazoned on them fluttered in the gentle breeze. Tristan stared, open mouthed, as they were led through the courtyard. Far off on the other side, behind a sturdy fence, soldiers in a training yard fired arrows at straw dummies faster than Tristan could see. He ran his tongue over his lips, and almost reached back to touch his bow, eager to join them. Cries of *"Nock!"* and *"Draw!"* and *"Loose!"* rang through the air.

"You will wait here," the guard said suddenly, turning with the rigidity of a seasoned soldier and walking up the steps to the castle doors. He held a brief, muttered conversation with the guard at the door, then turned again and beckoned the other soldiers to bring Lir and Tristan.

They glanced at each other.

As they approached the door, the guards stopped them again. One of them pulled Tristan's bow and quiver from him.

"Wh- wha—that's mine!" Tristan argued weakly.

"It's broken," the guard pointed out, noting the crude knot in the string.

"It... it's still mine."

"Weapons will be returned to you later," the guard said.

One of them gave him a reassuring smile, but it didn't reassure Tristan. He watched his bow being handled by more guards and felt a strange possessiveness overcome him.

"Be careful with it," he warned. The guards looked at him. A couple of them smiled at each other. Tristan sensed no menace.

Lir handed over a couple of small knives, and once the guards appeared satisfied they were no threat, led them inside.

The interior was brighter than Tristan had been expecting. A grand, open throne room, long and narrow. More banners hung from the walls, and statues of various birds in flight stood proudly behind the soldiers that lined the carpet. At the far end of the room, a set of steep steps led up to a marble throne under a sweeping archway. There, stroking the fantastic plumage of a red and gold bird, sat a young woman with fair hair.

"Lir Mac Conmara of Ériu's Isle and his companion, Your Grace," said a quiet advisor to her left. The woman smiled and beckoned Lir and Tristan closer. The bird beside her crooned softly.

"You stand before Queen Morrigan, Daughter of the Dragon, High Priestess of the Old Ways, and Queen of Tír-Na-Nóg," an advisor called to Lir and Tristan as they approached. Tristan felt his heart leap into his throat, and couldn't help but stare.

The queen was much younger than he was expecting. She looked a little older than him, but he knew that was probably an illusion. She was most likely many decades old. Her long, white gown left her muscled arms bare. She possessed a feminine strength, echoed in a white bow and quiver of arrows that sat at the side of her throne. A golden headdress of chains glittered on her brow.

"You're a fisherman?" the queen asked. Lir nodded and Tristan tore his eyes away to stare at the floor.

"And you were at Tumbling Bay yesterday?" she asked.

Lir nodded and mumbled, "Aye, Your Grace."

"Speak up," she said. Tristan caught the hint of

amusement in her voice and couldn't stop himself from smiling.

"Aye, Your Grace. I was at Tumblin' Bay yesterday," he repeated, and looked up at her. Morrigan smiled at him.

"I received a message from Melusine this morning. She tells me that you threatened four of her foot soldiers and called them—what did she say, Falconbane?" she leaned over to her advisor, who unrolled a rather damp-looking scroll.

"Erm, hm," Falconbane rumbled, reading through the message quickly. "'Scaly water-rats', Your Grace."

Morrigan laughed, and then cleared her throat.

"Well," she said, apparently trying to suppress a smile. "That's imaginative."

"Your Grace," Lir said, looking highly relieved. "I know I was in no position to deny the merrows their right, but this lad is—"

Morrigan stood suddenly, and Lir started and fell quiet. Her eyes wide and her mouth open in stunned silence, Morrigan descended the steps and approached Tristan, who felt his heart pound in his throat. He tried to avoid staring into her eyes, but it was hard when they glittered like forest pools.

"It... can't..." she whispered, then broke into laughter. "Thomas Rhymer's son? You look exactly like him!"

CHAPTER 15

"No games, Erlik"

T HE COLD NIGHT rippled with the fragrance of honeysuckle and witch hazel. Mab stood at her balcony, gazing at her slumbering city below. The silky silence embraced her. She rubbed her arms against the chill, and with a sigh, she turned back into her chamber before the wintry air stole into her chest.

After closing the doors to the balcony behind her, she approached the fire. Fingers danced over the soft velvet of her chair, and she sat to watch the flames devour the wood. Red shapes mirrored in her dark eyes, her pupils huge like a hunting cat.

"You should have left me in that cage."

A strong hand wrapped around her throat and lifted her back to her feet. She choked his name, and Erlik grinned wickedly and kicked her chair aside. It crashed against the wall and tipped over, knocking small trinkets off her dresser. She fervently scratched at his hand, drawing blood, but he dragged her towards her bed.

Say something… say you will allow me.

He threw her down on the bed. She bounced into the furs, but he clambered on top of her and clamped his mouth onto hers.

It's time you were tamed, Wolf-Queen.

"Erlik!" her voice held no plea or beg, only a command. Her resolve gave him pause.

"Mab?" he whispered, and stared into her crystalline eyes. She glared back at him, and the power of her gaze punctured his mind.

Fire blistered his brain, and he staggered back away from the bed. He pressed the heels of his hands into his eyes, trying to quell the blazing storm behind them. Pressure built in his head.

"Mab!" he screamed. "Make it stop, please!"

"Erlik, wake up."

He snapped open his eyes with a sharp intake of breath. He blinked a few times to clear his vision, and found Mab sitting on his bed, staring at him.

"I would say 'good morning', but it does not appear to be so," she said calmly.

"Mab?" he slowly sat, staring at her as if wanting to confirm her existence.

"Yes, that is my name," she said as she peeled an apple with a small knife. Erlik looked around. A basket of food sat beside her, full of bread, meat, cheese, and fruit. "You have said it often enough."

"I—" Erlik stared at her. The dream had been so... *vivid*. He hadn't done such wicked things... had he?

"What is it?" Mab pressed when he said nothing. She offered a brass plate, the apple now sliced into segments and arranged neatly. He pushed it away.

"I dreamt—awful things," he croaked, and took the pitcher of water she offered instead and gulped it down. "You're lucky to not be troubled by dreams."

"*Lucky* is perhaps not the word I would use," she said. Erlik blanched; that had been a bit too callous of him.

"Did I say anything? In my sleep?" he asked. Mab shook her head and bit into a segment of apple with a half-shrug.

"Just my name a few times," she said. "You looked distressed. I did try to wake you, but you always were a heavy sleeper." She reached forward and brushed his hair out of his eyes.

Instinct overcame him. Erlik grabbed her wrist. Her eyes narrowed for a brief moment and she tipped her head back. He released a long, slow breath and relinquished his grip when she tugged her arm away. She made a thoughtful noise, and he gulped.

"What is the matter?" she asked suspiciously. Erlik's eyes darted and he tried to slow his breathing to a normal rate, but his heart was racing.

"Nothing, just… nothing," he said quietly. He looked up at her suddenly. "You came back."

"I did," she said. "And, as promised, I brought some more food for you, and a change of clothes. The ones I brought you yesterday were too big."

She picked up the pile of clothes and laid them out at the foot of his bed.

"Get dressed; there is much we need to discuss."

Erlik pulled the shirt over his head and fastened the tunic around it. Both fit him better than the first shirt she'd brought, and he felt much more comfortable. Yet when Mab gestured for him to sit, he gulped and felt restricted, as though a noose had tightened around his neck.

"The sorcerer, Maleagant," Mab began. Erlik shifted.

"Wait, Mab," he raised a hand to stop her. "Before you speak, there's something I should tell you."

She tilted her head, "Oh?"

Erlik paused, unsure of how to proceed.

"Maleagant visited me last night," he said at last.

Mab's eyes widened briefly.

"How did he know you were here? Were you hurt? What did he say?" she asked. Her words came too quickly for her to be indifferent. His heart skipped a couple of beats, and he forgot to keep his genuine smile hidden.

"You almost sound concerned," he said. Mab frowned.

"No games, Erlik. Answer me."

His smirk slipped.

"He knows you want me to go to the Iron Keep. And he

wants me to bring you with me."

Saying it aloud made it feel so much worse. Mab leaned back, looking pensive. She made a thoughtful noise again.

"I see," she said slowly. "Did he say why?"

"No."

Mab shook her head. "No, I cannot imagine he would," she said. "He seems like a secretive man. And secretive men are dangerous."

"Well, quite," Erlik agreed. He inhaled slowly as his thoughts tumbled like ships on a stormy sea, and he gazed at her, trying his hardest to keep his anxiety from showing.

"Although I suppose it does help me decide on the next course of action," she said. Erlik released a sigh of relief and smiled.

"You'll go back to Elphame," he said, nodding.

"I will come with you," she said at the same time.

A long silence, punctured only by the roar of the waterfall at the mouth of the cave.

"What?" Erlik asked in a dead voice, an eyebrow raising.

Mab blinked, then frowned.

"Return to Elphame? Why?"

"*Why?*" Erlik repeated, aghast. "Did you miss the part where Maleagant *wants* you at the Iron Keep?"

"No," she said patiently. "I am not stupid."

"He obviously wants you for something sinister," he said, standing. "I forbid you to come with me."

"Forbid me?" Mab stood up too, though her small stature made little difference in comparison to his. "Have you forgotten that you do *not* control me?"

"No man can tame you?" Erlik smirked. Mab blanched, blinking numbly for a few moments.

"That is not funny!" she snapped. Erlik's smirk vanished. He licked his lips.

"Still, it's my duty to protect you."

"Since when?"

"Since I married you, you obstinate she-wolf!" Frustrated, Erlik flung his arms down like a petulant child and stared hard at her, hands curled into fists.

Another long silence followed.

"I gave the ring back," she said quietly. Erlik detected her tone straight away.

"So?"

"So I am not your wife anymore," she said. Then, after a short pause, "Am I?"

Erlik tilted his head and gazed at her. "You gave me back a Binding Ring that had lost its magic. But you never annulled the marriage."

Mab blinked slowly.

"You are—" she swallowed. "You are still my husband?" she breathed. Her right hand crept to her left and rubbed her third finger. It appeared to be such a common habit that she didn't even acknowledge it.

"And you're still my wife," he said. "So I'll do everything in my power to keep you safe."

"I am well aware of the dangers of the Iron Keep."

Erlik frowned.

"Are you?" he asked. His voice was quieter now. "You seem more than willing to put yourself in harm's way. Why?"

"Maleagant is attacking my people," Mab said, the revelation that they were still married apparently forgotten in her concern for her seelie. "I have to *do* something. If you are not willing to help me, then I will go alone."

She gathered her cloak around her and strode past him, towards the cave mouth. Erlik grabbed her arm, and she froze.

"Let go," she said in a deathly quiet voice.

"Look at me," he said. She didn't move. "*Look at me!*"

She turned her venomous glare on him. He released her arm immediately. That look could have reduced him to ashes. He swallowed and stepped back. Not out of fear, but reverence.

"We'll go together," he offered.

The venom in her stare withered, and affection overcame him.

"Very well," she said. "We go together. I will send a

message to my council. We will be gone for almost a week."

You'll be gone far longer than that if Maleagant has anything to do with it, Erlik thought, but didn't voice his fear. He merely watched her, heart pumping dread through him with every word she spoke. Why did she have to be so stubborn?

You wouldn't love her if she wasn't.

A small smile tugged at Erlik's lips. The little voice in his head was right. He wouldn't adore her if she didn't have that stubbornness, that pride. Despite that, all he wanted was to shield her from the dangers she'd be blindly walking into at the Iron Keep.

"Faolan," Mab called as she moved to the cave's mouth. Erlik could just make out her voice over the roaring of the water. A muffled conversation followed.

Erlik chewed half-heartedly on a pear, and started to put the leftover food back into the basket, just as Mab re-entered and smiled at him.

"I have sent Faolan back to Elphame with the message," she said, and helped him gather their belongings. Erlik could only nod. He looked up at her and she approached him with a smile. Despite the dominant and persistent ache in his chest, and the fear that swamped him, he managed to return her smile.

CHAPTER 16

"Why did you release me?"

"W HIST!" ISOLDE HISSED as she peered from the door. "Broc!"

Broc opened his sleepy eyes and looked around.

"Hmm?" he mumbled. "S'm'one say m'name?"

Isolde chuckled as she crept into the circular study. Broc sat up and stretched, scratching his head with his claw.

"I've brought you a present," she said, pushing a small, soft square wrapped in muslin through the bars of his cage. Broc unwrapped the package and beamed.

"Honey cake! You're too good to me, little mouse," he said, gleefully tearing off pieces of cake.

"Better than earthworms?" she asked, grinning. Broc nodded, his mouth full. She picked up her broom and started to sweep the ashes of yet another of Maleagant's failed spells, when Broc beckoned her back.

"How goes the tunnel?" he whispered, brushing crumbs out of his fur. Isolde looked around to make sure they were still alone.

"It's ready," she said, barely able to contain her excitement. "We can go tonight, when they're sleeping!"

"We can't," Broc said. "Not tonight."

Isolde looked crestfallen, "Why not?"

"Something is happening," Broc said, casting his eyes

around the tower. "There's a woman coming to the Keep. I don't know who she is, and I'm not completely sure why they want her. I think she's important or powerful. Maybe some noble or… or witch, or *something*." He grunted in frustration. "I wish your sister wasn't so cagey when she spoke!"

"So?" Isolde pressed. Wrapping his claws around the bars, Broc stared at her. "What does it have to do with us leaving?"

"I think Maleagant means to kill her and use her to open the portal properly this time. We can't let that happen."

"I'll warn her," Isolde said at once.

"Be careful, little mouse," he said in a hushed voice, and gave a soft sigh. Isolde nodded.

"I heard they were preparing a feast, so they'll no doubt make a big fuss of her arrival," she said thoughtfully. Broc smiled inwardly. *Such a clever girl.*

"I suppose Maleagant will want me to serve her," Isolde went on. "I can warn her then. When I'm sure she trusts me, maybe she can come with us through the tunnel?"

"Maybe."

"I'll think of something," she said. Despite the worry in her eyes, she spoke with such determination, Broc almost believed they could do it. They could escape from the Iron Keep. They could have their freedom.

✧　✧　✧

ERLIK TUGGED ON his boots as Mab left the cave again to call a mount for him. As he followed her, he heard her shrill whistle and a gentle thud of hooves. From the mouth of the cave, he watched a supremely impressive stallion stride out of the glade's thorny bracken, its head held proudly high. A black banner draped over its chestnut rump, swishing whenever the horse flicked its tail. She took its reins when it patiently stood beside her gleaming stag.

Erlik approached and took the offered reins, but the horse snorted and backed up, anxiously pawing the dirt. Mab frowned.

"What is the matter?"

"Elvish horses don't like me," Erlik huffed, then, with a quick glance at Mab's fretting mount, added, "Nor does your stag, apparently."

The beast tossed its head and bellowed a guttural roar. Mab ran her hand over its neck and muttered to it, and it seemed to calm, though it still eyed Erlik with distinct dislike.

"What did you ride before?" Mab asked grumpily, trying to relax the horse with little success.

"Not Elvish horses," Erlik muttered, backing away so the horse would calm down.

After a long time, and a lot of coaxing in Mab's natural tongue, the horse permitted Erlik to mount, and they set off.

"Aren't you afraid of being recognised?" Erlik asked as they rode through the forest.

"And what if I am?" Mab countered. "Maleagant knows we will be coming."

They rode in silence for a while, listening to birdsong and the gentle swaying of the trees in the autumnal wind, until finally they were out of the forest and onto the plains. Erlik squinted under the bright coin of the sun.

"The Iron Keep is that way," Mab said, pointing into the distance. "If we follow the road towards Hunter's Oak, we can turn east towards the Keep."

"As you wish," he said. He scanned the horizon. Dread swallowed him. Throwing off the shiver that threatened his calm exterior, he kicked his horse into motion again.

The day wore on. The air grew cooler. As the sun slipped below the skyline, the sky blushing blood-red, Mab found a mound of weathered rocks by which they could make their camp for the night.

Noticing the frost beginning to form on the grass, Erlik conjured a roaring fire, and Mab sat opposite as the darkness gathered around them. They sat in silence, listening to the crackling flames. Wintry hands gripped them, and Mab eventually conceded that the night was too cold to sleep out in the open. With a clever twist of her hands, she summoned a cocoon of branches and roots from the earth to surround them. Another flick of her fingers, and a glamour settled over the branches, turning their form to a canopy of cloth and stitching, with a windbreak to keep out the worst of the chill.

"Something irks you?" Mab asked, after the sun had set completely and their only light became the glowing fire between them.

Erlik forced himself to stop twisting his hands.

"What makes you say that?"

Mab didn't say anything. They stared at each other for a moment.

He sighed, "I'm fine."

"You are afraid," she said.

"I said I'm *fine!*"

"But you are *not*," she snapped. "What is about the Iron Keep that has you so worried?"

"You know exactly what," he muttered sullenly. "You should be worried as well."

She paused. "He is dead," Mab said quietly, moving to sit beside him. The closeness of her brought her scent to his nostrils, and a shiver to his skin.

"I know," he said. "But the memory of him isn't."

Mab exhaled hard.

"I understand," she said. "But something terrible is happening at the Iron Keep. And my people are suffering for it. I must find out why. Even if it means..." she trailed off, and Erlik saw the muscles in her throat roll as she swallowed hard. He took her hand and squeezed it.

"You'd be willing to sacrifice yourself? For them?"

"For the smallest child," she agreed, without hesitation. Then, in a small voice, "You do not have to come, if you do not want to."

Erlik's heart dropped into his stomach. "What?"

"You do not have to come with me. You can leave now, if you want," she said. Her glittering eyes locked onto his like the gaze of a cat.

"Don't you realise the danger you're putting yourself in?" he said. Why wouldn't she listen to him? They could run away now, together, to the furthest corners of the world, and start afresh.

"What would you have me do?" she almost sounded sad. "I am trapped, choice-less. I need to find out what evil is brewing in the Iron Keep. I have sent men before you, and none have returned. If I send you alone, Maleagant will concoct some punishment for you for not bringing me. And, if what he said is true, Elphame is weakened, infiltrated by his own. He will find a way to get me to the Iron Keep, whether willingly or no."

Mab gazed at him and went on, "If we go together," she said slowly. "We can protect each other. But I will go alone, if necessary."

Erlik halted. Suspicion bubbled up inside him. He narrowed his eyes slightly.

"What game are you playing, Mab?" he said.

"No game, I simply—"

"Don't lie to me," he snarled. "Tell me truthfully, why did you release me?" He folded his arms and glared. He watched as the question lanced through her like an arrow.

"I—"

She blinked and hesitated, though her mouth moved as if wanting to speak. She licked her lips and swallowed hard. *Say it. Go on.*

"Do you want me dead? Like the rest of the fools you've sent to that wretched place? You said it yourself, Maleagant no doubt has some vile plan concocted. Who knows what he has in store for you, but what about me?"

He watched her squirming under his snarled words with twisted delight.

"You should have just let your precious *Champion* kill me, it would have been kinder," his voice rose. His words hurt her, he knew by her flinch. Yet he ploughed on, unrelenting.

"Say it, Mab. Why did you release me?"

"Erlik, I—"

"Tell me!"

"I missed you!" she shouted, rounding on him.

Her words echoed around in the little tent, but not as loudly as they echoed in his head. His heart pounded a hard tempo in his throat.

"Is that what you wanted to hear? How could you *ever* think I would want you dead?" she snapped, jabbing a finger into his chest. Her touch bolted lightning through him, igniting his nerves and blood with a flash of energy. It didn't hurt, but he fell back from shock. "Why would I release you from years of imprisonment only to send you to your death? Do you truly think me so *petty?*"

"Mab, I—I didn't think—"

"*That* is obvious," she slapped away his hand before he could touch her. "Think what you want. I know what is in my heart. Perhaps you should look at what is in yours."

She turned her back to him. Erlik said nothing for a long time, watching her.

"I missed you too."

He saw her shoulders drop, like a wolf lowering her raised hackles. But she didn't turn back to look at him. Erlik sighed. Neither spoke again, save for her muttering one word before falling into silence:

"Amadán."

CHAPTER 17

"The Crooked Mile would be the best route"

TRISTAN PUSHED THE food around his plate with his fork. Opposite him, Lir shovelled the meal down with great enthusiasm, beaming at Tristan when he caught him looking. Tristan returned his grin and turned his gaze to the queen. Smiling, she tilted her head slightly.

"Aren't you hungry, Tristan?" she asked, stroking the neck of her softly crooning phoenix.

"Aye, Your Grace," he said. "I'm just thinking about my mother and father."

"*Tch*, call me Morrigan," she said with a casual wave of her hand. "I don't like formality among friends."

She laughed, and Lir joined in, nodding in appreciation, cheeks bulging with food. Tristan's mouth twitched, but he couldn't help feeling nervous in her presence.

"Pardon, Your Grace—Morrigan," Tristan stumbled. "Might I be able to hire a carriage or a horse to take me to Elphame?"

"Of course," she said. She picked up a handful of grain and held it up for her phoenix to peck at. "The Crooked Mile would be the best route. I'll have something arranged for you, so you can set off whenever you're ready."

She turned and beckoned over a young page. As he approached, Tristan began to eat, not wanting to appear rude.

The page leaned down, Morrigan muttered to him, and the lad scampered off.

"You're welcome to stay the night, of course," she said, winking at Tristan. He gulped down a mouthful of food and blinked at her. Morrigan threw back her head and laughed. For a reason he couldn't place, Tristan was reminded of the dark-haired prisoner in the forest.

I shouldn't ask, it's probably a tetchy subject. The prisoner did say he'd been usurped. Maybe by Morrigan herself?

Tristan twisted his hands and chewed his tongue.

"Don't look so worried," Morrigan said, still chuckling. "It was only in jest."

"I know," he said. "I was just... I was thinking about when I was separated from my mother and father."

"Oh, yes," she said, leaning back casually. "I've been meaning to ask about that. How *were* you separated?"

"Wolves chased me," he said.

"Wolves?" Morrigan repeated, sitting up straighter. "How'd you manage to get the wolves angry at you?"

Lir sniggered, gesturing with his fork. "'S'what I said."

Tristan frowned and shrugged.

"Wolves are wolves, they chased me because I was there, probably near their hunting ground," he said.

"Every wolf in Albion answers to Mab," Morrigan said. "None of them would chase or attack a seelie, especially one related to Thomas Rhymer. You must've done *something* to provoke them."

"I don't think so," Tristan pushed food around his plate again, eyes lowered. "I was just talking. There was a man in a cage, and—"

Morrigan dropped her goblet. The sound of smashed glass echoed through the hall. Lir jolted so hard he bumped the table, sending food and wine spilling over the wood. Tristan stared.

"What?"

"He's alive?" Morrigan whispered. "You spoke to him?"

Tristan swallowed a lump in his throat. He couldn't tell if

Morrigan looked terrified or overjoyed at the news.

"I... yes, I did," Tristan said slowly. "Who is he?"

Morrigan's mouth barely moved, "My father."

A shiver rattled through the hall this time. Tristan felt immediately colder.

"Your father? He said he knew mine," he said quietly.

Morrigan let out a mirthless laugh.

"I suppose he did, in a way," she said bitterly. "He would do anything to get out of that cage."

Whispers scuttled around the room like insects. Tristan caught some of them.

"*Dragon King.*"

The cold spiked. Morrigan nodded.

"Erlik, the Dragon King," she said slowly.

"I thought he'd be dead," Tristan said.

"No," Morrigan grimly shook her head. "He's a god, he can only be killed by one of his own kind. He can only be contained, which he is. He *is* still contained, isn't he?" Morrigan's voice took on a sharp edge, and she narrowed her eyes at Tristan. He quickly nodded.

"I didn't free him; the wolves chased me away from the cage."

"Good," Morrigan sighed. "I can't imagine what would happen if he were ever released."

The great hall became silent. Lir lowered his fork and stared at his plate.

"I'll arrange a carriage for you in the morning," Morrigan said quietly. "Excuse me, I... I've lost my appetite."

She stood and pushed her chair away, and left the table. Before she vanished from the room, she paused.

"When you go to Elphame tomorrow, give your father my regards," she said softly. "You're all welcome back any time."

CHAPTER 18

"I had been wondering when you'd show up"

"**I** THOUGHT YOU said the Iron Keep had been rebuilt?" Erlik said as he stared with distaste at the Keep. They were still some distance away, but the hill upon which they had paused gave a good vantage.

Mab raised her eyebrow at him.

"I did," she said. "I did not say it had been redesigned."

Immense, black, and dominating to the eye, the Iron Keep was an impenetrable fortress, crowned with jet spikes and teeming with crows, which feasted on the rotting corpses locked inside iron gibbets. Erlik snorted at her expression.

"Do you have a plan?" he asked. Mab hesitated. Erlik groaned and continued. "You don't have a plan?"

"Not necessarily, no," she said defensively. "But Maleagant is expecting us, yes?"

"This is too dangerous, Mab, we shouldn't—"

"I have no choice, Erlik," she said. "I must go in there. The Nuckelavee is still running free, its disease is spreading. I have to find a way to stop it. Not to mention the other beasts he has set loose."

Erlik sighed. Mab reached out. A spark flickered between their hands, and Mab retracted her arm quickly.

She urged her stag into motion again. The Keep's portcullis was open, making the place look like a skull about to swallow them.

Mab rode first into the courtyard, and dismounted, but there was no one in sight. She looked around and frowned.

"This is not right," she said. Erlik dismounted from his horse and cast his eyes around the courtyard too. "Where is everyone?"

No smiths or masons; no dog-handlers, no falconers; no stable-hands or ostlers. No guards or soldiers. Not a single person wandered the courtyard. Surely they couldn't all be inside? It was only late afternoon.

"Ah," called an oily voice. "I had been wondering when you'd show up."

Mab and Erlik both looked up sharply to the front doors, and saw the sorcerer descending the steps towards them. He spread his arms out wide as though in welcoming, although his beaming smile did not reach his eyes.

"Such a pleasure to welcome you both," Maleagant said. "And to see you together... well, it warms my heart to see you've settled your differences."

"Enough honeyed words, sorcerer," Mab snapped. "You have a lot to answer for."

Erlik put a hand on her arm.

Don't antagonise him.

Mab threw him a dirty look.

We do not have time for pleasantries!

"Please excuse my wife," Erlik said slowly. "It's been a long journey."

"Oh, but of course," Maleagant said, and the greasy, ugly tone of his voice sickened Mab. "You will find your room upstairs, one of my servants will show you the way."

Mab narrowed her eyes suspiciously and glanced at Erlik.

He is inviting us to stay?

Erlik looked down at her. *It appears that way. It gives us time to come up with a plan, at least.*

"Very well, that sounds—"

"Oh, you naughty thing, greeting our guests without me."

A beautiful woman with ash-grey hair descended the steps

with a slow and deliberate gait, and sauntered up behind Maleagant. The sorcerer turned to her, and put an arm around her waist.

"Ah, yes," Maleagant gestured to her by way of introduction, cheek muscle twitching. "My lover, Carman."

Erlik nodded his greeting to her, and she stepped forward and curtsied low to Erlik, her steel-grey eyes never leaving his face.

"An honour and a pleasure to welcome you here, my lord," Carman said huskily. Mab cleared her throat pointedly. Carman's eyes slid to her, and gave her an overly pleasant smile.

"Your Grace, such an honour," she curtsied to her, though not as low as she had to Erlik.

"There are matters we need to discuss, but we'll let you get settled in," Maleagant said, then gestured to a small, mousy-haired girl lingering anxiously in a doorway. "Isolde will show you to your room. You must join us tonight for the feast."

He smirked and turned away. His long robes swept out behind him as he and Carman strode across the courtyard, his staff echoing across the stones. Carman looked back at Erlik, and gave him a keen smile and winked. Mab frowned.

"She is very beautiful," she said coolly, raising her eyebrow. She took the reins of her stag and led it into the stable. Erlik narrowed his eyes.

"You can't be jealous, surely?"

"Not at all," she said, a little too quickly. "Just... aware."

Aware of the fact that she looks like the mother of your firstborn.

She kept these words to herself. The memory, though ancient, still stung. It made her chest ache more than she cared to admit to think of Erlik with other women. The women who bore him his numerous children. The women whom he'd denied loving, yet she couldn't help the jewel of envy lodge like a stone in her throat.

"My lord? My lady?"

The timidity of the voice startled her out of her thoughts,

and they both looked to find the mousy-haired girl staring at them from where she'd moved to the stable door.

"I'm to show you to your room," she said quietly. After closing the half-gate to keep their mounts stabled, Erlik threw a quick glance at Mab, and wrapped his arm around her waist to walk beside her.

"I HOPE THE room is to your liking, my lady," the girl said, twisting her hands. Mab stood in the centre of a small bedchamber, though it contained a bed large enough for two. Erlik stood at the window, staring into the courtyard.

Mab nodded at the girl.

"It is, thank you," she said. "Your name is Isolde, yes?"

Isolde nodded, looking surprised that Mab had remembered her name.

"Yes, my lady," she said. Mab tilted her head and approached her. She gently cuffed the girl's chin to look up from the ground. They were the same height.

"Stand up straighter, *luichín*," she said kindly. "Only then, when you look people in the eye, will you see people of your own quality and value."

"You shouldn't encourage a slave to look higher than her master," Erlik said slowly, turning from the window to approach them both. Mab frowned at him.

"Isolde is no slave," she looked back at the girl, as though to reassure her, "no matter how Maleagant treats you."

Erlik leaned closer to her.

"We're not here to rescue wayward girls," he hissed in her ear.

Mab threw him a dirty look, then looked back at Isolde, who seemed confused.

"I know you are worth more than Maleagant. I can see it in your eyes," she said.

Isolde beamed at her, and gave her a small curtsey.

"You're very kind, my lady," Isolde said. Something in her face seemed to jar for a moment. Chewing her lip, she glanced between Erlik and Mab.

"What is it, *luichín?*"

"May I speak freely, my lady?" Isolde asked quietly. Mab looked surprised, but nodded.

The girl ran to the door and looked down the corridor. "I believe you're in great danger," she said, returning to face Mab, speaking faster now. "The master and mistress spoke at great length about a woman arriving at the castle, I think he means you. Though he didn't mention your—erm... your c-companion?"

Isolde cast a shy glance at Erlik, seeking the right title for him.

"Her husband," he sharply corrected her.

"Yes, my lord, my apologies," she curtseyed again. It seemed to be such a nervous habit of hers around Maleagant that she couldn't help herself. Mab gestured for her to continue.

"You need to leave as soon as you can," she said, then lowered her voice even further. "There's a tunnel, we – that is, me and my friend, Broc – we're going to use it to escape. You should come with us."

"I am grateful for your assistance child, but we cannot leave," Mab said, a slight frown creasing her brow. "There is dark magic emanating from this Keep, and it is infecting my land and my people. I must find the source and put an end to it."

"The portal, my lady," Isolde said, even quicker now. "That's what he intends with you. He wants to open a portal to the realm of the dead. We don't know why, but he's going to use you, maybe even kill you, to do it."

Mab struggled to repress a hard shudder. Spidery fingers of fear danced along her arm and down her back. *It is the cold,* she told herself. *I cannot be killed by a mere sorcerer's tricks.*

"It appears the girl is right," she heard Erlik's voice, as though from far away. "It's too dangerous for you to stay here. We should leave now rather than later."

"I cannot," Mab said. "If Maleagant has been opening the

portal and releasing the monsters, then we must find a way to stop him. Even without me, he will continue to open the portal and release even more beasts into my realm."

"But—"

"At least if I am here, we can find a way to stop this."

"What if he succeeds, my lady?" Isolde asked.

"Then I will bear the responsibility," she said. "It is my duty to protect my people, I intend to do so."

The girl nodded, and Erlik heaved a sigh.

"Then..." Isolde trailed off and twisted her hands. She inhaled and ploughed on. "You should go to Maleagant's study, in the western tower. He keeps his notes there. I can't read them, but my friend Broc is there too, he might be able to help."

"I admire your bravery, child," Mab said warmly to Isolde. "I ask that you remain near me this evening at the feast. Should the worst happen, we can protect you. And your friend."

Isolde shyly smiled, and withdrew a key from the folds of her dress.

"Here, take my key. It's for the study. I have a copy so I can clean up the messes of his failed spells and potions."

"He does not appear to be a very good sorcerer, if his work keeps failing," Mab smirked slyly at Isolde, who giggled and shook her head.

"I should go. Be safe, my lady. My lord," Isolde curtseyed again before leaving, albeit still looking anxious.

Erlik unfolded his arms as he crossed the room to close the door.

"You treat others too kindly, Mab," he said darkly. "It'll get you in trouble one day."

"I treat the downtrodden with respect, I see no harm in that."

Erlik huffed.

"So, now we know what Maleagant plans for you, and a means to investigate," he said. No matter how long she'd known him for, it always startled Mab to find him looming over her.

"Indeed," she said. "Such foul magic. To open the Gates of Annwyn would require great sacrifice."

"I still think we should leave," Erlik said, but continued as Mab opened her mouth to retort. "But I know you won't. It infuriates me that you should put other lives before your own."

"How can I not? I am the queen; I will protect my subjects until my last breath."

"What do you intend, then?"

Mab inhaled slowly. "We need to investigate his study."

"I'll go," he said at once. "You will have to hold Maleagant's attention for a while. We already know he has an interest in you."

Mab pulled a disgusted face, and Erlik grinned.

"Not *that* kind of interest, thankfully," he said. "Though he must be blind or mad not to. Talk with him, distract him. I'll try and find whichever room he took for his study."

"Very well," Mab said. "Find anything you can relating to the Nuckelavee. Maleagant's notes, journals, anything. Come back and meet me here in an hour."

"As you wish, *a múirnín*," he said. Mab blinked at her language coming from his lips. She offered him a warm smile and nodded, and he leaned forward to press a kiss to her forehead.

Erlik poked his head out of the door and looked both ways down the corridor.

"Go, now. And be careful," he said.

"*You* be careful, clumsy ox," she replied, unable to keep the affection from her voice.

CHAPTER 19

"The spirits in this Keep are restless"

"M ALEAGANT," MAB CALLED, striding along the corridor towards him. "I wish to talk with you."

The sorcerer stopped in his tracks and paused before turning to look at her with that ugly, condescending smile. Yet a muscle twitched in his jaw.

"But of course, my lady," he said. "In regards to...?"

Mab paused. *Keep him talking. Keep him distracted.*

Slowly, she said, "I wish to apologise for my behaviour when we arrived." The words almost stuck in her throat. "It was rude of me to snap at you in such a way. I hope you can forgive me."

"Forgiven and most assuredly forgotten, my lady," Maleagant waved a hand, and gestured for her to walk with him.

"You are kind," Mab went on. "I am curious as to why you chose the Iron Keep as your settlement," she said carefully. "I assume you know the history of this place?"

"You'd be correct in that assumption," Maleagant said. "As for why I chose it? Why, mere convenience, my dear lady. This Keep has been empty for years. Many people still believe it to be haunted."

Mab made a "hmm" noise, and Maleagant looked down at her.

"You don't believe in ghosts, my dear?" he asked, smiling still.

"Not in this Keep, Maleagant," she scoffed. "Any spirits here have long since moved on."

"As I understand it, you had a hand in that," the sorcerer stopped their walk, and stared hard at Mab. She narrowed her eyes and returned his stony glare. Maleagant went on: "You've been to this Keep before, haven't you? You were… *influential* in the removal of its former owner."

"Ancient history, long forgotten by many," Mab said in a low voice.

"And yet the memories and consequences of the act live on," Maleagant taunted further. He touched one of the stone walls, and his voice dropped to a whisper. "These walls *bleed* with memory. The spirits in this Keep are restless. Perhaps you can help me give them the closure they so desire?"

Maleagant curled a lock of her hair around his finger. Mab slapped his hand away, repulsed.

"I know what foul magic you intend here, sorcerer. Why do you seek to open the Gates?"

"We all have our secrets, *witch*," Maleagant said mockingly, his ugly smile returning.

"Do not call me *'witch'*," Mab growled. "Tell me, or I shall discover it myself."

"I do hope you and Erlik can join us for the feast later. It will be quite an enjoyable evening, I think."

He turned away and strode up the corridor, leaving Mab seething and confused.

✧　✧　✧

THE CARRIAGE TRUNDLED along the stony road, jostling Tristan and Lir inside like wooden puppets in a box. Queen Morrigan had gifted them with new clothes, baskets of food and a handful of guards for the journey. Tristan picked unnecessarily at the fabric of his new tunic.

"Pack it in," Lir chuckled, rubbing his sore backside as the carriage rattled over a particularly bumpy patch. "You're makin' me nervous."

"Sorry," Tristan mumbled. "Doesn't fit."

"Aye," Lir agreed soberly. "I know what you mean. Never worn anything this fancy afore." The fisherman yawned. "Give me a poke when we get there, will you?"

Lir laid his head back and tried to sleep, but the jostling carriage proved too much, and he ended up begrudgingly partaking in word games with Tristan to pass the time.

Finally, after beating Lir for the fifth time in a row, Tristan caught sight of a magnificent white city in the distance. He jumped to his feet and banged his head on the ceiling of the carriage, causing Lir to laugh so hard he fell out of his seat.

Rubbing his sore head, Tristan scowled at Lir and sat back down, eagerly watching the city get closer and closer. Lir watched him with a smile.

The whiteness almost blinded him. Much larger and grander than he could ever have expected, Tristan couldn't keep his mouth closed, nor his eyes still.

As in Tír-Na-Nóg, banners and flags fluttered in the breeze around Elphame, except instead of birds, the sigil of this city heralded a howling silver wolf on a purple field.

The portcullis opened once the carriage approached, so their progress went unimpeded. They trundled on, and Tristan immediately felt the road become smoother. He looked out of the carriage window and saw all foot traffic pause and turn to look at the carriage as it rolled by. He sat back, but Lir waved, clearly enjoying himself.

"Nice place," he said, blowing a kiss to a fair-haired woman in the crowd. The fisherman sat back with a satisfied grin. Tristan nodded in agreement.

"Why's everyone staring?" he asked, almost to himself. Elphame was a bustling city. Surely it would receive hundreds of visitors, traders, and craftsmen a day?

"Think about it, lad," Lir pointed to the avian decor. "The crest of Tír-Na-Nóg is painted on every door. We're in a bird cage, in a den of wolves."

Tristan shivered, suddenly remembering Lir's fear of Mab. What was it he'd called her? *She Who Rides The Battlefields?*

He pushed those thoughts away. All he wanted was to find his parents. The city's elegance went unnoticed as he scanned the crowds for any familiar face.

"Where do you think my parents will be?" he asked finally, tired of searching and finding nothing.

"Not a clue," Lir said. "But I think there's a safe bet to start."

He pulled Tristan forward and pointed at the enormous white castle where the carriage seemed to be headed. Tristan let out a slow breath and sat back again.

Even if this mother and father weren't inside, perhaps Queen Mab would be. A cold shiver raced through his blood, but he couldn't tell if it was fear or excitement. *Maybe both.*

Both sat in silence until the carriage rolled to a stop, and a guard opened the door. Tristan stepped out into the courtyard and looked around, feeling a little lost. The castle of Elphame was much larger than the one at Tír-Na-Nóg, and he squinted as he raised his eyes to the blinding white stone.

"Queen Morrigan sent a magpie along with the message that you were on your way," called a voice. Tristan looked up as Lir stepped out of the carriage with a graceless stumble. An old man with long silver hair and pointed ears stood at the top of the steps leading into the castle. He made his way towards them, and Lir gave an awkward bow. Tristan was about to clumsily copy him, when the elder spoke again.

"My name is Elder Lightfoot, Steward of Elphame," he said, politely inclining his head. "Our queen is away on business, but I suspect she isn't who you came here to find." he said, with a knowing smile.

As if on cue, as though the gods themselves had planned it down to the last second, a cry came across the courtyard that made Tristan's heart leap into his throat.

"Tristan!"

He turned, so fast he felt he had broken his neck with the

speed, and saw her running at him, eyes shining, arms wide.

"Mother!" He ran, catching sight of his father behind her.

They met in the middle of the courtyard with a force hard enough to knock them both over, yet they remained upright, fiercely hugging for all to see. Tristan didn't care. He couldn't remember the last time she'd held him so tightly.

"Oh, Tristan," she mumbled into his shoulder, and he could hear her voice break. "Don't ever frighten us like that again!"

"I'm sorry, Mother," he said, suddenly feeling extremely guilty. "I won't, I promise."

"Promises, promises," she waved the words away and broke apart from him. "It doesn't matter, as long as you're safe. Thank the gods."

"You see?" his father said, beaming. "I told you he'd be alright." Yet Tristan could see his eyes were wet with relief.

"What happened, Tristan?" Thissy asked, brushing hair out of his face. "Where did you go?"

"I…" Tristan paused. He considered for a moment telling them about the man in the cage – Erlik. But something stopped him. Everyone assumed him to be dead. Better keep it that way. "I followed a stag and doe. I got lost. Lir helped me, he took me to Tír-Na-Nóg, and Morrigan… *Queen* Morrigan sent us here in a carriage."

As he spoke, he turned and gestured to Lir, who crept up behind him sheepishly.

"Well, the lad was lost, and I…" he mumbled, twisting his hands.

"Thank you," Thissy breathed out in a sigh of relief, and threw her arms around him. Lir looked momentarily horrified, then smiled when he felt the genuine warmth of her embrace.

Thomas cleared his throat.

"Come, Tristan," he said. "We'll get you cleaned up and settled in."

CHAPTER 20

"You're a kind lady"

AT THE HEAD of the table sat Maleagant, smiling smugly as he snapped his fingers, and Isolde moved forwards. She attended Erlik first and poured him wine from a silver pitcher. He saw Mab catch her eye and give her the tiniest smile of reassurance.

Erlik had found nothing in his search. Key clasped in hand, the Western Tower had eluded him. He returned after a fruitless hour, frustrated at himself, and handed the key back to Mab.

"How do you like the wine?" Maleagant asked, interrupting his thoughts. Isolde had just finished refilling his goblet, and had shied away to the shadows. Erlik nodded, taking a sip. Under the table, he felt a foot stroke his leg. He tensed and looked up to see Carman caressing the stem of her wine glass and staring at him with a hungry expression. He frowned, moved his leg away, and leaned closer to Mab. He rested his hand atop hers on the table. She looked at him curiously, and rewarded him with a little smile.

"If I may ask, Maleagant," Erlik heard himself say. "Why did you invite us to stay?"

Maleagant shrugged.

"Why shouldn't I?" he said. "We so rarely receive visitors here—"

"Even rarer that we should receive such a *handsome* guest," Carman said throatily. She ran her index finger along her jawline and down her throat, caressing the low hem of her gown.

Erlik swallowed hard. He felt Mab's hand tense inside his, and looked down to find her glaring so fiercely at Carman he was surprised the woman hadn't burst into flame. Carman cleared her throat and averted her eyes.

"Maleagant," Mab said, her voice sharp and cold as an icicle. "What happened to the people I sent to this Keep?"

Be careful what you say.

She ignored him.

"People, my lady?" Maleagant asked, in a voice that suggested innocence. "I'm afraid we've received no emissaries from the proud city of Elphame. Perhaps they were intercepted on the road?"

"By the Nuckelavee perhaps?" Mab responded frostily. Erlik squeezed her hand.

Mab, listen to me, be careful!

"Oh, I've heard about that monster," Maleagant said, spitting a cherry stone onto the floor.

"Enough secrecy, Maleagant," Mab said, standing. Erlik's hand felt cold and lonely without hers. "I would have the truth now. We here are all aware of your deeds in this Keep. Why are you trying to open the Gates?"

"The truth, my lady, is a fragile and beautiful thing," Maleagant stood as well and approached her. "If you truly wish to know what this Keep is capable of, come to my study in the morning, and I will show you."

That's a trap. Don't agree.

"Very well," she said.

Erlik could have slapped her. Instead, he pinched the bridge of his nose.

"Perhaps then we can spend a little time together, my lord?" Carman asked, quiet enough for only him to hear. Her foot had found his leg again. He pulled away, repulsed, but she didn't seem to care. Her smirk widened, and her eyes became heavy-lidded.

"Be assured, Maleagant," Mab went on. "If what I find in this Keep is insidious, you will regret inviting us to stay."

"Is that a threat, my lady?" Maleagant stepped closer to her. Erlik saw Mab's right hand clench into a tight fist, and stood hastily.

"I think we should retire. Come, Mab," he said, moving between the two. He took Mab gently by the arm and guided her away from the table, having no desire to eavesdrop on Maleagant's vile words to Carman.

✧ ✧ ✧

"WHAT WERE YOU *thinking?*" Erlik shouted, slamming the door closed behind him. "Do you want to get yourself killed?"

"Erlik—"

"This is madness, Mab," he said, grasping his hair. "And I know madness better than anyone."

"Erlik, would you—"

"We're leaving now. I don't care if we haven't found anything, I won't let him hurt—"

"*Erlik!*"

Her voice lanced through him like a shard of ice, and the hearth fire exploded, spitting sparks out onto the stone floor. One excited ember caught the corner of the rug, which started to smoke.

"Damn it, Mab," he muttered, and ran to the rug to stomp out the smouldering fire.

"Please, calm down, and listen to me," she said, her voice soothing and her arms raised as though to settle a wild beast. "We will not leave now, I have things to do."

"Have you listened to *anything*—"

"I have," she said loudly, interrupting him. "A plan. I will go and find Maleagant's notes or journal, *then* we will leave for Elphame."

Erlik folded his arms, "If I couldn't find anything, what

makes you think you can?"

"Because I suspect he has used sorcery to hide the entire tower," she said, and withdrew the key. "This key has the scent of magic on it. Isolde said his study was in the western tower, yet you could not find it. But we both know there *is* a tower. We have been there, long ago. If I go, I should be able to break through any enchantments he has used to conceal the tower, and locate his study."

Erlik raised an impressed eyebrow.

"You distract Maleagant this time," she said, peering out of the door. "Perhaps in a more incendiary way than I did?"

Erlik grinned again.

"Be careful, my love," he said. "I'll meet you back here. Then we can leave this damned place."

Mab paused and looked up at him. Then, to his immense surprise, she lifted herself onto her tiptoes and pressed her lips against his. She lingered there, and he inhaled her scent, wrapping his hand around the nape of her neck.

She broke the kiss first, lowering herself back to the flats of her boots. Erlik felt more dazed than if he'd drunk five bottles of wine. Mab pressed her lips together hard and nodded wordlessly, then hurried along the corridor, melting into the shadows.

MAB RACED PAST a window, catching sight of the fire in the stables she was certain Erlik had set. The hallways were dark, and every shadow looked like a looming threat, but Mab carried on.

Keeping clear of the sleeping quarters, her feet led her higher into the Keep. *Good to see my mind has not betrayed me,* she thought grimly. The centuries past had not faded the memories of the Iron Keep's design. *This way to the kitchens,* she recalled. *That way to the gatehouse.* Passing a cobwebbed door, she stopped, heart stomping in her chest. She ran her fingers over the rotted wood. Slimy, sickly green moss came away and clung to her fingertips.

My old chamber, she realised with a horrible jolt. Her fingers grazed the splintering wood. She knew in her heart it was dangerous to linger, but this room drew her curiosity.

With a quick glance around, she pushed the door. It resisted. Years of disuse and dirt had probably rusted the hinges.

I should not, she thought to herself. *There is nothing of use in there.*

Despite herself, despite the warning her heart was giving her, she waved her hand towards the door. A pulse of magic rippled the wood like water, and Mab stepped through.

Her old room was as expected: dark, dusty, filled with the stench of rot. Mab conjured a flickering purple flame to light her way. The dancing shadows on the wall made her shiver as she looked around.

Three of the four bedposts had snapped and fallen, and there was a long-abandoned rat's nest in the sunken bedding.

Curtains hung limp and torn, infested with moths which stirred irritably when Mab's light cast over them. The bookshelf had collapsed in on itself, and Mab felt a strange sadness when she saw the books had decayed into mulch.

A chill hand gripped her when she noticed the blood stains on the stone had remained.

This was where she had first admitted her feelings for Erlik. The moment she realised he loved her, and she loved him in return.

Her free hand trailed through the dust that coated the dresser beside the dilapidated bed. Had it truly been so many years since their first kiss, the first time he'd held her. When he'd shielded her against the rage of his brother, when the Lord of the Dead fell to Erlik's blade. And his hands shook as he told her to flee from him.

Run.

No, I will not leave you.

Mab, please, I… I can't stop it… run. Please.

But I… I love you, I cannot—.

Gods, Mab, run! Please!

A squealing rat ran out from under the bed. Mab jumped in surprise. She had lingered too long. With one final glance around the room, she left.

In the hallway, she extinguished her light and brushed the dust from her. This Keep was a waking nightmare; too eager to dredge up old memories. The very stone hungered for pain.

She pressed on, glad to leave the old room and the old memories behind.

HIGHER AND HIGHER she climbed, further into the Keep than she would have wanted. It seemed like the stone itself was whispering, hissing at her to turn around. She repressed a shiver. *Nothing to fear,* she repeated to herself several times.

Until, there, the scent of magic. Almost unperceivable. She halted and inhaled deeply. Unlike her magic, ancient and wild, this sorcery smelled false, artificial. Mab wrinkled her nose.

She lifted her hand and felt, against her palm, the gentle thrum of resistance. Not quite a glamour, that was fae magic. This felt more like a barrier. A curtain, a veil.

Veils can be torn.

Closing her eyes, she raised the other hand and breathed slowly. She summoned her own magic from deep within her, feeling that cold ache tug on her heart. Purple clouds blossomed over her fingers, clashing with the magic already in place. She pressed against the invisible barrier, and felt something break.

There was no sound, only a small pulse, and where once a blank stone wall stood, now an unremarkable wooden door appeared before her.

Smiling to herself, she withdrew the key and, with a quick glance over her shoulder, unlocked the door and slipped inside.

Closing the door gently behind her, Mab lit a few candles with a simple wave of her hand, and looked around the enormous room. The ceiling was painted with many moons and stars, and skeletal models of strange beasts hung suspended all around the room. There were jars and pots of gelatinous liquid, thousands upon thousands of books lining the walls, and one elaborate stone throne. Mab scoffed inwardly at the sight of it. *So Maleagant thinks himself a king?*

She moved around the room quickly and silently, trying to find something on the desks and tables that could tell of Maleagant's plans, but the place was so cluttered she had no idea of where to begin.

"You're up late," said a voice. Mab spun around, glaring into the shadows of the room.

"Who said that?" she called. A scrawny badger in a suspended gold cage stretched and yawned.

"I did," it said. Mab stopped and stared at it, raising her eyebrow. It sat back with a heavy thump and scratched its head. The cage swung gently.

Mab approached it.

"Who are you?" she asked.

"My name is Broc," the badger said, wrinkling its furry nose. "I used to be Steward of the Keep, until Maleagant changed me into *this*. I don't know why he doesn't just kill me."

"Isolde mentioned you. She did not say you were a badger."

"So you're the..." Broc rubbed his eyes again then frowned. "Why are you still here? Didn't she tell you to leave?"

Mab nodded. "But I cannot. There are things I must do first."

"Then make it quick. Maleagant has wicked plans for you."

"Tell me, then."

"Dark things, milady," he said, lowering his voice to a whisper. "He's obsessed with death and blood magic. He's been dabbling in forbidden magic for a long time now, trying to open the gateway to Annwyn."

"Does he have a journal?"

Broc pointed to a cluttered desk.

She turned and followed his claw-point, and picked up a string-bound notebook. She untied the fastening and flicked through it quickly, catching glimpses of drawings and sketches, and several complicated-looking equations.

"This is how the Nuckelavee was freed," Mab said, tucking the journal into her cloak. "He must have succeeded in opening the gateway, if only for a short time."

"Indeed, milady," Broc nodded. "They never speak too plainly about their plans, so I don't know exactly what they want with Annwyn. Isolde's sister, Carman—"

"*Sister?*" Mab interrupted, then shook herself. "No, forgive me, that matters little."

She inspected the lock, and found it much simpler than the one barring the door to the study. She focused her power, and the lock twisted and clicked open. "I have what I need. Wake Isolde. Go to Elphame with her; I will meet you there and find out how to transform you back to your true form."

Broc crept out of his cage and stretched.

"You're a kind lady," he said. "Too kind for this place."

With that, he jumped off the table and ran for the door, his claws clicking on the stone floor.

Mab watched him go. It had been a long time since anyone had called her *kind*. She turned and swept her eyes over the rest of the room. A large cauldron stood nearby, a foul stench belching forth. Mab pressed a hand over her nose and approached carefully.

The table was lined with phials and jars. Some contained only liquid. Others contained preserved parts of creatures long dead. A rat with two tails hung suspended in greenish, viscous fluid. A still-beating heart thumped pathetically in a jar full of blue liquid.

Mab turned her nose up. She couldn't help the sense of condescension at seeing his work.

Alchemy, she snorted internally. *This is why the magic smells so false. It is artificial, crafted in a workshop. Maleagant has no natural magic of his own.*

She knew she was being petty, but she couldn't resist a complacent smile.

Bookcases lined the walls. Mab approached and ran her fingers along the spines. She'd never heard of most of them.

And little doubt, she thought, when she realised the subject matter of most of the tomes. *Blood magic.*

She repressed a shiver of revulsion. Maleagant was tampering with both the most basic and the most forbidden of magics.

Mab gave the room one last, long, sweeping look, and turned to leave.

Her hand had barely touched the handle when the door swung open, revealing a smoke-burnt Maleagant.

"Lost, my lady?" he growled, reaching into his robe. Before Mab could move, speak or cast any magic at him, he threw a vial at her feet which exploded, and Mab's world faded to black.

✧   ✧   ✧

ERLIK PACED RESTLESSLY. Minutes had turned to hours, and Mab had still not returned. How long does it take to poke around in a dusty old room and find a journal? He should have gone in her stead. He should never have brought her to this damn Keep in the first place.

He had a wild urge to break something expensive. Managing to subdue his temper, he continued to pace. He ran his hand through his hair, the length tickling the base of his neck. He flexed his hands, unsure of what to expect when she arrived. He flung himself down on an elegant blue chaise and drummed impatient fingers against the arm. Anxiety burned under his skin.

What was taking so long?

The anticipation brutally reminded him of when, all those years ago, he'd waited for her to come to him, *if* she'd come to him, after he confessed how he felt for her. She'd asked for time. He'd granted it. But those unending, unknowing hours almost killed him.

There was a gentle knock at the door, and Erlik launched towards it, all his doubts immediately forgotten in a dizzying rush of affection. He threw open the door and heaved a sigh of relief to see Mab standing there.

"Finally," he muttered, and pulled her into the chamber. "Did you find what you were looking for?"

Mab nodded but didn't elaborate. Erlik raised his eyebrows impatiently.

"Well?" he pressed. "What did you find? What's Maleagant up to? Why does he want to open the Gates?"

Mab gave a silvery laugh and sat down on his bed, running her hand through her hair. Erlik watched her, apprehensive.

"Can't it wait until morning?" she asked, and beckoned him towards her. Erlik chewed his lip.

"We really should leave before then, Mab," he said, yet approached her and cupped her cheek, shaking off the uneasy feeling that had started to grip him.

"I don't think there's any harm in us staying the night, my love," she purred.

Erlik frowned. *There's definitely something not right.* He licked his lips.

"Are you... well?" he asked haltingly. *Did Maleagant do something to her?*

Mab gave the silvery laugh again. "Of course, I'm fine. You look thirsty. Here, let me fetch you some wine."

She stood and walked to the desk at the other side of the room. Erlik stared after her, eyes narrow. Yet he couldn't stop his eyes drawing to her swaying hips. When she turned back around, he lifted his gaze back to her face and saw her lips pulled into a smirk. She approached him and offered the goblet of wine she had just poured.

"Thank you," he said slowly. Eyes still fixed on her strange expression, he took the wine and sipped. It had a hard, bitter tang, and he coughed into the goblet. She smiled and tipped the base of the cup upwards, forcing the wine down his throat.

"Mab, what's wrong with you?" he choked, shoving the goblet away.

"There's nothing wrong with me, my love," she said softly. "I just missed you."

His mind furred as thoughts became disjointed. Erlik blinked hard and cleared his throat. He dropped the goblet and it clattered against stone. Wine spilled.

Something's wrong.

"Oh, look what you've done," she tutted and shook her head. She pushed his chest gently and he stumbled backwards, falling onto the bed.

She clambered on top of him and stroked his cheek, stray locks of her long hair tickling his face. Her sweet breath filled his nostrils, and he closed his eyes. The wine coursed like fire in his veins.

Something's wrong!

She leaned forwards to kiss him. Their legs entwined, and Mab's kisses became more feverish. Erlik couldn't think. Couldn't speak. He could only hold her, want her, take her. He watched her undress above him, and move with him until he entered her.

Something... is wrong...

CHAPTER 21

"Long is the day, and long is the night"

THE SMELL OF burning assaulted his senses first. Erlik opened his eyes and a sharp poker of pain rammed through his skull. He winced and sat up, cradling the back of his neck with a groan.

His eyes immediately found Mab, who paced like a captive wolf. He could see why she was so agitated; they'd dared to put her in a cage.

She breathed out a sigh of relief at seeing him wake. Erlik looked around and found himself in a similar prison, though he didn't recognise the room.

"Are you hurt?" she asked. Her voice was like a needle of pain behind his eyes, but his heart leapt at the sound. She was concerned for him.

"No... are you?" he asked. She shook her head. "What happened?"

"Maleagant found me here. This is his study. He dabbles in alchemy, and he used some sort of concoction, I suspect of his own design. It rendered me unconscious."

Confused, Erlik dragged himself to his feet and approached the bars that separated them. How could she have come to him when she'd been locked up here?

Before he got the chance to ask, Mab continued, "I have tried using magic to escape, but the metalwork seems similar to that of your cage in Wicklewood."

"But you came back to the room? We—"

"Here," she threw him something through the bars; something small and glimmering. He caught it in his left hand.

"I can weaken the enchantment, but I cannot pick the lock. I know you can. Try now, and we can escape."

He looked at the thing she had thrown to him. A hair pin. *Her* hair pin; an onyx wolf head with amethyst eyes. He'd tried to steal this from her, once. When they'd first met.

"Erlik," she prompted. "Hurry."

He nodded and rushed to the cage door. Leaning out, he pushed the spike of the pin into the keyhole and began to manipulate the tumblers inside. His face and hands began to burn. *Cold iron!*

Hissing, he withdrew.

"What is it?"

He shook his head like a dog shaking off a fly, and ran his hands over his face.

"Cold iron," he said gruffly. "Stings."

He sharply inhaled and struck at the lock again. Mab made a noise of concern, but he ignored her. He could do this, just a few more tumblers…

"Erlik, the door!"

He withdrew the pin and tucked it carefully into his sleeve, stepping away from the door in time to see Maleagant and Carman enter, both wearing insufferably smug looks on their faces.

No one spoke. Erlik watched Maleagant approach a workbench and busy himself with several bottles. The clink of glass was the loudest sound in the room.

"Well, now," Maleagant said, without turning around. "This is nice."

Mab stopped pacing and glared at the sorcerer.

"Release us, wretch," she spat.

Maleagant turned and cast an eye over her, nodding approvingly. A sickening surge of hatred rose in Erlik's chest.

"Well, you are such a feisty little thing," Maleagant said. "I can see why you like her, Father."

Erlik blinked. Mab stared. The silence was absolute.

"What?" Erlik finally managed to whisper.

"Don't look so surprised," Maleagant said, smirking. "I expect there are a hundred bastards running around Albion bearing your features, if your reputation is anything to go by. I don't expect you to remember my mother; she's been dead a long time, either way."

"What do you want?"

Maleagant gave a self-satisfied laugh that made Erlik's skin crawl.

"*I'd* hoped," Carman said, lounging on the throne pridefully, watching the exchange without a flicker of surprise. "The tainted wine at the feast would have rendered you unconscious. But you didn't seem to have drunk enough. Or you have a high tolerance for valerian root."

Maleagant laughed again, a simpering and ugly chuckle. Erlik balled his hands into fists.

"So I had to find another way," Carman went on. "You didn't seem to be receptive to my own charms, despite your reputation. So I had to assume a different face. I can't mimic the way she speaks, though. So we heightened the dosage in the wine for good measure."

"With a little help from me, of course," Maleagant put in. "I like to experiment, as you discovered tonight, my lady," he threw a nod to Mab now. "Alchemy is a tricky art to master, but a great boon."

"The combination seemed to work," Carman finished. "You were so easy to manipulate."

Erlik closed his eyes as horrifying realisation struck him like lightning.

"That wasn't Mab in our room," he whispered. Carman shook her head slowly, eyes fixed on him, curling a lock of hair around her finger. "It was you."

"Erlik?" Mab's voice punctured his heart. It wasn't small or meek or hurt, only confused. "What do you mean?"

"She disguised herself as you, and came to our chamber,"

he said, unable to look her in the eye.

"And you…" Mab stiffened. She didn't need to finish. Erlik nodded slowly. A cloud of purple fire blossomed at her fingertips, then dissipated as soon as it appeared.

"Forgive me, *a múirnín.*"

Silence stretched out between them.

"What do you want, sorcerer?" Mab asked again, her voice harshening to cold steel. Erlik marvelled at her rage. Had she slept with another man, he would have been destroyed.

"You shouldn't ask questions you already know the answer to," Maleagant said patronisingly. "It's not polite." He turned away and started mixing potions again on his work bench.

"Answer me!" she growled. "Why do you want to open the Gates of Annwyn?"

"She's clever," Maleagant said to Carman, still with his back turned. "We should keep her around."

"I'd rather we didn't," she replied, still with her hungry gaze fixed on Erlik.

"It's impossible, Maleagant," Erlik snarled.

"No, it's not, actually," the sorcerer turned again, crushing something in a mortar. Whatever it was, it emitted a foul stench. "It's quite possible. With enough blood, *anything* is possible."

"Blood magic," Mab hissed, and Erlik could feel her revulsion reflected in himself. Even during his novice attempts at necromancy, he never touched upon blood magic. "That is abhorrent, it is forbidden."

Maleagant sneered at her and shrugged.

"It was all thanks to you, my lady," he said. "The servants in the castle weren't enough."

That's why there's no one else here, Erlik realised, remembering how empty the courtyard was when they first arrived.

Maleagant went on, "So we took people from the closest villages. But mortal blood barely held enough power. Then *you* started to send spies. Just one *Fianna* spy held more power in his blood than twenty mortals."

Mab's lip curled and she screamed curses, launching herself at the bars, as if she could melt through them and destroy him. Yet the cold iron cage singed her skin, tainting her face and arms with cruel black marks. She grunted in frustration and pain and backed away, allowing her flesh to heal.

"The portal opened, though not for very long, I'm afraid. Long enough for the creatures to escape. The Dullahan. The Cú-Sith Hounds." Maleagant paused, and gave her a nasty grin. "The Nuckelavee."

"You will pay for this, you ditch-born maggot!" Mab spat.

Maleagant threw his head back and laughed. Carman joined in. Her silvery laugh annoyed Erlik more.

"Enough!" Erlik snapped. He slammed the flat of his fist against the bars, ignoring the hissing flesh. "Why do you want to open the Gates? What could you possibly want on the other side?"

Maleagant approached him slowly, condescending. Now that Erlik looked at him properly, his eyes did seem a little familiar. He tried to place the woman who'd been his mother, but he couldn't do it. There'd been so many...

"We want something that only the former lord of this Keep can provide."

Erlik's blood froze in his veins. Spiders of fear scuttled up and down his spine. White spots burst at the corners of his sight.

No.

He grabbed a handful of Maleagant's robes through the bars and pulled him closer, almost lifting him off his feet.

"You *can't*," Erlik said in a low voice. "You can't unleash him. You can't bargain with him. And you certainly can't *control* him."

Maleagant threw off Erlik's grip, ripping the cloak as he did so.

"I can do what I want!" the sorcerer shouted, suddenly losing his calm composure.

"No," Mab whispered. Erlik looked over at her. His heart plummeted; her eyes were huge, unblinking. Her hands clenched and unclenched. She stood rigid, her face drained and wan. Erlik's heart almost stopped in its cage. No one could inspire such fear in Mab. No one, except—

"Erlik is right," Mab went on, almost a whisper. "You cannot unleash him on Albion, Maleagant."

"Oh, I can," he said, eyes sparkling. "You see, only the Lord of the Dead can grant eternal life. Only the Lord of the Dead can promise I—*we* will never cross into his domain. All I need, my dear, is *you*."

"Why? Why would you possibly desire eternal life?"

"*You* have it. *He* has it," Carman sneered.

"We are Old Gods," Mab countered. "Do you think it is easier? Living forever? Do you think it will bring you peace? Or power? Do you know how curseful it is, to watch the world wither more with every blink of your eye? To see the ones you love decay and disappear? It is no boon to live forever."

"And yet you don't relinquish it?"

"He's right," Carman put in. "If it's such a curse, why don't you just lie down and *die?*"

Erlik winced; those words were bitingly cruel. Yet Mab took them in her stride.

"I have my people to protect."

"And you?" Maleagant turned to Erlik now. "Why do you keep on living eternally? What do you have to keep you alive? You have no one to protect. You have no one."

Without hesitation, Erlik looked at Mab. Mab lifted her eyes to his. Erlik shook his head.

"I have no choice," Erlik said.

Maleagant scoffed. Carman glowered at him.

Mab shook her head, "I will never help you."

"Oh, but you don't have to do anything, my lady."

Erlik recognised Maleagant's darkly hungry look all too well.

"The Heart of Magic Itself. Within my grasp, at last."

He reached through the bars, stretching his hand forward

to touch her face. Mab's eyes flashed with violet light, and Maleagant sharply retracted his hand with a yelp.

"Witch!"

Snarling, Maleagant turned away again, and grabbed a stone basin. He poured the contents of several vials into the basin.

"Long is the day, and long is the night," Maleagant muttered as the mixed potions belched out white smoke. "Long is the waiting of Arawn's might!"

Maleagant grabbed his staff from where it had been ledged against the table, and slammed it into the stone floor.

MAB CONVULSED AND fell forward onto her hands and knees. Fire raked her body like claws. Over the pounding blood in her ears, she heard Erlik screaming her name, but she couldn't look up. Her heart beat so fast she thought it might burst. A red haze fell over her eyes. She gasped for air, but every ragged breath felt like a noose had tightened around her throat.

She heard Erlik scream again, his voice breaking.

She forced her gaze up. Tears beclouded her sight. She'd never seen him so desperate. His eyes were frantic and wide as he pressed himself against the bars, trying to reach her. But fire coursed through her veins again, and she writhed against the pain like a burning snake.

The agony grew, higher and higher, until it reached her heart, and it felt like her entire being was aflame. Burning from the inside out. She finally released the blood-freezing scream she'd been holding back.

Then came a fearsome, gut-wrenching ripping sound, like flesh tearing from bone. Mab arched her back as the fire left her as quickly as it had come.

She slumped, trembling and breathless, and rolled onto her side. Hair partially covered her eyes, but she could see Erlik still straining to get through the bars to her. Ugly, black burns scorched his face and arms, only to fade when he moved away from the cold iron bars. She tried to get to her feet, but her arms didn't have the strength. She doubted whether her legs would even support her.

"Mab," she heard Erlik whisper. He looked horrified, his hair a mess from grasping at it in desperation, his hands bruised and blackened from wrenching at the cage bars. She started to crawl towards him, like a wounded wolf limping to her mate. But at that moment, her strength left her entirely, and she collapsed, trembling and panting on the stone floor.

"*Maleagant!*" Erlik roared in fury, but the sorcerer paid them no mind.

"*Oscail an doras go dtí an domhain fada-dhearmadta,*" he chanted, staff raised. "*Oscail an geataí an bháis!*"

Carman watched through widening eyes. She licked her lips. The flames in the braziers flickered and died, and a freakish whispering around them grew malicious and hostile. Blue tendrils of magic snaked from Mab's prone body and wove into the air above them. Erlik watched in despair as the tendrils joined together and formed a huge portal in the painted ceiling.

Blue and shining and brimming with screams of pain, the gateway throbbed with the thousands of souls desperate to fall through the veil and become real once more.

Maleagant grinned, eyes wide with delight, and raised his staff higher. A sleek black shape fluttered out from the Gates of Annwyn and alighted atop a bookcase. The crow ruffled its shining black feathers and cawed. Carman jumped, then looked at Maleagant.

"Did that bird just say—?" she began, but Maleagant waved at her to be quiet, and thrust his staff towards the portal. A bolt of lightning struck and pierced the thin membrane. A vile white worm wriggling into the realm of the dead.

"I seek the blood of the dragon!" he bellowed.

The screaming souls obeyed his command. With pitiful moans of pain and fear, they relinquished the prize and retreated back into Annwyn. The membrane stopped pulsating and vanished. Maleagant yanked back his staff, wrenching with it a pale body from the cold embrace of death.

CHAPTER 22

"We have demands already"

A BILLOWING SILENCE followed. Punctured only by a ragged gasp from the naked man on the ground. Maleagant and Carman looked at each other, and Carman cast another nervous glance at the crow.

"Stand," Maleagant commanded. The man didn't move. "I said, *stand!*"

"Enough!" the man croaked, yet slowly gained his feet, conjuring black robes around himself. "You cannot command me."

Carman stared, nose crinkled and mouth twisted, at the gaping, bloody wound that had killed him. The wound that hadn't healed since his death.

"How long has it been?" the man asked.

"Long enough."

"What reasons have you for summoning me?" the dead man asked, his voice deep, his words slow. Deliberate. Maleagant gave him a simpering smile and turned.

"Something for you," he said, gesturing to the cages.

The cages which now stood empty. Doors creaking.

Erlik froze in the doorway and slowly turned, supporting Mab who half-stood draped across his arm like a dying woman, her breath coming hard and fast.

Erlik held up the hairpin, his usual casual smirk only

slightly askew. Carman released a whine of annoyance.

"Brother."

All levity vanished with the word. Erlik dropped the hairpin, fingers now clumsy with fear. He wrapped his freed hand around Mab and subtly moved her behind him.

Voice shaking, he whispered, "Idath."

"How long has it been, little brother?" Idath asked.

Mab eyed Idath with wary disquiet. *'Little' brother indeed,* she thought to herself. It had been so long since she'd laid eyes on this monster of a man, she'd forgotten how Idath towered over them both. She failed to repress her trembling.

Bone-white hair fell far past his narrow shoulders. Each of his thin fingers ended in long, knifelike nails. Tall, pale, and slender, the very image of Death itself. Both brothers shared the sharp, cruel features resembling a crow, but Idath was the light to Erlik's dark.

Erlik ran his eyes over his brother, and Mab noticed him struggling not to step back in horror.

"How long, little brother?" Idath asked for the third time, his voice a quiet, thunderous rumble. Erlik gulped again and shook his head.

"I don't know," he said.

Idath took a step forward, and Erlik took one back out of instinct. He ran his tongue over his lower lip, as though furious at himself for betraying fear.

Mab saw Idath's gaze flicker to her. Their eyes met for a brief second. Her heart pulsed hard in her throat. Even at her full strength, she doubted she'd be able to face Idath.

"You married it?" Idath's lip curled in disgust. Mab blanched. *How could he possibly know that?*

Without a word, Idath lunged, grabbed Erlik's throat and squeezed. Mab inhaled sharply and stepped forward, but Erlik pushed her back again.

"You will pay for what you did, brother," Idath growled. "You *and* the Heart."

Maleagant cleared his throat. Idath looked momentarily confused, before realising who had made the noise. He turned, dragging Erlik with him.

"There are some things we'd like to discuss with you, Idath," Maleagant said. "For one, we desire a boon for releasing you."

"You will hold your tongue, boy," Idath released Erlik, who fell to the ground and scrambled back towards Mab. She took him immediately into her arms. "You will be rewarded when *I* see fit."

"We have sacrificed a great deal to bring you back to this world," Maleagant said petulantly. He stared up at Idath without fear. Had Mab seen it, she would have reluctantly applauded his gall.

"I am not ungrateful," Idath said. "But I will exact my revenge first. Then you shall be rewarded as only *I* see fit."

"We have demands already,"

"You will demand nothing of me, boy!" Idath roared.

"They're escaping!" Carman's shrill voice rang in their ears. Idath turned abruptly, small eyes widening. Mab and Erlik had almost made out of the door, footsteps silent and steady.

"Coward!" Idath snarled.

He raised a hand, but Mab was faster. She shoved Erlik aside and gestured wildly. A fiery serpent, writhing in purple flames, rose from the floor. Sparking and spitting, the magic encircled Idath and squeezed. As Idath roared in frustration, the snake lifted him from his feet and slammed him against the stone wall. Dust crumbled from the ceiling.

Mab waved her hands again, sending Maleagant and Carman sprawling across the room. One final gesture, and the snake slithered around the room, igniting it in violet flames. Mab smiled bitterly.

Let them burn.

"Quick, come," she turned and grabbed Erlik's hand. The snake had already erupted into purple smoke.

"*Witch!*"

Idath's voice was a bellow of a wounded bull.

Mab saw his intention before Erlik did.

HE WAS NEVER skilled with magic.

The inexplicably mundane thought crossed Erlik's mind before anything else.

He always had to resort to brute force.

The dagger clenched in Idath's hand didn't register. Idath's arm drawing back didn't register. The dagger spiralling towards him didn't register.

A Deathblade, forged in the depths of Annwyn. A death sentence for any being – mortal or god – who met its kiss.

The glinting point crept closer, yet still it didn't occur to him to move. His mind, his body, his very blood had frozen. Nothing responded.

Only one sound penetrated his mind. A sound that would never leave him, etched in his memory forever. It was only a small gasp, a dull and fleshy thump, a soft wail, but it would haunt him for the rest of his life.

Mab was in front of him. He could feel her trembling. She raised one shaking hand. *Blood.*

Erlik looked down at her. Yet her eyes were fixed on the leather-bound dagger handle protruding from her chest.

His world edged to a crawl. Rage exploded before he even knew it was building.

The room erupted into chaos.

Creatures born of flame crawled out of the blaze and burst into liquid fire. Jars of unknown fluid exploded. Erlik's eyes burned with black fury. With an anguished scream, he violently gestured, and unseen forces lifted Idath and slammed him into the ceiling.

He fell back to the ground with a hefty thud as Erlik approached, eyes on fire, ready to tear his brother apart.

"Erlik," Mab choked.

Her voice brought sense back to him. *No time.* Turning his back on Idath's prone body, he ran to her and lifted her into his arms and she moaned. She hissed in pain as he took hold of the dagger's handle.

"No!" she cried. Erlik froze. A bubble of blood burst at the corner of her lips. "Leave it… it is barbed. You must," she drew in a ragged breath. "You must get me back to Elphame."

"I will," he whispered. "Hold on, *a múirnín.*"

He hesitated. A swift glance behind him told him Idath, Maleagant, and Carman hadn't moved, yet he knew they shouldn't leave them to rebuild their strength. Half-formed plans raced each other through his mind.

Praying the fire would take care of Maleagant and Carman, and they'd deal with Idath once Mab was safe, Erlik tightened his grip on her and ran.

As he sped through the halls, beads of sweat appeared on Mab's face. Her face contorted in anguish. Blood dribbled from the corner of her mouth and sprayed his tunic when she coughed.

"You're going to be fine, Mab," Erlik heard himself say. "Keep your eyes open. For me, do it for me."

The Elvish horse snorted in distress when he entered the stable. He kicked its gate open for it to run free, back to the wilds. He paused, staring at Mab's stag.

How am I supposed to mount without hurting her?

Mab clicked her tongue before his thought had even finished. The stag lowered itself to its haunches and gazed patiently at him. Erlik released a breath of relief and swung one leg over the beast's back.

No reins. No bridle. No saddle. Gods, Mab, how do you—

"*Rith*, Oisín. Race the wind," Mab whispered. The stag snorted and regained its feet. It pawed the ground for a few seconds, and Erlik held Mab tighter. He gripped the stag with his thighs and leaned forward.

The stag bolted out of the Iron Keep and fled for Elphame.

CHAPTER 23

"It's him!"

A GROUP OF apprentices practised fire magic against a row of straw dummies. Each one looked around Tristan's age. The scent of burning straw filled the air, retrieving memories Tristan had hoped to forget.

"Soon enough," Thissy said, giving his shoulder a fond squeeze. "You'll have magic of your own. Then you can join in to practise your craft."

Realising she must have noticed him staring, Tristan felt the blood rush to his face. He nodded and raised the curry comb again. Epona tossed her head. Tristan sighed, pressing the comb to her mane, sweeping it downwards. Her hair was knotted, and he tugged gently.

"Don't worry about being left behind," Thomas put in, lowering the two buckets of oats he'd brought in. "Everyone learns their craft differently. You might do better at healing magic, like your mother."

Tristan wrinkled his nose. Thomas laughed and rolled up his slipping sleeves.

"I wouldn't turn your nose up at that, if I were you," he said. "Your mother has saved my hide with her magic more times than I could count."

"Maybe if you weren't so foolhardy," Thissy said airily, brushing down her own grey mare.

Thomas playfully scowled, and flicked a finger. A droplet of water leapt from the bucket and splashed her nose.

Thissy let out a soft "oh!" of surprise, then gave her husband a look of mock outrage.

Thomas smiled innocently. "Oh, Tristan did it."

"You are in *so* much trouble!"

"Uh-oh," Thomas said playfully. "Tristan, run! I'll fend off the dragon!"

Tristan laughed as his father tackled his mother, lifting her bodily over his shoulder. Thissy squealed with impish delight.

"The dragon is defeated!" Thomas yelled, and threw Thissy down into a huge pile of hay.

Tristan laughed. He felt like a boy again. Thissy emerged from under the hay, strands tangled in her golden hair. She grabbed Thomas and pulled him into the hay with her, but not before Thomas had grabbed Tristan's hand to pull him down too.

The three of them wrestled to be free of each other and the hay, unable to breathe from laughing so hard.

Finally, Thomas dragged himself to his feet and brushed himself down. Epona stamped her feet, snorting.

"What's the matter, old girl?" he asked, eyes still shining from mirth. He approached her to pat her neck, but she snorted again, tossing her head. Thomas frowned. "What do you mean?"

Tristan helped his mother out of the hay. She plucked strands out of his hair, watching the smile vanish from Thomas's face.

"What—" Tristan began, but his father looked up sharply.

"Quiet," Thomas said suddenly, not smiling at all now. "Do you hear that?"

The quiet rumble of a gathering crowd. Then, suddenly, one long, loud howl of despair.

Tristan's eyes immediately shot to the courtyard. The three stepped out of the stable to see a large crowd of seelie in the courtyard, encircling something.

Or someone.

AS THEY APPROACHED, Thomas saw every face was white and wide-eyed. Some at the centre of the group staggered back, pushing others aside in their attempt to move away. The rumble of voices grew to a cacophony around them. A huge, white stag reared back with a loud bellow, forcing the crowd to retreat further.

"It's him!" came a terrified cry, and several seelie fled the courtyard. Thomas pushed his way through the crowd, until he reached the centre, and his heart dropped like a stone. A chill lanced through him. He immediately turned back to face his wife and son. Tristan was standing on his tiptoes to see more.

"Don't let him see," he said in a low, urgent voice. Thissy nodded, shaking.

The man on the ground looked up sharply and glared at Thomas. Frenzied desperation filled his eyes as he clutched a woman's body close to him. Blood stained his shirt. His hands. Even his face. Thomas's eyes widened and he felt a sickening lurch roil in his belly.

"*You!*"

"Do something, *amadán*! Please!" Erlik said feverishly. "They won't listen to me!"

Thomas stared at the woman cradled in his arms.

Frail, weak, as though seriously ill or badly wounded. Her eyes were closed. Thomas couldn't even tell if she was still alive.

A dagger protruded from between her breasts. Erlik's shaking hands tried to stem the flow of blood that pumped sluggishly from the wound.

Thomas's heart pounded hard in his throat. He'd barely recognised her; he had never seen Mab look so diminished before. Her eyes closed. Her natural glow dimmed. The powerful scent of wood smoke and nightshade overwhelmed by the coppery tang of blood.

This is wrong.

"Thissy, fetch the guard," he hissed to his wife. "And physicians."

She pulled Tristan away. He complied this time. Thomas moved forwards, but Erlik clutched Mab closer to him.

"Don't touch her!" he spat. Thomas glowered and dragged him to his feet by the collar of his shirt.

Rage blinded Thomas to everything around them; he didn't care that people were staring, or that Erlik didn't fight back. He barely cared that Mab jarred so fiercely when she hit the ground that her face twisted in agony. She coughed and blood sprayed from her lips.

"What did you do to her?" Thomas demanded. Erlik snarled and pushed Thomas away. He kneeled beside Mab as guards rushed around them. Metal sang against leather as they drew swords against him.

Erlik raised his hands to show them empty, but Thomas took no chances.

"Arrest him!" he commanded.

"What?"

The captain dragged him back to his feet and bound his hands in iron chains to stop him conjuring any magic.

Erlik struggled and hissed in pain as he was dragged away.

"No! No, I need to be with her! She needs me! Rhymer! *Rhymer!*"

Shaken, Thomas watched until he was safely out of sight, then followed the guards carrying Mab into the castle.

CHAPTER 24

"She needs me!"

ERLIK HAD RIDDEN hard and fast over the moors, clutching Mab close to him. The cold air stung his face like slapping hands, but he rode on. The stag leapt over a laughing brook, and Erlik felt Mab almost slip from his grasp. He pulled her back to his chest, willing her to have the strength to hold onto him. The dagger rose and fell as her breaths grew shorter. Her eyelids fluttered.

I cannot heal it.

Erlik couldn't respond. He didn't know how. His heartbeat matched the pounding of cloven hooves as they rode towards the white city, looming on the moors up ahead. Dark, heavy clouds hid the afternoon sun, turning the day into night. His despair had seen to that.

A pack of wolves silently approached from behind, and ran alongside the stag. Erlik realised they weren't there to give chase. They were an honour-guard, there at the silent plea of their weakening mistress. The stag must have sensed their intention, for it gave no sign of distress.

Erlik kicked the stag and urged it faster as they approached the city. The gatehouse stood open and inviting, built into the great wall that surrounded the city. The wolves skidded to a stop at the brow of a hill and howled. The sound chilled Erlik's blood.

"Hold fast, traveller!" a seelie guard called from the battlements, raising his spear to a defensive position. Erlik ignored him, and rode through the gatehouse with fierce determination.

"Hold there!" the shout came again. Erlik heard more commands of other officers behind him, and the immediate rush that spilled out of the gatehouse and chased the galloping stag through the narrow streets.

Civilians parted swiftly as Erlik charged through, the stag's cloven hooves clattering on stone. He rode up the long pathway that led to the castle and burst into the courtyard, finally allowing the stag to slow to a stop. A curious crowd gathered at once as he slid down, and he collapsed into an aching heap in the middle of the courtyard. He clutched Mab close. Her breathing had become frighteningly slow.

"Someone, help! Please!" he begged. This was no time for pride; they stood around him, staring with open mouths at her limp body. Her blood soaked his shaking hands. Muttering grew to a rumble around him.

"What are you doing? *Help me!*" Erlik bellowed, looking around desperately, but the seelie just stared back at him. The crowd around them had swiftly grown, and Erlik bent his head over Mab's, trying to force away his shame and fear. But it overwhelmed him.

He threw back his head and released an excruciating cry of grief and despair, his whole body trembling with rage. At the seelie. At himself. Even at Mab. The stag whinnied and reared back, and the crowd stepped back as someone screamed.

"It's him!"

More fearful cries echoed in the courtyard. The crowd dispersed as seelie fled his presence. But there were so many of them, all curious to see who had entered the courtyard in such a dramatic fashion.

Erlik bent over Mab again, hiding his face and forcing away the pricking of angry tears in the corners of his eyes. He pressed his lips to her damp forehead and whispered fervently to her to wake up and help him.

"Don't let him see," he heard a voice say. A voice he found horribly familiar.

Erlik drew in a long, deep breath. Hatred and fury bubbled like acid in his throat, and his dark eyes narrowed. *Him.*

Erlik looked up, curiosity getting the better of him. He stared at the seelie family, but his concern for Mab overshadowed his hatred. His dishevelled hair fell into his eyes and he clutched Mab tighter to his chest.

"*You!*" He saw Thomas Rhymer's eyes widen in recognition, fear, and hate.

"Do something, *amadán*! Please!" he implored. He didn't know how else to address him. "They won't listen to me!"

Thomas stared at Mab's body in Erlik's arms, as unhelpful and dense as the other seelie around them. Erlik felt a surge of frustration.

"Thissy, fetch the guard. And physicians," Thomas told his faery wife, and she led their son away, although he kept stopping as though wanting to stay and watch his father. Thomas moved forwards to take Mab, but Erlik held onto her protectively.

"Don't touch her!" he said in a sharp voice. She was frail enough already. If the *amadán* picked her up carelessly, he'd no doubt cause her even more harm. But Thomas grabbed his shirt and hauled him to his feet. Erlik cried out "No!" when Mab fell to the ground. Blood sprayed from her mouth in a fine mist and dribbled onto her lips.

There was nothing he could do. If he fought back, the seelie would assuredly keep him away from Mab, when he might be the only one able to save her life.

"What did you do to her?" Thomas demanded. Erlik had to fight the urge to hit the idiot boy. How could he even *think* he'd harm Mab in such a way? The guards ran towards them, and Erlik pushed Thomas away roughly and kneeled down beside Mab.

But instead of coming to Mab's aid, they surrounded him, swords pointed straight at his heart. Erlik swallowed and raised his hands. He opened his mouth to protest that they should worry about Mab rather than him, but Thomas Rhymer spoke first.

"Arrest him!" he said. Erlik couldn't speak. He felt himself being dragged to his feet again and his hands chained. He couldn't cast. He couldn't do anything. Cold iron clamped icily against his flesh, disrupting any power he might have conjured.

"*What?*" he couldn't allow it. "No! No, I need to be with her!"

He struggled as more soldiers appeared to restrain him and drag him away.

"She needs me! Rhymer!"

He met with no reply. Fighting for his freedom, the guards dragged him out of the courtyard, away from Mab.

"*Rhymer!*"

CHAPTER 25

"You are so simple"

MALEAGANT GROANED AND pushed a pile of debris off himself. He sat up and looked around. Idath had already regained his feet, standing in the smouldering wreckage of the study. Maleagant stood and began picking through the blackened remains of his books and notes. Carman feebly shifted. She sat, and immediately wished she hadn't. The room whirled around her and she fought the urge to vomit. She dragged herself to her feet, pulling her ripped gown back up her shoulders.

"Why didn't you help?" she accused, glaring at Idath. "Now they've escaped!"

"I extinguished the fire before it burnt you to death," Idath said. "I consider that *helping*."

Carman's lip curled.

"I have struck the Heart with a Deathblade," Idath continued. "It will be unable to heal the wound inflicted, but I have little doubt my brother will find a way to save its life. It was always his weakness."

Maleagant collapsed into one of the few undamaged chairs, nursing his head. He conjured a cold, damp cloth and held it to the large welt on his temple, glaring at Carman as she began to pace.

"I am not as strong as I should be," Idath said quietly.

Carman scowled.

"You look strong enough to me," she said.

"I was much stronger than this. My powers are much weaker than they were," he said, flexing his long, thin fingers. "You must have done something wrong with the ritual to summon me."

Maleagant's cheek twitched, "I did everything right."

He started to stand, then hissed with pain and regained his seat. Carman stopped pacing.

"So what do we do now?"

"Does Elphame still stand?" Idath asked, still as a frozen statue. He hadn't turned to look at either of them.

Maleagant nodded, then winced again.

"Yes, the damned city still stands," he groaned.

"Then they will retreat there," Idath finally turned to look at them. "So that is where we must go. How many men do you command?"

Maleagant paused, and glanced at Carman.

"None," Carman finally said.

"None?" he repeated slowly. "Then how did you expect to take the city?"

"We didn't," Maleagant said. "We don't want Elphame. We want immortality, and magic. Powerful magic, to match theirs."

Carman knew instantly Idath understood who Maleagant meant. She desired magic, having never possessed it before. Maleagant had magic, yes, but not real power, like Mab's or Erlik's. He craved more. She craved *any*.

"Life and power," Idath said. He released a slow, mirthless chuckle. "Mortals. You are so simple. I will grant you what you desire, after I have my brother."

"That's not—" Carman began, but Maleagant waved his hand to silence her. Her eyes flashed. She had been about to declare the unfairness of Idath's offer. They had summoned him back to life, hadn't they? They had given him the chance to take his revenge on Erlik, and he'd wasted it. That wasn't their fault. He should grant them their desire *now*.

Idath's small eyes found her. She swallowed. Perhaps he could hear her thoughts?

"You will need magic, woman," he said. Carman's heart leapt into her throat. "I will give you magic."

"And me?" Maleagant sat up straighter. Carman threw him a filthy look.

"You will have your boon," Idath said. "When *I* see fit. Come, the Gates must be opened again, and my children released."

✧ ✧ ✧

THOMAS PACED BACK and forth outside of Mab's room as thoughts busied around his brain like flies. How had this happened? How had this been *allowed* to happen? Why was she out of the city in the first place? Where had she been? And why was *he* with her?

The door to her chamber opened, and one of the healers emerged, looking harried.

"Well?" Thomas asked immediately.

"We've managed to remove the blade," the physician said. "But magic doesn't affect the wound. We've had to bind it with yarrow and motherwort to lessen the bleeding."

"Lessen?" Thomas repeated. "Not 'stop'?"

The healer shuffled his feet and twisted his hands.

"Like I said, milord, magic doesn't affect the wound," he mumbled. "We've never encountered a wound or affliction that can't be healed in that way."

"Mab can heal herself!"

"Not in this state, milord, she—"

"Then do something else!" Thomas roared. He thrust a finger towards Mab's chamber. "She is your *queen!*"

He heard running footsteps approach from behind, but he didn't turn to look.

"If she dies on your watch," Thomas said darkly. "You'll have a lot more to worry about than what I'll do to you."

"She's not going to die," said a voice behind him. Thomas's heart lifted and he turned to face his wife.

Thissy looked breathless, carrying a basket packed full of bottles and dried herbs. Thomas took the basket to ease her burden, seeing her lurch with the weight of it.

"I can help," Thissy told the physician. "I was a healer and midwife in the mortal realm, where they couldn't rely on the Old Ways. I have knowledge of herbal concoctions that could work – or at least help."

A wall of heat met Thomas's face as they entered the room. A fire blazed white in the hearth. The room reeked of blood and motherwort. His eyes immediately went to Mab.

She lay still on the bed, a sheen of sweat glistening on her face. Though the foul weapon had been removed, a gaping wound in her chest lazily pumped out thick blood. Large red blooms stained the bed sheets around her. Her face was white, ghostly. Dark circles enrobed her sunken eyes. She didn't even look like Mab anymore.

Physicians fumbled around her, their hands slick and shaking, clumsy with frustration and worry. Linen bandages passed between them. A heavy jar full of yarrow gave off a pungent, spicy scent, but it wasn't enough to overpower the tang of blood and the bitter twist of motherwort.

"Here," Thissy moved them aside, and began to jostle the bottles she'd brought. Thomas handed those he'd taken back to her. She uncorked some with her teeth and began mixing her tincture on the bedside table.

Unsure of what to do with himself, Thomas asked, "Where's Tristan?"

"With Lir," Thissy replied, not looking up from her work. "I didn't think this was something he should see."

Thomas nodded. He could understand that. His own introduction to her had been ignoble enough. She deserved more dignity this time.

"Thomas?" came a croak from the bed. Everyone jumped. Mab's eyes had opened, and she stared at Thomas. Despite her ill pallor, her eyes still sparkled. Faintly.

"Mab," Thomas fell to his knees by her bedside. "Don't worry, we're going—"

"Erlik," she wheezed. "I need Erlik."

Thomas hesitated. "Mab, I… I don't think—"

Mab clutched at her chest. She drew in sharp, ragged, gasping breaths. Her face contorted with agony. A healer immediately offered her water. She pushed them away and turned to face Thomas again.

"Y-you must…" she choked out. Blood slid down her lips. Thomas looked for a cloth to wipe it away, but she grabbed his arm with surprising strength.

"You must," she tried again. "Tap into… tap into his power. Use his power to fuel your magic. Channel it. To heal me."

She dragged in a deep breath, and blood oozed out of the gaping gash in her chest. Thomas averted his eyes. The simple smock she wore did nothing to hide her modesty.

"I do not have much time," Mab went on, her voice growing to a weak whisper. "You must do this. Please."

At her last begging word, her eyes rolled back and fluttered shut. She collapsed back onto the bed. Thissy was first to attend. Thomas moved aside, his head ringing with her words.

Tap into Erlik's power? Would he even allow him to do so?

"Thomas," Thissy turned her back on Mab as the other healers bustled around her. A pulse of greenish gold light surrounded the bed. Though magic didn't affect the wound, they could still use it to cool her fever and perhaps ease her pain.

"You have to do as she says," Thissy said. "She's right. None of our magic can heal this. I don't know what caused this wound, but no doubt *he* does."

"What if *he's* the cause of this?" Thomas countered.

"What if he's not?" she said. "I'm not defending him, by any means. But if there's a chance we can save our queen, I want to take it. And we'll deal with the consequences afterwards."

Thomas sighed. Thissy lifted her hand and brushed her thumb against his face. He turned his head slightly and kissed the mound at the base of her thumb.

"You're right," he said. She gave him a weak smile.

"Of course I am," she said. "I'm your wife."

Thomas kissed her brow, took in a slow breath and left the room.

CHAPTER 26

"What do we need to do?"

DESPITE THE URGENCY, Thomas walked the halls with the slowness of a condemned man, his mind racing. Could he truly tap into Erlik's powers?

Blood pumped hot through his veins and thumped in his ears. He'd connected to Erlik years ago, when he first came to Albion. His mind's eye showed him the unwanted memories, the conversations that followed.

It's not poison, clever boy... it's blood... you're bound to him in ways you can't imagine.

Thomas shivered. He hadn't thought about Kali in years. Though her mad, drooling, giggling face was never far from his nightmares.

Your blood is strong, Father.

And?

Pure.

He was still bound to Erlik, even after all these years. True, the bond was weak, unperceivable even, but not gone. Never gone. But now, perhaps he could put that hated bond to some use. If Erlik allowed it, he could tap into his ancient power and use his magic to heal Mab.

If Erlik allowed it.

Thomas looked up, finding himself at the dungeon door. With a heavy sigh, he entered and descended the steps. The dungeon's cold air hit him like a wave. A few cells were occupied; pickpockets and drunken brawlers. One old man argued with himself in the corner. Thomas felt a stab of pity. That old man was in the wrong place. He made a mental note to speak to Lightfoot later about it.

Thomas approached the simple wooden door at the end of the dungeon, where the only prisoner to be personally guarded awaited him. Thomas nodded to the guards to allow him entry.

"Be careful, milord," one of them said. "This one whispers dark things."

Thomas nodded once more as the guard unlocked the door, and then stepped into the dimness.

As soon as he entered and closed the door behind him, Erlik looked up and shot to his feet.

"What's happening?" he asked immediately. "How is she? Is she well? Has she woken yet? I need to see her, I can help!"

He started forwards, but thick chains around his wrists and ankles abruptly stopped him. The chains jingled in the small room. Thomas cast his eyes towards them. *Cold iron,* he noted. *Stops him from using magic, at least.*

"She woke briefly," Thomas said quietly. He wasn't entirely sure why he was speaking so civilly to him, nor why he was indulging his false concerns. But Erlik's wide eyes and chewed lower lip shook his confidence more than a little. "She fell unconscious again, but Thissy—my wife, and the other healers, are looking after her."

"Do they know what they're doing?" Erlik began to pace. "It's a Deathblade, they…"

Erlik paused, and Thomas frowned at him.

"They what?" he prompted.

"I need to see her," he said instead.

Thomas shook his head, "Not possible, I'm afraid."

Erlik opened his mouth to fire back an angry retort, then closed it again. He resumed his pacing. His steps were short because of the chain; Thomas could see him struggling.

"What happened?" he asked. Erlik stopped and stared at

him. The silence was hard and uncomfortable. Thomas strained to not look away. He refused to yield first.

"We don't have time," Erlik said. "Let me see Mab, then we can tell you everything. I need to know if she's well."

"Not until you tell me what happened," Thomas replied, shaking his head. It was a dangerous and risky game, taunting Erlik like this. Time was against him. But he had to know the truth.

Erlik chewed his tongue, as if holding back a furious tirade. A long, heavy pause stretched out again.

"Please," Erlik said quietly. Thomas blinked; he'd only ever heard Erlik beg like that once before. "She needs me."

She asked for you, Thomas thought bitterly.

"She has us," he said aloud.

"You can't protect her!" Erlik rushed forward, losing his composure, but the chains yanked him back. Thomas retreated a few steps, hand flying to the sword on his hip, "Not from— not from what's coming."

"What? What's coming?" Thomas lowered his hand again, genuine curiosity piqued now. "What happened? Where were you? How did this happen?"

Erlik had resumed his pacing, looking for all the world like a dark lion sizing up his prey.

"Fine," he said finally. "I'll tell you."

Thomas leaned against the wall, "Make it quick, and make it honest," he said coolly.

"Mab released me," Erlik began. "She needed my help."

"Why—"

"Shut up, and let me speak," Erlik said, without vitriol. He sounded more weary than angry. "A sorcerer called Maleagant has taken residence in an old fortress called the Iron Keep. He was trying to open the Gates of Annwyn. And..." he paused and swallowed hard. "He succeeded."

Erlik inhaled slowly. His eyes darted. Thomas waited, aware of the seconds ticking by.

"The portal he opened released monsters, beasts that have ravaged Albion. Mab was frightened for her people, so we went to the Keep together to try and stop him."

"Did you?"

Erlik shook his head. He chewed his lip again.

"Maleagant unleashed more than just monsters. He's released my brother."

Thomas hesitated. He knew very little of the Lord of the Dead, but the name *Idath* had a tendency to sap all courage and warmth from the room. Thissy always shivered whenever she muttered his name in an oath, to guide a soul to his realm. Even Mab looked unnerved whenever someone said the name.

"Idath?"

Erlik nodded again slowly, his eyes still fixed on Thomas. The old madness that used to dance in them had burnt out. Now, he only saw a man. An old, tired, scared man.

"Idath wants vengeance on me. And Mab. He won't hesitate to destroy this city to get what he wants," Erlik said.

"That's why she released you?" Thomas asked. *Why would Mab go to Erlik, of all people, for help?*

"I know what you're thinking," Erlik said quietly. "But even if she didn't need my help before, then she certainly does now. You *all* do now. Idath will gather his strength and attack this city with all his force. Whether he finds Maleagant a help or a hindrance is trivial. Maleagant was the first drop of rain that precedes a thunderstorm."

Thomas had almost forgotten how eloquent Erlik could be. It was almost a song, the way he spoke. Deep, rich tones in an elegant and refined accent.

"What do we need to do?"

Erlik lifted his hands to show the chains.

"No," he said. "I told you my story. Take me to her."

Thomas felt his cheeks heat up.

"She asked for you."

Thomas saw Erlik's brow minutely twitch into a crease. The chains rattled again, and he glanced down. Erlik's wrists were burnt red and raw from the cold iron. A twinge of guilt poked Thomas in the chest, but he brushed it away. *This is Erlik. The Dragon King. The Poison-Hoarder. He deserves worse than this.*

"She asked for me?" Erlik repeated, his lip curling into a snarl. "Why didn't you bring me straight to her? I *told* you she needs me!"

Thomas tipped his head back, "I had to be sure."

"Sure of *what?*" Erlik shook his head. "Never mind, it doesn't matter. Take me to her, *now!*"

"For her sake," Thomas said. "Not yours."

Erlik nodded quickly, "Yes. Of course."

"Gaoler," Thomas called. The door immediately opened, and one of the guarding soldiers entered.

"My lord?"

"Fetch a set of sticklewort shackles," he said.

The soldier nodded, turned on his heel and left. Erlik looked wary, and frowned at Thomas.

"She asked for you," he went on. "Because she wants me to tap into your power so I can heal her."

The crease deepened between Erlik's brows. He briefly glanced at his hands.

"My magic would poison her," Erlik said quietly, as though to himself. He lifted his gaze to Thomas again. "It has to come from you. Her kind."

"You'll be chained on the way to her chamber," Thomas went on, and the door reopened. The soldier handed him a pile of chains. "Sticklewort has been tempered into these shackles to bind your magic. For now."

Erlik eyed them warily, then his narrow-eyed gaze rose to Thomas.

"Steel," he said, and Erlik held out his hands. Thomas paused, and then quickly swapped the chains. Erlik hissed with relief when Thomas let the cold iron fall away. Thomas almost apologised. Almost.

He released Erlik's feet from the shackles. He had momentarily thought he might receive a kick to the face for his efforts, but he remained as still as an obedient horse being shoed.

Straightening up again, he took hold of Erlik's upper arm and guided him out of the dungeon.

CHAPTER 27

"How dare you?"

THE WOUND GAPED, ugly and brazen. Her simple shift was now more red than white. Mab's pale face now only showed the smallest flickers of life; brief contortions of pain, soft sighs, eyelids fluttering as though dreaming.

Only Thissy remained at her bedside. She had done all she could. Mab's life now lay in the hands of the Old Gods. Thissy offered up a desperate prayer.

As though in answer, an urgent knock came to the door. Thissy wiped her eyes and answered.

She gasped and drew back.

The Dark Prince greeted her. Though no mocking smile adorned his face, no cruel trickery there; only desperation, fear, and worry.

"How is she?" Thomas asked, appearing beside him. Thissy swallowed and hesitated. Unable to speak, she shook her head.

"No," Erlik growled, and pushed past her. He approached Mab's bedside and kneeled beside her. "No, she can't die. She can't. *I won't allow it!*"

Erlik turned and beckoned Thomas closer.

"Rhymer," he said. "Come here, now."

Thissy gently pushed Thomas forward. Erlik beckoned again, more insistent this time. Thomas stared at his outstretched hand. Erlik had turned his eyes back to Mab.

"Don't worry, my love," Thissy heard him mutter. He took one of her hands with his spare one, and rubbed it. "You're going to be alright."

Thissy baulked. *'My love'?* She chewed her tongue. Her eyes darted between Mab and Erlik. As if he could sense her eyes, he turned his gaze on her, and she instinctively drew back. But Erlik turned instead to Thomas.

Thomas approached. Thissy saw him inhale as he unlocked the shackles that bound Erlik's wrists together. He dropped the chains on the floor. The resulting clatter didn't register with Mab; she remained still as a frozen effigy over a grave.

Thomas took Erlik's outstretched hand with disdain. Erlik stood, and closed his eyes, his head bowed. Thomas's shaking hand hovered over Mab's wound. He, too, closed his eyes.

Thissy watched. Nothing was happening. She drummed her fingers against her thigh and chewed her lip.

She approached the bed, finding Thomas's eyes squeezed tight in concentration. Erlik breathed slowly and deeply. She noticed him steal a glance at Thomas's hand, and frown when he saw no glowing light, no healing magic.

"What are you doing?" he snapped, and pulled his hand away. "Why aren't you healing her?"

"I'm trying!" Thomas retorted. He shook his hands and cracked his knuckles. Thissy winced.

"You're not *trying* very hard," Erlik said, gesturing to Mab.

"Maybe it's *you*," Thomas said bitingly. "Maybe your magic is too poisonous to be channelled."

Erlik narrowed his eyes at him. Thissy sensed this conflict wouldn't end easily. She looked down at Mab, who stirred in her uneasy repose.

"Mab explicitly told you to come to me for help, didn't she?" Erlik turned to face Thomas completely now. Thomas didn't retreat.

"What if she was wrong?" he replied, voice rising. "What if you're more wicked than she realised? Though that hardly seems possible."

"Watch what you're insinuating, *boy,*" Erlik snarled, and grabbed a fistful of Thomas's collar.

Thomas threw him off and pushed him away. Unsteady, Erlik staggered back, and bumped into the dresser, knocking several bottles of herbs over. Glass tinkled and shattered when they hit the floor.

Thissy felt her heart plummet into her stomach. *This isn't going to help!*

With a snarl, Erlik lunged forwards and tackled Thomas. Thomas grunted and wrestled Erlik's arms off and threw a punch at him. Thissy shouted in surprise when Erlik retaliated and landed three or four rapid blows to Thomas's face and stomach.

They fought on the floor like boys at play, but while the two men grunted and scuffled, Thissy's patience snapped.

She stepped around the bed. Glaring down at the pair of them, she gestured with her hands, a sweeping gesture, like she was pushing her way through a crowd.

Thomas and Erlik separated, sliding across the floor as if being pulled by ropes. Thomas hit the wall beside the hearth with a groan. Erlik hit the wall by the door and grunted, rubbing the back of his head. Thissy stood between them, arms still outstretched, turning her furious gaze on each of them in turn.

"How dare you?" she said in a low growl, surprising even herself. "*Both* of you! Our queen is dying and you're fighting like children! No, even *children* have more sense than that! You're like two dogs fighting in the street!"

Thomas thumbed blood from his mouth. Erlik gingerly touched the bruise by his eye. Both looked sullen but remorseful.

"You're right," Thomas said glumly. He got to his feet, grimacing. Erlik copied him. The bruise on his face had already faded, but his red-faced shame hadn't. He approached Mab's bedside. Thissy regulated her breathing to normal once again.

Thomas approached Mab's other side.

"I'm sorry," he said quietly. Erlik said nothing, but brushed a lock of hair from her pale face.

"Let's try again," Thomas said, and reached out his hand. Erlik was about to take it, when Thissy boldly stepped forward.

"No," she announced. "I'll do it."

Both men looked at her in surprise. Thomas warily glanced at Erlik's hand, then at Thissy's face.

"I'm not sure, Thissy," he began. She held up a hand to stop him.

"I'm not afraid, Thomas," she said.

"But," Thomas pointed out. "I thought it had to be me? I have the blood-bond with him."

Erlik pulled a disdainful face behind Thomas's back and turned back to Mab.

"You just assumed that," Thissy said. "Mab didn't say it *had* to be you. Besides, I'm the healer here. If anyone can do this, I can."

Erlik looked mildly impressed. Thomas stepped aside to make room for her at Mab's bedside. Thissy tipped her head back and, despite a brief moment of hesitation, stretched out her hand. Erlik narrowed his eyes, but Thissy saw determination there, not hatred.

He took her hand and held it firmly. His flesh was cold, but not unpleasant. Again, he closed his eyes and lowered his head, and Thissy held her other hand over Mab's wound.

Summoning her healing powers from deep within her, she felt a strange resistance. As though some kind of impenetrable barrier stopped her magic from reaching the wound to heal it. She concentrated harder, and focussed her power. The cold tug of magic on her heart began to ache, but something else began to overwhelm her. Some powerful, external force.

Erlik's power!

Thissy looked up, and saw him staring hard at her. His face was dark, but again, without hate. He gave an almost unperceivable nod, and looked down at Mab again. He swallowed hard, and closed his eyes.

A wave of cold engulfed Thissy's entire body. Her toes

curled within her boots, and her hair stood on end. Her palm now aglow with soothing golden light. Lightning crackled through her veins. White stars burst behind her eyes. The barrier began to break.

Hand shaking, she flexed her fingers, and tendrils of golden light snaked from her palm down towards Mab's wound. Tears pricked her eyes as the power ignited within her.

Her whole body trembled. Gasping for breath, she threw back her head and cried out, pain erupting inside her heart. The magic burned freezing cold. Blood pounded a thunderous tempo in her ears. Tears rolled hard and fat down her cheeks.

"Hold fast, you're doing well," she heard Erlik say. His voice was soothing, calm, reassuring. She forced herself to look at him, and found him staring at Mab. "It's working."

Renewed with vigour, Thissy poured all of her strength into a final jolt of magic. At last, the barrier broke, and the golden, healing light surrounded the wound. It became blindingly bright, and for a moment, Thissy thought her hand had burst into flame. She yelled in pain, and let go of Erlik's hand as she fell back.

"No!" he lunged forward to grab her, but she had already collapsed into Thomas's arms.

The golden light vanished, and Erlik desperately grabbed Mab's hand.

Let it have worked, Thissy silently prayed, and weakly staggered back to her feet. Thomas steadied her, keeping a tight hold on her. *Please, Gods, let it have worked.*

The golden light slowly vanished. Thissy dared steal a glance at the ugly wound. But it wasn't there. Only a torn hole in her shift remained. Thissy looked up at Mab's face. It remained passive, still and serene. Silence hung heavy in the hot room.

"Mab?" Erlik whispered. Thissy heard his voice break. "Gods, please... Mab..."

With a long, hungry breath, Mab's eyes snapped open.

CHAPTER 28

"Idath walks free"

"W**AT...ER...**" HER VOICE a hoarse creak. Someone – she couldn't see who through the haze – brought a cool cup to her lips. Despite the desperate desire to gulp it down, she had only the energy to sip it.

Every inch of her ached. Her chest most of all. She put her hand to the wound, but it had vanished. Only a throbbing bruise-like pain lingered there. She made to sit, but a gentle hand lay on her shoulder.

"Easy," came the soft voice. She looked up and her eyes strained to focus. All she could make out was a dark, blurry shape. She blinked, and Erlik's face came into view.

"Where...?"

"You're home," he said. His voice barely rose above a whisper. "You're safe."

"How are you feeling, Your Grace?" came another voice, female this time. Mab turned her head slowly. Familiarity warmed her heart.

"Thistledown," she said, and stretched out a hand to hers. "You have come home."

Thissy beamed and nodded, and looked to the man beside her.

"And Thomas," Mab smiled at him. She had thought his presence only a dream. "It gladdens my heart to see you both."

"Our son is here too," Thomas said, taking Thissy's hand in his. "But we thought it better to wait for introductions."

Mab blinked in surprise. "Your son?" she breathed. Thissy nodded again.

"Almost sixteen years old," she said, proud tears in her eyes. Mab carefully sat up straighter. She winced.

"Careful, my love," Erlik said. Mab had almost forgotten his presence. "It'll take time before you're back to full strength."

Mab swallowed. *We do not have time.*

Erlik nodded. Mab looked at him significantly.

"How are you feeling, Mab?" Thomas asked, repeating Thissy's earlier question. She realised she hadn't answered. She wasn't sure how to.

After a pause, she said, not entirely truthfully, "Much better, thank you."

Now that she saw him closer, she noticed he did in fact look a little older, his face a little fuller, jaw a little more shadowed, shoulders a shade broader. *He has a son now,* she reminded herself. It seemed impossible that the young lad who had ventured across the bridge and discovered his heritage now stood before her; a man, a husband, a father, the Champion of Elphame.

Silence for a moment, while an unspoken awkwardness gathered around them.

"I want to thank you," Mab said finally, sitting up straighter. "For working together. Despite the animosity between you, I am grateful for your unity in this."

Mab watched Thomas and Erlik throw untrusting looks at the other, and she inwardly sighed. *Not quite so unified yet, then.*

"I assume Erlik has told you what has happened?" she addressed Thomas. Erlik absently toyed with her fingers.

Thomas nodded, and glanced down at his wife before replying, "Idath."

Thissy started.

"What?" she nervously cast her eyes between the three others, lingering a second longer on Erlik. Idath was, after all, his brother.

Mab nodded, and pushed her bed covers aside, grimacing.

"We must summon the Queen's Council at once," she said. "Erlik and I shall explain everything."

✧   ✧   ✧

THE QUEEN'S COUNCIL gathered around the crescent-shaped table, an assembly of anxious seelie. Mab sat at the centre of the table. Every movement seemed stiffer, more controlled. As though she still wasn't fully healed. Yet she appeared to have made every effort to present a powerful figure to her council. Thomas knew from experience how important morale was to seelie-folk.

Her wary gaze moved between each person, watching her council for any signs of panic or worry. *And they have every reason to be afraid,* Thomas spitefully thought to himself.

Now that Mab was – relatively – safe, Erlik had lapsed into a sullen silence. He now sat directly beside her, eyes fixed on the table and idly carving symbols into the wood with his knife. The scratching sound was slowly driving Thomas to madness, and he wished Mab would stop him, but she seemed preoccupied. He wished Thissy sat beside him now; she could easily calm him with one gentle touch.

She and Tristan waited outside; only the highest council members had been allowed into the chamber this morning. As Champion of Elphame, Thomas had been granted entry. He had thought it would be reason enough to keep Erlik out, but Mab had insisted on his presence, despite the tension that hung thick in the air. Thomas released a loud sigh, and Erlik shot him a filthy look.

"Your Grace," Lightfoot said, his voice the first to puncture the silence. "Is it truly necessary to have the Dragon King here?"

Erlik stopped destroying the table and turned his venomous glare to the Steward.

"Yes," he replied in her stead. Lightfoot glowered at him.

"I will not speak to you, *nathair*," he said. "I won't have you poisoning these talks with your lies."

"What *lies*, leaf-ear?" Erlik snapped.

"Enough," Mab said, her voice cutting through the dissent in the room. The seelie looked up at her. Erlik threw one final, lethal stare at Lightfoot.

"We are not here to quarrel amongst ourselves," she said firmly. "If we do, then our enemies will surely destroy us."

"The only enemy I see, Your Grace," said a red-haired seelie Thomas didn't recognise. "Is *him*."

"Didn't you hear what she just said?" Erlik snapped. "We don't have time for infighting."

"You shouldn't even be here, Poison-Hoarder!" yet another seelie said, standing.

"You *dare* speak to me—"

More seelie stood to shout back at Erlik, who threw back his chair and leapt to his feet to defend himself.

This is chaos, Thomas wearily thought.

"We don't have time for this!" he said loudly, but his voice was lost in the cacophony. He stood up too, yelling to have himself heard.

"*Ciúnas!*"

An unseen hand stole his voice. He choked, but only wet sounds escaped his throat, no words. He turned to Mab to find her standing, her eyes blazing.

"Enough!" she said, her voice echoing louder than any of theirs could ever do so. The room had darkened without them realising, the flames on the braziers only glowing coals now. "All of you, *sit down*."

Each person in the room resumed their seats, meek and silent under her furious glare.

"A terrible danger is about to befall our city," she went on. "We *must* stand together, or we will fall."

She waved her hand, and Thomas felt a twinge in his throat and knew his voice had returned. Yet he dared not use it. The fires burned high again, and light returned to the room.

"Erlik and I have infiltrated the Iron Keep," Mab said. "We have discovered many secrets."

Erlik shuddered. Thomas looked at him, but Erlik kept his eyes on the table.

"A sorcerer, Maleagant, has taken residence in the Iron Keep, along with his lover, Carman," she said. Erlik grimaced this time. Thomas frowned at him.

"Through the most forbidden of magic," Mab went on, "Maleagant has opened the Gates of Annwyn, and unleashed monstrous creatures upon Albion."

"The Nuckelavee?" Lightfoot asked.

Mab nodded, "And more. The Dullahan rides free across the moors. An Each-Uisge threatens the waterways. The Cú-Sith hounds run wild, driven mad from being dragged across the veil."

That must have been what attacked us, Thomas thought, thinking of the evil dogs that had almost ripped him and Thissy apart.

"Monsters can be slain, my lady," the redheaded seelie said. Mab sighed.

"This may be true, Wildbriar," she said. "But not just monsters have been released from Annwyn."

She paused. Thomas saw her steeling herself. This pause wasn't for dramatic effect. Mab was genuinely afraid. She straightened in her chair.

"The Lord of the Dead has returned to Albion," she said clearly. "The Gateway has been opened. Idath walks free."

A shiver rippled around the table. Although Erlik had told him so already, it hadn't seemed real enough until Mab admitted it. Gooseflesh pricked his arms. The room felt a hundred times colder.

"The Lord of the Dead?" someone whispered.

"Black magic," came someone else's frightened voice.

"*Blood* magic," Erlik corrected quietly, twisting his hands.

"What should we do, Your Grace?"

"We are not without advantages," Mab's tone came clear as morning bells, though Thomas noticed she looked distinctly paler. "We have Maleagant's journal."

She stood up to walk around the table. Thomas saw a flicker of pain briefly shadow her face. As she passed Erlik, he took the leather-bound journal out from his pocket and handed it to her. Mab flipped it open and set it down on the centre of the table. From where he sat Thomas could just make out crude diagrams.

Thomas swallowed hard and pulled the journal closer so he could look through it. The drawings he found therein were gruesome: tools for draining blood from bodies; flayed men and the uses for their skin; various methods for slicing flesh and sawing through bone.

With a shiver, he pushed the journal back to the centre of the table. He caught Erlik smirking at him, and resolved to act less squeamish.

"Maleagant has all but stated he means war, therefore we must act fast," Mab said. "And Idath has made his intentions clear."

She said no more. Thomas looked curiously at her, but she shook her head, and Thomas understood: *Later.*

"And what of the Trickster, Your Grace?" Lightfoot asked. He cast a dark look towards Erlik, who scowled.

"Erlik is to remain here until this threat has passed," Mab said. "Once we are out of danger, once Idath is defeated, and Maleagant and Carman are either dead or contained, then we can discuss his fate."

"You're too kind," Erlik said, kissing his fingertips and gesturing towards her. The seelie glared at him.

"Are you sure you want him around, Mab?" Thomas asked carefully, not taking his eyes off the fallen prince. Mab returned to her seat at the head of the table.

"Yes, I am sure," she said with a note of finality. "Steeleye, send patrols to the outlying villages. Those nearest the Iron Keep are the most vulnerable. Caernarvon, Ravenstone, Whitehaven. There is little point in trying to take back those already attacked. No doubt the people there have either fled or been slain."

Her voice grew hard. Thomas knew it was painful for her to admit defeat, and even more painful to abandon her people, but he also knew why this was necessary. She was right; there was no point in risking soldiers for the sake of a burnt-down village, when the people there were likely already dead.

"We must also establish a warning signal. Lightfoot, send a ranger to the Tower of Glenstrae to keep watch. We require warning if any armies, Idath, or Annwyn beasts approach."

"What of the Nuckelavee, my lady?" Lightfoot asked. "The Mortasheen sickness is spreading faster and further."

Thomas caught Mab and Erlik glance at each other before she responded.

"We know little of the beast. But, as Wildbriar said, any beast of flesh and blood can be slain. Erlik, you are to study this journal and garner any information you can from it. Thomas, you will help him."

"*What?*" Thomas and Erlik said together. As though expecting this reaction, Mab had already pinched the bridge of her nose and raised a weary eyebrow.

"I have glanced through the journal. Some of the languages Maleagant used, no doubt to conceal his work, are very old. Languages only Erlik or I would be able to read," Mab explained. "And I have other matters to which I must attend."

"So why can't I work alone?"

"For once in my life, I agree with him," Thomas said.

Mab raised her hands to silence them both. Erlik slumped back in his chair and scowled like a petulant child. Thomas folded his arms and huffed.

"Whether you like it or not, you two *must* learn to work together," she said. "This is a small task. If you cannot do this, how can you expect to fight together against what is coming?"

Erlik glared at Thomas for a moment.

"Fine," he muttered darkly. Thomas didn't trust himself to speak; he only nodded. Mab gave them both a smile.

"Good, then the council is adjourned," she said. The seelie slowly stood and filed out. Only Erlik and Thomas remained seated, neither too eager to start working with the other. Mab looked between them and heaved another sigh.

"You are both being very childish," she said, folding her arms like a mother admonishing two little boys.

"I am not," Erlik mumbled, staring at the table. Mab's mouth twitched into a smile. She held out her small hand for him. He reached for it. She offered her other hand to Thomas, and he took it in his calloused one.

"I need you both in these dark days," she said softly. "Thomas, you are my Champion, and the defender of this city, but you must learn that you cannot do everything by yourself, and learn to forgive those who have proven their willingness to change."

Erlik gave him a smug smile, and Mab turned to him.

"Erlik, there is so much history between us. To even *begin* to describe what I feel for you…" she trailed off. Then shook herself and continued. "You must learn to let go of your pride, and accept help when it is offered."

Now it was Thomas's turn to look satisfied at Erlik's huffy expression.

"It is time to lay aside old quarrels and stand together. Neither of you are as strong or as clever as both of you combined. You must learn to work together, peacefully, amicably. I doubt you will ever be friends, but perhaps your bond is stronger as rivals."

Erlik sniffed irritably but said nothing. Mab took her hands away and smiled at them both.

"You should work in the library, it will be quieter. Please try not to kill each other."

"I make no promises," Thomas said quietly. Erlik smirked.

"Well," he said. "Won't this be interesting?"

CHAPTER 29

"A snake doesn't care who it bites"

THISSY ENDLESSLY PACED outside the council chamber, twisting her hands as she went. Tristan watched her, unsure of what to say. His father had gone into the chamber a while ago, along with the man from the cage, and a small woman dressed in a black and purple gown that glittered like stardust. They still hadn't emerged, and his mother grew more and more anxious with every passing minute.

"He shouldn't be in there with them," he heard her mutter as she passed him. "It's not safe."

Tristan twisted his hands too. Yes, Erlik was arrogant, but he seemed amicable enough. He hadn't mentioned the encounter with him to either of his parents. He wouldn't know where to begin. *Oh, by the way Mother, when I wandered off in the forest, I happened to run into Erlik in a cage. You know, the man that everyone around here is either terrified of or absolutely hates? We chatted; charming fellow, bit full of himself.* He didn't imagine that would go down very well.

And that woman, the small one in the black gown, that must've been Mab, Tristan realised. He hadn't managed to catch a glimpse of her face, but the scent that washed over him when she passed... Tristan shivered. The smell of the night air, when he'd stand under the stars and gaze at the flickering blue lights above. The smell of wildflowers and wood smoke, distinct and refined.

His mother sat down beside him with a sigh.

"I hope your father knows what he's doing," she said, then looked at him as though she'd just noticed he was there. "Are you alright, Tristan? Are you hungry? Tired? Do you want anything?"

"No, I-I'm fine, Mother," he said. She gave his hand a squeeze.

"Don't worry," she said, absent-mindedly.

"Mother, are *you* alright?" Tristan asked.

She looked at him, then leaned forward and kissed the top of his head, but didn't say anything.

They sat in silence for a while longer. The enormous doors blocked out all noise from inside, so Tristan couldn't even overhear any conversation. He was desperate for answers. He wasn't a child; he wanted to know if they were in danger. More than that, he wanted to *help*.

The chamber doors opened at long last, and a crowd of seelie bubbled from within. All muttering darkly to each other. Each face looked ashen and afraid. *Erlik couldn't cause this much fear among them, surely?* Tristan thought to himself. If he'd been in the chamber with them, he *must* be on their side?

Thissy stood on tiptoe to try to see over the lake of heads emerging, but she slumped back down when the doors shut, and there was no sign of Thomas. Or Mab. Or Erlik.

Tristan's heart began to race. What if Mab had some kind of special task for his father? Something important that perhaps Tristan could help with?

After a few more agonisingly slow minutes, the doors opened again and his father stepped out. Thissy leapt to her feet and ran to embrace him, but stopped dead and retreated slightly when Erlik emerged behind him, and gave a small smirk.

"Mistress Rhymer," he said, with a slight nod that resembled a bow. Tristan stared at him. He looked distinctly more regal now that he was out of his cage and cleaned up. Tristan had no trouble believing that he was a prince, albeit an unpopular one.

"Erlik, enough," said the dark-haired woman who walked out behind him. Thissy curtseyed low to her, and sensing the weight of her presence, Tristan sunk into a deep bow.

"You must be Tristan," she said as she approached, and took his face in her cool hands. He noticed her slender fingers ended in long, sharp nails, and he repressed a shiver when he realised how close those talons were to his throat. "I have heard a lot about you. I am Mab, Queen of the Old Ways."

"And I've heard much about you, Your Grace," Tristan mumbled, then cleared his suddenly dry throat. Mab was extremely beautiful. "It's a great honour to meet you at last."

"Such a polite child," Mab said approvingly. She nodded to Thomas and Thissy, who beamed and glanced at each other proudly.

"I see you've found your way home, *amadán*," Erlik said.

Tristan gulped. *So much for that secret.* He forced himself to meet his mother's eyes.

"What?" Thissy put her arm around Tristan's shoulders. Tristan gently shook her off and shuffled his feet. "You've met him?"

"Oh, yes, didn't he mention?" Erlik said, smirking at Tristan's discomfort.

"Why didn't you say anything?" Thissy asked him. Tristan quailed, and averted his eyes to the floor.

"I didn't think it was important," he mumbled. He caught Erlik rolling his eyes.

"Don't blame Tristan, Thissy," Thomas said darkly. "A snake doesn't care who it bites."

Erlik frowned and folded his arms.

"Now, now," he said in a patronising voice. "Have you forgotten we're on the same side?"

"You're on nobody's side, *nathair*, except your own."

Thomas scowled hard and stormed past. Mab sighed. Erlik raised his eyebrow at her and gestured at Thomas.

"You want me to work with *him*?" he said.

"Stop antagonising him, then," Mab scolded, then

indicated he should follow him down the corridor. Erlik huffed.

"Fine," he said, and turned away to follow Thomas. Mab watched him go, and exhaled slowly, looking weary.

"Your Grace?" Thissy asked quietly. Mab didn't look at her, but nodded to indicate she was listening. "You—I mean, Thomas and the Dark Prince are to work together?"

Mab nodded again and still said nothing.

"And he is allowed free rein of the castle?"

Another nod.

"Is that… wise?"

At last, Mab looked at her, her expression becoming one of catlike awareness, as if she knew something others didn't. Tristan couldn't tell if he was frightened of her or beheld her in wondrous awe.

"Perhaps not," she said, sucking in a deep breath. "But perhaps, sometimes, wisdom is overvalued."

She turned her gaze on Tristan now, and he felt his heart expand and plummet.

"Hmm," she said, eyeing him up and down. "A strong lad. What skills do you possess?"

Despite her being shorter than him, Tristan suddenly felt three inches tall under her crystal-cold scrutiny. His heart thundered, and he feared she would hear it in the silence. Suddenly, he realised he recognised this feeling. He'd experienced it staring into the deep, old, mournful eyes of the white doe in the forest.

"I…" suddenly, his mind was empty. He stumbled through his thoughts, but the only skill that immediately leapt to him was his ability to pick locks. And he was certain the queen wouldn't be impressed with that. He panicked. *Say something! Anything!*

"He's an expert with a bow, Your Grace," his mother prompted, and Tristan heard the pride in her voice, and felt his cheeks grow warm. He resisted the urge to slap his own forehead. *Of course.*

"An archer?" Mab sounded impressed. Tristan dared to

look up, and found her smiling at him, albeit a smile that hid a secret. He nodded, blushing harder.

"He does not say much, does he?" she said. Tristan heard the laugh in her voice. "Very good. We will make great use of you in the days to come."

The queen turned away and walked away from them.

He turned to his mother only to find her chewing her lip and twisting her hands. Tristan swiftly deflated.

"Mother?" he said, and she started. "Are you sure you're alright?"

She gave him what she apparently thought to be a soothing smile and nodded.

"Of course, Tristan," she said. "Come, we have work to do."

CHAPTER 30

"The veil between worlds is thin here"

BLUE-TINGED MIST SWIRLED as a little boat sliced through the lake's mirror-like waters. Maleagant and Carman stared up at the ruins as they approached through the silent night. The ancient castle was decrepit; a black skeleton of itself rising from the deep. Idath raised an arm, and the little boat gracefully glided towards the shore.

There was no breeze, yet Carman felt something rustle her hair as she disembarked. She spun, almost sure she'd heard voices in the darkness. Idath swept past her, heading into the archway of the dilapidated castle. Maleagant followed, and Carman trailed behind, eyes darting for signs of movement in the shadows.

"The magic I gave you is powerful, but short-lived," came Idath's deep voice from up ahead. "You will use it as I instruct."

"While I'm not ungrateful," Carman began, in a voice that bled ingratitude, and scowled when she missed her footing and stumbled up the crooked stone steps. She brushed the grime from her hands. "When are you going to give us the boon we *asked* for?"

Maleagant shot her a filthy look.

"When I have exacted my revenge," Idath replied, as he strode fearlessly through the dark. "When my brother and the Heart both lie broken at my feet."

Carman made a noncommittal noise, lifting the hem of her skirts to avoid a slimy puddle.

Idath led them into a large circular space that put Carman in mind of an open-air theatre. He slowly paced the ring, circling a tall cairn of loose stones in the centre.

Cold fingertips of fear tickling her neck, Carman looked around. Now certain she could hear whisperings all around her, coming from every shadow, though she couldn't make out what they were saying. She shivered, and something that sounded like a child laughed in a dark corner. Maleagant looked up sharply, his eyes narrowed. Carman walked closer to him, but refused to admit her fear of the dark.

"Just shades, my pet," he said, patting her hand. "The veil between worlds is thin here."

Maleagant waved his staff and the whispering grew fainter as the braziers around the arena burst into flame.

Idath approached them. Carman struggled not to shrink away. Although he hid it well under his layers of robes, Carman had seen the gruesome gaping hole on his chest: the wound that had claimed his life and had never healed during his time in Annwyn. Congealed blood clung like jelly to the shredded skin. Carman gagged whenever she thought of it.

"I will open the Gateway," Idath announced. "You will use your new magic to stabilise it while I summon my children through."

Maleagant nodded silently. Carman chewed her lip. A twinge in her belly made her feel nauseous. She opened her mouth to speak, and the ground lurched under her. Throwing out her arm, she grabbed Maleagant to steady herself. Her free hand touched her forehead, finding it hot and clammy.

"Carman?" Maleagant held up upright. "What's wrong?"

"I-I don't know," she said. Idath made another noise, and looked her up and down and scoffed.

"What is it? What's wrong with her?" Maleagant asked, sounding more frantic than Carman had ever heard. Already the dizziness in her head was passing.

"It is not my domain," Idath said with an unamused snort.

"Though I recognise it when I see it."

"Recognise what?" Maleagant impatiently snapped. Idath raised an eyebrow and turned away, saying nothing more.

Carman stood up straight, still swaying slightly.

"I think… I think I'm better now," she said. It was only a small lie. She still felt sick, but her head was no longer spinning. Could this be thanks to her new magic?

"I am not a patient man," Idath said pointedly. "Do not make me wait any longer."

Still a little unsteady on her feet, Carman approached the place Idath had marked out for her. Maleagant stood opposite, a few feet away, still throwing her the odd glance. Together, the three formed a triangle around the cairn.

Idath raised his arms and bellowed words Carman couldn't understand into the night. Her stomach roiled again, and she forced herself to stay upright. The air above the cairn split apart, and once more the blue throbbing portal appeared before them. Maleagant raised his staff, and Carman lifted her arms. She closed her eyes to concentrate. Maleagant had given her brief and simple instructions on how to summon her new magic on the journey here.

She flexed her hands, curling her fingers and uncurling them. A cold ache tugged on her heart. She forced herself to take control of it.

Magic crept through her veins towards her fingertips, like ice water tingling along her arms.

Cold pain engulfed her cramping hands as magic burst from her fingers, and tendrils of power touched the portal.

"It is failing!" Idath shouted over the pained moans of the dead. "Keep it stable!"

The twinge in Carman's belly became a sharp pinch, and she groaned and bent double, clutching her stomach, losing her grip on the magic tendrils, weakening the already dying portal.

"Carman!"

"Hold fast, woman!" Idath bellowed in anger.

Something hot and sickly pushed its way up Carman's throat, and she turned and fled the courtyard, still doubled over.

"YOUR WOMAN IS corrupted," Idath sneered in disgust as he watched her run. As soon as she had vanished from sight, ugly retching and splattering sounds rang through the stone arena.

"What's wrong with her?" Maleagant twisted his hands, caught between wanting to help her and disgust at the noises. "Is it the magic you gave her?"

"No, it is not," Idath looked down at Maleagant. "Can you not tell?"

The sorcerer frowned at his father's brother. He shook his head.

"Your woman is with child," Idath said.

Maleagant choked on air, "*What?*"

"Your woman," Idath said again, slower. "Is with child."

"B-but that's not possible!" Maleagant said in a strangled voice. "I-I can't—"

"The child is not yours," Idath said. "It is my brother's."

Maleagant's already pale face turned white.

"But... how could... that's not..."

"Stop your gibbering, boy," Idath snapped. "It matters little. What matters is why my powers are not to their full extent. You *must* have mutilated the ritual to summon me. I cannot even transform."

"I did everything right!" Maleagant stamped his foot like a child. Idath raised a thin eyebrow at him. A muscle in one of his hollow cheeks twitched.

"Regardless, I am not as powerful as I should be," he said quietly. "My children must be released, and if we three cannot open the portal, then *I* must garner more power. The Heart of Magic Itself should suffice."

CHAPTER 31

"You will feel the pull of magic"

"I CAN BARELY read this handwriting, let alone understand the language," Thomas muttered. The library had swiftly emptied once Erlik entered, so they had silence in which to work. Only the librarian remained, watching carefully from behind the shelves. Her fair hair was so long it gently teased her ankles as she walked, and Thomas caught her looking at Erlik with shy interest.

The two men sat by a window to catch the last few hints of light through the glass. A few candles glimmered in the gathering dark.

Erlik wasn't listening. He stared out the window, watching Mab in the courtyard below, absent-mindedly rolling an apple between his hands. It seemed surreal that barely two days had passed since he'd kneeled in that very courtyard, clutching her frail body close to his.

Now, clad in silver armour comprised of a metal corset and vambraces over a shining black gown – more ornament than actual armour – she watched Rhymer's boy firing arrows at a target with amazing skill. He smiled; even from afar, he could see the admiration shining on her face. Even the way she stood had him hypnotised, hollow-backed, head held high and proud. She had removed her fine jewellery and adornments, and her hair flowed freely in the breeze.

"Look at these drawings," Thomas said, and laid the journal down on the table. Erlik didn't look up. Thomas leaned closer to the journal and squinted.

"I need you to translate this," he said, and moved the journal across the desk, tapping at a paragraph. "What does it say?"

Erlik still didn't look. Thomas frowned.

"Erlik, are you listening?" he asked, moving the journal closer. "Erlik? *Nathair!*"

Erlik snapped his head to him, looking mildly surprised.

"Are you listening?"

"That's a strange way to start a conversation."

Thomas pointed at the journal in annoyance, "What does this say?" he asked. Erlik puffed out his cheeks with a heavy sigh and picked up the book, squinting at the untidy handwriting.

"It's about the Nuckelavee," he said, eyes scanning the words. "Maleagant didn't mean to unleash it, or any of the other monsters that followed. They were accidents, when he was looking for my brother."

"So he doesn't know how to kill it?"

"It appears not," Erlik lowered the journal again and began to riffle through the pages. "Though this isn't the only entry in there."

"He managed to capture its image, look," Thomas put his hand out to catch a turning page, and traced a diagram with his finger.

A frightful amalgamation of horse and rider; even in picture form, the monster sent chills down Erlik's spine. A skinned horse, with the torso of a skinned man affixed to its back, as though a legless rider sat mounted. Neither head bore muscle or sinew, only hollow skulls. Both mouths were overfull with a forest of needle-like teeth. The arms of the rider hung down past the flanks of the horse, and ended with sharp spears instead of hands. The front two legs of the horse ended, not in hooves, but in enormous talons.

Erlik leaned in closer. The human half of the Nuckelavee

had been drawn with its mouth gaping in a scream, though he couldn't tell if it were from pain or anger.

"Listen to this," Erlik said when he noticed a passage beside the drawing. "'I killed the spy the Wolf-Queen sent, but this morning's experiment still failed. I thought he would have enough power in his blood. Although the Gate opened, it didn't remain so for long. Still, it was more successful than any previous attempts, and the Gate opened long enough for a score of hounds to escape.'"

"We need to tell Mab about this," Thomas interrupted.

"She knows. But hold, there's more," Erlik went on. "'I thought I caught a glimpse of the Lord of the Dead earlier, but there were too many souls eager to escape the portal. I tried to summon him through, but the blood-to-blood spell didn't work. I'll need stronger magic to summon such a powerful being.'"

"That's why he wanted Mab there!" Thomas said.

"Will you *stop* interrupting?"

"Sorry, go on."

"'The dogs went mad when they emerged. We managed to leash them enough to get them out of the castle. The Dullahan is capable of speech, thankfully, and clever enough to understand. She gave us no further trouble, and left the Keep of her own accord. The only thing that caused any real threat was the Nuckelavee. Its breath carries some sort of disease. Carman was affected at first, but one of my rare books described a remedy for a similar poison. A few tweaks to the ingredients and I managed to cure her of the sickness. Although I was unable to restore the red of her hair, she has shown no other adverse effects.'"

Erlik flicked through the pages, and finally with a triumphant *"Aha!"* he pointed at a yellow page. There listed several ingredients and preparation instructions, below a heading of *Mortasheen Remedy*.

"We might not know how to kill the damn thing yet," Thomas said. "But at least we have some defence against it now. Come, let's take this to Mab."

✧   ✧   ✧

MAB WATCHED TRISTAN successfully hit every target before him. His mother stood nearby, anxiously chewing her lips. Mab had assured her several times that this was no test, and that she simply wanted to observe his skill.

"You are very talented, Tristan," Mab called, when Tristan perfectly executed a tricky shot from a good distance. Tristan turned and beamed, lowering his bow.

"Thank you, Your Grace," he said. Mab smiled. The boy seemed more confident with a bow in his hand. *Such is the way of most men*, Mab thought wryly. *So much bolder when armed.*

"It's getting dark, Tristan," Thissy said, approaching. "You won't be able to see the target soon."

"Just one more shot?" Tristan glanced from his mother to Mab, as though asking for permission.

Mab smiled and nodded once.

"Very well, but this will be your most difficult one yet," she said, and waved a hand. The target's three wooden legs cracked, splintered, and sprang to life, the board scuttling about on the cobbles like a freakish spider.

"If you can hit this last shot, I will grant you a new bow from my personal armoury," Mab smiled.

TRISTAN WATCHED THE target scurry about, half-unnerved and half-fascinated, but eager to try. The board's movements were erratic: he couldn't tell where it would run to next. He nocked his arrow once more, and drew back the string, concentrating for any pattern it might demonstrate.

His eyes ran down the length of the arrow. His breathing slowed. His fingers ached from holding the string, but he never let his aim quiver. Tristan ignored all noise around him, the clashing of steel from training soldiers, his mother quietly muttering support, the simple cry of a bird overhead. He loosed.

Too late, he knew he would miss. The board scampered the opposite way Tristan anticipated. His heart sank. Tristan cursed the target, the arrow, the bow, himself. Everything he could think of.

Everything slowed to a crawl. Tristan felt a tug on his heart, an ache that became a burn, and fire spread from his chest down to his fingertips. Goosebumps tingled over his arms and a prickle crept up his spine, over his scalp. Tears burned in the corners of his eyes. His hand, his arm, vibrated with effort.

The arrow in midair exploded into flame, curved in its trajectory, and veered left, towards the shivering target. It struck, and the board shattered. Splinters of charred wood flew through the air.

Tristan froze. He looked at his mother who clapped and cheered, then to Mab, who gave him a genuine smile.

"Your magic has manifested," she said. "Welcome home, Tristan Rhymer."

Tristan looked down at his hand, still clutching the bow, his knuckles white. He couldn't speak. Was this what magic felt like? It coursed through his veins, enhancing his senses: now more alert than he could ever imagine.

This is it! I have my magic now! It feels so—

He felt a strange tingle on his scalp. An approaching storm thickened the air, the electric charge prickling his skin. His hands trembled. He felt suddenly weak, like he was recovering from a sickness. His fumbling fingers dropped the bow with a clatter and he bent double, groaning.

"Easy," Mab said soothingly. She approached him. "Do not allow it to overwhelm you. Breathe deep, and breathe slow. It will take a few days for you to become accustomed to it."

Tristan nodded. He still felt a little unwell, and thought he should probably sit down, *soon.*

"Then, once you feel you have more equilibrium," Mab went on. "You can join the other apprentices to learn how to control your power, and develop your skill even further. And," she added, "I believe I owe you a reward. Such an impressive feat deserves more than a new bow. Go with your mother to the armoury, I will meet you there."

Tristan shakily nodded and approached his mother. She bounded towards him and wrapped him in a proud embrace. Tristan barely heard her excited words of encouragement over his thumping heart.

MAB WATCHED THEM leave. She knew the boy would exhibit his magic soon, but she had not expected it to be so explosive. It had been a long time since she had witnessed such a powerful display of first-time magic.

She waved a hand and reassembled the target board. It stood unmoving, looking no worse for wear.

"Get this ridiculous leash off me, you stupid man!" shouted a male voice. Mab spun, her hand automatically flexing into fistfuls of fire and ice. Two guards approached, one half-dragging a pale, frightened-looking girl by the arm, and the other struggling with a badger on a leather restraint.

"Please, we haven't done anything wrong," the girl begged as they were brought before Mab. "We were told to come here—"

"Silence, girl," the guard snapped. They stood before Mab, who subdued her magic. "Your Grace, we found these two just outside the city gates. They claim to have come from the Iron Keep."

"They have," Mab said. "But upon my request. Release them."

She nodded to the guards, who let go of the two. Isolde bent down to untie the leash from Broc's middle. She gathered him up in her arms and straightened again.

"You-you're Queen Mab, aren't you?" Isolde asked in a small voice. Broc visibly shivered in her arms and huddled closer to her. Mab nodded. Isolde quickly sunk into a clumsy curtsey.

"You have no need to be afraid," she said as Isolde rose again. "I am the same woman you met in the Iron Keep. Only now you know my name. Come, follow me."

Mab turned away and led them from the courtyard into the castle's main hall. Isolde seemed too busy looking around at the beautiful, lavish decor to watch where she was putting her feet, and tripped often. Broc nibbled her fingers to make her concentrate, but she was clearly too distracted to care.

"You will be our guests here. This good lady will show you to your chambers," Mab said, gesturing to a smiling red-haired girl beside her when they stopped. "You will find all you need in there, but should you require anything, ask one of the chambermaids."

"Thank you, my lady—I mean, Your Grace," Isolde said, and curtseyed low again, a little more gracefully this time. "We'll make ourselves useful, I promise. Won't we, Broc?"

The badger nodded, then looked sheepishly at his claws. Mab smiled.

"Maleagant has used alchemy to change your form, yes?"

Broc nodded again.

"I am afraid I must think on this," she went on. "I am unsure how to reverse magic caused by an alchemical concoction. There are many factors involved. I would not wish to turn you into something worse."

Broc's eyes immediately widened. He looked uncertainly up at Isolde. Mab leaned in conspiratorially.

"'Twas a joke," she smirked. "Have no fear, I will return you to your human form. Give me some time to," she paused and pulled a disdainful face, "*research* the exact alchemy involved."

"Thank you, Your Grace," Broc bowed his head in Isolde's arms. The serving girl gestured for them to follow her.

"Mab," came another voice from behind her, and Mab turned around to see Erlik and Thomas approaching. *So they have not killed one another, that is a relief at least.*

"How are you feeling?" Erlik asked first. Mab smiled, but said nothing.

"We've found a remedy to the Mortasheen," Thomas said, taking the book from Erlik and offering it forward to show her.

"Well, *I* found it, but I'm letting him share the praise,"

Erlik said with a shrug. Thomas rolled his eyes.

"Thank you," she said and returned the journal to Thomas's hands. "Thomas, take the recipe to Aoife and the other herbalists. We need this distributed to as many villages as possible."

Thomas nodded and bowed to her, then, after a pause, gave a curt nod to Erlik, and left the room. Mab looked up at Erlik and sighed a smile.

"Thank you," she said again, quieter this time.

He frowned. "For what?"

"For working with Thomas without doing something…" she trailed off.

"Stupid?" he finished for her. She nodded, laughing.

"Quite," she said.

He smiled and brushed his thumb against her cheek.

"As if I could ever say no to you," he said.

"And thank you for saving my life," she added. Erlik lowered his hand.

"As much as I'd like to take all the praise for that too, I wasn't the only one who helped."

"I know," she said. "But still. I imagine the seelie treated you with a certain degree of mistrust?"

"Somewhat," Erlik muttered, rubbing his wrists. Mab looked down at them, and put her hands in his.

"There is something I wish to discuss with you. Wait for me in my chamber, I will meet you there."

CHAPTER 32

"I didn't do it"

TRISTAN GAZED AT the rack of bows with hearty envy. Intricately carved recurve bows, simple long bows, and a few mechanical crossbows he was itching to try out.

"Have any caught your fancy?"

Tristan jumped. He hadn't heard Mab enter. His mother curtseyed, and Tristan attempted a low bow.

I really need to practice that, he thought. Mab smiled. A man that Tristan didn't recognise stood beside her.

"Aodhán is to fit you with new armour," she said, catching his gaze. "Something light, but sturdy."

"Thank you, Your Grace," Tristan said, then added sheepishly, "I... I've seen a bow I like."

Mab's lips twitched. Tristan pointed to a recurve bow, stained dark green and carved with twisting vines and leaves.

"It is a beauty," she agreed. "It is yours."

Tristan felt a giddy rush of childish excitement that he fought to keep under control.

"Aodhán will measure you," Mab continued, still smiling. "I have some business to attend to."

"Thank you, Your Grace," Thissy said softly, and Mab nodded to her, and left.

Aodhán approached with a measuring rope.

"An archer, hmm?" he asked. Tristan nodded, beaming.

"Which is your main hand?"

Tristan gestured with his right hand, and Aodhán brought the rope up to measure his arm.

"Good, that makes everything easier," he said, lining up the rope. "I once made a belt for a left-handed swordsman. Never again. Worst job I've ever done…"

Tristan watched him grumble away to himself as he worked.

✦   ✦   ✦

ERLIK COULDN'T KEEP still. He paced restlessly, twisting his hands, running fingers through his hair, chewing his tongue. He sat down by the fire, only to tap impatiently on the arm of the chair and stand up again.

When he heard the door open, he leapt to the sound like an over-eager pup. Mab entered, wearing an amused smile.

"You look tense," she said. Erlik heaved a sigh.

"What took you so long?" he asked. Mab tilted her head coolly.

"My attention cannot always be on you."

Erlik pulled a face and turned away.

"What did you want to talk to me about?" he asked, resuming his pacing. *In your bedchamber, of all places?*

Mab inhaled deeply.

"Idath," she said. The name clanged like a bell in the silence. Erlik froze as a chill hand gripped his throat.

"What about him?" he heard himself say, as though from far away. His voice sounded eerily calm for how deeply his terror ran whenever he heard the name.

"I know how much you fear him," she began slowly.

"I am *not* afraid of him," Erlik snapped, proud of his still voice. Mab looked wearily up at him.

"Please do not deny what I see plainly," she said. "I can see the fear in your eyes when you hear his name."

"Mab, I'm—"

"Yes, you are," she said sharply. "I am too."

Erlik slumped. Hearing Mab admit her fear somehow assuaged his.

"We need a plan," she went on. "Idath will not sit idle for long. He will attack Elphame, perhaps even Tír-Na-Nóg. We must warn Morrigan, and prepare both cities for invasion."

Erlik marvelled at her. *She has such a clever grasp on things,* he thought. *She could easily rule the world if she wanted.*

"If Idath was difficult to defeat when he was alive, I hate to imagine the trouble we will have now that he is dead," Mab continued. "Perhaps our best chance would not be to destroy him, but to imprison him?"

"What about my cage? In Wicklewood?" Erlik prompted, wanting to feel useful. But Mab shook her head.

"No," she said. "Even contained, it is too dangerous to leave him in Albion. He must be returned to Annwyn."

Erlik nodded. "Good idea," he said. Then, after a brief pause, "How?"

Mab looked disheartened.

"I do not know," she admitted. "I had hoped you might remember something from the time you dabbled in necromancy?"

Erlik chewed his tongue. He barely remembered any of the spells or rituals from when the madness had gripped him tightest. It had only been a short-lived attempt at that black magic – not quite blood magic but close enough for discomfort – and his one and only success had yielded a wild monster. *Abarta, the Doer of Deeds,* Erlik thought to himself. *I swore I'd never attempt that sort of magic again.*

"I don't remember much of that time," Erlik said, shaking his head. "I could perhaps try something, but it would be reckless to try and open the Gateway without practice. Look at what Maleagant unleashed."

"Good point. And that is another thing," Mab noted. "We need a plan to deal with these monsters roaming Albion."

Erlik produced the tattered journal and laid it on her writing desk. "The Dullahan can speak, she might be persuadable. And the Cú-Sith seem to fear storms; they can be shaken with thunder and lightning."

"You speak as if you've faced them before," Mab asked at once. Erlik faltered.

"I-It's all in the journal," he said, shrugging as casually as he could. Mab narrowed her eyes in suspicion.

"Is that so?" she reached for the journal, but he moved it away, avoiding her eyes.

"Erlik?" she prompted. He sighed.

"That first night," he said slowly. "When you'd released me, and I was in the cave? Just after Maleagant had left, I needed some space and air to clear my head. So I went for a walk."

He paused. Mab made a noise to indicate he should continue.

"I heard howling, and thought it was maybe your wolves. I was going to return to the cave, but I heard shouting. Fighting. I knew no sensible creature in Albion would take on your wolves, so I went to investigate."

"And you encountered the Hounds?"

"Yes. Attacking your Champion and his wife."

Mab baulked.

"Thomas—never mentioned—" she began, the words failing in her throat.

"Why would he? They survived. We've had other things to worry about."

"And you… you saved them?"

Erlik nodded. "I was wearing a hood. He thought I was you."

"Why would you not tell him it was you?"

"And have him think I care?" Erlik scoffed. Mab's face shone with a genuine smile. Erlik's heart doubled in size at the sight. It filled him like warm wine on a cold night.

"We should send a message to Melusine," she said, tactfully moving on. "The Each-Uisge is attacking her people as well as mine. They must be warned so they can prepare for its next attack."

"Then that leaves the Nuckelavee," Erlik noted. Silence hung heavy. He allowed her time to think before breaking it.

"I will look through some books," she said at last. "Perhaps there will be something in my library."

"And," Erlik said. "What about…"

He hesitated.

"Idath," she finished for him. She sighed. "In truth, I do not know. How does one kill that which is already dead?"

Erlik repressed a shiver. Memories flooded his mind.

The night had been hot and thick with furious words. Blistering rage had swallowed him, had guided his hand. Mab screaming; telling him – telling them *both* – to stop, to talk it out, to remember they were brothers.

He remembered driving his blade into Idath's chest. The sickening crunch of crushed bone. Skin and muscle ripping as the blade sliced into him. The hot gush of blood that followed and drowned his hands. The first time he had watched life drain from someone's eyes. From his *brother's* eyes. Silence pounded hard against his eardrums. A vile, demonic voice in his crumbling mind bidding him turn his blade on Mab next. *Hurt her. Kill her. Take her life as you took his.* Unable to drop the sword from his shaking fist.

"Go, Mab—!"

"Erlik?" her voice came as a blast of cool air. He raised his gaze to hers. There she stood, lovely and clever and wild, his she-wolf wife, concerned for the pain in his eyes.

"I was just thinking," he said quietly. Mab nodded understandingly. "I don't want to see you hurt again. I want to protect you."

"I can protect myself," she said softly. He knew she didn't mean it as a rejection of his offer, but as a declaration of her freedom. That didn't stop the annoyance from creeping around his throat.

"Not from Idath," he said. "You said yourself, you're afraid of him."

"A cornered wolf is more dangerous than a dogged hunter. You should know that better than any."

"Meaning?"

Mab hesitated. Her eyes, clearly without thought, flickered briefly to the bed. Erlik frowned.

"Oh," he said. He swallowed the lump in his throat.

She still thinks, after all these years...

"I didn't do it," he said quietly, his eyes meeting hers. Mab stopped short, brow creasing the tiniest fraction.

"What?"

"What you think I did that night," he paused, then inhaled slowly. "I didn't do it. I couldn't take what wasn't freely given."

"I-I do not... I—"

This had struck her hard, he could tell. He spoke again quickly.

"The Binding Ring had sapped your strength, and you fell faint," he said. "I took you to bed. I could have—I could have done what you think, but I didn't. I would *never* do that to you."

He dared look at her, and saw her eyes filled with relief. His heart lifted.

"Why did you let me believe so?" she breathed, taking slow and careful steps towards him. "I hated you for *so* long."

Erlik shrugged, "I tried to tell you, the morning after," he said tentatively. "Then I realised what you'd done to yourself, with the hemlock. I panicked. Your safety became my main concern, not whatever you thought of me."

"How do I know you are not lying?"

"Look at me," he said. "Do you truly believe me capable of—of that?"

He couldn't bring himself to say those awful words again. The ugly taste of them lingered in his mouth like sour wine.

Mab gazed at him. Her pupils were huge, her eyes sparkling.

"You..." she trailed off. Wetted her lips with her tongue. Tried again. "You have done so many terrible things. Wicked things. To me, to my people, to your own family."

Erlik sighed and hung his head.

"But no," she finished. "I do not believe you could be

capable of such a *cruel* thing."

He looked up at her. He found her smiling. A watery smile, truly, but a smile.

Erlik brushed her cheek with the back of his fingers, and then traced the shell of her pointed ear.

"May I?"

She hesitated. He waited.

She opened her eyes, and one brow quirked up.

"Yes."

With a sharp intake of breath, Erlik lunged and, wrapping his hand around the nape of her neck, pressed his mouth hard onto hers.

Mab staggered back a few steps, then regained her feet and responded with enthusiasm and passion. She lifted herself up onto her tiptoes and wrapped her arms around his neck. He pulled her closer to him, pressing the length of his body against hers.

Erlik lifted her off her feet, and carried her to her bed, still kissing her with such desire he was amazed the room hadn't set ablaze. His heart thumped hard against the cage of his chest. As he lowered her down, he pulled away and stared into her wild, wild eyes, now hooded with love and desire. She tenderly caressed the rounded shell of his ear, so unlike her pointed one, and he smiled.

Without a word, without him asking the question, she smiled and nodded, cupping his face with her taloned fingers.

Smiling, he leaned in and worried her neck with his teeth. Mab shivered and grew tense when his tongue brushed the sensitive tip of her pointed ear, and when a fragile mewl escaped her lips, he knew every nerve in her body had exploded in white fire.

Mab arched her back and Erlik dragged in a hoarse gasp, fumbling in his attempts to undress her as fast as possible.

Her fingernails raked his skin as he peppered her neck and chest with kisses. He nipped, and she released a most un-Mab-like whine. A low chuckle rumbled in his throat, and his gaze met hers. Her lip curled into a wicked smile as she wrapped her legs around him, and pulled him closer to her.

CHAPTER 33

"Oh, I like her!"

"So, how does it feel?"

Tristan's brushed tangles out of Epona's silver mane. The horse tossed her head when he didn't reply. He was still getting used to the sound of her voice. He wasn't sure what he expected when he first heard her speak, but it was gentle and soothing, almost motherly. Tristan wondered if she'd ever foaled, but it felt rude to ask.

"It's comfortable," he said slowly, rolling his shoulder. The stiff leather of his new cuirass creaked. "It'll need wearing in though, but once I've—"

Epona snorted, "I wasn't talking about the armour," she said. "I was talking about the *magic*."

"Oh," Tristan lowered the brush. He flexed his free hand; he wasn't entirely sure of how much control he had over the magic he summoned. "It's... different."

"Good different?" Epona pressed, turning her head to gaze at him. Tristan paused before answering. He smiled and rubbed her nose.

"Yes," he said, still looking at his hand. "Good different. It'll just take some getting used to."

The courtyard had emptied once darkness had settled, but sleep was the furthest thing from Tristan's mind. Magic buzzed under his skin.

"I was wondering if I'd see you again," said a honeyed, deep voice. Tristan jumped, making Epona snort. Or perhaps it was the *Cat Sidhe* that spooked her. The beast sat above them in the hayloft, gazing down at them with warm golden eyes. Firelight from the lit braziers reflected in those eyes, giving them an otherworldly gleam. Its fluffy tail swung lazily.

Tristan grinned.

"Likewise," he said, and the cat pounced down from the loft on silent paws and walked with perfect balance along the fence that separated each stall. "I thought you didn't like coming to Elphame? Because of the wolves?"

"Things change," the *Cat Sidhe* said, ignoring Epona's snort of dislike. "The smell is stronger on you now. I take it you've come into your magic?"

Tristan nodded. The cat smiled, showing off those pointed teeth.

"Perfect," it purred. "Got any eggs?"

Tristan shook his head and frowned.

"Why do you care if I have magic or not?" he asked.

The *Cat Sidhe* flashed its white teeth at him again and released a little chuckle.

"You're going to need magic to face what's coming."

"And what's coming?"

"Death."

Tristan's smile slipped. The cat gave him a slow blink.

"Death?" Tristan repeated slowly. It nodded. Epona kicked her front hooves. "Are you being overly dramatic on purpose?"

The *Cat Sidhe* sharpened its claws against a wooden post. "You have magic now, Tristan Rhymer. I hope you learn to use it well and wisely. And quickly."

"Begone, pest," Epona snorted, and stamped irritably. The cat yowled and hissed at her, then with a flick of its fluffy tail, jumped down from the post and darted away.

Tristan glowered at the horse. "What did you do that for?" he asked crossly. "It was just starting to spill its secrets!"

"Don't trust the *Cat Sidhe*, Tristan," Epona said. "It's more trouble than it's worth."

"Oh, what a beautiful horse!" said a new voice. Tristan turned to find a pretty girl with wild brown hair standing in the stable's doorway, holding a scrawny badger in her arms.

"She is, yes," he said. "Talkative, though."

Epona huffed and twitched her tail, but said nothing.

The girl gave a shy giggle and approached. The badger jumped out of her arms and into the piles of hay to hunt for any mice the *Cat Sidhe* hadn't already caught.

"May I?" she asked. Tristan nodded and held the curry comb out for her. The girl took it and swept it across Epona's neck coat.

"She's very well-behaved," she said. "Good strong flanks, nicely shod hooves, shiny coat, no sign of disease... she's a prize."

"Oh, I like her!" Epona said smugly, lifting her head higher and letting out a small whinny.

Tristan laughed. "She said she likes you," he told the girl. She giggled again. It was an adorable noise, and Tristan found himself grinning.

"Do you know much about horses, then?" Tristan asked.

"Just a little," she admitted, sweeping the comb through Epona's mane. "My father was an ostler when I was a little girl. He used to let me and my sisters play with the horses."

Tristan nodded, watching her expressions change from nostalgia to sadness, and wondered if her family were still alive.

"She must be an elvish horse," the girl went on before he could ask. "I've never seen one up close before."

Even if he'd had no idea of his heritage, growing up with a horse that never aged, whose mane shone like molten silver, and whose hooves rippled in beautiful mother-of-pearl would have given Tristan some clue that his family were not exactly of the mortal world.

Instead of saying this aloud, however, he merely patted Epona's rump absent-mindedly.

With a rustling of hay, the badger poked his head out of the straw with a squealing mouse in his jaws. He crunched it down and bounded over, jumping into the girl's arms. She made a small "oof" noise when she caught him. Despite being distinctly scrawny, the badger must have still been some weight.

"Oh, this is Broc," she said, nodding to the badger in her arms. "I'm Isolde. Pleased to meet you."

"Likewise," Tristan said. "I'm Tristan. Rhymer. Tristan Rhymer."

He tried his hardest not to slap himself in the forehead.

Isolde blinked and looked surprised, and glanced down at the badger.

"Rhymer? As in... Thomas Rhymer? The Champion of Elphame?" she asked, her grey eyes wide. Tristan nodded, feeling a little uncomfortable. His father obviously cast a large shadow. It would be hard to step out of it.

"He's my father," he said, a little more snappish than he intended, so smiled to soften his tone. Isolde looked awestruck.

"Smith's Hammer," she whispered. Tristan shrugged slightly. "So this must be Epona?" Isolde reached out and patted the horse's nose, who gave her a playful nudge.

Tristan nodded again, his insides squirming with delight at the noise she made, and gave her an awkward smile. Isolde offered him a shy one in return.

"This city is very beautiful," she said. "Have you lived here all your life?"

"No, I lived in a village called Ercildoune, just over the bridge," he said. "I was raised in the mortal realm. My magic has only just manifested." He wasn't entirely sure why he was telling her all of this, but she politely nodded and looked interested. "What about you? Have you lived in Elphame your whole life?"

Isolde glanced at the badger, and it shuffled in her arms.

"We've only just arrived," the badger said. Tristan blinked again and his forehead creased.

"The badger talks?" he said slowly. *Not that I should be surprised,* he thought to himself. Isolde nodded and gave him a cheery smile.

"Oh, he's not really a badger," she said.

"No, I'm just *stuck* this way," Broc mumbled sullenly and folded his front paws. Isolde gave him an affectionate scratch behind the ears.

"Queen Mab said she'd change you back once she's figured out how," she chuckled. "Why don't you go find her? She might be in the library?"

"It's a little late, don't you think?" Broc said. "I can't disturb a queen this time of night."

Isolde made a *hmm* noise and frowned. Broc's face twisted into a thoughtful expression, glancing between Tristan and Isolde, then lightly nipped her fingers and jumped out of her arms again.

"I'm heading to bed. Don't get into too much trouble with your new friend, little mouse," he sang as he bounded off.

"He's not always so grumpy," she said. "He just wants to be human again."

Struck with a sudden courage, words tumbled from his mouth before he could stop them.

"Would you like to ride out with me, Isolde?"

Isolde blinked in surprise. "Now?"

"Tomorrow," he said with a reassuring smile. "I'll meet you here in the morning. There's a little grove of trees just outside the city gates I saw on my way here."

"Oh, that sounds nice," she beamed. "Do you have a smaller horse than Epona though? I'm afraid I'm not a strong rider."

"I'll go slowly," Epona promised.

"You can ride with me," he said to Isolde. "Epona says she won't go too fast."

"SHE SEEMS LIKE a sweet girl," Thissy said warmly, looking down into the courtyard, watching Tristan and the girl part ways.

"Tristan certainly seems to think so," Thomas grinned, hooking his arm around his wife's waist. "I knew they'd get along. And when am I ever wrong?"

Thissy made a thoughtful noise.

"Would you like the comprehensive list, or just the finer points?" she asked sweetly.

"Oh, how amusing," he said, and playfully nudged her. She laughed, and they stopped to look over the balcony at their son again.

"You should go with them tomorrow," Thissy said, with a trace of anxiety in her voice. "Just to be safe."

"I'll let you break that news to him over breakfast," Thomas chuckled.

Thissy's brow creased in concern. "You jest, but with Idath on the loose in Albion, is it safe to let Tristan go riding outside of Elphame's walls?"

Thomas sighed. He kissed her brow and smoothed away the wrinkles of doubt with his thumb.

"A compromise? I won't go with him, but Lir will. We'll talk to him in the morning, *a ghra,*" he said. "Don't fret, Tristan is a smart lad. He takes after his papa."

"Hmm," Thissy quirked her eyebrow at him. "That's what worries me."

Thomas chuckled.

"Come, it's getting late," he said. "We've got a lot of work to do tomorrow."

CHAPTER 34

"He's been released into Albion"

DAWN BROKE OVER Elphame with the sweet crispness of a summer apple. Tristan hummed jovially to himself, head held high, as he made his way down to the main hall to break his fast.

As he entered the hall, he spotted his mother and father at the end of a long bench, muttering over untouched bowls of porridge. Tristan bounced towards them and took a seat beside his father, who pushed a bowl towards him.

"Good morning," Tristan smiled, sprinkling blueberries into his bowl. His mother gave him a strained smile, and his father patted her hand. The happy bubble in Tristan's chest deflated.

"What is it? What's wrong?" he asked.

His mother straightened her back. "Nothing's wrong, *a páiste.*"

Tristan squinted suspiciously, and pushed his bowl away.

His father inhaled deeply and copied him, then turned to him. Tristan was forcibly reminded of the time he'd been told his beloved cat Tufts had been run over by a wagon.

"Tristan," Thomas began. Tristan swallowed hard. *Who could possibly be dead?*

"Do you remember when you were younger," Thissy took over, "and I took you with me when I attended to the old farmer who lived at the other side of the river?"

"Mister O'Donoghue?"

"That's right," she went on, smiling easily now. "Do you remember what happened?"

"He'd..." Tristan strained to remember. "He'd fallen on his pitchfork when the pigs got loose, didn't he? Got himself a nasty gouge in the leg?"

"That's right," Thissy said again. "And by the time we'd gotten to him, the wound had festered and we couldn't save him, do you remember?"

"I remember," Tristan said uncertainly. "Why are you asking me?"

"Do you remember when I offered the prayer to the Lord of the Dead? To guide his soul to Annwyn?"

"The Lord of the Dead; you mean Idath?"

A cold shiver ran through the now-silent hall.

Thomas lowered his voice, "Yes, Tristan. Him."

"What about him?"

"He's no longer confined to Annwyn, Tristan," Thomas said slowly. "He's been released into Albion."

Tristan took a few moments to process this. If his mother offered prayers to guide souls into peace, what would be so terrible about the Lord of the Dead?

"And that's... bad?" Tristan asked dumbly.

"Yes, Tristan," Thissy said, taking his hand. "When we pray to Idath, it's to get his attention and distract him from the new soul entering his realm."

"Why would he need to be distracted from that? Surely he'd look after them, right?"

Both Thomas and Thissy grimly shook their heads.

"I'm afraid not, Tristan," Thomas said. "Idath doesn't look after the souls in Annwyn. He... well, I don't think anyone is really sure what he does with them, but needless to say, it's not a pleasant thing to become one of his thralls."

"And now he's here? In Albion?"

Both nodded again.

"We'd rather you stay close by for now," Thissy said.

"But I was going to—" he broke off and blushed a little. He cleared his throat and tried to sound older, more responsible. "Isolde and I were going for a ride. I have my magic now. I can look after us both."

"Tristan, you're not trained," Thissy said, but Tristan pulled away from her touch.

"I'm not a child anymore," he argued, looking to his father for help. Surely he would understand, wouldn't he?

And Tristan swore he saw a flicker of recognition in his father's eyes.

"If you must go," Thomas said slowly, and Thissy's eyes snapped to him. "Take Lir with you."

"What can he do that I can't?"

"A spare set of eyes and hands won't go amiss."

"He doesn't have any magic. He's only human!"

"Your father was *only human* when he first came to Albion," his mother gently pointed out. "Think of all the things he did."

Tristan suddenly realised how recently he'd been *only human*. The words deeply shamed him. But it was too late to take them back now.

"He's half-seelie, it doesn't count," Tristan folded his arms and leaned back in his chair, averting his eyes.

"Please, for your mother's sake, take Lir with you," Thomas said.

Tristan sighed through his nose.

"Fine," he said. Then, standing up, "May I be excused then? I'll have to find Lir if he's coming with us."

Thomas nodded, and Tristan grabbed a pear and shoved it in his pocket, then left.

"I HOPE HE doesn't do something reckless," Thissy said, chewing her nail.

Thomas pulled a plate of bacon closer to take a couple of rashers.

"Reckless? *Our* son? Never," he said dryly.

"Maybe you should follow them…" Thissy trailed off when Thomas gave her a look.

"*A ghrá*, he's right," he said. "He's not a child."

"He's not even sixteen!"

"He's agreed to take Lir with him, that's a reasonable compromise."

Thissy continued to chew her fingernails but said no more.

I hope you're right, she said in his head.

The hall steadily filled with people as they sat in silence. Thomas looked around. Every face looked pale and wan; apparently, news of Idath's release had spread quickly. Seeing the seelie so terrified did nothing to assuage his own fears. Once, he would have easily said the most dangerous creature he'd encountered was Erlik. Now, his confidence in that was shaken.

Idath was a god. More than that, he was a *dead* god. His heart felt heavy at the thought of facing him. His skill with magic was meagre at best. His sword arm was his best defence for his family and his queen, and what could a sword do against that which was already dead?

CHAPTER 35

"Begone, foul thing"

MAB LAY AGAINST Erlik's chest, her fingers lightly tracing his seven-pointed star tattoo. Her eyelashes tickled his skin when she blinked. Smiling, he ran his hand up her arm, looking down at her with deep adoration.

He inhaled deeply. The musky smell of him lingered on her, intermingling with her own divine and intoxicating scent. She drew in one long breath, a smile curling her lips.

His back and shoulders stung where she'd raked her nails. He was certain she'd drawn blood, but he couldn't resent her for it. Her touch had been like fire, her kisses near drove him back to madness, her wild scent still burning inside his nostrils.

She leaned over him to kiss his chest.

"Say something," she said softly, her lips ghosting across the tattoo over his heart.

"Such as?" he asked, his voice husky with longing. She looked up at him and gave him a mysterious smile. *Gods, that smile,* he thought to himself. *It could make a man do anything.*

"Anything," she said, looking down again, nuzzling against his chest like a cat. He smiled and brushed his fingers through her hair. He spotted a small bruise under her jaw where one of his kisses had nipped a little too hard. It would vanish shortly, he knew.

"Anything?" he repeated. His brain was too muddled, too

fogged, too full of thoughts of *her* to make coherent sense. She smiled and pressed her body against his. She felt so small beside him; he wanted to wrap his arms around her and keep her there forever, safe and warm and loved.

"Mab," he whispered, and she looked up. "What happens now?"

"What do you mean?"

"With us. With me," he said. "When this is over, what happens to me?"

"Oh, must we talk of such things?" she said softly.

"Please," he muttered against her tousled locks. "I want to know."

"Later." Her eyes found his, eyes softer than he'd ever seen them. There was no wintry coldness there, no sharp disdain, no mocking laugh.

"As you wish" he sighed. Then, noting a conflicted frown appear on her face, gave her a reassuring smile and nod. "Truly."

"Then for now," she said slowly. "You will stay with me."

Erlik smiled and quirked his brow, looking intrigued.

"And will your leaf—"

He stopped himself with a quick bite to the tongue. He licked his lips nervously, halting the smile at the sudden ferocity in Mab's eyes. *There she is; my she-wolf.*

"Will your seelie allow it?" he corrected himself. Mab shifted back into place, her hair tumbling over his chest. He tilted his head slightly to watch her.

"I do not know," she said, her fingers lightly tracing patterns again. "But regardless, we need you here. *I* need you here."

Erlik smiled and kissed the top of her head, the only part of her he could reach without disrupting her gently dancing fingers. He reached to his neck and pulled off the chain that held the ring close to his heart.

"Then this is yours, if you want it back?" he offered the ring to her, and she frowned, confused. "It's no longer a Binding Ring," he explained. "Its power was broken when the

Binding was. It's just a ring now."

Mab smiled and held out her hand. He slipped the ring onto her finger, and the circle of silver gleamed comfortably in the firelight. He smiled; she looked so content. He kissed her again, his hand tracing over her body, lightly caressing the curve of her breast down to the flat of her belly, lost in thoughts of what could be.

She smiled, and rested her hand against his jumping heart. He repressed a shiver. Her fingers could do things to him that no other woman could. How could he ever have mistaken Carman for her? *No*, he told himself sharply. *Don't think of that.*

Mab shifted upwards and kissed him. He bit her lip gently and she pulled away, chuckling.

"Come, we should get dressed," she said, rolling away from him out of the bed to stand.

Erlik heaved a theatrical sigh, and Mab smirked and took his hand to pull him to his feet.

They dressed quickly. Mab braided her hair into a long plait that fell past the small of her back, and Erlik stood still for a few moments, admiring it.

"Stop staring," she said, the corners of her lips twitching. Erlik jolted. He hadn't even realised he'd been doing so. Smiling, he approached her and ran his hand up her arm.

"I can't help it," he said, casting his eyes over her, and sighed again, this time in the brief happiness he found in her arms. "What did I do to deserve you?"

"Something wicked, no doubt," she said dryly.

Erlik leaned forward to kiss her, but before his lips could brush against hers, three sharp blasts on a horn came from far away. Mab pulled away, and Erlik grumbled under his breath. She threw open the doors to the balcony and stepped out.

"What's the matter?" he asked, approaching her from behind.

"'Tis the signal from the Tower of Glenstrae," she said.

Erlik squinted into the distance. There was no sign of an approaching army. Only half a dozen figures stood on the horizon. A couple appeared to be mounted, and the rest on foot. The tallest figure turned Erlik's blood to ice-water. A now familiar wave of fear prickled on his scalp. An instinctive arm went around Mab's shoulders.

A large black crow fluttered down onto the balustrade of the balcony and preened. Mab stared at it, and Erlik tried to shoo it away, as though frightening the crow would also frighten away the approaching threat.

"Begone, foul thing," Erlik snapped.

"*Liar!*" the crow screeched, and flapped its wings angrily at him as it took to the air.

"Why are they here?" Mab wondered aloud. "With no army?"

"I don't know," he admitted. His tongue felt thick and clumsy; fear had gripped him by the throat and strangled his voice.

Mab looked up at him. The fear in her eyes fed him strength, and burnt away the cold terror that locked him tight.

A sharp knock rapped on Mab's door, three times.

"Enter!" Mab called, despite Erlik's small choked noise of protest.

Thomas strode in, his sword sheathed in the belt around his waist, but without any armour.

"Mab—"

"We know," Erlik said. "We heard the signal."

Thomas cast his eyes between them both. His brow furrowed and his eyes narrowed in suspicion.

"Don't look at us like that, *amadán*," Erlik said.

"We will ride out and meet them," Mab said, stepping back into the room.

"What? No!" Erlik said at once. "You almost died the last time we faced them!"

"We will not be alone this time," Mab said. "Thomas, prepare a small guard to accompany us. We will meet them under a sign of peace."

"*Peace?*" Erlik repeated, stunned. "Mab, have you forgotten—?"

"I have not," she said. "But if we do nothing, they will

return with an army and ransack my city."

Erlik sighed in defeat. She was too stubborn to talk out of an idea.

"Very well," he said. Mab nodded to Thomas, and he glanced between the two. Despite the animosity between them, Erlik could tell the *amadán* was in agreement with him.

"Are you sure about this, Mab?" Thomas said. "Everything you've ever told me about Idath—"

Mab raised a hand to stop him and gave him a catlike blink.

"I know, Thomas," she said. "This will not be easy. But I have faith in you. You are my Champion, and the defender of Elphame. We will do this together."

She nodded encouragingly as she spoke, and Erlik saw the boy swell with pride. He bowed his head to her, snapped his heels together like a trained soldier and left. Erlik shook his head and sighed in exasperation.

"We cannot meet them in open battle," she preempted, and he nodded. "It is futile. But the city must be ready if they decide to storm it. You, Thomas, and I will go out and meet them, with a handful of my personal guard, to discuss peace."

Erlik sighed and ran his hand through his hair, hands trembling.

"He won't accept peace," he said softly. "He knows only chaos. We both barely escaped his rage last time."

"I know, *a múirnín,*" she said, looking out onto the horizon. "But if he was killed once, he can be killed again."

CHAPTER 36

"Your quarrel is with me"

CARMAN'S PULSE THUMPED in her temples. Nausea threatened to overwhelm her again. She wanted nothing more than to run back to the Iron Keep and lock herself away. Had she gotten her own way, she would have turned tail as soon as Idath had broken the news to her and sought out a tincture or potion to get rid of the wretched, unwanted thing inside her.

But Idath had other plans. She was bait now, to tempt Erlik out into the open for Idath to toy with.

Perhaps then, she hoped, *I'll get the immortal life I want.*

Maleagant smirked when several figures appeared over the crest of the hill, and Carman struggled to remain still when the thing inside her belly felt as though it *moved*. Idath and Maleagant looked at her, and she uncomfortably shifted under their gaze. A wave of sudden exhaustion washed over her.

The figures grew closer, and Carman arranged her face to hide her discomfort. Erlik and Mab approached them, with a young man Carman didn't recognise, and a few soldiers she assumed to be the witch's personal guard. Despite everything, she smirked to herself.

MAB APPROACHED THE group, her heart thumping harder with

every step. Idath stood as intimidating as ever, yet her sight had been overtaken by the horde of monsters that surrounded him.

The Cú-Sith dogs stood beside him, snarling and drooling, red-eyed and copper-eared, their white bodies monstrously contorted and draconic.

A headless woman sat mounted on a headless horse. *The Dullahan*, Mab realised. The rider carried her own head under her left arm, and bore a whip fashioned from a backbone, curled innocently on her belt. For now.

Mab stopped a good distance away from the hideous party, her steps halted by the sight of the third monster, which pawed restlessly beside Idath. What she had originally thought as another mounted rider was not truly so.

The Nuckelavee reared back on its skinless legs, kicking the front talons with evil menace. The rider upon it had no lower half, but instead the body melted disgustingly into the horse's back. Muscle and sinew writhed with every movement as it trotted restlessly in circles on its four repulsive legs. The grass and earth it touched was scorched; brown, and withered.

It took all Mab had not to turn away, though she couldn't disguise her horror and disgust at the sight of it.

"I'm glad to see you've recovered, my dear," Maleagant said mockingly as she approached.

"Yes," Mab bit back, momentarily disregarding the monsters. "Thank you for your concern."

Maleagant laughed. Carman ran her tongue over her teeth and smirked.

"I've brought my pets," Maleagant went on. "I see you've brought yours."

He gestured to the guards around Mab. Erlik scowled and crossed his arms.

"Sorcerer," Erlik acknowledged. Mab noticed that he avoided looking at Idath. She too could feel the wrongness of his being. His very presence offended her, her magic reacting against his abhorrent nature.

The laws of magic have been broken.

Mab chanced a glance at Idath. But he kept his eyes fixed

on his brother, his hands constantly clenching and unclenching, as though he longed to strangle him.

"So you managed to keep her alive, Father," Maleagant commented. Mab felt Thomas double-take beside her.

"You failed to mention that," he hissed a whisper to Erlik.

"'Tis not important, Thomas," Mab whispered back.

"Oh, Thomas the Rhymer?" Carman said, the first words she'd spoken since they'd arrived. A smug smile crept onto her face. "The Champion of Elphame, lapdog to the great Queen of the Old Ways."

Mab glared at her, eyes ablaze, and was pleased to see Carman squirm under her stare.

"Be silent, *striapach*," Mab said darkly.

"She has fire in her belly, this one," the Dullahan said. All eyes turned to her. Her voice echoed weirdly. "I would like to play with the beauty awhile."

"No," Idath said. His voice silenced all around him. Even the dogs cowered. "The Heart is mine, as is my brother. You may toy with any of the others."

"We have come to discuss peace, Idath," Mab said, standing up straighter. "Not to exchange threats."

"Silence," Idath said. "I will speak with only my brother."

"We have something of yours, Father," Maleagant said, and Mab noticed his voice waver ever so slightly. She frowned. "When you fled the Iron Keep, you left it behind."

Carman smirked.

"A little token, to remember our night together," she said, and her hands went to stomach and rested there.

Mab's eyes widened and her lips parted in shock. An envious knot tied in her chest, and her breath caught in her throat. She looked at Erlik. His face had turned white, mouth twisted with disgust. He said nothing, only looked at Mab for forgiveness.

There is nothing to forgive, a múirnín, she thought to him. *She tricked you. The blame is hers alone.*

"Why are you doing this?" Mab asked quietly. She cursed the wretchedness in her voice. This was no time for weakness, for vulnerability.

Carman began to laugh. Maleagant joined in. Only Idath stood stoic and unsmiling.

"We've told you already, witch—" Maleagant began.

"Do *not* call me witch, sorcerer," Mab spat. "I was not speaking to you." Her eyes never left Carman. "Carman, why are *you* doing this? What wrong have I ever done you?"

Carman shifted. Her eyes darted. "It-it's not about *you*—"

"It must be," Mab said. "You take great delight in watching me suffer, why? How have I crossed you to give you cause to hate me so?"

"Because you have *everything!*" Carman screeched suddenly. "Everything I could *ever* want, you have! Life, power, magic, *everything* I've wanted since I was a child! You could never understand."

Carman inhaled slowly. Mab didn't speak. She had the feeling Carman wasn't finished.

"When I was a little girl, my parents would tell my sisters and I about the Heart of Magic Itself," Carman went on. Mab tipped her head back and frowned. "How it had been a spirit of air and darkness, which ran through the fabric of the world like water. Until the Great Smith captured it in a jar, and forced it inside a doll made of clay. And he gave it to the Old Gods to shape. They carved it into the likeness of a beautiful woman, and sent her back down to our world to rule over Elphame, the shining silver capital that lay at the heart of Albion."

Mab repressed a shiver. It was so disconcerting to hear her life as a fairy tale, a bedtime story for children.

"But when my sister Vivienne began to show signs of magical promise, and my parents..." her face grew dark and twisted with envy. "They lauded and praised her above all things. 'Oh, Mab, Mab, the merciful and great, the Heart of Magic Itself, thank you for this blessing! A mere mortal, gifted with magic?'"

Carman sneered, "Why her? Why *her* and not *me?*"

"You misunderstand, I do not bless mortals with magic," Mab shook her head. "There must have been some faery blood in your family, long ago. Magic manifests in mortals whenever it wants, there is no conscious force behind it. It is erratic."

Carman clearly wasn't listening.

"I saw you, you know," she said, her eyes agleam now. "When I was a girl. My parents took my sisters and I to a Beltane festival."

Erlik shifted in discomfort and cleared his throat. Mab glanced at him.

"I doubt you'd remember. It would've been just another festival to you." Carman went on. "I watched you and thought you were so beautiful, so powerful. You barely had to blink and magic just obeyed you, easy as that," Carman snapped her fingers. "It was like you had the whole world in your grasp. You could've anything you wanted. *Anything*."

Carman expelled a gush of air through her nose and sneered, "But now I have something *you* want. How does it feel, witch?"

"Do not call me witch!" Mab growled.

Maleagant, who had been listening intently, laughed aloud at her words.

"What happened to Vivienne?" Thomas asked curiously. All eyes turned to him. He shrugged as though the answer didn't bother him.

"She drowned," Carman said. She said it so easily, as though losing a sister meant nothing to her. "Her precious *magic* couldn't save her from the lake behind our house."

"It matters not," Idath said. "Brother, you and the Heart will return with me to the Iron Keep."

"Leave Mab out of this," Erlik said. "Your quarrel is with me."

"You are wrong, brother," Idath approached Erlik, crossing the unspoken neutral plain between both sides. Thomas put his hand on his sword and moved to draw it, but Mab stopped him, carefully watching Idath.

"You took my life, but the Heart was the cause," Idath said. "Because of the both of you, I have spent centuries rotting in Annwyn. In the cold, and the dark, and the anguish of the

Land of the Dead." His voice rising in volume, rotted teeth grinding together so hard Mab imagined she saw them crumbling away.

Idath grabbed Erlik's throat.

"Did it feel good, brother?" Idath snarled. "Did it feel good *murdering* me?"

"Enough!" Mab said sharply, taking a step forward.

Idath looked down at her, and a cruel sneer curled his lip.

"You have become so weak, little brother," he said. "You have let your *feelings* rule you."

Erlik struggled hard against Idath's grip. "Leave her alone, Idath."

"I will not, Erlik," Idath hissed, and lifted Erlik off the ground by the throat. He choked, and Mab gasped as his boots kicked fruitlessly at the air, fingers scrabbling at Idath's hand.

"Idath, stop this now!" she commanded, but he laughed, a deep and booming noise that seemed to shake the ground. With a growl, Mab twisted her fingers to encase the monstrous being in ice, but although frost plumed from the earth below and crept up around his legs, it appeared to have no effect on him.

He laughed again; Erlik's eyes rolled back in his head.

"No! You cannot take him!" Mab made to rush at Idath, but an invisible force impeded her way. Thomas unsheathed his sword and started forward, and the Dullahan unrolled her freakish whip and cracked it. A blinding flash of white spotted their vision. Robbed of sight, Thomas groaned and covered his eyes, along with the guards behind him.

"Idath, stop!" came Maleagant's voice through the blindness, and Mab turned to the noise in confusion. Blinking furiously, she made him out through blurry eyes. She saw Carman, pale and wan, half-collapsed into Maleagant's arms. "Take him back to the Keep and finish him there!"

"Be silent, sorcerer," Idath snapped.

He rolled his neck and shoulders. Mab heard a sickening crunch of bones and withheld her grimace.

"Mab—Morrigan—sh-she doesn't... Tír-Na-Nóg—" Erlik

managed to choke out the warning, although he seemed to be losing consciousness fast. Idath's small eyes widened in rage.

"A *woman* sits on my throne? The great city of Tír-Na-Nóg is prey to a woman's whim?" he asked in a low voice. With an angry growl, he dropped his brother. Erlik fell heavily to the ground, collapsing in the dirt, gulping down air and massaging his bruised throat. Mab rushed to his side.

"Albion has grown weak and wretched in my absence, and the absence of my children," Idath said, looking in disgust at the white city. "No longer am I confined to the limits of Annwyn. Soon, my children will share in my freedom; when I break open the Heart of Magic Itself and regain my former strength, I will rule once again, and this world will tremble at the mere mention of my name!"

"Enough, demon!" Thomas drew his sword, prompting the guards behind him to do the same, but, with the look of a man desperate to flee, Maleagant twisted his hand. Thomas's own hand mimicked it; there was an audible snap, and Thomas screamed and dropped the sword, clasping his broken and useless wrist in his other hand. Mab helped Erlik stagger back to his feet, but, seeing her distraction, Idath stepped forward and easily batted her away, as though she were nothing but a fly in the air.

Erlik looked up sharply, his eyes full of hate. He gave a roar of fury and clumsily drew his own sword, lunging at Idath. Surprisingly nimble, the dead man dodged the attack and returned the blow.

The Cú-Sith leapt forwards, tearing at Elphame's guards.

Mab gestured to the sky, and shouted *"Anfa!"*, and thick black clouds gathered. Thunder rattled the sky, and rain began to belt down upon the warring group.

The hounds shrank back at the sound of thunder. Whimpering, tails tucked firmly between their legs, the dogs backed away from their prey and fled onto the moors. Maleagant cursed their retreating backs.

The Dullahan flicked her wrist, and her whip cracked again. Mab and Thomas shielded their eyes from the blinding light, momentarily disoriented. Laughing, the headless woman circled the group, harming only their sight whenever her whip lashed the air.

The Nuckelavee, however, dug its bloody talons into the softening ground, snorting and whinnying. The rain hissed and sizzled on its skinless flesh, and it screamed in pain. Foolishly, Mab caught herself staring for a fraction of a moment; why would the rain cause it such agony? A blast of foul-smelling breath issued from the horse's mouth, singeing the dead grass at its feet. Mab's heart thumped hard in her throat.

The Mortasheen!

Without thinking, she gestured at the earth with both hands, and a wall of roots and thorns sprang up from the ground, surrounding the creature in a cage.

Erlik and Idath still fought, seemingly unaware of everything around them. While Idath was the taller of the two and obviously stronger, Erlik was quicker, and seemed blinded by his rage. His attacks flew wilder and wilder, flurries of steel and magic, throwing handfuls of black fire one moment and swinging his blade the next.

Two guards lunged for Maleagant and Carman, but she weakly raised her hand. Fire flickered at her fingertips; it wasn't enough to set the guards ablaze entirely, but small spurts of fire erupted from their arms and shoulders between their metal armour. Ignoring the weak flames that quickly sputtered to nothing, they approached, but Maleagant wielded his staff like a pike, and attacked both at once.

Mab's eyes swiftly moved over the group; her guardsman holding strong against Maleagant's attack; the Nuckelavee clawing at its wooden prison, foul breath withering the roots for it to escape; the Dullahan laughing madly as she circled, never engaging in combat; Idath and Erlik battling with such ferocity they could quite easily kill each other. Again.

She moved forward to help him, but Thomas held her back.

"No!" he said, his face ashen with pain, holding his broken wrist close to his chest, his sword hanging uselessly in his other hand. "Mab, wait—!"

Mab stopped short. Maleagant had plunged his hand inside his robes and pulled forth a small bottle. She recognised it at once and took a step back, but too late.

He flung the bottle. She raised her arms instinctively, but the glass smashed at her feet, and noxious rust-coloured fumes rose around her. A metallic scent invaded her nostrils. Her chest ached and screamed as her eyes burned and rolled back. The world turned to dusty darkness around her.

CHAPTER 37

"I know what must be done"

MAB STIRRED IN Thomas' arms just as he entered Elphame's gates and the portcullis closed behind them. "Where...?"

"Mab!" Thomas lowered her to the ground. "I didn't think you'd wake so quickly. Maleagant used some kind of... *potion* on you—"

"He experiments with alchemical concoctions," she croaked, swaying on the spot and putting a hand to her forehead. "He has done it to me before. I think it is some form of cold iron, weaponised into a miasma. What happened? Where is Erlik?"

"He stayed behind."

"*What?*"

She moved towards the gate but Thomas stopped her.

"Move aside, Thomas," she growled. "We have to go back for him."

"No, my duty is to keep *you* safe."

"I can still save him!" she threw him off and glared at him. Thomas felt his temperature rapidly increase. Sweat beaded on his forehead, and he avoided her gaze; it felt like she was trying to set him alight.

His right arm throbbed with pain, and had swollen up in clouds of purple and blue. His fingers were useless, and he selfishly hoped Thissy would be waiting for him at the castle to heal it quickly.

"Let me go back," Mab snarled at him. A crowd was gathering now.

"No, Mab," he said sternly, taking her arm to steer her towards the castle. "I won't let you risk your life for his!"

Mab glared at him and threw his grip away. He sucked in a sharp breath when her hand caught his broken wrist. She froze, eyes full of guilt and regret.

"Elphame is in danger, Tír-na-Nóg is in danger. What's one life against the lives of every citizen in both cities?"

Mab growled, then, lowering her eyes and her hackles, heaved a heavy sigh.

"I am sorry," she said quietly. "You are right. But I cannot leave him, I must go back."

"You can't," Thomas said, forcing as much sadness into his voice as his dislike of Erlik would allow. He knew how Mab felt about him, even if he didn't understand why. "At least, not now. We need to warn Morrigan. They need to know what's coming, they need to be prepared."

Mab sighed again.

"Very well," she said. "I will inform her. You must ready the soldiers. I fear what Idath has in mind."

Thomas hesitated, and Mab nodded at him. "I know what must be done."

"Mab," Thomas put his hand on her arm. She stiffened and he removed his hand immediately. "What Idath said, about... breaking you open?" He felt disgusting just repeating the words.

She paused.

"He'll come after you too."

"I know."

"What if he uses Erlik as bait?"

"He will," she said, her gaze lowered. "That is likely the reason we were allowed to escape. But that does not mean I must abandon him. Idath will lay a trap for me, with Erlik at the centre. But I will not walk in blindly. Let me think for a while."

Thomas sighed, "As you wish."

The nibbling worry didn't abate, but he felt the depths of her despair would trigger her temper, so decided it best to leave her to her thoughts. His broken wrist would have to wait. He nodded once and turned away. He knew Mab was too hard to cry, but he could have sworn her eyes held a slight glimmer that wasn't there before as she returned to the castle alone.

"*A ghrá!*" called a voice behind him. He turned and saw Thissy push through the crowd towards him. With a rush of relief and affection, he ran to embrace her, careful to move his broken wrist aside. "What's happening?"

She took his broken wrist almost out of instinct and started to heal it. Thomas winced when he felt the bones fuse together, but the warming sensation under his skin eased the pain a little.

"Idath has taken Erlik captive," he said quickly. "Mab thinks he'll be using him as bait to lure her out. He wants to open the Gates of Annwyn again. He mentioned Tír-Na-Nóg though, so Mab has gone to send a missive to Morrigan to warn her. She wants me to ready the army in case of attack."

"No, Thomas," she whispered. "Tristan hasn't returned!"

His heart dropped into his stomach. "I'll go find him."

"No, I'll go. You need to stay here, prepare the soldiers, and protect the city. Do your duty as Champion," she reminded him.

Thomas flexed his fingers as she spoke, the bones of his wrist now fully healed.

"I can't let you go alone, it's too dangerous—"

"He's our *son*, Thomas," she said in a low voice. "I'll fight Idath himself for his sake."

Thomas's chest swelled with pride and love. He kissed her hard, and they parted; she towards the stables, and he towards the barracks.

"LIGHTFOOT," THOMAS CALLED for the elderly seelie. "Send an ambassador into the central city to warn the civilians. We need to set up a barrier around the city walls to keep them safe."

"Does Idath mean to attack, then?" he asked anxiously, and Thomas explained again, starting to grow weary of repeating himself.

"I assume Mab is sending word to Morrigan?" Lightfoot twisted his hands in fear. Thomas nodded, then paused and lowered his voice.

"Lightfoot, I need to confide in you," he said, casting his eyes around for eavesdroppers.

"Of course, what is it?"

"I think Mab is going to try and rescue Erlik by herself," he said. Lightfoot blanched.

"Why?"

With a sigh, Thomas went on. "I know it seems like madness, but Mab loves him. I think she wants us distracted defending the city while she slips away to the Iron Keep to save him."

"You mustn't let her go, Thomas," Lightfoot said. "You have to talk her out of it. It's too reckless!"

It seems recklessness is the norm these days, Thomas thought.

"I've already tried, she won't listen to me."

"I'll talk to her then, she can't be allowed to do this."

"I don't know what you can say that I already haven't, but you're welcome to try."

Lightfoot gave him a weary nod and turned to walk away. Thomas watched him leave and heaved a deep sigh. Closing his eyes, he prayed to the Old Gods to be kind to them, and even offered up a small prayer for Erlik, if only for Mab's sake.

✧　✧　✧

"FLY SWIFTLY, MY sweet," Mab said to the magpie. "Morrigan must be warned as soon as possible."

It ruffled its feathers with a cackle. Mab stroked the blue-green shimmer of its feathers, and it took off, carrying a scroll in its claws. She watched it disappear into the sky for longer than she should have, but the tower's quiet solitude calmed her restless mind.

Idath had not killed Erlik, she would have felt it. She would have known. She had tried many times to communicate with him through their minds, but had been met with only silence. Perhaps Idath's unnatural presence was blocking their connective magic. She wondered vaguely if Erlik had been trying to reach her, too. Rage threatened to boil over, and she desperately wanted to incinerate something, but instead she took a deep breath and exhaled slowly.

Be calm, Mab, she told herself. *Erlik still lives, there is still time to rescue him. Although I do not wish to think what tortures they are subjecting him to…*

She pushed such thoughts away. Idath would no doubt exact a vicious punishment on his brother as vengeance, but Erlik was strong; they would not break him. They could not break him. *They will not break him.*

The tower around her trembled, and dust crumbled from the pointed ceiling. She inhaled. The tremors ceased.

They will not break us.

✧   ✧   ✧

ERLIK LOST TRACK of how long the beating lasted. Idath's boot and fists sank into his chest and stomach several times, and he was certain several ribs had broken. He weakly coughed, and the coppery tang of blood filled his mouth.

Idath kicked him once more, and Erlik groaned and rolled onto his back, panting and wincing, clutching his aching body. The sky was like an open ocean above him, and he longed to lose himself in its depths.

"Enough, Idath!" he heard Maleagant's voice nearby. "We need to return to the Iron Keep, Carman is sick."

Oh yes, we must help poor Carman, Erlik petulantly thought.

He pushed himself to his hands and knees and wiped his mouth with the back of his hand. He stared at the smear of blood for a moment.

Idath slowly circled him. Erlik took shallow breaths; his chest burning, and his sides too tender to try and stand. He kneeled instead, and somewhere in the back of his mind he felt a shade of sour irony. *Kneeling before my own brother,* he thought bitterly.

"I have thought long and hard about what atrocities I would visit upon you, brother," Idath said. Erlik tipped his head back and inhaled through his mouth, closing his eyes. "You took everything from me."

"She was never yours, Idath," Erlik said thickly, opening his eyes again to stare at the sky once more. The cool remnant specks of rain pricked his face, and he lowered his head again with a wince. "I couldn't let you kill her—"

"It was its duty!" Idath bellowed, and lunged forward. Then he seemed to regain his composure, and held himself back. Instead, he glowered and continued to circle his brother. "That was why it was *created!* To die in service to the Old Gods!"

"In service to *you,* you mean?" Erlik snapped, as harshly as he could muster. "She's not a tool you can use and discard, Idath. She was created to rule the world below the skies, not for you to use to fuel your own ambitions."

"You foolish boy," Idath sneered. "You fell in love with a golem, a clay doll given breath. I almost pity you. You are nothing. The *Heart* is nothing. When it comes to me, trying to save you, I will break it open and gain the power it holds within."

"*Stop!*" Erlik's palms flared with black fire, and his eyes burned with hatred and rage. A sea of pain bloomed through him and he groaned and fell forward onto his hands. He heard Idath laugh. The sound forced an old, old fear into his heart.

"It is time that I reclaim what was stolen from me," he heard Idath say.

Erlik's hands clenched at the earth beneath his palms,

grabbing fistfuls of dirt in his anger.

A heavy fist seized Erlik by the hair and dragged him to his feet. He had to bite his tongue to stop himself from crying out as shards of agony sliced through him. Idath wrapped his hand around his throat and squeezed hard.

Erlik looked his brother in the eye. Idath could always tell when he was afraid, and the years in Annwyn hadn't changed that. He knew that Idath could see his fear.

"We shall return to the Iron Keep," Idath said. "Let us see how much you *love* your pet doll."

Hands bound, with a rancid cloth shoved into his mouth to silence his silver tongue, Erlik was dragged along behind Idath, Maleagant, and a staggering Carman.

CHAPTER 38

"I don't take sides"

TRISTAN WATCHED FROM the darkness of the trees. The beating was brutal, and Tristan winced with every contact. The creature laying into Erlik could only be described as a ghost; tall and ashen, the dead man could only be Idath. Tristan's heart fluttered frantically in this throat. Two others stood nearby, but he didn't recognise them.

A rustle of leaves beside him. A twinkling of charms on a rope. Tristan's heart almost stopped when the *Cat Sidhe* appeared from the undergrowth beside him.

"I did warn you that Death was coming," the cat said dryly, tail swishing in the leaves. It sat beside him and gracefully licked its front paw.

"Why aren't you more terrified?" Tristan kneeled down and whispered to the cat, not taking his eyes off Idath.

"Because I'm not standing in his way."

"So you're on his side?"

"I don't take sides."

Tristan withheld his frustrated groan, "Then why are you here?"

"Got any—"

"If you ask me for eggs one more time, Cat—"

The *Cat Sidhe* swiped his face with its paw.

"Be quiet," it growled. "Got any ideas on how to get past

him?"

Tristan blinked at the cat.

"No," he admitted. "Do you?"

The cat stood and scratched its horns against the tree. Tristan held his breath in case the noise attracted Idath.

"I told you," the *Cat Sidhe* said, sitting beside him again, eyes narrow. "I don't take sides." It paused. "You could wait until he leaves."

"That's preferable."

"He may have already seen your horses," the *Cat Sidhe* pointed out. "Though if that were the case, you'd likely already be dead."

"What would you do?"

"Me?" the *Cat Sidhe* sounded amused. "I'd lay low until he's gone and then scurry home as fast as my four legs could carry me. If I had a home, that is."

"I like that plan best," Tristan gave the *Cat Sidhe* an extremely grateful head scratch. "Next time you're in Elphame, I'll find you the biggest, fattest chicken eggs I can find."

"Good," the cat nodded and blinked, then, with a flick of its fluffy tail, disappeared once more into the darkness.

Tristan turned his eyes back to the group. Idath had dragged Erlik to his feet and was in the process of binding his hands. They seemed about to leave. His heart thundered so loud he feared they could hear it.

As silently as he could, Tristan shuffled back into the dark foliage, then darted back to the clearing where Lir and Isolde remained.

"Well?" Lir asked loudly as soon as Tristan emerged from the bracken. "What's all the racket?"

"*Shh,*" he hissed quickly; Idath was still too close for comfort. "We need to get back to Elphame."

"Now?" Isolde sounded disappointed.

"Well, about an hour ago would have been preferable," Tristan said, not too overwhelmed with fear to notice the way his heart jumped at the disappointment in her voice. "But yes, as soon as we can. Idath is just outside the city, we need to wait until he's gone, then we can hurry back to Elphame."

Lir swallowed hard. Isolde's eyes widened at the name.

"You two stay here again, I'll check to make sure he's gone."

Lir and Isolde muttered to each other as Lir helped her mount his horse instead of Epona, and Tristan crept back to his hiding place in the edge of the wood.

One foot in front of the other, as slow and silent as fog, Tristan steadily eased his head out from behind the tree. The plain was clear. Tristan scanned the horizon. If he squinted, he thought he could just make out the blurry shapes of Idath and his company and captive.

He returned to the clearing, not caring for noise anymore.

"They've gone, come," he said, mounting Epona. Lir and Isolde trotted up beside him. "Let's go."

The trio rode out, Tristan first, still scanning the plain for signs of danger. All looked clear, and he gestured for Lir and Isolde to follow him.

Suddenly, a blast of fire knocked Tristan from Epona. She whinnied and reared back in fright. A chilling laugh reached his ears.

"*Tristan!*" Isolde jumped down from her horse and ran to him. Lir reached to grab her and haul her back, but missed.

"What have we here?" sneered a voice, and Tristan looked up to find the tall, pale man approach. Erlik, beaten and bruised, struggled against his bonds behind him, wincing in pain.

"H-how—" Tristan stammered. He tried so hard to quell the tremor in his voice, but it was almost impossible. Every crumb of air seemed to have been sucked out of his lungs. Cold washed over him like a deluge.

"A cloaking spell hid our presence from your eyes. We heard you talking from the wood."

"*Sister!*" a sick-looking woman tilted her head at Isolde, then sneered. "Wretched girl! How dare you leave the Keep? After everything I've done for you!"

Isolde helped Tristan to his feet but said nothing.

"Maleagant, bind them," Idath said. "They can join my brother in his torment."

Erlik writhed harder, mumbling something through his gag. Idath gave him a filthy look. The other man – slimy, sycophant-looking with a nervous twitch in his eye – waved his staff, and Tristan felt his hands snap behind his back, rough rope wrapping itself around his wrists.

"And the horseman," Idath barely had to raise his head to look at Lir, still mounted. His horse circled nervously. Lir seemed to be taking everything he had not to bolt. Tristan prayed his courage held. Idath sniffed disdainfully.

"Mortal," he said. "Imperfect. Insignificant. The scraps from the Smith's forge, barely worthy of note, and certainly not worthy of Albion. Maleagant, dispose of it."

Maleagant had been listening to Idath disparage mortals, and a sour look twisted his face. His shoulders hunched, and sullenly he clenched his raised hand into a fist.

Lir's head snapped to the side, neck broken.

Isolde turned her face sharply away, releasing a low moan. Tristan couldn't speak nor move. He watched, almost in slowed time, as Lir's body slumped and fell from the horse. The beast fled, too skittish to remain any longer.

"You killed him," Tristan said in an empty voice. Idath gave him a disgusted look and approached Epona now.

She shied away as the dead man approached, her ears back and her eyes wide and rolling. Her teeth bared.

"A fine horse," he said, somewhat approvingly. "Elvish in breed, I believe. It would be a shame to kill it."

"Don't touch her!" Tristan found his voice, and was answered with a blow to the face. He felt his nose pop, and blood gushed into his mouth.

"Tristan, no!" Isolde's voice was full of fear and sorrow. "Leave him alone!"

Idath dragged her to her feet and thrust her towards Maleagant, who bound her tightly.

Tristan suddenly felt something hot around his wrists. He withheld his cry of surprise, and his eyes found Erlik. The prince's eyes were locked on his, and he gave the tiniest nod.

He used his magic! Tristan realised. *But why on me, and not himself?* Idath wasn't looking at him. *I need a distraction.*

Erlik seemed to hear him. He writhed against his bonds and managed to work one arm free, and the gag slipped from his mouth. He thrust his hand towards his brother, and he erupted in black flame.

"Run, Tristan!" Erlik bellowed over Idath's scream of rage and pain. Tristan halted. He sought Isolde, who struggled against Maleagant's grip. Erlik gave a grunt of frustration. "I'll look after the girl, just *go!*"

Epona bit Tristan's arm, catching only cloth, and pulled him away. Tristan staggered. But the flames around the tall man were dying down.

Hating himself, Tristan leapt up onto Epona.

"Go, Tristan! *Now!*"

Bolts of fire and deadly daggers whirled past his head as Epona sped away. He ducked as a flaming arrow whistled past his ear, and he desperately patted down the fire; the smell of burning hair stung his eyes.

Epona ran, faster than he'd ever ridden a horse in his life, until the anguished screams and yells fell out of earshot, and Elphame's gates came into view.

"You knew that boy, brother," Idath sneered, staring after the retreating horse.

"He was a coward, he fled," Maleagant said with a cold laugh, holding Isolde tight enough to bruise her.

"At my brother's instruction," Idath said, turning his eyes on Erlik, who wheezed in pain. Idath approached him and forced him upright, then backhanded him across the face. Erlik staggered, broken body screaming in protest.

"Who was he?"

Erlik straightened and said nothing, but spat a glob of blood in Idath's face.

Idath wiped the offence away. He re-tied the bonds, and

shoved the gag back into Erlik's mouth.

"Come," Carman said. "When we return to the Keep, I will have words with my little sister."

Isolde trembled. Erlik tried to catch her eye. He intended to keep his promise to the boy, though he wasn't exactly sure why. But the girl kept her gaze fixed on the ground, too terrified to speak another word.

CHAPTER 39

"He has changed, Lightfoot"

MAB THREW HER cloak around her shoulders as she strode through the corridors. The journey to the Iron Keep would be long, but enough time had been wasted already. Thomas would be preparing the army to defend the city from whatever vile Annwyn-spawned creatures could attack. The last battle for control of the city had not been easy, but it had been simpler. So much simpler. Seelie against unseelie. Now...

Morrigan would receive her message and command her armies to do the same; but this task, Mab thought, she must undertake alone.

"Your Grace?"

She stopped in her tracks, and her head snapped to the noise.

Lightfoot approached her meekly from a doorway. She must have walked right past him.

Yet, as he approached, she'd never seen him look so afraid of her before. The sight unnerved her. Why would he have reason to fear her?

"The remedy for the Mortasheen sickness has been distributed among the people. There is a little left. The herbalist is awaiting a shipment of burdock root. Here, you should take this."

He handed her a small bottle of red liquid, which she

uncorked to gingerly sniff at. She coughed.

"Most potent," she said. Lightfoot's lips wobbled into a smile.

"That means it's strong," he said. "There... is also something else I wished to discuss with you."

Mab tilted her head and gestured for him to continue.

"The Dragon King, Your Grace," he said. The words echoed sharply in the empty hallway. Mab said nothing. She straightened her back and tipped her head back slightly.

"I fear his influence over you may be clouding your better judgement," Lightfoot went on. "I... I understand you have some affection for him, but—"

"I have not sacrificed the love for my people for the love I bear for Erlik," Mab said coldly.

"Love?" Lightfoot sighed and ran a hand over his face. "Mab, please remember how the seelie suffered under his rule. How can you love a man like that?"

"He has changed, Lightfoot," she said. "He is not the same man he once was."

"He will never change, Mab," Lightfoot's voice grew hard. "Men like that don't change."

"You are wrong," she said, the braziers in the corridor dimming. "Look at the good he has done. He could have left that first night I freed him. He could have left many times since. But he has stayed by my side, he has even saved Thomas's life, without thought of reward or advantage. Tell me those are not the actions of a changed man?"

"You're blinded by your emotions, Mab."

"And *you* are blinded by your prejudice."

"He's brought the Lord of the Dead to our very doorstep!" Lightfoot argued. "Perhaps it's best to let Idath keep him—"

"No, Lightfoot!" Mab said. "Even if we let Idath keep Erlik, even if we let him torture him to madness and death, Idath will not stop there. He will come for Elphame next, then for Tír-Na-Nóg, and then anyone else who stands in his way, until he rules Albion as a wasteland of salt and ash and bone."

"How can you be so sure?" Lightfoot asked. "He may just

keep Erlik alive to torture, and leave Elphame and Tír-Na-Nóg alone."

Mab shook her head, her jaw set in anger. "I will not leave him with that beast," she said in an icy voice.

Lightfoot sighed. His shoulders dropped.

"I care about you, Mab, as if you were my own daughter," he said quietly. "I don't want to see you hurt again. And I know what you plan to do."

Mab hesitated, and Lightfoot took her silence as an opening.

"I know you plan to go back to the Iron Keep alone," he said. "Please, for the sake of Elphame, for the sake of my own health, take Thomas with you."

"I am not a child, Lightfoot," Mab began, her eyes averted. Lightfoot nodded knowingly.

"I know, Mab," he said. "But you appointed Thomas your Champion. Let him act as one. Think on it, before you do something rash."

He bowed and left her. Light returned as the braziers glowed warmly again. Mab heaved a sigh and closed her eyes.

Foolish girl, she thought to herself. She gave herself a mental shake and regained her composure, then strode off to the barracks to find Thomas.

But a more youthful voice drew her attention instead. A desperate cry for help.

"MOTHER!"

Tristan's voice pierced Thissy's heart like an arrow. She ran out of the stable, having just finished saddling a horse, and found Tristan bursting into the courtyard alone. Blood streamed from his nose.

"Tristan!" she ran to him and grabbed the rein to calm Epona. She could almost feel the fear emanating from both. "What happened? Where's Lir? And Isolde?"

"Mother—" Tristan dismounted, staggering when his feet hit the ground. "Idath—Idath was there, and a man and a woman, I think she said it was her sister, they took Isolde! We have to get her back!"

"Tristan, be calm," Thissy took his arms to steady him, and put one hand over his obviously broken nose to heal it. Tristan brushed away the drying blood around his mouth.

"They had Erlik as well—he's the reason I escaped! He distracted them, but they killed Lir and—" Tristan babbled on.

"Oh, Tristan," she pulled him close and hugged him. "You're lucky to be alive!"

"It doesn't matter about me!" he pushed his mother away. "We have to save Isolde and Erlik!"

"I am glad someone agrees with me," Mab's voice rang through the courtyard. Thissy turned to see her descending the steps towards them. "How did you escape, Tristan?"

"Erlik—" Tristan swallowed and began again. His guilt overwhelmed him. "Erlik used his magic to free me, and distracted them so I could escape."

Mab sighed, and her face softened.

"I told Lightfoot he had changed," she said quietly, more to herself. "Erlik's sacrifice has bought us a little more time, but Idath intends to use him as bait in a trap to lure me to the Keep. Nevertheless, we must rescue him, and Isolde. Idath will no doubt exact revenge on him, and Carman is less than gentle with her sister."

"What is it? What's happening?" a badger's claws clicked upon the stone as Broc bounded towards the group. Thissy stared at him.

"Broc!" Tristan greeted the badger, ignoring his mother's confused mumble. "Isolde's sister has taken her back to the Iron Keep!"

The badger's eyes grew wide with fright. "Carman has Isolde? That *witch!*" Broc snarled, then shrank back from Mab. "Oh, no offence meant, Your Grace," he added meekly.

Mab scowled.

"None taken, as I am no witch," she said. "But I am afraid I have had no chance to look into reversing your curse."

"It's fine, Your Grace, you've had much more important

things to worry about than a silly old badger," Broc said, without sarcasm.

Mab nodded, this time with a smile.

"Thank you for understanding," she said. "Perhaps once I change you back, you could assist Lightfoot with steward duties? He could use an apprentice."

Then her demeanour changed to one of business-like authority. "Now, I had thought to embark to the Iron Keep alone, but through another's wisdom, I have come to realise that would be a foolish endeavour. Come, we must find Thomas as soon as possible."

CHAPTER 40

"Your face offends me"

"**A**GAIN! HIT HIM again!"

Erlik couldn't see Carman, with his head bowed low and his eyes closed in exhaustion, but he could picture the expression on that beautiful, heartless face. She seemed to have recovered once they'd returned to the Keep, and Maleagant had given her some tincture to soothe her unsettled stomach.

Erlik stood upright, stripped to the waist with his arms chain-bound above his head.

The whip lashed across his back again. Erlik bit down on his tongue to stop his scream escaping. He felt the tickle of blood trickling down his back. He slumped forward. Only the chains kept him on his feet, but even that was crippling; broken ribs screamed at him, and a burning sensation filled his whole torso. *Just to lie down and rest...*

Maleagant's lashes had been biting enough, but once Idath had taken hold of the whip, Erlik felt like every sting flayed off his flesh. He had so far managed to stay silent, though he feared his restraint was about to snap.

The return to the Iron Keep had been suspiciously short. They'd brought no horses, and Erlik feared he wouldn't be able to walk all the way back without a show of weakness. Despite that, it seemed they'd been walking for less than an hour when the skull-like Keep came into view. No doubt Idath's eagerness to cause unspeakable pain to his brother had come to fruition, and he'd cast some Annwyn-borne magic to get them there all the faster.

He pitied the girl – Isolde, he remembered. She hadn't said another word during the journey, but he could almost taste the fear rising from her. Her hands had shaken so badly, Carman could barely tie a rope around them.

Once they'd arrived at the Iron Keep, Erlik and Isolde had been led through the dungeon, the massive room filled with hideous torture devices, spikes and wheels and racks and a huge upright coffin lined with needles. Erlik repressed a shiver as he'd passed them. He couldn't recall these items ever being here when he was younger. These must be Maleagant's devices, sequestered away in the darkest, most hideous corner of a keep already dripping with blood.

Isolde sat in a cramped cage on her own, watching Erlik's flogging with wide eyes, fearing her turn under the vicious bite of the whip. Yet so far, Idath had taken pleasure in torturing only his brother, and the vile company appeared to have forgotten about the girl. For now.

"Fetch the brand," he heard Idath say suddenly, and Erlik's head snapped up. There was an eager shuffling of feet, and the *shing* of something heavy and metallic being removed from a fire. Idath appeared in front of Erlik, and his stoic face showed no joy or satisfaction, though Erlik knew he was enjoying every sick moment of this. Unlike Carman, who appeared at his side to hand him a large, glowing brand, failing to hide her cruel smile. Erlik couldn't read the backwards word on the brand, and he swallowed hard and tipped his head back as he glared at his brother.

Idath's face twisted as he thrust the brand forward onto Erlik's chest. The scream that he'd managed to contain for hours now ripped from his mouth without control. His flesh sizzled and seared as the brand moulded onto his skin.

Idath pulled the hot metal away, and Erlik slumped, panting and moaning in agony. His head flopped forward and his damp brow creased when he read the word now scarred into his flesh from upside down.

Kinslayer.

Slowly, Erlik lifted his head and glared at Idath. With the mask of hatred gone, the Lord of the Dead held no emotion on his face again, but Carman ran her tongue over her teeth.

"What should we do to him next?" she asked eagerly. Erlik threw her a filthy look, but didn't have the energy to muster a sarcastic remark.

"Let him rest," Idath said. Both Maleagant and Carman looked at him, and even Erlik frowned. "Put him in a cell for the night. Then we shall begin again in the morning. He is the lure that will draw the Heart of Magic Itself to me, he cannot be destroyed yet; the Heart will know, and will not come. Not even to retrieve his body. But if there is a chance it believes it can save him, then it will try."

"Did you hear that?" Carman took hold of Erlik's face and dug her fingers into his cheeks. He swung feebly in his chains. "She won't come for your broken body if we kill you now."

Erlik tried to spit in her face, but his mouth was too dry. Instead, he stayed silent and stared her down. She broke first, and looked away, thrusting him away from herself.

"What about Isolde?" Maleagant's voice rang through the dungeon. Isolde's head snapped up, having hid her eyes from Erlik's torture.

"She has to be punished for leaving," Carman said. "Fetch her forward, Maleagant."

"No..." Erlik managed, though it came as an exhausted croak. All heads turned to him. "Leave her."

"You want to take the punishment for her, Father?" Maleagant sneered. Even Idath's lip curled.

"Such weakness, brother," he said coldly. "Oh, but you promised the boy you would protect her, did you not? Bring me the girl. Put my brother in the dungeon, so he can listen to her screams."

Too tired and sore to struggle, Erlik could only silently curse Idath as Maleagant unbound him and dragged him away.

✧　✧　✧

THE CELL WAS filthy, dark, and damp. A quiet scuffling told Erlik that he was also sharing the dungeon with several rats. He considered hunting them down and snapping their necks just to get some peace and quiet, but he was too weary to even move.

He sat in his windowless cell, deprived of sleep, food and water, and thought of Mab. She must have sent a message to Morrigan by now, but it seemed Idath would prefer to spend longer torturing his brother, rather than assaulting his former city. Erlik sighed heavily, and the scabbed brand on his chest cracked and started to bleed again. He swore softly and tried to stem the blood with the single scratchy blanket he'd found in the corner.

A shrill scream rang through the dungeon. Erlik suspected it could be heard from the other end of the Keep. He didn't know Isolde well, but he wouldn't wish her fate on anyone. She was barely out of girlhood, yet she faced torture from the Lord of the Dead himself. A strange sense of protectiveness came over him.

"Erlik?"

His head snapped up at once, and he scrambled forward to clasp the bars of his prison. His hands sizzled around the cold iron and he let go at once with a hiss.

"Mab?" he breathed. "What are you doing here? How did you get in? You shouldn't have come!"

"Hush my love, I am not truly here," she explained in a whisper. "I am here in spirit only; my physical form is still in Elphame."

He reached through the bars to touch her, and his hand sailed gently through hers. A ghost in the dark.

"I cannot stay long, I do not have much time in this form," she said. "I wanted to be sure you were still hale. And to tell you that I am coming to save you."

"What?" Erlik stood, and winced when his body

agonisingly protested. He kneeled again. "No, Mab! It's what Idath wants, it's too dangerous! You can't come here!"

"I will not be alone," she said softly. "There will be others. Tristan is insisting we come for Isolde, but he wants to repay you for saying his life as well."

Erlik felt a surge of surprise. *Rhymer's boy?*

"Stay strong, my love," she said. "I will come for you."

Her image faded, and Erlik reached out again, as though to grab the remainder of her essence and keep it with him. *Stay strong, my love...* her words echoed in his head. He wasn't entirely sure if he could do as she asked. She had always been stronger than him.

The dungeon doors rattled and swung open, and Carman entered, dragging Isolde behind her.

Carman flung Isolde into the cell opposite Erlik, and the girl cringed and cowered in the corner, clutching her hands close to her chest. Every finger looked broken. Her eyes puffy and face red from sobbing.

"Who were you talking to?" Carman turned and glared at Erlik.

"The rats," he snapped. "I prefer their company to yours."

Carman's cold laugh rang out. Erlik felt rage bubble inside his chest. Despite the agony in his torso, he lunged through the bars for her, but she stepped back. The cold iron sizzled against his flesh, and he stepped away.

"Begone, bitch," he spat sullenly. "Your face offends me."

Carman tutted and mockingly shook her head.

"And here I thought we could spend another lovely night together," she said.

"Don't pretend you wanted this any more than I did," Erlik growled in response. "You seduced me under the guise of my wife for sport, and look where it got you. A little magic in your fingertips, and a half-breed whelp in your belly."

Carman said nothing, but ran her fingers along the bars. Erlik watched her, wanting to break them all as she broke her sister's. He sat on the floor, trying not to wince as he pressed his lacerated back to the stone wall.

Erlik took the moment to stare at her. *This vile woman carries my child,* he thought bitterly, feeling sick at the notion. *Another bastard.* She certainly looked unwell. There were purple crescents under her eyes, and her grey hair looked lank and far less lustrous than before. Erlik wondered with morbid curiosity about the child; he'd never bedded a human before, only seelie or unseelie. Would the child have magic? Or would it be like its mother; powerless, bitter, and short-lived?

"What are you staring at?" Carman's sharp voice interrupted his thoughts.

"I was picturing your head on a spike," he lied, and offered her a twisted, false smile. Carman laughed.

"What an awful thing to say," she said with a pout. "You hate me now, but in nine moons time—"

"Five."

Carman paused. "Five what?"

"Five moons time," Erlik sighed, almost too tired to explain. "Children borne from Old Gods mature faster. Even if it doesn't have my magic, it still has my blood. Therefore, *five* months."

He couldn't be certain of the exact timespan of course; but by past experience, it certainly made sense to believe so. Five months, six months at the most, and yet another child with his eyes would exist in Albion.

And not a single one of them with the one woman he truly loved. Erlik hated himself, suddenly and entirely.

"You're lying!" Carman snapped, looking suddenly unnerved. Erlik laughed, although pain racked through him again.

"Why would I lie about that?" he asked. "You look upset, maybe you should go lie down. After all, you're going to need your rest."

Carman growled, her lip curling into a snarl.

"Have your fun now, King-In-Rags," she sneered. "Tomorrow, you'll be taken back to the dungeon, and Idath will use every device in there to torture you. We'll break your body and your mind, so when your precious she-wolf comes for you—" Carman gave a self-indulgent laugh. "*If* she comes for you, she'll find only a gibbering mess."

Erlik said nothing. His smirk had slipped, and he stared at her with a cold, if slightly worried, expression. Carman laughed at him.

"Sweet dreams, Dragon King," she said, and left him, alone and afraid, in his dark cell.

CHAPTER 41

"It can be lonely"

"YOUR GRACE?"

Morrigan looked up. She lowered her quill as her Master of Birds approached, a magpie perched calmly on his arm.

"What is it, Swiftwing?"

"A message from Her Majesty, Queen Mab," Swiftwing held out a small, rolled up parchment. The magpie chittered. Morrigan took the message and scanned it quickly.

She hummed for a few moments, then, eyes resting on a single word, her heart dropped like a stone, and she sank back into her seat.

Idath.

"Falconbane!" she called, and he appeared at her side at once. "Send runners to every unseelie village and spread the word. The Lord of the Dead has been resurrected. We must be prepared for war in case he strikes at Tír-Na-Nóg."

"Idath *lives?*" Falconbane spluttered. Morrigan nodded.

"Resurrected," she grimly corrected. "He's taken up his old residence at the Iron Keep, and taken my father captive. Queen Mab intends to mount a rescue," she said. No one spoke, but a single word lingered on every lip like a drop of poison.

Why?

"We will stand with Elphame against whatever comes.

Brief the soldiers, and inform the civilians."

"At once, Your Grace."

Morrigan stood, and Falconbane hesitated.

"Your Grace?"

"If my uncle walks Albion again, it means that powerful magic has been invoked," she said thoughtfully. "Magic not of the Old Ways."

Morrigan paused and chewed her lip. Then moved away from her desk and strode towards the door.

"I need to speak with our librarian."

"Why, Your Grace?"

"To make sure she didn't burn my father's old books on necromancy."

✧   ✧   ✧

THOMAS SAT AT the head of the crescent-moon-shaped table, listening intently to the emissary that stood before him.

"News obviously travels fast," Lightfoot said suspiciously, sitting beside Thomas.

"The sorcerer Maleagant passed through our realm not two moons ago, with chaos in his wake. Our king has been observing his machinations in secret ever since."

"Why did you not send word?" Thomas asked.

"We were awaiting word from our spy. Unfortunately, he had been discovered and slaughtered by the sorcerer. We were not aware until his blood-drained body recently washed up on Achnahaird shore."

Thomas inclined his head to offer his condolences. Misthaven spies were regarded almost as highly as royalty for their ability to pass undetected. For Maleagant to have found the spy and killed him did not bode well.

"His Grace King Herne sent me here to inform Queen Mab of Maleagant's foul magic. But as I grew closer to Elphame, I heard of Maleagant's deeds. I have therefore come to offer, not fresh news, but aid."

"Your alliance to Elphame is both appreciated and accepted," said Thomas. "Return to your forest and your king, and thank him for his offer. We will certainly make use of your assistance in the coming days."

The warrior gave a short, respectful bow, and turned to leave, carrying his helmet under his arm. The impressive headpiece was adorned with the antlers of a stag, indicating his position in his army. Thomas watched the warrior of Herne leave, pondering the horned king himself.

"Thomas," Mab called from the door. "Come." Without another word, she beckoned him and vanished from sight.

"Lightfoot," Thomas leaned over to the steward. "I need you to see to the rest of the council matters. Accept any help on offer. I'll be going to the Iron Keep with Mab."

"As you say," Lightfoot nodded, then put his hand on Thomas's arm to halt him as he rose from his chair. "Look after her," he added. Thomas nodded soberly.

"WE MUST RIDE for the Iron Keep as soon as possible," Mab said, striding along the corridor towards the armoury. "We have already wasted enough time."

"Slow down, Mab," Thomas said. "Have you thought this through? We'll need soldiers to storm the Iron Keep. Maleagant and Idath are deadly enough, even *without* an army, and we don't know if they've summoned any more monsters from Annywn."

"We will not ride out with soldiers," she said. "If we arrive with an army, Idath will kill Erlik and Isolde before we even enter the Keep. We must rescue them *first*, then march on the Keep."

The Rhymer family walked behind her, and she could tell they all intended to go with her. Tristan insisted upon it, wanting to rescue Isolde. And she knew Thomas and Thissy would be loathe to see their son put himself in danger.

"And you're sure he received your message?" Tristan strode behind her with a determined, stony look on his face.

He clutched his new bow tightly.

Mab nodded.

"I am," she said, and said nothing more on the subject.

Once they'd entered the armoury, Thomas immediately approached the straw dummy bearing his heavy armour. Thissy took down a lightweight leather studded cuirass, easy enough for her to wear and still wield her magic.

"You are all certain in your intent to come with me?" she asked, and the room fell silent. All eyes turned to her.

"Of course," Thomas said, as though it were obvious. "Why wouldn't we?"

Mab smiled.

"I just wanted to be sure."

"Do you have a plan, my lady?" Thissy asked, buckling the leather armour around her chest, and turning to Thomas to help him tie the cords of his vambraces. Mab hesitated. Erlik had asked her something similar on their first night at the Keep. Her answer had been the same.

She shook her head, "No, I do not," she admitted. As soon as the words had left her mouth, she realised how foolish her actions had been. She had no plan on rescuing Erlik; she had been led by blind vengeance.

"Well," Thomas said slowly. "You've been to the Keep before. How should we get inside? Once we do, how do we find Erlik? Once you find him, how do we escape?"

"The tunnel," came a voice from the door.

Mab turned to find Broc clambering up onto a table. He pushed a couple of daggers aside and sat down with a thump.

"I told you of it, when we first met, do you remember?" Broc asked Mab. "The tunnel that Isolde opened, in the pantry. It's how me and Isolde escaped."

Mab's face lit up.

"Perfect, we can enter and leave the Keep without having to go through the front gates," she said. "Broc, will you tell us how to find the entrance?"

Broc paused, then nodded. He scratched behind his ears with a hind leg.

"I'll come with you, Your Grace," he said. Mab gave him an uneasy smile.

"I appreciate the gesture, Broc," she said gently. "But I cannot ask you to come with us. You are no soldier, you are a steward. More than that, a *badger*."

"I can still fight—" Broc began weakly.

"I am truly sorry, Broc," she said. "You can be most helpful now by providing us with the entrance to the tunnel."

Broc sighed. "You're right," he said. "I'm no use to you in this shape."

As Thissy laced Mab into her silver armour – light and engraved with vines – Broc outlined the entrance of the tunnel to Thomas.

"Thank you," Mab said at last to them all. "I do not know how I will repay this loyalty, but I will try. Come, we must be on our way as soon as possible."

MAB PATTED THE neck of her stag as she waited for the others to mount. The beast seemed almost as eager as its mistress to be on the move, and pawed at the ground often. She clicked her tongue when Tristan's horse tried to chew his sleeve rather than let him ride it. The sturdy horse snorted and finally allowed Tristan to mount, with much muttered swearing.

"Why must we ride?" Tristan called out. Mab turned her gaze on him. "Isn't there a way you can use your magic to get us there more quickly?"

Mab nodded grimly, "There is a way, but for me alone. I would need to wait for you all to catch up with me. It is also rather painful, and I would rather conserve my strength for the battles ahead. We ride together."

Tristan swallowed hard.

"I'm ready," he called. Mab nodded again. She waited until Thissy had settled onto her grey mare before kicking her stag into movement. The thundering of hooves was almost enough to make Tristan lose his grip, but he held on tight, and squeezed his legs around the horse as it followed the others.

Tristan had only ever ridden Epona; this horse seemed to have an agenda of its own. He felt as though he were flying, though possibly the most uncomfortable flight he could ever have imagined. His thighs chafed against the leather saddle, and the cold air slapped against his face as the city streets rushed past. The main gates passed by, and suddenly he faced the vast expanse of the open moors, and Elphame slowly vanished below the horizon.

"WE WILL REST here tonight," Mab said, as she tied her stag's reins to a tree branch. "You are all weary from the ride, and I would rather you gather your strength tonight."

They had stopped riding a little while ago, and everyone except Tristan had dismounted. He was cold, stiff, and extremely uncomfortable.

Once his feet hit solid earth, he staggered. His hands were tender and red from holding the reins so tightly. The muscles in his legs had seized up and felt as though they were on fire as blood rushed back into them. He moaned in pain and sat on a grassy hillock, kneading the flesh of his thighs to get the feeling back into them.

Mab curled her hands, almost a beckoning gesture, and branches and roots grew with creaking ancientness into a cage around them. With a clever pulse of magic, the sylvan cage became fabric and stitching. Tristan stared when he realised; she was making a windbreak for them.

"The nights are cold here," she explained, when she caught him looking.

"How far is the Iron Keep, my lady?" Thissy asked, bringing forth an armful of firewood.

"Not far now," she said from the mouth of the tent. "We should arrive in the morning."

Looking into the distance, she let out a soft sigh and closed her eyes.

THE NIGHT CLOSED in around them. Thomas had disappeared for a while, and returned with a couple of rabbits. Thissy skinned and dressed them, and Tristan set about making up the fire. He struggled with sparking the flint, until he remembered. He sensed Mab's eyes on him.

Tristan cleared his throat and rolled up his sleeves. Hoping his mother and father were too busy focusing on their own tasks of laying out the bedrolls, he closed his eyes and concentrated.

He hovered his hands over the kindling. A tinny buzz sounded in his ears. His fingers grew numb and stiff with cold.

"Do not exert yourself," came Mab's voice. "Men require years of training before they can use magic as freely as women. It will exhaust you if you try."

Tristan felt his face flush. He took his hands away.

"I just... wanted to try," he mumbled. Mab smiled and approached.

"Fire is always easiest to channel first," she said, kneeling beside him. "Given the initial manifestation of your powers, I believe it will be easier for *you* to channel it through your bow. Remember when you set the arrow aflame?"

She offered her hand, giving him her dark, strange smile. Thissy and Thomas had stopped to watch. Mab's skin was cool, and as he placed his hand in hers, he could feel the gentle pricks of her nails against his wrist. He pushed a shudder away.

"Of course, if you tap into magic directly from the source, it will be easier to summon," she said, nodding pointedly at his other hand, which had been resting on his thigh. Tristan frowned and followed her gaze. He yelped and fell back. Only Mab's strong grip kept their connection. His left hand was engulfed in a flickering white flame. He lifted it closer. He could feel the warmth on his face, and the white light reflecting in his eyes, but he felt no pain. No stench of burnt flesh, nothing. Only a gentle tickling, like dipping his hand into a trickling brook or running through a cool breeze.

Eyes wide, he turned back to Mab, who smiled. She guided his hand down to the kindling, and it ignited. She let go, and

Tristan's hand immediately extinguished, though the embers took root in the wood and grew into a comfortable campfire.

Tristan flexed his fingers multiple times, caught between staring agog at them, and at Mab.

Night settled in, and their portions of rabbit had been cooked and consumed. Tristan began to feel his eyelids grow heavier.

The firelight grew small despite his insistent prodding. Thomas and Thissy drifted off to sleep, but Mab stayed awake, a sentinel statue at the edge of their camp, looking out onto the moors.

Tristan watched her, caught between fascination and fear. There was an ancientness about her that terrified him. How long had she walked this earth, he wondered. How many lifetimes had she witnessed? How many loves had come and gone, flickering out like candles in the breeze.

She turned to look at him, as though she could sense his eyes on her. He looked away quickly, embarrassed to have been caught staring. Her breath was a gentle scarf of mist in the night, and she sat down beside him.

"You are curious about my life?" she asked simply. She didn't sound angry. Tristan almost breathed a sigh of relief.

"I—yes, Your Grace," he said slowly, cautious of his words. "I was wondering what it must be like to live forever."

"Please, call me Mab."

She paused before answering his question.

"It can be lonely," she said. It sounded so simple, yet sadness coloured her tone.

"My…" Tristan paused, then felt bravery grip him. "My father told me about Erlik. About what he did. To you."

The words seemed to halt themselves before escaping his lips. Mab turned her crystal gaze on him.

"Oh?" she prompted, as though she knew this was not the end of his questioning. Tristan fidgeted with a loose thread.

After a short pause, "Why do you want to save him?" he asked. Mab raised an eyebrow at him.

"That is not what you wanted to ask," she said, with a

ghost of a smile twitching her lips.

"I—" Tristan baulked. He shook his head. "No, I'm sorry. I don't mean to pry."

"'Tis nothing to apologise for," she said, and Tristan had never seen her look so kind or speak so softly. He suddenly felt warm, comforted, like she was a firm but loving aunt in whom he could confide.

"I... I wondered," Tristan licked his lips and began again. "I was wondering why you love him?"

Mab looked up at the sky. A blanket of cold blue diamonds burned above them. Standing, she approached the edge of their camp again. Tristan wondered if, despite her words, he had struck a particularly raw nerve.

"Did you know that wolves mate for life?" she asked. Tristan blinked. Mab looked over her shoulder at him, and Tristan shook his head. Mab offered him a mysterious smile.

"Get some sleep, Tristan," she said. "You will need your strength for tomorrow."

Tristan nodded and lay down beside the last glowing embers. He kept his eyes on her until sleep overtook him, and he drifted into dreams of wolves and wild woodlands.

CHAPTER 42

"It appears the witch has tamed her wild dog."

ERLIK THREW HIMSELF into a waking state with a sharp intake of breath. He slowly sat up and rubbed his eyes with his knuckle. With no idea whether or not the sun had risen yet, he ran his hand through his tangled hair and tried to ignore the rumbling of his empty stomach. Though it would be impossible for him to starve to death, it would still be a deeply unpleasant experience.

Groaning, he used the wall to help him stand, his mind too busy to try and make sense of his situation. In the opposite cell, Isolde hadn't woken yet. She lay twitching and whimpering in her sleep, twisted fingers blossomed in clouds of purple and blue. Erlik felt a twinge of guilt, and, selfishly, fear of what would happen to *him* next. Perhaps it would have been better if Mab had left him in the cage.

No, he thought immediately. *I would endure a thousand nights of torture at my brother's hands if it meant I got to be with Mab again.*

He paced, happening to glance down at the brand on his chest. It had scabbed over during the night, and Erlik silently blessed his quick healing. His fingers gently touched the hardened knot of bloodied flesh, and he winced. The wounds on his back didn't pain him so much now; the humiliation burned more, so palpable it could be bottled.

At the soft clatter of keys, Erlik stopped pacing. The bright flare of a torch burned into his eyes. Maleagant appeared first, carrying the torch and a jangling set of keys. Carman followed, wearing the despicable smirk that Erlik longed to wipe away with a well-placed slap. Idath came last, every bit as cold and stoic as only the dead could be.

"Good morning," Erlik said, voice filled with sour sarcasm.

Carman gave him a sneering laugh; he reciprocated with a filthy look. How could he ever have thought that face beautiful? He realised now that it was a cruel mask, a harsh, painted facade of beauty. Even when she smiled, it looked like sneering, like she believed everyone to be beneath her. She strode past Erlik's cage and rattled a dagger against the bars of Isolde's prison. The girl awoke at once, releasing a soft yelp of fright as she did so, and shrank back.

"Easy, sister," Carman said in what Erlik assumed was meant to be a soothing voice. "We're not here for you. You can rest for now. But you need to learn your lesson, so tomorrow, we'll heal up your fingers so you can get back to work."

Erlik's heart dropped into his stomach.

Maleagant unlocked his cage and Idath stepped inside. Erlik took an instinctive step back, then silently cursed. Idath cast his icy blue gaze over Erlik, taking in the numerous wounds he'd inflicted.

"How well are you healing, little brother?" Idath asked, voice emotionless as ever. Erlik frowned.

"Oh, fine," he snapped. "Thank you for your concern."

"You cannot use your silver tongue to get out of this, Erlik," Idath said.

"Perhaps we should cut it out instead," Carman smirked. Erlik glowered at her.

"So you can keep it for yourself, whore?" he asked. Idath backhanded him, and he staggered back several steps. His body cried out, the bruising around his torso still flared in an angry display of colour.

"Don't hurt him!" Isolde cried from her cell. All eyes

turned to her. She hesitated, then shrank back into the darkness. Erlik's brow creased slightly, then he wiped the blood from his mouth.

Idath said nothing, and merely circled him with a twisted look of disgust.

"You say her name in your sleep," Maleagant said quietly. Erlik's blood turned to ice. He knew exactly who he meant; he dreamed of Mab most nights.

"And?" he asked in what he hoped was an offhand voice.

"You care for it," Idath muttered. Erlik wasn't sure if Idath deliberately referred to Mab as "it" to antagonise him, or if he genuinely believed she wasn't real. Either answer was enough to cause him to despise his brother even further.

"That's no secret, Idath," Carman jeered. "That's how I was able to seduce him so easily. He likes her face too much to complain whenever he sees it."

"And look where that got you," Erlik snapped. "Carrying a bastard you don't even understand." He turned to face his brother. "Why do you associate with them, brother? They're nothing but petty thieves."

"Then you should appreciate the familiarity, *Attercop Aetheling*," Idath said, and snatched him by the arm and marched him from his cell.

Carman made a cooing noise when he passed her, and Erlik reached out to grab her throat, but Idath clicked his fingers and Erlik felt his hands snap behind his back and press together. A thick coil of rope wrapped around his wrists and bound him tight. He struggled to move his hands, but the knots stretched and strained and held firm.

"Keep walking, Father," the sorcerer said coolly. Erlik locked eyes with him.

"I've killed one of my sons before," he said in a low voice. "You won't be the first."

"You're in no position to make threats," Maleagant responded. Erlik leaned in close to Maleagant and whispered to him.

"You don't know what you've unleashed," he said. "You're

walking a dangerous path, Maleagant, and you're playing with things you don't understand."

"I can control him," Maleagant sneered. Erlik glanced at Idath and noticed his small eyes narrow in hatred.

A flicker of an idea fluttered through Erlik's brain like a bat. Idath despised being leashed, ever since their youth.

"No one can control him," he said. He silenced when Idath pushed him into an unpleasantly familiar room. The torture devices glinted evilly in the dim light. Erlik exhaled slowly as he tried to decide which one he would most like to avoid.

THE LASHINGS DIDN'T last as long this time. Erlik eventually lost count of how many times the whip kissed his flesh. The old wounds opened again and bled freely down his back. Once, Carman brought him a cup of water and pressed it to his lips, but he gave her a filthy look and spat back at her; it only earned him another lashing.

At last, when the lashings subsided, and Erlik slumped forward with only a trace of consciousness, his chains were loosened and he was allowed to collapse. The room spun around him. He swallowed the foul words he yearned to throw at them, knowing it would only result in another lash.

Instead, he lay on the floor, panting like a weary dog. He groaned when he tried to move. He expected them to laugh, but no one made a sound. He felt spidery hands lift him up and plant him on his feet. Erlik staggered and fell forward, but Idath caught and steadied him. Erlik frowned and forced his eyes open. What was this show of brotherly affection?

Idath looked down at his brother, and Erlik stared back at him, brow creased with agony and confusion. Idath said nothing, and walked Erlik backwards until he felt his legs hit a chair. Idath pushed on his shoulders, forcing him to sit. At once, Maleagant clicked his fingers, and the rope once more sprang up, binding his wrists and ankles to the arms and legs of the chair.

Too tired to feel fear, Erlik looked up at his brother and

gave him a confused look.

"If you want information from me," he asked. "I don't know anything."

"No one is arguing that," Idath said, donning a heavy gauntlet. "But I need no information from you, brother. I torture you, not for secrets, but for vengeance."

"Haven't you already exacted it enough already?" Erlik asked, his eyes watching the gauntlet with apprehension. The knuckles were hugely prominent, and he didn't like the way Idath kept flexing his fist. Idath looked down at him, and Erlik found himself straining against the ropes that bound him to the chair.

Idath's fist came like a war hammer to the face. Erlik's head snapped to the side. He felt his nose pop and spurt blood. Yet a wave of warmth washed over him, and he slowly looked up to see Maleagant shrouding him in golden light. He frowned, and his nose gave an unpleasant crack as it snapped back into place. Was he... *healing* him? Why?

As Idath struck another blow, Erlik suddenly understood through a haze of excruciating pain. For every strike Idath administered, Maleagant would heal him, so the pain would keep coming. An unending cycle, until one of them got bored or tired. And Idath had the stamina of the Old Gods. This could last forever, if he wanted it to.

The hours turned to days, it seemed. Erlik tried everything to make his torment end. Bribery, blackmail, threats, persuasion. But they were either too clever or too cruel, and none of them cared.

The blows concentrated on his face, breaking his jaw and nose more times than he could have counted. There had been no pause, no relent, no chance to rest. Again and again the beatings came, Idath seemed to have no end of hatred he wanted to inflict on his brother.

Erlik found it easier to simply retreat into the recesses of his mind, allow the madness to return, counteract every vicious blow from Idath with a gentle caress from Mab. Every glow of healing was a kiss from her soft lips. He kept his eyes closed, picturing her face, her delicate fingers dancing over his skin, her hand toying with his hair—

"Enough," came Carman's voice. Erlik cursed her mentally for breaking his concentration, and he opened his eyes but said nothing. Carman approached and ran her fingers across his cheek. He narrowed his eyes.

"You're weaker than I expected, Father," Maleagant said. Erlik looked up at him. "It appears the witch has tamed her wild dog."

"Don't... witch," Erlik mumbled to his knees. A tendril of bloody spittle dropped from his lips.

"You have gone soft," Idath said. "You would not have broken this easily years ago. Your time with it has made you frail, brittle. Like a mortal."

Erlik looked down again. He felt a growl building in his throat, but he was too tired to make a sound. Instead he sat still, listening to their taunts and their mockery, refusing to believe it.

"Did you think if you were kinder, then she would keep you?" Maleagant asked. Erlik kept his head down and closed his eyes.

"Why would I keep you?"

Erlik snapped his head up to see Carman had taken Mab's form and voice again. Her face looked false and unnatural, and it didn't suit the cruel look she'd adopted.

"You're a murderer," she continued. "A liar. A thief. I *despise* you."

Erlik screwed up his face and turned away.

"No," he mumbled. "Not true. Not her. *Not her.*"

Carman-Mab laughed, and Erlik forced himself to look at her. Before he could speak, she waved a hand in front of her face, and her appearance changed. She became a younger, black-haired girl in red, with a thin scar marring her cheek.

"*Kali?*"

Deep down, Erlik knew it wasn't her, that it *couldn't* be her, and that it was only a trick. But in his sleep and food deprived delirium, it was easier to accept her as real.

"You sent me away, Father," she said. After years of not hearing her voice, Erlik blinked at the sound. He had almost forgotten the curiously mad lilt. "You banished me and condemned me to death. What kind of wretched father *are* you?"

Her face changed again, to a man's this time. Erlik's eyes widened and he swallowed hard.

"You're a filthy hypocrite," Monstrance said bitterly, looking repulsed. "You reviled me for swearing loyalty to Mab and the seelie, and yet here you are, ready to suffer in service to her."

Erlik shook his head and kept his eyes down. *This isn't real!* He forced himself to think of Mab, but her face with that taunting, cruel smirk just swam before his eyes. *Don't... no... ignore it... not her!*

"Father," another voice punctured his thoughts, and he forced himself to look up. Malik shook his head, staring down at him with a disappointed face. "What have you done?"

"N-no..." Erlik stammered. His fragile resistance began to crack, and he felt splinters of uncertainty puncture his mind. Malik's face melted into another, and Erlik had to choke back a moan of guilty despair.

"You betrayed us all, Father," Corvus said. "You're cruel and evil. How could you kill me?"

"No more... please..."

"Father?"

Morrigan looked down at him with such pity in her eyes, he felt his heart would break.

"Father, how could you kill Corvus?" she asked. Erlik shook his head. "I loved him, I loved *you*. How could you betray me like that?"

"Morrigan, my princess, my sweet, my little girl... I'm sorry—please—"

"How could you?" she whispered. "How *could* you?"

"Please, no more!"

He moaned and lowered his head, desperate to loosen the cuffs around his wrists and curl up in a pitiful ball on the floor.

Frantic drumming filled his head, a low thrum, and he slowly realised it was his own heartbeat, pounding a frenzied tempo in his ears. He shook his head to rid himself of the memories that plagued him, but their voices echoed like mockingbirds.

"No more, I beg you!"

He opened his eyes.

Erlik sat alone in his cell. He looked around, but he was most definitely alone. Isolde wasn't there. He would have easily assumed it had all been a dream, but for the agonising pain of torn flesh all over his body. How did he get back here? Had he passed out?

"*A múirnín.*"

Erlik lifted his head slowly. His brain adamantly told him that it wasn't her, screamed that she wasn't real, she was just a vision, but when he saw her smile, his heart leapt into his throat. He returned her a small smile, and he couldn't help but believe it *was* her.

"Mab."

Still smiling, she kneeled beside him, cool fingers touching his cheek. He closed his eyes, taking in a sharp breath, inhaling her scent; he could feel her, smell her. This *must* be true. She said she'd come for him.

Her fingers left his cheek and crept down his arm, taking his hand and pulling him to his feet. His broken ribs screamed in protest, but he looked down at her once he had staggered to his feet, and she gave him a somewhat mischievous grin, and pulled him away.

At once, the walls of the cell melted away. Bright sunlight burned his eyes and a cool breeze tousled his hair. Mab pulled him through bustling crowds of seelie, celebrating some festival. He felt Mab's hand leave his, and saw her throw him a wickedly cheeky smile as she danced away into the crowd. He looked around, frowning, and looked down at himself.

He was clean, finely dressed, unmarked, and unscarred. He stared for a long time, not quite understanding. Was this a dream? It seemed so real.

Someone pushed past him and he stumbled forward. He

righted himself and prepared to glare at the insolent seelie, but he faltered at the wide grin the man gave him.

"Oh! Apologies, Your Grace," he said with a humble yet familiar air. "I didn't see you there."

He bounced away, laughing with the other seelie. Erlik stared after him. That seelie had greeted him… almost like a friend? It *had* to be a dream. The seelie despised him; none would *ever* speak to him so cordially.

He looked into the crowd and saw Mab dancing with juvenile delight. He had never seen her so happy and carefree. The smile on her face made the ageless queen seem somehow younger, brighter, less likely to set someone ablaze. Erlik moved towards her, drawn to her giddy happiness like a moth to a flickering candle.

Mab waved him over when she saw him, and pulled him into the crowd to dance with her. He laughed – he couldn't stop himself – and pulled his hands out of hers.

"I don't dance, Mab, you know that," he said, and she gave him a reassuring smile and stood on her tiptoes to kiss him. The softness of her lips startled him. If this was a dream, it was his most vivid yet. Unless… perhaps it wasn't a dream? Perhaps it was real? Maybe the Iron Keep had been a horrific nightmare. His doubt began to ebb, and as he gazed at Mab, he felt strangely detached, as though he might float away.

"Come," she said, and took his hand and led him away from the crowd, towards a raised platform where two carved wooden thrones sat awaiting them. Mab sat down in one and gestured for him to join her in the other. As he did so, he couldn't take his eyes off her; she was, in every way, perfect.

"You look beautiful," he said at last. His voice echoed weirdly, but he found he didn't care. Mab smiled at him and reached over to take his hand and press the palm to her mouth. She wrapped his hand around the kiss. Her eyes glittered warmly, so unlike their normal icy piercing darkness.

"Your Grace," her steward – Lightfoot, was it? – approached the platform, leading a small boy by the hand. Mab looked down and smiled at the boy. She stood and leaned forward to pick the child up, balancing him on her hip with expertly maternal care. Erlik stared at her, confused.

"What is the matter, little one?" she asked, laughing softly at him. The boy rubbed his eyes, as though just waking from a deep sleep.

"I couldn't sleep, *Mamai*," he mumbled softly.

Erlik froze.

He stood abruptly, and Mab looked at him in concern.

"Is something wrong, my love?" she asked. Erlik couldn't speak for a moment, and his limbs locked stiff.

"He—he's your son?" he managed to choke out. Mab gave a soft, silvery laugh.

"How much wine have you *had? Our* son, my love. Our little Merlin," she said, and gently nuzzled the boy's nose. He giggled, despite his obvious tiredness, and kissed his mother's cheek, arms around her neck.

Erlik felt his throat constrict. He staggered forward a step and stared at the boy. He was dark-haired and pale, like both of his parents – *parents?* – but he had inherited Mab's glittering eyes and the gentle contours of her face.

"We don't—I don't understand. Mab, this—this can't be—"

Erlik's heart thundered like a thousand galloping horses. Her son... *their* son... he was perfect. Everything he could ever want lay before him. Beloved of Mab, beloved of their son, beloved of their kingdom. He could stay in this dream world forever.

"This—this can't be real," Erlik said quietly. The sound of the cheering seelie pressed into his ears like pressure before a storm. It built behind his eyes and he dug the heels of his palms into his eyes, wanting to wake up from this twisted dream.

"Of course it's real, my love. How can you say that?" she said, reaching out to cup his cheek gently. He staggered back from her touch, shaking his head. Mab recoiled as though burned, and the look of hurt in her eyes shattered his already fragile heart.

"Erlik, what is it?" she asked.

"Papa?" Merlin blinked at him. Erlik moaned.

"Begone, phantoms," he said, throwing as much assertiveness into his shaking voice as he could muster.

He turned away and jumped down from the platform, pushing his way through the crowd.

"Erlik!" he heard Mab shouting his name but he ignored her, as much as it killed him. He heard her begging him to come back, to not leave her again. As he pushed through the crowds, the seelie faces began to twist and change into masks of loathing, each of them jeering at him, screaming for his head and his blood, and Mab's voice became a harsh *bean sídhe* wail. He put his hands over his head and crouched to his knees, screaming to drown out the noise of the angry crowd around him. He curled up on the ground as forests of legs pressed in around him, blocking out the warmth and the light, suffocating him, drowning him in hate and blood and fire.

"No! No more. No more!" he moaned. Their voices began to fade, and he dared to glance up. He was alone again, surrounded by darkness. No dim light of the dungeon, no sound, no smell, just him, alone in the void. He gulped and looked around, but there was nothing. He heard his own ragged breathing, and his racing heart thump in his ears.

Erlik pressed his palm against the ground. It felt hard and cold to the touch, like stone or metal, he wasn't certain which. He stood up again and took a nervous step forward.

As soon as his foot lifted, an unearthly and familiar scream pierced the darkness, and he spun around, his eyes darting in the pitch black, frantically seeking the light.

"Mab!" he would know her voice anywhere. "Mab, where are you?!"

"Erlik, help me!"

He twisted towards the sound and ran, stumbling, tripping over his own feet in desperation to reach her.

She screamed again, and there was a sickeningly wet thump, followed by silence, and he skidded to a halt.

"Mab?" he called, voice echoing in the nothingness. "Mab, say something! Where are you? *Mab!*"

He turned on the spot, panting, running his hand through

his hair. His ears picked up the sound of ragged whimpering, and his head immediately snapped to the sound. He staggered towards it, and saw her.

Gasping for breath, Mab lay on her back, her shaking, bloodied hands clutching at a dagger between her breasts.

All at once, Erlik felt the world crumble and fall away. Time edged to a crawl, and before he could stop it, an anguished scream fell from his mouth.

Not again.

He fell down beside her and lifted her into his lap. Too weak to make any sound louder than a whimper, Mab shuddered in his arms, struggling for breath.

Erlik held her close and wept, muttering incoherent words that begged her not to die. He wouldn't allow it, he *couldn't* allow it, that she can't, she *mustn't*, die.

Not her. Never her.

"*No!* Gods, no, not again, please," he sobbed. "Don't close your eyes. Don't leave me alone, not after everything. My love, don't die... stay with me, please! *Please!*"

Mab gazed up at him, her trembling hands brushing his cheek, leaving bloody smudges where her fingers grazed his skin.

She shuddered and lay still, and Erlik felt the last thread of his sanity snap. The threshold that had withheld the old madness within him broke. And without Mab, without *her*, to keep him grounded, he broke too.

He let out a long, throat-tearing scream, and tasted blood at the base of his tongue. He bent over her body and held her tighter, and her body collapsed into ash.

"No," he croaked. "Not her. Please, gods. It should be me. Please. Not her, not her. Not her..."

He stared at his empty, dusty hands, her ashes floating into the air to catch and stick to the tears on his face. Slowly, Erlik curled up in a ball on the floor of his dark, empty cell and wept, begging forgiveness from those he could no longer see.

CHAPTER 43

"That place is drowning in evil"

"HIS BODY IS broken, his mind will soon follow," Idath said slowly, sitting as far from the warmth of the fire as possible. "If it is not destroyed already. It will not be long now."

"Is it wise to leave him alone?" Maleagant asked. Carman sat by the fire, watching the flames. The growing *thing* shifted inside her belly, and she fought the urge to throw up.

"It is best to let him wallow in his own misery for a while," Idath said. "Let his memories plague him, let his pain and guilt consume him. It will break him all the faster."

"How do you know?" Carman challenged. "Your domain is death, not madness."

"Our mother," Idath addressed her through gritted teeth. "Manaie, was the Mother of Madness. She planted the seed within him – within us *both* – long ago. He does not know. He thinks himself merely susceptible to it."

"What do you intend to do with him, once he's completely driven to it?" Maleagant asked.

"I will send him to Annwyn in my stead. Let him suffer in the cold and the dark for a change. Let him feel the agony of having everything you ever wanted *ripped* from your fingertips."

Idath's face had twisted. His teeth bared like a dog, small

eyes wide and cold.

He continued, "Perhaps, once I am done with this world, I will return there, and I can torment him in my own domain for eternity."

The crackle of the fire drew Carman's eyes. She watched a fiery log crumble to ash and send sparks into the air. Curiosity gnawed at her almost as incessantly as sickness did.

"What's it like in Annwyn?" she asked quietly. She wasn't sure he'd heard her at first.

"Why? Do you intend to venture there?" Idath said, after a while. Carman slowly shook her head, and even Maleagant looked up out of curiosity. Idath made a noise that could have been a sigh.

"There is a darkness there that does not break," he said softly. "Imagine your world as it is now, but forever trapped in the night, with no moon, no stars. The only light is from the white mist that hangs over the Sea Without Shore. The air is heavy, thick with the sounds of weeping, and the mournful souls wander there in pain and despair, lost in their misery."

"When I first found myself there, I constructed a great castle in the sky, built from the blackened foundations of Annwyn itself, a mighty floating fortress where I can observe my deathly domain."

Another log burst into ash in the grate.

"My powers are far greater in Annwyn than they are here. There, at my full strength, I can change my shape, and assume my natural form, in which I feel more comfortable."

Maleagant frowned, and shared a glance with Carman.

"Your natural form?" he repeated. Idath looked up and his lip curled.

"Yes," he said. "How do you think I move from my floating castle to the ground below? One cannot fly without wings."

Carman put her hand to her clammy forehead and sucked in a sharp breath.

The gnawing twinge in her belly became an unpleasant thump.

Erlik's words echoed in her ears.

Five moons. Gods, Carman, what have you gotten yourself into?

"So what should we do about the witch?" Maleagant asked Idath, interrupting Carman's thoughts.

"The Heart? What of it?"

"You don't think she'll come for him?"

"Of course it will come for him," Idath said, and something close to a mocking leer pulled at his lip.

"What should we do then?" Maleagant pressed.

Idath laughed. Carman's blood froze. The hairs on her arms stood upright. No other sound had ever frightened her more. It was chilling, mirthless, utterly devoid of warmth.

"What threat does it pose?"

Maleagant frowned. "She still has the most powerful magic in all of Albion. And what if she brings an army? This keep is held together with the barest of magic. It can't withstand Mab, her army, and any allies Elphame has. No doubt Tír-Na-Nóg will answer her summons, and Morrigan's archers are formidable."

"Stop babbling, boy. The Heart will bring no army, no allies. It is far too proud," Idath said in a low voice. Maleagant looked unconvinced.

"But what if—"

"Enough of your fretting, sorcerer," Idath snapped. "Allow my plans to come to fruition, and we shall watch as Elphame falls. And once the shining capital falls to me, the rest of Albion will follow suit."

The fire crackled lower and lower as they fell into silence, watching and mistrustful of each other.

✧　✧　✧

THERE IT STANDS, Thomas thought to himself. The Iron Keep stood gaunt and stark against the grey sky. He suppressed a shudder.

"That place is drowning in evil," Epona said, and anxiously

pawed at the ground. Thomas patted her neck.

The portcullis had been left open, and Thomas felt an enormous sense of apprehension wash over him. Why, in such turbulent and uncertain times, would Maleagant leave the gate to his Keep open and unguarded? Was it an invitation to a trap?

Definitely a trap, Thomas thought. *But we knew what we were heading for.*

"I do not know what to expect when we enter," he heard Mab say. He sat up straight and looked at her. "We must be cautious. Stay together, and trust each other. If anyone is separated from the others, make for the gate as quickly as possible, and we will meet you outside. Once we have Erlik and Isolde, then we leave. We do not linger, we do not engage Maleagant or Idath. And if anyone encounters Carman," Mab paused and Thomas noticed her hands tighten their grip and her expression harden. "Cripple her if the opportunity arises. I will deal with her later."

"Understood," Thomas said. Thissy and Tristan nodded.

"Come," Mab turned her stag away from the entrance. "Thomas, show us the way to the tunnel."

Thomas guided Epona into motion. He led them to a small cavity in the wall that Broc had outlined for him. Large enough for a slender person to squeeze through. Thomas hesitated.

"Mab?" he said slowly, and she looked over her shoulder at him. "You and Thissy might be able to fit through there, but..."

Mab eyed his bulky armour, and then looked back at the tunnel. She dismounted and approached the mouth of the passage. With a deep breath, she raised her hands, palms facing outwards. Trembling, she slowly separated her hands as if pulling aside a curtain made of lead. The tunnel shook, loose stones crumbling free and scattering on the ground. At last, with monumental effort, Mab had widened the tunnel enough to allow enough room for them all.

"Leave the mounts here," Mab commanded. Clearly not in the mood for caution, she rushed into the opening without a moment of hesitation.

Tristan swiftly followed, obviously eager to assist. Thissy went next, hissing unheeded words of vigilance to her son. Finally, only Thomas stood outside. He took in a huge gulp of air, then ploughed forwards into the gap.

At last, they emerged; Thomas blinked to adjust his eyes to the new light. Glancing around, he found the surroundings to be a dingy pantry.

"Come, this way."

She quietly led them through the pantry door and into the kitchen. There were no staff there. Silence reigned.

So far, so good, Thomas thought to himself.

"Where is everyone?" Thissy whispered, voicing his own thoughts.

"Maleagant slaughtered everyone in the castle," Mab whispered back. "He used their blood to fuel the gateway to Annwyn."

Thissy's face whitened.

"Blood magic," she choked.

Thomas's hand found the hilt of his sword, and he noticed Mab constantly flexing her fingers, as though ready to conjure at a moment's notice. Sparks ignited and fizzled out at her fingertips. Instinctive.

"They will have him in the dungeon, no doubt," Mab said quietly, then beckoned them to follow her down a sloping corridor. "Come, I remember the way."

"Have you been here before, Mab?" Tristan asked. "Before this whole thing started, I mean? Before Idath was released."

Mab stopped mid-stride. Thomas gave Tristan a stern look. Mab turned her gaze on him, but Thomas noticed a small smile tugging at the corners of her mouth, and he remembered she'd always had a fondness for innocently curious minds.

"When I was very young," she said. She turned and continued walking, a little slower now, more cautious. "It was in this very Keep that Erlik and I first confessed our love for each other."

Thomas felt a memory spark to life. He recognised this

story:

Mab had been betrothed to Idath, but her affection fell instead on his younger brother, a trickster and a rogue. Mab's heart had been stolen, and she took his in return. After they'd confessed their love, and Idath had discovered it, brother fought brother until the younger slew the elder. Erlik's hands had been stained with his brother's blood, which caused his banishment from the House of the Old Gods, and Mab had fled. Realising he'd lost both his place among the Old Gods, *and* the woman who loved him, Erlik fell deep into a crippling madness, which caused the war that had lost Thomas his father.

All lives are connected, somehow, he thought. *We're all just pawns on the chessboard.*

"So this Keep was Idath's?" Tristan asked, a boyish font of curiosity. Mab nodded.

"Once upon a time, yes," she said wryly. "It became abandoned after Idath's death. Stories of ghosts do little to encourage new inhabitants."

Thomas shivered. At the mention of ghosts, he anxiously glanced around. The air somehow seemed cooler. Mab gave him a reassuring smile, and ploughed deeper into the darkness ahead.

CHAPTER 44

"Not her!"

THE LACK OF guards grew steadily more unnerving. Mab followed her memory through the corridors with patient, deliberate steps. The others followed, their footsteps almost as quiet as hers.

Thomas brought up the rear, and Mab silently praised his loyalty. She had expected much more resistance from him in this. Any attempt to rescue Erlik should surely have warranted harsh words and questions about her sanity. Yet he remained at her side, vigilant and faithful as ever.

Mab's hands twitched at every tiny sound. Every footstep gonged louder than a beating drum; every scurrying rat sounded like the chattering of laughter; every breathed sigh became a cruelly hissed word.

As they descended, and the air grew colder and coppery-tanged, her heart gave a hard and painful jerk. The chilly air nipped her fingers. She flexed them again. The reek of blood spiked and she forced herself to repress a gag.

"*Gods*, that smell!" she heard Thissy whisper behind her. She glanced back to see her covering her nose and mouth with a hand.

"Come," Mab ran her tongue over her lower lip. "We cannot be much further away."

Conjuring a small violet flame on her palm as a light

through the darkness, she hurried on.

"To the east... lies Aryndel..."

Mab stopped dead, and Tristan almost walked into the back of her.

"What is it?"

"Hush, listen," she said, her heart beating an irregular tempo in her throat. *I know that voice!*

She took a few steps forward, and felt a rat scamper past her boots. The shock rattled her more than the fright.

"Cathedral on the moor."

Thomas pushed past the others to lay his hand on Mab's arm. She couldn't face him. She beckoned the others to follow her as quietly as possible, and pressed on.

"West is... Brackenpeth."

The mantra pressed into her ears. She shook off the chill that raced through her entire body. *When did it become so cold?* The purple flames glinted on something metallic just ahead. Something moved in the darkness.

"Home of barbarian shore."

Mab couldn't breathe. His voice was so close now, but the smell of blood and fear overwhelmed her other senses. She carefully reached into the darkness to feel for that glinting something, and her fingers hit something ice-cold. So cold it burnt. *Cold iron!*

She hissed and retracted her hand almost immediately. Then, sucking in a breath between her teeth, she pushed through the darkness to wrap her fingers around... a metal bar? *A dungeon cell,* she realised.

He's here.

Her flesh sizzled and hissed, and she pulled away once more, cradling her blackened fingers.

"To the north... hides Trimsaran."

Mab gestured with her flame-filled hand. Purple fire leapt from her palm and onto braziers that lined the walls.

Light filled the cage. Mab froze. Her racing heart stopped.

His hair dishevelled, tattered and tangled like the branches of an ancient tree. Stripped to the waist. Dried blood stained the skin of his bare chest and shoulders. His eyes sunken hollows. Muttering to himself in the lonely darkness. A metal collar around his throat bound him to the wall by a short chain.

But worst of all, a vision that chilled her to her core, a sight that wrapped its glacial, bitter fingers around her stopped heart, were the shards of silver in his hair.

The Mortasheen.

The room span. The floor lurched. Mab staggered, but Thomas's hand steadied her.

"Easy, Mab," came his soothing voice.

"No," Mab moaned. She tipped her head back and gazed down at the pitiful figure on the ground. She could not bear this sight. It broke her heart to see him so beaten. *Tamed*, she realised. *My dragon has been tamed.*

She moved forward, ignoring the cruel hissing of cold-iron against her flesh as she pressed against the bars.

"*Where mystic men grow white,*" he mumbled.

"Erlik, look at me," she said. "*A múirnín*, come, look at me."

"*To the south lurks Wicklewood,*" he finished, idly drawing in the dirt. "*There, dead boys go to fight.*"

"He's mad," Thomas whispered in realisation behind her. She could have incinerated him where he stood, but she knew it wasn't fair to take out her frustrations on him. Instead, she tried the door. *Locked, not surprisingly.*

"My lady?" Tristan's voice sounded small and meek behind her. *He is afraid of me*, she realised with a painful jolt. "May I?"

Mab frowned, until she saw him produce a small bent pin from his pocket. She gave him a sharp nod. Licking his lips, Tristan kneeled and fiddled with the lock. His fingers barely touched the cold iron, dancing over the metal as swift and silent as a weaver. Mab stood like a cat watching her unsuspecting prey, drumming her fingers against the back of her other hand.

Thissy blew into her hands to keep them warm. Thomas wrapped his arm around her. She huddled against him and gave him a smile. Mab couldn't help the seed of jealousy sprout inside her. Loving gestures came so naturally to them. It was an easy sort of love; no shouting, no clawing, no bruised throats or cut lips. Utterly devoid of turmoil. Thomas caught her eye, and Mab averted her stare. Her relationship with Erlik seemed so chaotic in comparison. Their love was volcanic. Smouldering and cold at the same time. Never gentle or sweet, no stolen glances or secret whispers. Just ancient, destructive, impossible. *A wolf and a dragon. My dragon.*

With a quiet click, Tristan stood up, looking pleased with himself.

"I used to pick the lock on our pantry door to get to the biscuit jar," he said smugly, and moved away. Mab sighed with relief and stepped forward. Wrapping her cloak around her hand to avoid touching the iron, she tugged open the door and stepped inside. She hesitated.

"I need some time alone with him," she said. Thomas looked momentarily annoyed, then glanced up the corridor.

Nodding, he said. "As you wish, Mab. But be quick, we still need to find Isolde."

Thomas turned, guiding the others away, to wait for her at the end of the corridor.

Mab paused, and then kneeled down. Erlik didn't look at her. His red, glassy eyes fixed on the ground. He'd carved symbols and words into the earth with his torn nails. His lips dry and cracked, he looked older and more tired than she'd ever seen him.

"*A múirnín,*" she whispered.

"Sweet one," he translated in a slurred mumble. She gently touched his shoulder, afraid to startle him. His skin was icy, and Mab immediately took off her cloak and threw it over him. He inhaled deeply.

"Scent is hers. But not her. Not her. Not real. Not her," he said. Mab sighed deeply.

"Erlik," she said, slowly and gently. "We have come to take you home."

She reached out again and tried to lift him to his feet, even just to his knees, but he went rigid at her touch and shied away. She retreated at once, hands raised to show she meant him no harm.

"Not her. Not her. *Not her!*" Erlik screeched, his eyes dancing wildly.

He scrambled away, and pressed his back to the wall, ripping her cloak off him as though it had burned. The chain snapped taut, and Erlik whined like a wounded pup. Mab's eyes widened, and she crept a little closer, as close as she dared.

"Easy," she said, her voice quiet and soothing. She kept her hands raised before her, as though approaching a wild and angry animal. She made shushing noises. "I am here now. You have nothing more to fear."

An angry red burn on his chest caught the light. Raw, shiny, red, a word branded into the flesh to proclaim his crime. She squinted to read the word in the dimness.

Kinslayer.

Fury rose like bile in her throat. Her hands clenched, and her vision blurred. *How dare they disfigure him in such a way? Weaken him with torture so he cannot heal himself? I will avenge this. A thousand fold.*

Mab took several deep breaths to calm herself.

"Erlik, look at me," she said. He obeyed, and tilted his head like a dog. He deeply inhaled her scent and closed his eyes as if to enjoy it more.

"It smells like her," he shook his head. "But it's not her. Can't be her. Not her."

Mab stared at him and gave a soft sigh. She crawled forwards and sat down in front of him, threading her fingers into his. His eyes fixed onto her hands, and he blinked hard and fast.

"Not her," he begged. "Please, not her."

Mab took in a sharp breath. Why did he keep saying that? She shook her head.

"Erlik, please, look at me," she said. "Trust me. I am no vision, I am *real*. We are here to take you home."

"*No!*" he snarled, and pushed her away. "Still here—*not her!*"

How can I possibly convince him, when all he sees are ghosts?

She sighed, gazing at him while he calmly ignored her and resumed drawing in the dirt, mumbling to himself, looking every inch like a mad beggar. Mab glanced at Thomas whispering to Thissy and Tristan. Their time was short, and she was painfully aware of the moments they were wasting. She looked at her hands, as though the answer lay in the intricate curves and lines of her palms. She had never felt so powerless. Her eyes fell to the ring on her third finger. She turned her hand over and gazed at the beautiful silver band, catching the lilac light of her fire.

"Erlik," she said softly. He twitched and threw her an evil glare, as though furious at her for interrupting. "Do you remember when we first met?"

A long, cold silence followed. At last, he nodded. An infinitesimal bob of his head that would have gone unnoticed if she hadn't been staring so intently at him. His eyes never left hers.

"Do you remember the first words you ever said to me?" she asked. He nodded again, and she could have sworn a slight smile curved his lip. Her heart lifted. "What were they? Say it for me, now."

Again, a long silence followed. She didn't speak. She was too afraid to. Too afraid to lose this tiny grasp she had over his sanity.

"Forgive me, my lady."

She nodded, an encouraging smile on her face now. He stared at her through shadowed eyes; she couldn't fathom the emotion there. He looked weary, though there was more than just a glimmer of hope lurking in the darkness.

"Do you remember that day?" she pressed. He nodded once more. Mab stretched out her hand, a pale and ghostly shape in the firelight, and a silver cloud enveloped her fingers. Snaking out to reach him, misting over his face like fog. His pupils grew wide and black as memories, *both* of their memories, flooded his mind.

CHAPTER 45

"Forgive me, my lady"

IMPISH LAUGHTER RANG high and clear through the lower town, clanging against stone walls like tolling bells. Four thieves launched out of the market square, faces covered by black cloth, pursued by several shouting guardsmen.

One of them, at the head of the group, slipped into a narrow alleyway. Vaulting up the walls like a spider, he slipped through an open window into a mercifully empty room. The others followed, hiding in alley's shadows until the guards had passed. The leader poked his head out, hanging with easy skill from the window. He ripped off the black cloth covering his face and gulped down fresh air. Dark hair tumbled out, curtaining sharp cheekbones and jaw. Black eyes sparkling with mischief, thin lips curled into a sly grin.

The others crept out of their hiding places and looked up at him, laughing.

"You can come down from your tree now, little kitten," one mocked, taking off his mask too, revealing a pockmarked face and large nose.

"Actually, *Abrothennes*," the leader smirked, jumping down from his perch. "I was protecting my investments."

"Oof, full name basis," Abrothennes said. "I must be in trouble. Or you're about to propose?"

The leader snorted. "In your dreams, *Broth*," he said,

utilising his nickname this time. He upended his satchel, spilling out a mound of gold coins. The other two removed their masks too and sat in a circle, counting out their share.

"Wasn't there more than this?" the leader flicked the last coin away uncertainly.

"Would've been more if Vex hadn't been such a noble bastard," Broth said moodily. He nudged the man beside him, one with coal-black hair and a stoic demeanour.

"I don't steal from the poor," he said. "Only from those who can afford it."

"Where's the fun in that? There's your share, Cricket," Broth added, pushing a pile of coins towards the youngest member, a youthful lad with fair hair and bright eyes. "And yours, *my lord.*"

Though his voice heaved with sarcasm, he looked up towards their leader with deference. Despite the quiet of the alley, Broth's voice was met with a hissing hush.

"Erlik?" Vex asked. "What's the matter?"

"Shh, listen," Erlik stood and approached the entrance to the alley. He glanced back and jerked his head towards the oncoming bustle. The others scooped their coin into purses and jumped to their feet.

"What's the matter? Guards?" Cricket asked, an undeniable and youthful lilt of fear in his voice.

Erlik grinned, "Better. Look!"

The group peeked out into the street. Six black horses, draped in strange heraldry, bore proud soldiers in silver armour. The lady's youthful retinue followed behind on their own snowy horses.

At the fore, a finely dressed woman rode a huge white stag with sharp antlers to rival the branches of a tree. The woman's eyes swept the street with more than a hint of disdain.

"Seven," Broth whispered.

"What?"

"You fancy seven of those girls," he grinned, and nodded at the white-clad maidens.

"No I *don't,*" Erlik pulled an annoyed face, and turned back to watch the woman on the stag. "Nine, actually," he added in a disgruntled mutter.

Cricket snorted, and Vex elbowed him.

Erlik, meanwhile, was mesmerised. The woman on the stag was incredibly beautiful. Like a glittering star, so distant and cold. Like frozen moonlight. She seemed unsuitably dressed for Tír-na-Nóg's notoriously chilly autumn days.

"She's brought plenty of guards," Broth pointed out. Vex frowned and made a disapproving noise, and Broth rolled his eyes. "Oh, don't tell me: you don't steal from women?"

"Only their coin," Vex said, casting a dark look at Erlik, who seemed unfazed. "Besides, we *just* pulled off a heist. Why risk another? Without forethought? Without planning?"

"The most exhilarating heist is an unplanned one," Erlik turned back to them with a grin, and they gathered around him conspiratorially. Vex groaned, yet leaned into the circle with the others.

"How should we play it?" Broth asked.

"Want me to play hungry orphan again?" Cricket asked. Not four days ago, Cricket had used his youthful looks to trick a small gaggle of noblewomen into thinking he was a lost, orphaned child. While they cooed around him, the others lifted what they could from their purses. But Erlik shook his head.

"Not this one. I think—"

"Street fight? Blind beggar?" Broth interrupted eagerly. Vex clipped him across the head. Erlik smirked. He straightened up and quirked his eyebrow, and the others grinned with him. After straightening his collar, he brushed a hand through his hair and brazenly strode out into the street.

MAB PULLED SHARPLY on the reins, and her stag snorted and stamped. The dark-haired stranger who'd stepped out before her didn't seem cowed by her furious glare. Instead, he gave her a deep bow. Mab's breath caught in her throat as he rose again. He had a surprisingly honest smile, though now it was more of a smirk. His dark eyes twinkled as they lingered on her face.

"Forgive me, my lady," he said, his deep voice husky. "I was so overwhelmed by your beauty, I forgot myself."

Mab raised an eyebrow, and despite herself, felt a slight blush warm her cheeks. The young man was very handsome, with his sharp features and oceanic eyes. He approached her stag and patted its nose gently. The beast snorted with dislike and nudged his hand away, snapping as though to bite.

"If I may enquire, beautiful lady," he said. "What brings you to our modest city?"

Before Mab could speak, one of her guardsmen spoke up sharply.

"Begone, vagabond! Our lady does not speak with the likes of you."

The young man looked deeply offended.

"Vagabond? Nay," he said, dipping another courteous bow to the guard. "I'm merely a humble farmer, smitten by a beautiful lady, and curious as to her business—"

"Her business is no concern of yours. Begone, I said," the guard repeated, hand resting on the hilt of his sword as though in warning.

The young man took no notice, and took the insult in his stride.

"But has the lady no voice? I'm yet to hear her speak," he said. Mab kept her eyes fixed on his. "No doubt her voice will be as lovely as her face."

"Insolent dog," the guard said, and drew his sword.

"Enough, Faolan," Mab said. Her cheeks still felt warm, but now with anger as well as flattery. "I will not have our arrival to the city announced with violence."

The guardsman paused, then reluctantly sheathed his sword.

"Forgive me, Your Grace," he said.

Mab took small pleasure in seeing surprise and dismay cross the young man's face at hearing her title. Her cool eyes met his, and she tipped back her head.

"You are insolent," she agreed. "But you are no farmer.

You are a *thief*. Your companions are thieves. Instruct them to return what they have stolen from my entourage at once."

The young man baulked. His eyes darted in panic. Mab followed his gaze, as did her guards.

Three thieves froze. Three pairs of eyes stared at Mab. Three pairs of hands caught in the satchels of horses and purses of maidens.

"Scat!" one of them shouted, and they dropped their stolen items and fled. The young man before her, no doubt their ringleader, almost managed to flee. But Mab lifted her hand, and he froze in place as though rooted to the ground. Ice crept over his boots, rendering him immobile.

Mab raised an eyebrow at the young man, who stared at her, dumbfounded. After a few seconds, he affected an elegant smile and shrugged.

"Can't blame us for trying," he said, and winked at her. "Do you, ah… plan on thawing me out?"

Despite herself, Mab laughed. This young man was very charming. She gestured again, and the ice melted away. He shook one of his dripping boots free, and nodded his gratitude to her.

"I'm impressed," he said. "How did you know?"

Mab raised an eyebrow.

"Farmers have coarse hands and tanned faces from working in the sun all day. May I suggest using 'librarian', it suits you a little better," she said. Her heart gave a little flutter when the man laughed softly and ran his tongue over his teeth. His eyes drifted over her.

"I'll know for next time," he said. "I didn't catch your name?"

"Perhaps because I did not throw it," Mab coolly spurred her stag into movement again and ushered her entourage onwards.

"Will you throw it now, then?" he called. Mab allowed herself a little smile.

"No," she called back, without looking back at him. She could hear the smile reflected in her voice, but didn't bother disguising it. "I will not."

"Please?" he shouted, almost out of sight now. Mab looked over her shoulder at him. He still looked impressed, almost intrigued, by her.

"I am Mab," she said with a smile, and urged her stag into a quicker pace. "Queen of the Old Ways."

CHAPTER 46

"I expect you to keep your end of our bargain"

I DATH'S MOUTH SPLIT into a hideous smile, revealing shiny black teeth.

"It is here," he said slowly. Maleagant sat up straighter, and Carman's head snapped up from inspecting her long fingernails.

"What should we do?" she asked, fear colouring her voice. Maleagant glared.

"I will let them think they have won," Idath said. "Before I crush them into oblivion." Idath stood, joints grotesquely snapping and crunching.

Maleagant stood too, and Carman put her hands on the arms of the chair to push herself to her feet.

"No," Idath said. "You both will remain here."

"What? Why?" Maleagant demanded. "This is as much my plan, and my castle, as it is yours."

Idath narrowed his eyes.

"You are weak," Idath sneered. "And your magic is frail. You will only get in my way."

His long, white fingers gently rubbed the torn flesh of that awful open wound on his chest. A viscous droplet of congealed blood quivered and clung to his finger as he pulled away. Maleagant twisted his face in disgust and glanced at Carman, who retched and staggered out of the room. Maleagant paused until she had left earshot.

"I released you so you could give us what we wanted," he snapped in a low voice. "I gave you the chance to exact your revenge, and you've taken long enough. I expect you to keep your end of our bargain."

"We have made no bargain, sorcerer," Idath sneered. "You have imagined this alliance, and now you expect me to adhere to it?"

"I expect you to be grateful!"

"I am not ungrateful, boy," Idath grabbed Maleagant by his collar and lifted him so they were eye-to-eye. "I repay my debts, and I reward those who live in faithful service to me. I will honour you with the boon you have requested. When *I* see fit."

Idath dropped him, and the sorcerer crumpled. Without another word, he scrambled to his feet and smoothed down his robe. With a huffy look, he followed Carman out of the room.

✧   ✧   ✧

"ISOLDE!" TRISTAN HISSED, peering into each dark cell. "Isolde, where are you?"

He made sure he remained within sight of Mab's purple fire braziers. But the dungeon was a maze of dark corridors, and he couldn't help the anxious thumping of his heart in his throat.

"Tristan?" a quiet voice pushed its way through the darkness. Tristan's heart leapt.

"Isolde, is that you?" he hurried forwards. "Where are you? Call again!"

"I'm here, Tristan, this way!"

He shot to the sound of her voice, at the end of a row of empty cells.

"Isolde!" he rushed to her cell, cursing the brazen clang of the bars and the faint hissing of cold iron against his skin. He stopped short at seeing her bruised and swollen fingers. *Broken.*

"What have—did *they* do that to you?" he growled.

"Tristan!" she shuffled forwards, her eyes gleaming with hope. He noticed she ignored his question, but kept her twisted fingers close to her chest. "Oh, thank the gods!"

"Come, I'll get you out!" Tristan bent down to pick the lock again. "The others are fetching Erlik. Once we have you both, we can get out of this horrible place."

"Is he alright? They've done terrible things to him," Tristan heard the sob in her throat. He knew she couldn't help feeling some form of gratitude towards Erlik. He too wanted to thank him for keeping his promise, and for saving his life. And a thousand other things that he couldn't think of in the moment.

Isolde went on, "They moved us away from each other," she said. "But I could hear them torturing him. It was so awful."

"I know. Mab is helping him."

"Queen Mab is here?"

Nodding, Tristan stood and opened the rusted door with a grating scrape.

"Come, we'll go get the others and leave this damn Keep for good."

"M'FHÍORGHRÁ," MAB WHISPERED, and gently pressed a bottle to his lips. The contents must have tasted bitter and sharp; Erlik gagged even as he swallowed.

"This is the remedy to the Mortasheen," Mab explained. "Idath must have infected you somehow."

"I-I didn't..." Erlik cleared his throat. Mab offered him some water, which he eagerly gulped down. "I didn't even realise he'd done so."

He seemed a thousand times more lucid now. Mab could have wept with relief when he had locked eyes with her and whispered her name. She thanked every god she knew when he wrapped his freezing arms around her and muttered into her hair.

But she reminded herself of where they were. Now was not the time for reconciliation. She had to remain hard until they had left the Keep. For all their sakes.

Mab nodded soberly, "I am afraid I cannot restore your hair." She pulled gently at a lock of silver to show him. He shrugged it off.

"A small price to pay," he said. Mab smiled. She knew what he meant. *A small price to pay to see each other again.*

She made to stand, but her eyes ran the length of the chain that bound Erlik. He tugged at it, as if to show her its strength. Mab followed the links with her hand. The chain was forged strong and thick, but the lock—

"Tristan?" she called, and the boy appeared at once without noise. Isolde behind him. Mab marvelled at the lad, and his uncanny ability to be utterly silent when he wanted. *This boy would make a wonderful spy.*

She beckoned him closer and gestured to the chain.

"Can you pick this lock?" she asked. Tristan nodded and kneeled down. He fumbled with the collar at Erlik's throat. She half-expected Erlik to throw some scathing comment his way, but his next words surprised her.

"You use a pin?" he asked quietly. Tristan nodded but said nothing, eyes fixed on his work. Erlik made a thoughtful noise. "I had a little set of tools. I made them myself from fishhooks and old scraps of metal from the smithy." Tristan nodded again. "I still have them, even though I haven't used them in decades. When we get back to Elphame, you can have them."

Tristan looked up at Erlik in surprise. The collar clicked and fell away with a jingle of chains.

"I—thank you," he said. Erlik returned his smile.

Gingerly he stood, brushing himself down. His knees buckled, and Mab caught him, wrapping his arm around her shoulder to share his weight. She strained with exertion, too small to bear it.

"Thomas, help me."

Thomas obeyed, moving past Thissy and Tristan to take his other side. Erlik drew back and stared at him with a furrowed brow.

"What are you doing here?" he asked. He turned to Mab before Thomas could speak. "What's he doing here?"

Thomas rolled his eyes.

"For her sake, not yours," he said dryly. Erlik smirked as though sharing some private joke. Thomas returned it. Mab's brows lifted in surprise.

With a wince, Erlik took a step, but his wounds cracked and bled freely again. Mab removed her cloak to press it to Erlik's wounds when Thissy tentatively moved forward.

"Would you like me to heal him, my lady?" Thissy asked. Erlik recoiled, and Thomas jerked him unnecessarily, making him hiss in pain. Mab raised her hands to quieten them all.

"Thank you, child, but no," she said. "Seelie magic would poison him, and he is weak enough already."

Thissy nodded, and then looked around. A pile of clothes lay nearby, and she rummaged through them until she found a shirt. She thrust it into Erlik's hands. Shivering, he pulled it on.

"We have Isolde," Tristan said. "We can leave now, can't we?"

"Is she well?"

Isolde nodded, and Tristan put his arm around her.

"Her fingers are broken, though—"

"Oh, I'm tougher than I look, my lady," Isolde said shyly, and Mab gave her a motherly smile. Thissy took her hands, healing the broken bones in a warm, golden-green glow.

Mab led them out of the dungeons, extinguishing the flames in the braziers before they left. No one spoke, pausing every so often to listen carefully for approaching guards. Or worse.

They shuffled out of the castle as quickly and as quietly as possible; Mab hurried them along with little patience, until finally they emerged in the kitchen. It felt colder than before.

"The secret passage is this way," Mab whispered to Erlik, leading them to the pantry. She pulled aside the cabinet, and stopped short.

Enormous stones blocked the passageway. Moss grew

over the rocks, as though the passage had been barricaded for years.

Erlik groaned wearily and leaned against the wall. Thomas gently lowered him, and took to Mab's side.

"What is it?" he hissed.

"Idath," she whispered back, eyes roving over the mossy stones. "He knows we are here, and has sealed our escape."

"Can you use your magic to break it down? Or open another?"

"Perhaps," she said slowly, though she had little confidence. Annwyn magic was monstrously different to hers. Her power came from life. Faith. Belief.

She cast her eyes over the stones again. She gave herself a little shake. She had widened this tunnel earlier, and moved mountains with her power. Surely a blocked passageway would give her little trouble?

Mab raised her hands. Erlik's ragged breathing shivered in her ears. She closed her eyes. Exhaled slowly through pursed lips. Magic coursed through her veins. But the familiar cold ache in her chest became a chilling pain. Bitter ice gripped her hands.

"Mab?"

Erlik's faint voice sounded so far away. The ache became a blunt agony. Mab's breath caught in her chest. She couldn't breathe. Couldn't speak. Couldn't tear her hands away to break the bond of magic that had latched onto her very soul. The parasitic Annwyn magic pulsed, draining every drop of her strength.

"Something's wrong."

"Help her!"

Someone yanked her away, and she fell back into Thomas's waiting arms. Stumbling to the ground, she collapsed into him, gulping down the cool air. Something warm dripped onto her lip, and she touched her philtrum to find wetness. She brought her hand away. *Blood.* She felt Thomas grip her carefully, and brush the hair from her face.

"Mab, you're hurt."

Easing her breathing, she looked at Erlik, "I cannot undo it," she said. "Idath's magic… it was draining my life."

She wiped the blood away from her nose and regained her feet, using Thomas's strength to steady herself.

"Will you be alright?"

"Yes, I am well," she cleared her throat and cast one final look over the blocked passageway.

"Perhaps if we combine our magic—?"

"No," Mab said sternly. "We cannot compromise ourselves further. Erlik is too weak, and this magic would overpower all of us. Especially you three."

She eyed the Rhymer family. They were so fragile. So *small*. While not human, they were not immortal either. The weight of danger settled around her shoulders like a woollen cloak. Why had she asked them to accompany her? Suddenly, entirely, she hated herself.

"Conserve your strength. We will need to leave through the main door. Come, we must be more vigilant now."

Tension tautened the group, and Thomas helped Erlik to his feet again. All followed Mab as she led them back out of the kitchen.

Still, no one impeded their journey. No guards. No Idath. No Maleagant. No Carman. Yet the air was stagnant and thick with anticipation. Like the sky moments before erupting into a thunderstorm.

At last, the group crept through the front doors and emerged into the main courtyard. Everyone shivered. Winter air wrapped around them and tendrils of cold crept through their cloaks. Mab put up her hood.

She clicked her tongue. After a few moments, their mounts trotted into the courtyard, her stag at the head.

She helped Erlik mount behind her, and he wrapped his arms around her waist. The beast snorted in dislike at his presence.

Strategies and half-formed plans scattered through Mab's brain.

Return to Elphame. Help Erlik recover. Send a message to

Morrigan. Muster the army. Summon our allies. Raze the Keep. Destroy Idath. Somehow.

"Come," she called. Thomas followed first, turning Epona towards the open portcullis.

But with a great screeching grind, the huge metal gate slammed down, sending a cloud of dust and dirt into the air. The mounts reared, whinnying in fright at the sound and too-sudden movement.

"*Go socair anois!*" Mab commanded in a strong voice. The beasts tossed their heads and rolled their eyes, anxiously pawing the ground.

Dust choked the air for a few moments. Once it settled, every pair of eyes looked frantically around.

Mab's heart dropped. Erlik's arms tightened around her waist. His breath hitched.

They were trapped.

"Have you not stolen enough from me?"

Idath's voice sapped any remaining warmth from the air. All eyes turned to him.

"Return my brother," he said, and although his voice was quiet, it rang hard in their ears like a tolling bell.

"Never, Idath," Mab called back. "We are leaving with him and Isolde."

Idath laughed. The sky darkened and a cruel wind picked up.

"I care not for the whelp," he replied. "Return my brother to me, and I will let you leave with your pathetic little lives."

Mab felt Erlik's grip slacken, and she sharply glanced over her shoulder at him.

"No. He will not have you," she hissed, then looked up at Idath. "You will not have him!"

She waved a hand at the ground, and the stone steps split. Fiery tendrils snaked up from the earth and encircled Idath.

"All of you, hold the fire in my stead," she commanded, and nodded to the flames. Thomas, Thissy, Tristan, and Erlik, weak though he was, poured their magic into her fire, keeping it burning. It blazed with brilliant colour and light. Mab jumped down from her stag and approached the portcullis.

Planting her feet firmly, she slowly raised her arms, and flipped her hands so her palms faced the sky. Her magic extended, invisible and ancient, and latched onto the solid metal gate. No dark and deathly magic impeded her here; only age, metal and weight.

Magic surged through her veins, cold and terrible. Her hands began to shake. Her face twisted with effort.

"Faster, Mab!"

She ignored the voice. She didn't even know to whom it belonged.

With a reluctant groan, the portcullis crept upwards. Mab's arms vibrated hard with struggle, but she persisted.

Inch by agonising inch, the gate lifted. Until at last, it locked into place. Mab sagged. Her arms fell and she released a long, aching breath. With a staggering step, she turned back to find the fire still burning, but only just.

"Come!" she called. The others lowered their hands, allowing the fire around Idath to burn out. They would have a good head-start, at least.

Erlik turned the stag and approached her, and before she could mount, a braying, callous laugh stole her attention.

The Nuckelavee burst into the courtyard through the open portcullis; the Dullahan galloped towards them, the human head under her arm laughing; half a dozen Cu-Sith hounds stormed in, baying and howling, red mouths drooling.

The flames around Idath died away at last, and he descended the steps.

"Return my brother to me," he said again. "If I have need to say it once more, the beasts of Annwyn will destroy you."

CHAPTER 47

"Stop calling me 'witch'!"

"**Y**OU WILL NOT have him!" Mab shouted again. Thomas heard the tremor in her voice, and it chilled his bones; Mab feared so little, to see her fear of Idath crippled his resolve. If Mab was afraid, then the rest of them should be terrified.

The Nuckelavee snorted and dug its claws into the soft ground. Thomas swallowed the lump in his throat. He could smell the monster from here: the sickly stench of rot and corruption. He fought to withhold his choking retch.

"He is blood of my blood," Idath said, reaching Mab first. "I will always find him. I will have my vengeance."

"I will see you destroyed first," Mab snarled, eyes darting as though seeking some aid from the earth, the air, the sky, anything. Yet she didn't retreat. She looked impossibly tiny next to him. Thomas's heart almost stopped. He wanted to scream at her, to get away, move away. He was much too close.

"You have always been a thorn in my flesh, witch," Idath growled. Before she could cast any magic, Idath grabbed her throat. His spider-like hands tightened. Lifting her off her feet, small eyes narrowed and black teeth bared, he slammed her hard back down to the ground. Her body smashed like a ragdoll on the stone and she slumped in a heap.

"*Mab!*" a chorus of voices rang through the courtyard.

Erlik leapt from the stag, which revelled in its freedom and fled the courtyard, away from the Annwyn monsters. The others followed Erlik's example, and a herd of frightened horses followed a frightened stag.

The beasts of Annwyn saw their advantage.

Erlik reached Mab first. The Cu-Sith hounds leapt at him, booming and yowling. He swatted the first one away, and the others surrounded him, a growling ring of sharp teeth and claws.

Thomas drew his sword, and pushed Thissy behind him out of instinct. But with a fierce whip-crack, the Dullahan screeched her wild laughter and galloped towards him.

"No escape, handsome thing," she sneered. Thomas cast his eyes over her black, spiky armour. He saw her eyes glowing a freakish yellow. Up close, he noticed black smoke spewing from her neck where her head had been severed. Her horse snorted. Its breath steamed in the cold air. It, too, seemed hungry for death.

"Why do you follow him?" Thomas asked her quickly. Maleagant's journal said she was intelligent. Perhaps intelligent enough to reason with?

"All in Annwyn follow the new king," she said with a grin.

Thomas halted. *The* new *king?*

She cracked her whip and her horse screamed and reared up. Thomas countered the whip with his sword and it grated haltingly against the shards of bone. The Dullahan laughed and charged.

Thomas dodged, grabbing Thissy and pulling her away. Thissy flung a handful of green flames at the horsewoman's back. The fire petered out as it danced over her leather-clad shoulder blades.

She turned her horse and grinned at them. Its eyes gleamed red.

"That tickled, my beauty," she sneered. "Dare you to do it again?"

She charged again and this time the horse barraged into them both, knocking them to the ground. It reared again.

Thomas rolled away just as those pointed hooves came driving back down into the cobbled dirt.

The Dullahan cracked her whip. Thissy staggered back, her hands over her eyes. Seeing her weakness, the Dullahan turned on her first. Her bone-white blade lifted high.

"Thissy, *down!*" Thomas yelled, running at her and tackling her just as the sword came down. Rather than slicing his flesh open, it struck his spine like a club.

He roared with pain and went down. Thissy caught beneath him. Hearing no crack of broken bones, Thomas forced himself back upright.

Suddenly, the Dullahan released an unearthly screech of pain and hurtled forward to the ground. A blackened, gaping hole smoked on her back. Her body disintegrated into a pile of grave-hungry insects. Her horse screamed in distress at losing his rider, and bucked wildly around the courtyard.

Backing away, Thomas sought his rescuer. His eyes found Tristan, bow string quivering, smoke still curling in the air. He had frozen in rigid shock.

"Tristan!" Thissy launched to her feet. Thomas almost laughed with relief. She ran to him and took his hands. "Well done, now take Isolde somewhere safe and hide!"

"I don't want to leave," Tristan argued. "I can fight!"

Thomas saw the Nuckelavee approaching out of the corner of his eye, and his heart dropped into his stomach.

"No, Tristan!" Thomas bellowed. "Listen to your mother. This isn't about *you*. Take Isolde and hide!"

With a glance at the frightened girl, Tristan nodded, then grabbed Isolde's hand and ran. The Nuckelavee noticed.

Turning its monstrous face towards them, it pawed at the ground, leaving deep gouges in the soft dirt. It's awful, skinless face split into a hideous grin.

Thomas shouted, a wordless yell to get its attention away from Tristan. The monster turned its eyeless gaze on him instead. A mixture of relief and horror flooded him. He could barely fight the Dullahan. How was he to fight this beast?

"Thissy, any ideas?" he whispered, afraid a loud voice

would provoke it to charge. He glanced at her when she remained silent.

She looked up at him, "Pray."

His hand found hers. They backed away from the horse-monster as it slowly approached with exquisite delight at their horror.

"*Enough!*" Mab's voice rang sharp, clear through the courtyard. Her voice echoed, eyes glowing with amethyst-coloured light, ancient fury wrought into every inch of her face.

"Lord of the Dead," she hissed. "You will *not* hurt them."

"Mab?" Erlik's voice came as a breathy whisper; even he looked terrified of her. He beckoned Thomas and Thissy to move away from her. The hounds still surrounded him, but their twitching noses were turned on Mab now.

Darkness fell. The sky grew black. The Cu-Sith flattened their ears and whimpered, tails tucked between their legs. The Nuckelavee cantered anxiously, its freakish neighing laughter dying away. The Dullahan's horse snorted and reared up, and – still riderless – vanished into black smoke. Only an echo of its scream remained.

Mab's hands convulsed into claws, trembling with the weight of immense power. A deep rumble shook the ground. Idath locked eyes with her.

"Do you think your Pagan tricks frighten me, witch?" he sneered, baring his black teeth again.

Mab's face contorted into a monstrous mask of rage. Her hair flew about her face like snakes. Her entire body shook with fury.

"*Stop calling me 'witch'!*" Mab screamed, and the sky split apart.

Forked lightning struck the tallest tower of the Iron Keep, splitting it like a log. Thunder shuddered through the sky as fire, stone, and lumber rained down. Black clouds threw down their hardest showers. Dust became sludge.

The Cu-Sith yowled in fear and pain as they fell, crushed beneath stone. Mab turned her fiery gaze on the Nuckelavee. A wave of rainwater drudged up from the muddy earth and formed a suffocating dome around the beast.

Idath snarled and moved towards her. Mab gestured to him instead, one arm still extended to sustain the rainwater. Instead of her faithful earthy roots and branches, thick chains wriggled up from the ground like black worms and wound around Idath and bound him.

The roots of the Iron Keep, Thomas realised. *Of course!*

Mab's rage must have been strong enough to force the cold iron into obedience, for the chains bound Idath tight enough that he couldn't escape.

Rainwater pressed in around the Nuckelavee, and the beast screamed. Even under the bubbling watery dome, Thomas could hear its sizzling flesh. The monster reared, but it was its own undoing, for the water pressed in ever closer on every side, forcing it to kneel. One of its arms raised to try and press through the rain, but with a fierce squeal of agony, retracted its burned spear-like hand.

"Begone, foul creature!" Mab curled her taloned hand into a fist. And the bubble of water compressed fully around the monster, burning the Nuckelavee's skinless flesh until nothing was left of the monster except for a charred, waterlogged carcass.

"ISOLDE, STAY HERE," Tristan ran his thumb across Isolde's cheek. "I need to make sure my parents are alright."

"Tristan, wait!" she pulled him back. The sky above them grew black as storm clouds gathered above them. Tristan glanced once at the entrance to the courtyard before turning back to face her. Isolde shivered next to the crumbling stone wall that surrounded the castle. He unpinned his fur cloak and wrapped it around her.

"Please, be careful," she said. "And..." she paused and chewed her lip. "If you see my sister, please, try to convince Queen Mab not to kill her."

Tristan blinked, then nodded.

"I'll try," he replied. Isolde nodded in reply, knowing he

couldn't make the promise. She watched him dash away and sighed, her head bowed. Then, feeling a hand tug on her arm and pull her to her feet, she released a little "oh!" of surprise when Tristan kissed her gently.

"Stay safe, I'll come back," he said, dashing away again, torn between looking at her and looking at where he was going.

Isolde's face glowed red as a burning coal as she sat back down.

IDATH STRUGGLED AGAINST his bonds. Mab's hands twitched, her eyes narrowed in hatred and fire. Erlik appeared behind her.

"Mab, you can't kill him!" he said. "He's already dead!" Erlik grabbed her arm, and, even in his weakened state, managed to pull her away. "We need to retreat while he's bound and regroup."

"But—"

"Look at *them*, Mab!" Erlik snapped.

Mab turned her gaze, briefly, at Thomas and Thissy. Dishevelled, bloodied, and breathless.

Thomas sheathed his sword and glanced back at Idath. "The beasts are dead, but you and Erlik are both weak, we—"

"Father!"

All heads turned to the shout. Tristan skidded into the courtyard, eyes scanning for danger. Mab turned, distracted. Idath needed no other moment.

With a grating roar, he burst free of his chains, black links scattering and sinking into the mud.

"*No!*" Mab's eyes returned to Idath, but it was too late. He thrust a gnarled hand towards her, and Mab felt all control over her body leave her. She lifted into the air, arms and legs pulled taut.

"You dislike being called 'witch'?" Idath sneered. "Suffer then the demands of your creation, Heart of Magic Itself!"

He curled a finger, and Mab felt herself rip asunder.

CHAPTER 48

"There is a way"

THERE COULD BE no greater agony than this. Her entire being, her very soul, was aflame. She was blinded by the surrounding white light. Light that she herself emitted. Light that came from deep within. She felt her throat tearing with a tortured scream, but she heard nothing.

The deafening clang of an enormous hammer. The bending, breaking, moulding, of new life from intangible essence.

She had been content as ethereal vapour, part of the fabric of the world, intertwined with the air and the ground, the fire, the darkness, the seas and the sky.

Why must she suffer now?

A voice calling her name.

Her name? Had she a name?

The voice screaming. Cracking with heartbreaking despair. It begged for her life, for her freedom. It begged an unseen force to release her.

Only laughter answered.

The voices… they all sounded so familiar.

She felt her heart race. The light pulsed behind her eyes. A steel spike of agony rent her skull. A forest of thorns erupted in her chest. Blood thumped hard in her ears. Her head felt like it might split in two. The voice called her name again.

Her name.

It was now choked with tears.

Why must they suffer?

Why must I suffer?

"*Peata,*" a soft voice broke into her mind. "I heard your suffering call."

A figure approached through the light. Arms outstretched, as though welcoming. Warmth spread through her chest.

"*Peata,*" the figure said again, and as it grew closer, its features became more defined.

"*Mamaí,*" Mab whispered. The childish word came to her before she could stop it. She found she need not use her voice for this. "I do not know what to do."

Danu, the Mother of the Heart of Magic Itself, smiled warmly. She cupped Mab's face in her warm hands.

"You are so strong, *Peata,*" she said. "You have suffered. You have taken so much burden. But there is great wisdom, great power, inside you."

"I am afraid, *Máthair.*"

Danu nodded. "I know, my child," she said. "As are we all. If Idath succeeds in his quest, he will not only destroy you and Erlik, he will be able to enter the House of the Old Gods and destroy us all."

"I cannot defeat him," Mab admitted. "He is too strong."

Danu smiled mysteriously.

"There is a way," she said. "The Great Smith will send you a sign. A gift. It will help you defeat the Lord of the Dead."

"But—"

"You must trust me, *Peata,*" Danu said, and stroked Mab's hair. The warmth in her chest spilled out into a smile, despite the torturous agony that wracked her body still. "Watch for the fire from the sky. You will know it is time."

The blinding light that clouded Mab's vision began to fade, and with it, Danu herself.

"I love you, my little Mab," she said.

Mab felt her heart swell. "I love you too, *Máthair.*"

Cold air flooded her body, and Mab felt herself falling.

Erlik watched helplessly. Mab's body remained prone, suspended in the air above them like a broken puppet. Her mouth wide in a soundless scream. Her limbs pulled taut. White light surrounded her like an aura, but there was nothing healing about this.

"Idath!" Erlik shouted. "Please, I beg you! Let her go!"

Idath laughed hard in retaliation, and said nothing. Thomas and Thissy clutched each other and stared at Mab. There was nothing any of them could do against such immense power.

"Idath, please!" Erlik tried once more, his voice breaking. Idath merely swiped his hand and flung Erlik against the wall.

He landed with a heavy thump, his already weary body aching.

"No," he whispered, shaking. He couldn't help her. He couldn't save her. He couldn't—

Then, as if by divine providence, as if the Old Gods had finally forgiven his transgressions, everything happened at once. An unseen hand pushed the point of a sword through Idath's chest from behind. His laughter stopped, replaced instead by a choked, wet gasp of surprise. He looked down at the blade protruding from his body. Tristan appeared from behind Idath, eyes wide and hands shaking. He stepped around him, eyes fixed on the blade.

Mab fell. *Mab!* Erlik leapt to his feet and dove to catch her. Her slumped body landed heavily into his, but he felt the warmth of her flesh, her beating heart, and he almost laughed with relief. He held her close. Her eyes fluttered open.

"We can defeat him," she whispered. "There is a way."

Before he could question her delirious mumbling, he heard voices around them.

"Tristan," Thissy hissed, beckoning him away from the dead man. He ran to her, and she embraced him.

Idath's wet, sticky chokes for breath returned to laughter. Slowly at first, then louder and harder, until the stones of the Iron Keep shook. Erlik held Mab closer, and Thomas clutched Thissy and Tristan.

Idath convulsed, and the silvery blade glowed red, blisteringly hot, and melted away to nothingness before their eyes. Idath slumped, as though expelling a particularly vicious poison. Then, head still bowed, he turned small, red eyes on Tristan.

"*Whelp.*"

Tristan vanished from Thissy's arms. Idath stretched out his hands, fingers curled into a claw as if choking an invisible enemy. In a blink, Idath's fist was full of Tristan's throat, and the boy scrabbled at his hand.

"Bring my brother to me, and I will return the boy to you," Idath said in a low voice. "Fail, and he will die."

Idath vanished, along with Tristan, leaving only horrified silence in his wake.

CHAPTER 49

"It is a wise man who fears the unknown"

TRISTAN FORCED HIS hands to stop trembling. His breath to slow. His heart to stop racing. Black smoke cleared from his vision, and his feet hit solid ground. With barely time to allow his eyes to adjust to these new surroundings, Idath's cold hands dragged him through stone halls. A ruin, battered by storms. Tristan could hear sloshing waves against a shore.

The roof of this ancient ruin had long worn away, and an icy wind keened through the empty halls. The freezing air bit deep into Tristan's flesh. Idath dragged him through a half-destroyed archway into what looked like an old arena.

Tristan had heard stories about the Romans across the sea, who threw heretics into pits like this and forced them to fight enormous, vicious cats. Tristan almost considered the irony; he too, it appeared, would be fighting for his life against a monster.

Only this monster had a different agenda.

Idath dragged Tristan to the centre of the arena where a stone cairn stood beside a dead tree. With a click of fingers, ropes bound Tristan to the tree. His quiver and bow fell from his shoulders. They clattered to the ground, a few feet away. Idath ignored it. Perhaps because he knew no mortal weapons could harm him. Tristan wondered – not for the first time – what *could?*

Tristan said nothing. He'd tied enough snares in the forest and caught enough rabbits to know what he was now. *Bait in a trap.*

He shivered. Whispers came from every shadow, every corner. A skittering, high-pitched laugh danced off the stone.

Idath looked up.

"Silence," he spat. His deep voice echoed through the arena. The whispers and laughing stopped at once.

Idath turned to him, "Are you afraid, boy?"

Tristan swallowed and tilted his head so he faced the sky.

"Yes," he said truthfully. Idath nodded, as though he appreciated the honesty.

"Good," he said. Tristan looked at him in surprise. "It is a wise man who fears the unknown."

Night shrouded the courtyard like a velvet cloak, though one that offered no warmth.

"Do you know where you are bound, boy?" Idath asked, his voice quiet, as if he didn't want to frighten him further.

"The Gates of Annwyn," he replied. Although no one had told him, he felt in his heart he was right. The very air felt… *wrong.* Perhaps his new magic gave him insight. It vibrated under his skin. Telling him this place was unnatural. That Idath himself was unnatural. The Lord of the Dead nodded.

Idath circled the cairn, running his fingers over the stones.

"Indeed, but it is more than that," he said, and faced Tristan again. He looked deep into those sharp, wintry eyes. "This is my tomb."

A chill hand gripped Tristan's throat. He had been bound to a gravestone.

Idath continued, "This is where my body was interred after my wretched brother killed me. And this is where I will return the favour."

"And I'm the lure on your line?" Tristan asked. Idath sneered.

"You are smart, boy," he said. "I hope your mother and father are as clever."

"What do you mean?"

Idath gave him a nasty smile, showing his blackened teeth. He raised his hand and rubbed the torn flesh of his chest. Tristan tried not to stare, but it was grotesquely fascinating.

"You are indeed, the *lure on my line*," he repeated with a simper. "Your mother and father will come to rescue you. The Heart will follow for fear of their lives, and my brother, in turn, will follow *it*."

Idath began circling him again.

"Their hearts are weak and weighted by love. The Heart will be the cause of my brother's death, just as it was the cause of mine."

"I thought you said Erlik killed you?"

Idath narrowed his eyes at him, as if trying to decide how much to tell him. He sniffed.

"Erlik's hand carried the sword, but the Heart's voice guided it," he said coldly. "It told my brother it *loved* him." Idath spat the word like a disgusting curse. "I had planned to break it open and procure the magic inside. But my brother would not allow it. He tricked himself into thinking he loved it."

"He does love it—*her*," Tristan argued quietly. He knew he was treading on thin ice in talking back to him, but the Lord of the Dead seemed more interested in telling his story now.

"He does not love it," Idath replied, slowly pacing. "He cannot love it. It is not real. It is a clay doll, a puppet, a golem. The Heart of Magic Itself, carved into the shape of a woman."

Tristan frowned. How could that be so? He had seen her bleed. He'd seen her pain. She had thoughts and feelings like any other woman, any other *person*. Though he had yet to see her cry, he'd seen the hurt and love in her eyes, he'd seen her anger and her happiness. He'd seen her laughter, her strength, her pride. She was more real than Idath realised.

As though reading Tristan's thoughts in his expression, Idath sneered and spoke again.

"It is but a vessel for the magic it harbours," Idath continued. "The Old Gods were foolish to put such power in the form of a frail and small creature. A woman has no place on a throne, or in possession of great magic."

"But you do?" Tristan challenged. He regretted his words at once, when Idath turned his red gaze on him. He leaned closer to his face, close enough for Tristan to smell his foul breath. The stench of one who'd been dead too long.

"I do."

✦ ✦ ✦

"MALEAGANT!" ERLIK BELLOWED, kicking open every door in the Keep. "Show your miserable face, you coward!"

"Erlik, slow down!"

Mab chased after him. Thomas and Thissy had gone to retrieve Isolde and bring her inside. Now that Idath had vacated the Keep, it seemed less cold within the stone walls.

Empty room after empty room, and Mab finally caught up to Erlik. Face pale, hair dishevelled, silver armour scuffed. She wanted nothing more than to lie down and rest. Her limbs ached with exhaustion.

"We do not have time to seek out Maleagant and Carman," she said. "We must return to Elphame and regroup. You are still weak, as am I."

"I won't let that boy down again," Erlik said, shoving another door open, and slamming it closed when he found nothing. Mab watched him in surprise. She daren't speak her mind, but she knew how Erlik reacted when he cared about someone. Especially when that someone was in danger.

"Then we must find out where Idath has taken him," Mab said aloud.

"And we will," Erlik pushed open another door, only to find yet another empty room. "What better way than to find those who summoned him in the first place?"

Erlik was already halfway down the corridor, another six doors kicked open as he went. Mab rolled her eyes. *Bull-headed, stubborn...*

"With the noise you are making," she called, storming

towards him. "They will likely have already left the Keep for a safer sanctuary."

Erlik kicked a door; it remained jammed shut. He raised an eyebrow.

"You think so?" Erlik said, glancing at Mab. He kicked the door again. It remained unyieldingly closed. He thrust all his weight against it, grunting with effort, and Mab sighed and pushed him away.

"Allow me," she said. She waved her hand over the door, and the wood rippled like water. With a wry smile, she stepped through the door. Erlik followed her.

Her eyes met a dark room. A small, somewhat pathetic fire in the hearth illuminated Maleagant and Carman's frightened faces.

Erlik sneered as he strode past Mab. "How cosy. A little warren for a pair of frightened rabbits."

Maleagant stood up to fight, but Erlik grabbed his collar and shoved him against the wall.

"Tell me where Idath has gone," Erlik spat in his face.

"I-I don't—" Maleagant stammered. Erlik slammed him against the wall.

"Stop babbling," he said. "Where has he *gone?*"

Once more, Maleagant stammered but couldn't find the words. Mab marvelled at Erlik's outburst. She had never seen him so protective of anyone other than her. Thinking on it more, she could see how Erlik would feel a kinship with Tristan Rhymer. A roguish, charming lad, skilled at stealth and easily a wonderful thief or spy.

Carman's voice broke into her thoughts.

"We don't know! We don't know where he's gone!" she cried, voice shaking. Mab threw a piercing glower at Carman. "Be silent, harridan," she snapped, and Carman clamped her mouth shut at once.

"Thank you," Erlik nodded to Mab and then turned his attention back to Maleagant. "Now, where were we?"

"I swear, I don't know where he is!" Maleagant managed to choke out.

"You're lying!" Erlik shook him hard.

"I swear! I don't know!" Maleagant wept. "Please, Father, I don't know!"

Mab could watch no longer. Maleagant looked so pathetic, so pitiful.

She laid a hand on his arm. "Erlik, let him down. He knows nothing."

"He stood by and watched as Idath tortured me," Erlik spat. "Should I ignore *that?*"

"No," she said in a calming voice. "I too have my own score to settle with them *both*. But look at him."

Erlik did so. Maleagant's face was wet with tears and mucus, scrunched up in fear and misery. The very picture of a sorry mess.

"Let him down," she said again, gently.

Erlik let out a noise of disgust and let go. Maleagant dropped to the floor, his head in his arms, sobbing.

"Come," she said. "Leave them to their misery."

She took his hand and guided him out of the room.

"Mab?"

Thomas's voice rang clear through the halls. Mab followed the sound, Erlik after her, until she found the issuer.

Catching up to each other, Mab eyed what remained of the Rhymer family.

Thomas had removed his armour so could run and move more freely. He looked so much smaller without his plate. So much like the boy he'd been when they first met. He'd kept his mail shirt and gambeson. It would've been a foolish venture to proceed without any form of guard.

Thissy's eyes were red and puffy, but she was set with steely determination. A frown constantly creased her brow. Her hands had clenched into fists.

"Where is Isolde?" Mab asked.

"When the mounts fled," Thomas said. "They ran to her. She managed to calm them down. She's taken Epona and returned to Elphame with the other horses. And your stag."

Mab nodded her gratitude. It seemed silly to worry about a

beast, but she did care for Oisín.

"Have you found anything?" Thomas asked, breaking her thoughts.

Mab shook her head, "Only Maleagant and Carman—"

"But they don't know anything," Erlik finished for her. "They'll be no use to us."

"Won't they?" Thissy growled. Mab blinked.

This was no longer the placid girl who was once too frightened to ask if she could leave Albion and be with Thomas. She was now a mother, a she-wolf defending her cub. She would walk through fire for her son. And, it appeared, she was prepared to do just so.

"Where are they hiding?" she asked. Erlik beckoned her. She strode after him, hands still balled into fists.

Once at the door, Erlik gestured.

"After you, Mistress Rhymer," he bowed slightly to her. It would have been mocking, but for the gleam of genuine respect in his eyes.

Thissy pushed on the door. It didn't move. She touched the wood. Mab's magic had faded.

Mab moved forward, hand outstretched, but Thissy had other designs. She balled her hand into a fist, and her hand alighted with dancing green flames.

The door exploded. Erlik dove at Mab to shield her from the shards of splintered wood. Thomas grabbed Thissy and pulled her away.

The dust and splinters settled. The remains of the shredded door hung limply from the hinges. Maleagant and Carman once more stared at the intrusion with frightened eyes.

"We told you, we don't know anything!" Maleagant began. Thissy stormed in.

"Where is my son?" she hissed. Dust had settled on her face and in her hair. She looked a hundred years older.

"I—" Maleagant's eyes darted between her and the others. "I already told you, I don't know!"

"Thistledown, we have already—" Mab began. Thissy

snatched her clawed hand at the small fire. Embers followed her command and surrounded Maleagant's head. His face glowed red, his face already sheen with sweat.

"*Where is my son?*" she screamed.

The embers glowed brighter. And crept closer.

"Tell me where I can find him, or I swear I will burn you alive," she whispered, voice hoarse.

"I s-swear, I-I don't—"

"*We don't know!*" Carman screamed. All eyes turned to her. Her face flushed. Mab narrowed her eyes at her; despite the pitiful situation she'd landed herself in, Mab despised the woman. "Please, we don't know! Just leave us alone!"

Thissy *hmph*'d and pushed past the wretched woman. In the hallway, Mab could hear Maleagant still sniffling and Carman muttering.

"What now?" Thomas said, taking his wife's hand. It didn't quell the furious determination in her eyes.

"There may be something else," Mab said, looking thoughtful. "I have a shade of an idea. Come, follow me."

THE ROOM WAS almost completely destroyed. Black marks scorched the walls. The painted ceiling was smoke-burnt. Even the air still hung heavy with ash.

The four carefully picked through the debris in the crumbling study. Over a fallen beam and joist. Through the ashes. Stepping over the sickly contents of smashed jars. Erlik noticed a heart beating weakly in a pool of green liquid. Even as he stared, the thing pumped one final time, then faded to grey, withered and dry.

"There's nothing here," came Thissy's quiet voice, as Mab stepped carefully around the room.

"What was your idea, Mab?" Thomas called from the other side of the room.

Mab directed her answer to Erlik, "Do you recall when Idath said you were '*blood of his blood*'?"

Erlik tried and failed to withhold his wince.

"I do, though I'd rather not," he said. Then his face lifted. "Blood-to-blood, you mean? A tracking spell?"

Mab pulled a face.

"You know I hate that word," she said.

"Tracking?" Erlik grinned at her. Mab gave him an amused smirk despite herself. His heart swelled at seeing her smile again.

"But yes," she went on. "We used it once, do you remember? Magic that uses blood to find those who have been lost."

"I don't think Idath has lifeblood left in him," Erlik pointed out. "He is dead, after all."

"True," Mab agreed, and cast her eyes towards Thomas and Thissy. "But Tristan is not."

THE FOUR STOOD around a stone basin, filled to the brim with crystal clear water. Mab held out the knife for Thomas. He hesitated in taking it.

"You're sure this will work?" he asked, chewing his thumbnail. Mab nodded.

"Quite certain," she said. "We can use both you and Thistledown to find Tristan. Given he has both of your bloodlines running in his veins, it will give us a better chance, more likely a clearer image of where Idath has taken him."

"It's just," Thomas paused. "Blood-to-blood sounds…"

He trailed off. Erlik expelled a snort.

"Squeamish?" he smirked.

"No," Thomas retorted. "It's just… blood magic—"

"True blood magic is used to control the minds and wills of others," Mab said, offering the knife again. "This is simply a means of connecting your living bloodlines, to seek Tristan's location."

"Oh, for goodness' sake!"

Thissy snatched the knife and drew it fluidly down her forearm. Thomas winced as she held the wound over the basin and let the red liquid splash into the water. She shoved the knife into his hands, even as she healed her own arm.

"We'll never find Tristan if we stand around talking about it," she snapped. And Thomas saw once more the fierce, motherly determination he'd always loved in her. He took the knife and mimicked her motion. The wound stung like a hundred nettles. His blood dribbled into the water, muddying it dark red. Mab leaned over the basin.

"The image is forming, but it is dark," she said.

"Here," Erlik conjured a handful of fire and held it close to the basin. The four crowded closer.

An image of Tristan formed. Alive, awake, though his face was white as snow. He appeared to be sitting, bound to a large dead tree. Idath came into view, circling him. His mouth moved, though the image remained silent. The view muddled and went dark, and suddenly all that remained was a basin of bloody water.

"No!" Thissy pawed the water, splashing it everywhere. "It wasn't enough! I can't tell where he is! We need to do it again!"

"No, we don't," Erlik said quietly. He turned his back. "I know where they are."

"Erlik?" Mab asked.

"Idath has returned to his resting place," he said. "His grave. At the Gates of Annwyn."

CHAPTER 50

"You are weak"

THE SLIVER OF moonlight barely lit their way. The water was silent as the silver boat glided across its glassy surface. Mab stood at the stern, while Thissy sat at the prow, anxiously wringing her hands. Her eyes darted around the darkness, chewing her lips until they bled.

She hadn't said a word on the journey to this dark crystal lake. The sun had crept to the horizon and sank beneath it by the time they reached their destination. The walk had exhausted them, yet they pressed on.

Thomas and Erlik sat together, each leaning on their respective gunwales. This little boat had no mast or sails, no rudders or helm. Mab had called it from the depths as they stood at the water's edge, a little pebbly beach for the mysterious boat to berth.

The small craft sliced silently through the water, guided and kept afloat by Mab's small hand motions. She had summoned a small basket of fruit, berries, and nuts, but no one felt particularly hungry.

Erlik lifted his head and gazed at her. She seemed at home here, in this shimmering darkness. During the day, she appeared to be a scrap of glittering night, dropped from the sky into an unfamiliar and ungrateful world. Had they not been slowly sailing towards their possible doom, he would have been calmed by her presence.

"What is it?" she asked quietly, her voice breaking the silence of night. Erlik blinked; he hadn't realised he'd been staring. He shook his head.

"Nothing," he mumbled, and looked down at the water again.

Something bright and silver flashed beneath the surface. Erlik did a double take.

"Rhymer, look," he grabbed Thomas' arm and pulled him over to his side. "There's something in the water."

Thomas squinted, then shuffled back when the silvery something flickered past again.

"Mab," Thomas looked at her. "We're not alone."

"Here," Thissy's voice was quiet and broken, thick with tears, but strong enough to draw their attention. All eyes turned, and found, hanging from the boat's prow, her arms folded around the breast hook so she could speak, a silver-haired merrow; skin glowing blue beneath the light of the moon, eyes violet and shining.

"Hail, Mab, Queen of the Old Ways, Empress of Albion, and the Heart of Magic Itself," the merrow said. "I bring a message from Melusine."

Mab nodded, "Speak."

"The Each-Uisge has taken the life of your Steward and his company," she said. "Their bodies were found in Smuggler's Haunt, and returned to Elphame by Captain Bonney."

All eyes turned on Mab. Her ashen face like marble in the cold air. She inhaled, long and slow.

"How?"

"We believe it to have been a diplomatic mission to Misthaven and King Herne," the merrow said. "But we cannot be certain."

Mab nodded.

"I cannot thank you for this. But you have done me a service," she said. The merrow bowed her head.

"Your Grace," a gentle splash followed her words as the merrow departed.

Mab turned instead to Thissy, "Lightfoot raised you as his own. If you wish to mourn him, I can return you to Elphame, and we will go on to save Tristan."

Thissy stood, unsteady in the rocking boat.

"Lightfoot is dead," she said in a hard voice. "Tristan is alive. He needs me more."

Mab nodded in tense agreement.

"Mab," Thomas said carefully. "If Lightfoot is dead, then Elphame has no leadership. *You* should go back."

She shook her head.

"I cannot," she said. "Not now. I must see this through. The end of Idath is my responsibility, just as the rescue of your son is yours. The Queen's Council will assume leadership for now. And if I do not return…"

She fell silent, and no one dared speak. Mab swallowed and waved her hand again, and the boat resumed its movement towards the dark shape looming through the shadows.

"THERE IT IS," Thissy said at last. Thomas stood up and eyed the huge edifice emerging from the blue mist.

Black with age, the ruin looked ready to crumble to the ground. Their little boat nudged the shore, and Thomas and Erlik disembarked with a splash, pulling the boat further onto the beach. Thomas extended his hand to help Thissy climb out of the boat, and Mab stepped onto the pebbles, boots crunching. The air seemed to grow colder, and Thomas saw Thissy clutch her cloak around her.

"This place," Thissy said, and shook her head, shivering, unable to continue. She didn't have to; Thomas could feel it too. The veil between worlds was thin, and a pulsing aura around the entire island felt invasive. He felt as though the darkness itself was pressing around him, trying to suffocate him.

"Come," Mab said, and pushed forward into the blackness of the ruins. Thomas marvelled at her for a moment. Every living creature in Albion feared Idath, and Mab and Erlik had reason to fear him most of all. Yet she ploughed on, into the darkness, towards danger. She was a wilful creature, full of pride and purpose.

Thissy grabbed his hand and kept a tight hold on it, and he could feel her fingers trembling in his.

With Mab leading the way, footsteps light and certain, at last they found an open courtyard; Thomas found it to resemble an arena, with a stone cairn in the centre. Cold air wrapped around him, and the darkness seemed to intensify, as if it could sense the presence of life and despised it.

"*Tristan!*" Thissy shouted, and pushed past Thomas. Mab hissed, her eyes darting for Idath. Yet he could not be seen, and Thomas dashed after his wife.

"Tristan," he said softly as he skidded to a halt beside him and knelt down. Tristan's head lolled to the side, and Thomas pressed his fingers to his son's throat.

"He's alive," he breathed a sigh of relief. "Thissy, he's alive."

"Thank the gods," she clutched Tristan tight. "Tristan, *a páiste*, wake up."

His eyes cracked open and he groaned. Blinking, he sat up as best he could; Thomas tried to summon a weak flame to burn away the ropes binding Tristan, but he'd never had a strong affinity for summoning such magic, and drew his dagger to saw them off instead.

"Mother!" Tristan's eyes widened. "Father, no, it's a trap!"

The words had no sooner left his mouth, when a powerful gust of wind lifted Thomas like a ragdoll and threw him across the arena. He slammed against the blackened stone wall and slumped to the ground.

A dark chuckle echoed from the shadows, and Idath emerged like a ghost. Thissy pulled Tristan to his feet and away from Idath. Tristan tripped over his bow and scrambled to pick it up.

"Idath!" Mab's voice rang through the night. He turned his gaze on her.

"I knew you would come," he said. "I told the boy how love has made you frail."

Thomas looked up slowly, his vision blurred. Thissy bent over him, Tristan beside her, helping him to his feet.

Idath was a monstrous creature, towering over them all like a statue, as pale and dry as bone. The only splash of colour about him was the red, gaping wound in his chest.

"You are the Champion of Elphame?" Idath mocked.

"Leave them alone!" Thissy commanded, but the waver in her voice belied her bravery. Idath sneered and easily swatted her away.

"THOMAS, *NO!*" HE heard Mab call, but her words went unheeded. Thomas drew his sword and aimed for Idath's heart, but the dead man knew it was a blind attack of rage, and easily prepared for it.

Thomas lunged with a roar. Idath dodged, surprisingly nimble for such a large man, and swiped Thomas across the back with one of his claw-like hands. Thomas staggered, suddenly realising that he was prey to be toyed with.

He brought up his sword again, but Idath took hold of the blade. The metal made a hideous noise as Idath crunched it into uselessness, and Thomas gulped hard and took a step back.

"You are weak," Idath said, but got no further. Thomas flicked his hand, and his fingers blazed with red fire, which he threw straight at Idath's face.

The flames billowed around his head, and he roared like a wounded bull, staggering back, his hands flying to his face to claw the fire away.

Thomas saw his chance. He ran for Thissy and Tristan, and dragged them to their feet.

"Separate!" he shouted to Mab over Idath's bellowing, and ran with his family into one of the ruin's dark corridors.

Mab nodded and grabbed Erlik's hand to drag him behind her, fleeing into darkness. Erratic bolts of fire bounded through the air like birds, some hitting their monstrous target and others flitting into the night to fizzle into nothing.

IDATH'S LUMBERING FOOTSTEPS grew quieter as Mab and Erlik vanished into the shadowy maze. Pausing for a moment to catch their breath, they took shelter behind a wall that had managed to stay almost intact.

In the brief moment of solace, Erlik pulled Mab into an embrace, wrapping his arms tightly around her. She buried her face into his chest.

"What do we do?" she said, her words mumbled. Erlik shook his head.

"I don't know," he admitted. "We have Tristan now. We can escape and flee to Elphame?"

"Idath will follow," Mab said, pulling away. "He will lay waste to the city. I cannot endanger my people. We must stop him here, tonight. And the only way to do so is to return him to Annwyn."

"You said there was a way," Erlik said. "At the Keep, when you fell. You said there was a way to destroy him for good."

Mab paused, then nodded.

"I had a… a vision," she admitted. It sounded foolish to say it aloud. "My mother, she came to me."

Erlik raised an eyebrow.

"I am not mad," she said, pre-empting his mockery. "I know I saw her. She told me the Great Smith would send us a sign, a gift. She said to watch for the fire in the sky."

She stole a glance around the corner to see if Idath had followed them. Her heart fluttered frantically like a trapped bird against a cage of ribs.

"We don't have time to wait for signs," Erlik said carefully. "Maybe your first instinct was right. Maybe we don't destroy him, we just contain him."

"But how do we open the Gate?" she asked. Erlik shrugged.

"I've no idea," he said again. "Maybe Maleagant—"

"*Brother!*"

The bellow stole the air from her chest, and Mab grabbed Erlik to silence him and pressed her back against the wall. She could hear Idath's heavy breathing as he approached. A slither of fear raced down her spine. She cast her eyes around, and saw, above them, dangling shreds of moss and ivy.

With a clever twist of her fingers, the ivy rapidly grew down towards them, until it formed a curtain of plant life, covering Mab and Erlik and shielding them from view.

They remained still, statues in the dark, barely breathing. Idath's shape appeared in front of them. They held their breath. Mab closed her eyes.

A soft tumble of rocks. Idath's head snapped to the noise.

A rat? Mab thought. She didn't care. It stole Idath's attention, for he moved on, a dark and dangerous predator.

Mab released a long slow breath and opened her eyes again. Erlik let go of her hand, and she flexed her stiff fingers.

"Come," she whispered, parting the curtain of ivy. "Let us find the others."

CHAPTER 51

"Into death, even?"

T HOMAS CLUTCHED THISSY'S hand so tight, her fingers had turned white. They had fled deeper into the cold ruins. Further from the safety of the boat. Further from Erlik and Mab. Further from Idath's rage.

Tristan flitted behind, light as a cat in the shadows, quiver bobbing on his shoulder.

The ruins seemed to creak around them, but no sound reached their ears to suggest Idath was behind them. *He must've pursued his brother,* Thomas thought, and found himself both blessing their own luck and cursing Erlik and Mab's.

Finding a small alcove to hide themselves in, the three ducked into the shadows and rested against the wall; hearts pounding and breath burning in their throats.

Thissy swallowed.

"What do we do?" she asked, and Thomas knew what she really meant: *how do we help Tristan escape?*

"I don't know," Thomas admitted. "If we loop around, maybe we could reach the boat?"

"No," Tristan said, standing straight after having bent double to catch his breath. "We can't leave Erlik and Mab. Besides, Idath knows this place better than we do. He'd find us before we reached the shore."

"Tristan," Thissy said, wrapping her hands around his face.

"I know you want to help, but this is beyond even us. If we can get you to safety—"

"Then I'd sit in Elphame, waiting for Idath to come and kill us all, spending my last few hours utterly wracked with guilt for having left my parents to die," Tristan snapped. "I'm not leaving this place without you, or without Erlik and Mab. And since we can't leave, we can only stay and fight. If we die, then we die fighting, and die together."

Thissy blinked away her tears. Thomas's chest burned, not with breathlessness this time, but pride.

"IDATH!"

The furious bellow ripped through the night. Thomas, Thissy, and Tristan froze. Idath would surely follow that shout. It was the nature of every thinking creature to respond to its name, but Idath would ignore the name and follow the *challenge*. The pure confrontational anger within the voice would be enough to pique Idath's attention.

Do they dare respond to it as well? Thomas took a few tentative steps, and Thissy grabbed his arm.

"It could be a trap," she warned. Thomas gazed at her for a moment.

"Stay here," he said. "Tristan, stay with your mother. *Don't argue*," he added, when Tristan opened his mouth to protest. The boy closed his lips again and nodded.

Thomas withdrew his dagger and followed the sound of the shout, trying to ignore the pulsing blood in his ears.

"THAT SOUNDED LIKE—"

"I know."

Erlik and Mab shared a glance. The shout had startled another large rat into scurrying across their path. The skittering of its tiny paws made her skin crawl.

"How did he find this place?" she asked.

"More importantly, what does he want?" Erlik said, throwing a glance down a dark hallway.

"Let us find out," Mab stepped past him and towards the

darkness, but Erlik lunged forward and pulled her back.

"*Whoa*, there" he said, like he was calming a horse. Mab raised an eyebrow at him. "I didn't realise madness could take you so quickly."

"Meaning?"

"He called for *Idath*, so Idath will follow the noise. You'll walk right into his path," he said.

"So what should we do?"

"I'll go find out what he's doing here, you stay," Erlik said, gently pushing her backwards under the ivy. Mab resisted.

"Mab," he said slowly, almost like a warning.

"Erlik," she replied, matching his tone. "I will not stay here while you risk your life."

"I'd be careful," he began, but Mab cut across him.

"We go together," she said, and took his hand. He gazed at her, and her eyes glittered with wildness. There was fierceness there, and obstinacy.

"Into death, even?" he asked quietly.

She nodded.

IDATH'S HEAD SNAPPED to the call of his name. The voice was laced with desperation and provocation. A summons to battle. He turned, cold seeping into his muscles, stiffening his movements. He would answer this call, and perhaps the shout would be enough to draw out his curious, cowering quarry.

His footsteps heavy, he stalked the dark corridors, small eyes darting to and fro for signs of his brother. At last, he emerged into the arena, to the sight of Maleagant, supporting Carman who hung off his arm like a dying woman.

A cruel smile curled Idath's lips.

"You must help her!" Maleagant demanded, half dragging Carman with him as he approached.

"Must I?" Idath replied.

"She's *dying!*"

She certainly looked that way, but Idath knew better. Idath had granted her this gift, a taste of magic. But his power was drawn from Annwyn, and a living soul could not sustain death magic for long. Idath's gut twisted with bitterness. *The desire to live will always outweigh a desire to die.*

"She is not," Idath said aloud. "The magic within her is dying."

"But you said—"

"Had your woman not entangled herself in my brother's bed sheets, perhaps she would have retained the magic for longer," Idath said, raising his voice to make sure Erlik heard him, wherever he be hiding nearby. "But her body is rejecting the magic all the faster, because she is with child."

"How?" Carman croaked. Her eyes were sunken pits in the clammy paleness of her face.

Through gritted teeth, Idath said, "Because the soul of your unborn whelp carries magic, and it is warring against that which I gave you."

"My child will have magic?" Carman's eyes seemed to alight with greed; she had a means now of accessing power. This wouldn't be a child to her, only a tool.

"No," and Idath took great pleasure in watching her face fall. "It will *carry* magic."

Before Carman could retort, a noise stole Idath's attention. Barely a breath, hardly a whisper, a gentle puff of air that suggested someone was close. His head snapped to the noise.

"The Champion of Elphame," Idath called. "Come, face death."

Idath saw the Champion's hands twist on his dagger hilt.

"Let my wife and son go," he demanded, taking a slow approach towards Idath. A curious quirk tipped Idath's brow.

"They hold no interest to me. I seek only my brother and the Heart."

"What will you do with them?" the Champion had almost reached him now. Idath narrowed his eyes. This conversation felt forced. He said nothing in reply, only took two short steps towards the Champion.

THOMAS SAW ERLIK and Mab on the border of his sight. He forced himself to keep staring at Idath, to keep him talking, to keep his attention. Erlik whispered something to Mab, and she vanished into the shadows, still out of Idath's sight.

"What will you do with them?" Thomas repeated, when Idath didn't reply. His small eyes were thin with suspicion, and Thomas's heart dropped hard into his stomach.

"I will do what I intended to do centuries ago," Idath said slowly. "I will break open the Heart of Magic Itself, and my brother will witness his *love* destroyed before his very eyes, knowing it was only a golem, harbouring the most powerful weapon ever created."

"Mab is stronger than you realise," Thomas said, standing straighter. "She can't be broken so easily."

"I have heard enough blather from you, boy," Idath sneered, and lunged forward, hands like huge white spiders in the darkness.

Thomas twisted and spun away, blade careening wildly. He slashed at Idath, but no blood spurted from the open wounds. How could it? The man had been dead for centuries.

Idath stumbled, but recovered swiftly, and charged at Thomas like a bull. Thomas thought wildly of when he fought Erlik's son Balor. *At least Balor had a sense of honour.*

The mundane thought had barely crossed Thomas's mind, when a boulder the size of a small pony, wreathed in black flame, smashed into Idath, and sent him sprawling across the courtyard with a furious roar.

Thomas lifted his gaze and found Erlik, fingers aflame with dark fire; nimble movements lifting more rocks and boulders and firing them at Idath, burying him beneath a steadily growing cairn.

Erlik offered Thomas a curt nod, and beckoned him away.

"Father!"

Both Thomas and Erlik reacted to the shout, but it was for Erlik's attention. Maleagant sat, Carman's head in his lap, hair plastered to her forehead with sweat. Thomas sheathed his dagger and approached them, but Erlik laid a hand on his arm to stop him.

"Don't trust either of them," he warned darkly. He cast a glance back at Idath, buried beneath a small mountain of boulders. He'd bought them only moments.

"Take her away from here, Maleagant," Erlik said. "Find a village and live out the rest of your pathetic life in quiet and unassuming peace. *And*," he added, "never meddle with powerful magic again."

"Thomas!"

"Father!"

"Erlik!"

All heads turned to the tangle of voices, as Thissy, Tristan, and Mab emerged from within the ruins, and ran towards Thomas and Erlik.

"Where's Idath?" Mab immediately asked, as Thissy and Tristan ran into Thomas's embrace. Erlik gestured to the gently shifting hill of rubble.

"We need to open the Gates of Annwyn," Erlik said, and at once, all eyes turned to Maleagant.

There was a silent pause before he realised.

"Wh-b-but I can't," he mumbled. "Not again. It needs blood—blood magic. I needed a hundred men last time just to—"

"You *butchered*—?!" Mab began, starting towards him in a rage, but Erlik held her back.

"Then we need to find another way," Thomas began, but a bursting roar silenced him. The cairn of rocks burying Idath exploded, and the man himself emerged, dusty and dishevelled, and furious as a storm.

"You used *blood*?" he snarled, and held out a curling fist. Carman vanished in a wisp of black smoke with a fading echo of a yelp, and Maleagant's body lifted from the ground, like a marionette, and dragged itself towards Idath.

The dead man grabbed Maleagant by the collar and shook him hard.

"Idiot boy!" he growled. "*That* is why I am not as strong as I should be! You used *blood*, instead of *life!*"

Before any of them could move, Idath lifted Maleagant from the ground and held him skyward, as though offering a sacrifice to the stars.

"Long is the day, and long is the night," Idath bellowed. "Long is the waiting of Arawn's might!"

Maleagant erupted in bright red flame, his form convulsing, screaming a long and wordless shriek of agony. Idath began to laugh. The sound bounced off the ancient stones and echoed all around the ruin.

"Behold! My children, my army, my fellows!" Idath bellowed, and the Gates of Annwyn opened above him.

CHAPTER 52

"What do we do?"

THE SKY SPLIT apart in virescent hues, a pulsing flame gushing forth like a hungry river, eager to devour all in its path. Idath raised his arms, screaming in victorious splendour, yet his voice was drowned by tumultuous roaring loud enough to shake the pillars of the ancient circle.

"What was that?" Thomas bellowed, arms raised and straining to see against the raging wind and darkness. Mab cast a terrified glance at Erlik, who tore his eyes away from the pulsing hole in the sky to return it.

A melanic talon punctured the veil, slowly at first, then widening the gap for the creature to emerge. The rest of the claw followed, scaled like a lizard, monstrously huge. A second, taloned paw broke through, tearing through the thin membrane that separated the two worlds. With a sweeping gesture, the veil broke, and the dragon fell into the world of the living.

The ground shook with the weight. Landing awkwardly, wings bent and crumpled under its bulk, the dragon struggled to right itself. It roared and snapped at nothing, frustrated at itself, like a beetle on its back.

Obsidian scales glittered like precious stones, gleaming in the darkness. The dragon found its feet and stretched its enormous, leathery wings wide. Like sails, they filled at once with air currents, ready to take the beast on its first flight across the skies of this realm. Digging its claws into the soft earth, the dragon turned its opal eyes on each observer in turn.

"No sudden movements," Erlik said in a low voice.

Idath's pale form appeared through the darkness like a ghost.

"It has not come alone," he sneered, pointing to the portal. There, with each pulsing beat, another dragon – green, this time – clawed its way out of Annwyn. Idath's bellowing laughter rang through the night.

"Take to the skies once more!" He howled. "Burn the earth! Boil the seas! Incinerate every last being you see!"

Idath spat the words with malice, his eyes wide with insanity.

More and more dragons tore free of Annwyn, wings immediately lifting them into the sky. They circled like vultures, ignoring the easy prey below, relishing in their newfound freedom, before each going their own way and soaring off into the night.

"What do we do?" Erlik whispered to Mab.

She had frozen, her eyes wide, fixed and staring at the portal. Her breast heaved, lips parted, no words came from her.

"Mab," Erlik took her hand when she said nothing. "What do we do?"

She looked down at his fingers curled into hers, then lifted her eyes to his.

"I do not know," she whispered, with a slight, frightful shake of her head.

She released her hand from his and gazed at her shaking hands in despair.

"*A múirnín?*" Erlik whispered. She looked at him, her heart fragmented. His dark, liquid eyes filled her with sorrow. His thumb brushed her trembling jaw.

Mab looked again to the portal, still pulsing and vomiting out dragons. Every moment she hesitated, another beast tore itself from Annwyn and flew free into Albion. Idath stood below the gateway, watching with twisted delight each time another dragon was borne into the world.

Thomas, Thissy, and Tristan cowered behind a broken pillar, tightly clutching each other, eyes squeezed shut as if hoping to black out the terrors of the night.

Mab felt a hard, heavy weight drop in her chest, as if her fractured heart had become stone.

She had sworn to protect her people. *These* were her people, her most beloved, and she was failing them. They shook violently, fear tightly agrip. Tristan's eyes cracked open, and sought her. Pleading. Desperate. Terrified.

"No more," she whispered.

She gently released herself from Erlik's grip and stepped out into the centre of the arena. The stone cairn that stood as Idath's grave undid itself, every pebble that made up that loose pyramid dismantled. The stone pillars unravelled, from boulders to gravel, darting from her path as though the rocks themselves feared her, and struck Idath's back and shoulders.

He turned, a manic grin flashing black teeth and wicked intent. His smile slipped slightly when he saw Mab approaching him with slow, deliberate steps.

"You are frail, witch!" he snarled. "Your exertions have exhausted you. The love you carry for those around you has softened you. You are weak, fragile, and you are powerless before me!"

"I need not prove myself to you," she said, her voice deep with age and power and fury, shaking the foundations of the ruined castle. He paused and took a half-step back. Her eyes flashed with bright, violet light. The wind whipped her hair around her face; a demon of the most ancient world. "But if you think me fragile, then you are wrong. If you think me weak, then you are wrong. And if you think me powerless, then you have already lost!"

She thrust her hands downwards around her, and the faithful magic she bore plunged deep below the surface of the soil and fed life to dead roots. A great rumble thundered around them. Idath staggered.

The ground split. A horned snout burst forth. The rest of the creature emerged. A winding, worm-like body. Teeth longer than a man's arm. An enormous beast, formed of roots and trees and compacted earth. A dragon, yet not a dragon. Gnarled and black sylvan bonds to obey the mistress of magic. A forest come to life.

It turned its stone eyes on Mab, who cowed it beneath her ferocious glare. It turned to Idath, rounding its whole snaking body to face him.

Parting its beak, it bellowed a high-pitched roar at him, sounding like the cracking of ancient branches. Idath reeled. Mab raised her right arm, her head low and her eyes burning, breath fast and hard.

"Tristan!"

The voice held no interest to her. She saw out of the corner of her vision, the boy had crept from his hiding place, gazing in awe and reverence.

"Tristan, get down!"

The voice came again, but once more she ignored it. The boy would realise the danger soon enough. High above, wind currents from the dragons beating wings dragged up leaves and debris into a swirling maelstrom.

Mab curled her hands, and the snake-beast slithered around Idath. His small eyes widened when he realised the intent. The roots ensnared him, curling and growing around him, lifting him from the ground, higher towards the Gate.

"No!" Idath screamed, thrashing and writhing against his bonds.

The hungry portal extended cobalt tendrils of magic to snare him and inhale him back to the realm in which he belonged.

"WITCH!"

ERLIK HAD ANTICIPATED this. He had seen it coming for a long time now. He knew, he had always known, that Idath would not go peacefully back into the realm of death.

Erlik had watched her, his miracle, his *wife*, the loveliest and fiercest and strongest among all, as she'd done this most impossible task alone. He'd considered aiding her. But what could he do compared to her? Her power, her spirit, now inflamed with wild, ferocious, protective love, was exquisite. Beyond compare. Next to her, his magic would seem like mere parlour tricks.

But even she had her limits.

The forest-dragon she'd conjured was already crumbling. Idath was trapped, caught halfway between this world and the next, his snarling face and left arm still free.

He'd taken control of one of the magic coils that had bound him, but one was all he would need. He lashed out with it, like a whip. It sharpened, pointed, became a silvery metallic blade. Like the tail of a scorpion, its stinger forged into a Deathblade.

Idath issued a wordless roar of victory. The tendril thrashed wildly, and Tristan Rhymer released a high scream of agony.

All eyes turned to him. His bow dropped to the ground, blood staining its wooden grip and limbs. He clutched his hand close to his chest, bending double like an old man. Erlik caught sight of his shaking right hand, shredded and torn by the Deathblade.

Thomas and Thissy screamed in horror and ran to their son. Mab cast a single glance their way. The distraction gave Idath the opening he needed, and thrust the tendril of magic towards her. The instigator of his suffering, and the victim of his ire.

Erlik's world slowed to a crawl. Instinct took hold. A primal impulse. Not to attack, but to *protect*. He saw her eyes widen, but knew in his heart she wouldn't be fast enough.

Without thought, without words, Erlik shoved Mab aside.

The tendril of magic wrapped around his ankle, hot and white pain coursing through him at the touch. It tripped him onto his back, and dragged him towards the rapidly closing portal.

Mab scrambled to her feet and ran after him.

"No! No, Erlik!" she dived onto her front, grabbing his hands to halt his ascent. "No! Gods, no, *please!*"

She staggered to her feet, still gripping his hands, pulling him back as hard as she could. But the tendrils pulled harder. Her boots scraped in the earth as their strength began taking her too.

"*No!* You will not take him!"

"Mab, let go!"

"No!"

"Let go or we're both lost!"

"*Then we are both lost!*"

Erlik had no more words. The pain of the deathly magic had taken them. He could only cast his eyes over her one last time, and take in all he could of that moonmilk face, now twisted with despair; her glittering moonlight eyes, now overfull with fear; those soft, sweet lips that had kissed him with such passion, now mouthing wordlessly.

Either she let go, or they would both be pulled into the cold and dark realm of Annwyn. Only one choice lay before him.

"Mab," he said. "I—"

He pulled his hands out of her grip.

Mab fell back with a grunt. The portal dragged Erlik and Idath inside and sealed shut, leaving nothing but silence in its wake.

EPILOGUE

"Run."

S ILENCE REIGNED ABOVE all in the cold and empty arena. The curved moon hung above, crystal white, a mocking smile cocked on a curious face. Mab slowly regained her feet, her eyes fixed on the patch of sky above her where, only moments before, a pulsing gateway to the realm of the dead had taken her heart.

No.

No, he cannot be gone.

"Mab?"

The word cleaved her fragile senses like a blade. Her fingers twitched, curling into claws. Her breast heaved.

"Mab, is he..."

Someone – she didn't know or care who – approached her. She felt the hesitation of that someone as they decided against putting a hand on her shoulder.

"He's gone, Mab."

No.

Someone was breathing heavily. A steady *drip-drip-drip* of blood.

"Thomas, we need to go—Tristan—his hand. Thomas, please!"

The boy was badly hurt. Mab swallowed, but the lump in her throat threatened to choke her. She tried desperately to think of the words to say, to deny what her eyes had seen, that Erlik couldn't be dead, he *wasn't* dead. She wouldn't allow him to be dead. That they still had so much left to do.

"Mab?"

There, again, the intrusion. The clear voice that punctured her thoughts. The questioning lilt that drove away memories of Erlik's face, when all she wanted was his arms around her.

Thomas appeared in her peripheral vision, through the haze of dark hair that partially obscured her sight. She lifted her gaze, and turned her head slightly to look at him.

"Run."

She whispered the word through gritted teeth. She didn't want him or his family harmed. They hadn't wronged her. If anything, their presence was calming. But now, in this black moment of pain and despair, she didn't want to be calm.

"Thomas," she said in a low voice, shaking with the effort of holding back her rage. "*Run.*"

She saw his face pale. He said nothing more, merely swallowed and nodded, then rushed back to his family.

Once out of sight, Mab was unsure how long she could contain her fury. She heard his voice, quiet but loud enough to reach her ears.

"Come, we need to go," he said, and she could picture him ushering his wife and swiftly paling son away. "*Come,* now, we need to go, now!"

"W-what—what about—"

"No, Tristan, come on!"

She heard their footsteps grow quieter, and gave them a few minutes to scramble into the little boat and begin to row away.

She wanted to help Tristan. She wanted to feel something for him. But the black, ancient agony was building too high and too terrible for her to feel anything else for anyone else.

Her jaw ached from clenching her teeth so hard. Lightning crackled at her fingertips, arcing from her clawed hands to the ground. She took a few steps, each movement a monumental effort. The wind lashed leaves around her, tangling in her wild hair. The dead tree creaked and groaned, as if it longed to lift its roots and stride away.

Until, at last, the last cord of her willpower snapped, and she released her fury into the world.

The scream came first; a *bean sídhe* wail that echoed from time immemorial, built from centuries of pain and loss, every woman who had ever lost her beloved, recognised and remembered in this primordial storm.

The island shook. Stones loosened from the foundations. Mab's outburst of pain and fury reflected around her, and the arena exploded. Fire and stone rained down.

Clouds formed above her, broken with lightning, thunder rattling so close she felt her insides shake, her heart thumping so fast she felt it might burst. A red haze clouded her vision.

The tears came after. Blistering hot, like fire, scorching her cheeks and burning behind her eyes.

With barely a pause for breath, another scream tore from her throat. Ruthless and unrelenting, filled with fury and so high it almost seemed soundless.

Every wolf in Albion howled at the sky in acknowledgement of their mistress's pain. Stags and wild horses whinnied and snorted and reared, eyes rolling in fear as their world darkened around them. Rabbits and foxes fled into their burrows and dens.

Far away, in Elphame and Tír-Na-Nóg, citizens watched from their windows as the skies grew dark, and rainfall began to drown their cities.

Mab collapsed to her knees. Sodden by the rain, she watched the bubbling mud around her. Exhausted, she lifted her gaze to the sky.

"I will find my way to Annwyn," she decreed to the storm. "I will bring him back, and nothing – *nothing* – in this realm or the next will stop me."

High above her, the last dragon to escape Annwyn circled, its roar distant, echoing, lonely and lost.

Dear Reader

Thank you for reading *The Age of Magic*. If you enjoyed this book (or even if you didn't) please consider leaving a star rating or review online. Your feedback is important, and will help other readers to find the book and decide whether to read it, too.

Acknowledgements

They say it takes a village to raise a child. No one told me it was the same for novels. *The Age of Magic* could never have come about without the love and support of those around me. When I first wrote *The Old Ways*, I always told myself that I'd write one and be done with Albion; I wanted a single standalone fantasy novel and that would be it. Fortunately, the masses demanded a sequel. And by masses, I mean my friends and family. And by sequel, I mean a trilogy.

To my Mama Bear, who is still diligently, faithfully, and stubbornly "waiting for the movie". And to my Papa Bear, Teller of Dad Jokes, still with that uncanny impression of Gollum. You're both weirdos. And I love you.

To Nyx, my best friend, fellow writer, fellow fantasy connoisseur, and fellow 'queer-coded, long-haired, brown-eyed boy' enthusiast, (you have your Blackbeard, I have my Munson), and to our many writing sessions in various cafes across the North-East. You're also a weirdo. And I love you also.

And to my husband, James. I honestly don't know where I'd be without you. You're my love story. You make the rain fall in my dusty heart. All my treasure maps lead to you. You're the biggest weirdo, and I love you the most.

(Also thanks for rescuing me from spiders. Keep up the good work, champ.)

And lastly, to Sara, for not letting me quit when I lost faith in myself. It must have been hard not letting me float away like a stray balloon on a windy day, but your support and encouragement means the absolute world to me. Don't tell anyone I said this but I love you too.

About the Author

Born in 1990, England native RK Summers is a great lover and hoarder of books. Her love of the literary world began at five years old, when, as a ridiculously serious child, she wrote her first 'story' about a dancing tree, complete with a bittersweet ending as a lament for the loss of fairy tale magic. She was subsequently not a popular child.

During the Goth years of fourteen to nineteen, between the emotional teenage poetry, she also attempted a vampire/demon novel which she did actually manage to finish. But sadly, it was so agonisingly Emo that reading it back years later caused physical pain.

Thus began the Age of Albion.

Cut to 6 years later, and RK's debut novel The Old Ways was released into the world.

Her minor life goal is to read fifty books per year. Her major life goal is to be recognised in the street as "that author what wrote them books" or something to that effect. She would also like to one day pen a trippy and disturbing fiction featuring an alliance between Alice Liddell, Dorothy Gale, and Wendy Darling.

In her free time, she enjoys purple things, baking, afternoon tea, book forts, old witchcraft, and Celtic folk music. Her vices include Marvel movies and video games. She currently lives in the North East of England, with zero intentions of leaving her bleak, windswept, and salt-stung homeland.

More From This Author

The Old Ways
(Tales of Albion: Book 1)

Something snapped. He let the arrow fly.

The night Thomas Rhymer's young sister is stolen away by shadows and smoke, he discovers there's more to life than the fields and forests he knows so well. If he has any hope of rescuing Alissa, he must first cross into a realm where magic is lifeblood, and where shadows dance with dragonfire.

With the help of the seelie faery Thistledown, Thomas embarks on a treacherous quest, deep into the heart of war-raved Albion. But getting his sister back means pledging aid to Mab, the usurped Queen of the Old Ways, against the tyranny of the Dark Prince.

Yet danger and deceit lie around every corner, and some secrets are better left untold.

Available from all major online and offline outlets.